An English Squire

By

Christabel R. Coleridge

An English Squire
by Christabel R. Coleridge

Copyright © 2023

All Rights reserved.

ISBN: 978-93-59951-38-6
Published by

DOUBLE 9 BOOKS

2/13-B, Ansari Road
Daryaganj, New Delhi – 110002
info@double9books.com
www.double9books.com
Tel. 011-40042856

ABOUT THE AUTHOR

Christabel Rose Coleridge was an English author and editor of girls' magazines. She was born on May 25, 1843, and died on November 14, 1921. Sometimes she worked with author Charlotte Mary Yonge. She had strong ideas about how women should behave in society. Christabel was born at St. Mark's College, Chelsea, while her father, Derwent, was teacher there. She is the granddaughter of the poet Samuel Coleridge. She got her name from the poem "Christabel" by Samuel Coleridge. Coleridge lived her dream of becoming a writer, but for a while she helped her brother Ernest run a school. After that, she wrote and published more than 15 books. The first was Lady Betty (1869), a history story for kids. The story of Minstrel Dick (1896) takes place mostly in the court of Edward the Black Prince, who is dying, in Berkhamstead in the 1400s. She wrote fiction that showed how morally concerned she was, and the Society for Promoting Christian Knowledge released a number of her books. Charlotte Yonge was a friend of Christabel's. Charlotte and Christabel were linked through Mary Elizabeth Coleridge, who was also a member of Yonge's informal group, the Goslings. Among the books they worked together on were "The Miz Maze" and "The Winkworth Puzzle: A Story in Letters, by Nine Authors" (1883).

CONTENTS

Preface

In bringing this tale in a complete form before the public, I should wish it to be understood that it arose out of a series of conversations with a friend who suggested the character of Alvar Lester, to the original invention of which I can lay no claim whatever. He came to me from his Spanish home, and I have done nothing with him but turn him into an English Squire.

C.R. Coleridge.

PART ONE
Home Life

"A little more than kin, and less than kind."

Chapter One
The Lesters of Oakby

"Young barbarians all at play."

Some few years ago Mr Gerald Lester was the head of a family of good blood and position, and the owner of Oakby Hall, the great house of a village of the same name in the county of Westmoreland. The border line between Westmoreland and Yorkshire crossed his property; but his house and park were in the former county, for which he was a deputy sheriff and justice of the peace.

He was not a man of very large fortune, and Oakby Hall was not a show place, but a well-built mansion of the last century, with some architectural pretensions, and standing in the midst of that sort of wild and romantic scenery which, perhaps more than any other, fixes the affections of its inhabitants. Oakby, at any rate, was very dear to its owner.

The great sweeps of heather-clad moor, the fell sides, with their short green turf, the fertile valleys, had a character of their own, inferior as they were to the better-known parts of Westmoreland.

Oakby village was situated in one of the largest of these valleys, and the Hall lay low on the side of a hill over which the well-planted park stretched on either side. The house could be seen all the way up the long carriage drive, for it was only shut off from the park by an iron railing, within which the turf was mown close and fine, instead of being left to be cropped by sheep and cattle. The gardens were at the side, and there were no trees in front of the house but one oak of great size and beauty. There was a wide carriage sweep, and the space between this and the house was paved, and on either side of the front-door was a stone wolf of somewhat forbidding aspect—the crest of the Lesters.

The grey stone house thus exposed to view was stately enough, and though too open and free to be exactly gloomy, this northern front was bleak and cold, especially on a frosty winter twilight, when the light was dying away in the distance, and the piece of ornamental water and the pleasant bits of woodland, beyond were not distinctly visible. No such thought ever crossed the minds of the young Lesters, who came back to it from school and college as to the dearest of homes; but to a stranger, a little doubtful of a welcome, it might perhaps look formidable.

Within doors a blazing fire and abundance of rugs and skins made the hall the most attractive place in the house, both for dogs and men; especially between the lights, when there was little to do anywhere else, and all were tired with their day's work, or ready to discuss their day's amusement.

Just before Christmas play was legitimate; and the young Lesters, skates in hand, had just returned from the lake, and were grouped together round, the fire, noisily praising and criticising each other's recent performances.

"I never should have had a tumble all day if Bob hadn't come up against me like a steam engine," cried the one girl, a tall creature of sixteen, big, fair, and rosy.

"I came against you! That's a good one. Who could keep out of your way?" ejaculated the aggrieved twin brother. "You can no more guide yourself than—."

"A balloon," put in the more softly accented voice of the eldest brother present, as he unfastened his skates from the neck of his great Saint Bernard, who had dutifully carried them home for him.

"Now, Cherry, that's not true!" cried the girl in loud indignation. "Of course I can't be expected to do figures of eight and spread-eagles like you and Jack."

"I saw an American fellow the other day who skated twice as well as either of us."

"No? All! I don't believe that!" from the girl.

"But then they've ice all the year round," from Bob.

"I daresay they can't do anything else," from Jack.

"Jack always is so liberal!" from Cheriton; and then, "Hush! here's the squire."

It was sometimes said that no one of the young Lesters would be so fine a man as his father; and certainly Mr Lester was a splendid specimen of an English gentleman, though the big Jack rivalled him in inches, and promised equal size and strength, while Cheriton, who was of a slighter build, inherited his blue eyes and brilliant colouring. But they were his own children—every one fair, and tall, and healthy; and their characteristic differences did not destroy their strong resemblance to each other and to their handsome father, who now stood in the midst of them with a foreign letter in his hand, at which the children glanced curiously.

He was not much above fifty; his hair and beard, which had once deserved to be called golden, had rather faded than grizzled, his skin was still fresh and healthy, and his eyes bright in colour and full of expression; the level brows met over them. His children, as has been said, were curiously like him—Annette, or Nettie, as she was commonly called, perhaps the most so. Although she was big and unformed, she had the promise of great beauty in her straight sulky brows and large sky-blue eyes, resplendent colouring which defied sunburn, and abundant yellow hair. Her nose was straight and fine, like her father's, but her full red lips were a trifle sullen; the contour of her face was heavy, and though she looked well born and well bred, she lacked the refinement of intelligent expression. But if her great blue eyes looked stupid and rather cross, they were as honest as the day; and at sixteen there was still time for thoughts and feelings to come and print themselves on this beautiful piece of flesh and blood.

She was very untidily though handsomely dressed, and had the awkwardness of a girl too big for her age; but as she stood leaning back against the oak table, there was such vigour and life in her strong young limbs as to give them a kind of grace. She had a low voice of refined quality, but she spoke with a strong north-country accent, as did her father. In the brothers it was much modified by their southern schooling. The twin brother, Robert, retained, however, a good deal of it. He was a heavier, less handsome likeness of her, and might have been described as a fine lad or a great lout, according to the prepossessions of the speaker. The next brother, John, or, as he was usually called, Jack, had, at nineteen, hardly yet outgrown the same ungainliness of manner; but his height, and the strength trained by many an athletic struggle, could not fail to be striking; and though he had something of the same sullen straightness of brow, the eyes beneath were thoughtful and keen. There was no lack of mental power in Jack's grave young face, and he was a formidable opponent to his schoolfellows in contests of brain as well as of muscle.

Cheriton, except that his brows arched a little, so that he could not attain to the perfection of the family frown, and that he was an inch or two shorter and much slighter, was so like Jack that when he was grave and silent his brighter colouring and the moustaches to which he had attained were, at first sight, the chief points of difference between them. But then Jack's face to-day would be his face to-morrow, while Cheriton's expression varied with almost every word he spoke, so that he was sometimes said to be the image of his father, sometimes to be the one Lester who was like nobody but himself; while, now and then old friends wondered how this handsome young man came to have such a look of the mother, who had been no beauty, but only a high-minded and cultivated woman. He was his father's favourite, and somehow his brothers were not jealous of the preference. "Cherry," as they called him, was the family oracle, though he risked his place now and then when his utterances were not in accordance with the prevailing sentiment.

Mr Lester's expression was now dark enough to indicate annoyance of no common kind; but it did not take much to make him look cross, and if his sons and daughter had not known that there was an unusual speck on the family horizon, they would have surmised that the keepers were in disgrace, the newspaper late in arriving, or that they themselves had unwittingly transgressed.

As it was they were all silent, though Cheriton looked up with a question in his eyes, and the twins glanced at each other.

"I have had a letter from—your brother; he has started on his journey, and will be here in a day or two."

No one spoke for a moment, and then Cheriton said,—

"Well, father, I shall be very glad to see him. It's a good time for him to come, and I hope we shall be able to make it pleasant for him."

"Pleasant for *him*," growled Bob.

"It won't be at all pleasant for *us*," said his sister. "Fancy a foreign fellow interfering in all our concerns. And Granny says he's sure to set us a bad example."

"Ay," said the father, "you lads needn't be in too great a hurry to get up an intimacy."

"There's not much fear of that," said Cheriton.

"Ah, my boy," said Mr Lester, turning to him, "you take it very well; but it's hard on you; no one knows better than I do."

"As for me," said Cheriton, with a shade of the characteristic family gruffness in his much pleasanter voice, "you know it has always been my wish that he should come, and why should we set ourselves against it?"

"He ought to have come sooner," said Jack.

"That's no affair of yours, Jack," said his father sharply. "Don't be so ready with your comments. He is coming now, and—and I'll hear no more grumbling. I'm hanged if I know what we are all to make of him, though," he muttered as he left the hall.

"He'd better not interfere with me," said Bob. "I shall take no notice of him."

"Poor fellow!" said Cheriton satirically. "I won't kiss him, I declare," cried his sister.

"Now you boys, and Nettie, look here," said Cheriton seriously. "Alvar is our father's son and our brother. He is the eldest, and has his rights. That's the fact; and his having lived all his life in Spain doesn't alter it. And if his coming is strange to us, what will it be for him? Isn't it an awful shame to set our backs up before we see him? Is it his fault?" Cheriton's influence in the family was considerable, and the younger ones had no answer to his arguments; but influence and arguments are weak compared to prejudice; and no one answered till Jack grumbled out,—

"Of course we must do our duty by him, and perhaps he'll improve."

"On acquaintance," suggested Cheriton, with half-suppressed fun. "Suppose he's a finer fellow than any of us, and a better sort altogether. What shall we do then?"

"Oh, but he's a foreigner, you know," said Nettie, as if this settled the question. "Come, Bob, let's go and see the puppies fed."

"What I say is," said Jack, as the twins went away and left their elders to a freer discussion, "that the thing has been left too late. Here is Alvar,—twenty-five, isn't he?"

"Yes; he is only two years older than I am."

"How can he turn into an Englishman? It's all very well for you to chaff about it, and lecture the young ones; but the squire won't stand him with patience for a day; there'll be one continual row. Everything will be turned topsy-turvy. He'll go back to Seville in a month."

Cheriton was silent. He was older than Jack by nearly four years, and perhaps should not have attributed so much importance to the grumbling of his juniors; but his wider out-look only enabled him to see that their feelings were one-sided, it did not prevent him from sharing them; and the gift of a more sympathetic nature did but make him more conscious of how far these feelings were justifiable. Home life at Oakby had its difficulties, its roughnesses, and its daily trials; but what did this signify to the careless boys who had no dignity to lose, and by whom a harsh word from their father, or a rough one from each other, was forgotten and repeated twenty times a day? He himself had hardly grown into that independent existence which would make an unkindness from a brother an insult, an injustice from a father a thing to be resented beyond the day. It was still all among themselves, they knew each other, and suited each other, and stood up for each other against the world. They were still the children of their father's house, and that tie was much too close and real for surface quarrels and disputes to slacken it. But this stranger, who must be the very first among them all, yet who did not know them, and whom they did not know, who had a right to this same identity of interest, and yet who would assuredly neither feel nor win it!

Jack accused his father of having acted unjustly to them all; the younger ones rebelled with a blind prejudice which they did not themselves understand. Cheriton was vividly conscious of the stranger's rights, yet shrank from all they claimed from him; to the father he recalled resentment, weakness of purpose, and a youthful impulse, from the consequences of which he could not escape. The grandmother upstairs, no inconsiderable power in the Oakby household, formulated the vague distaste of her descendants, and strongly expressed her belief that a foreign heir would grieve his father, corrupt his brothers, and ruin his inheritance.

And now who was this foreign heir, this unknown brother, and what was the explanation of his existence?

Chapter Two
The Son and Heir

"Love should ride the wind
With Spain's dark-glancing daughters."

Some six or seven and twenty years before the date when his sons were thus discussing their elder brother's arrival, Gerald Lester, then a young man fresh from college, had been sent abroad by his father to separate him from a girl, somewhat his inferior in rank, for whom he had formed an attachment. He was not then his father's heir, as he had an elder brother living, and he was supposed to be going to make his way at the bar; but though well-conducted and brilliantly handsome, his talents and tastes were not of an order to make success rapid or certain, and such a marriage as he had contemplated would have been, though he had a small independence, peculiarly inexpedient. Though at times passionate and defiant, he was not a person of much strength of will; and he yielded to the pressure put on him, partly from sense of duty—for he was by no means wanting in principle—and partly because it was too much trouble to resist.

The affair, however, left him in an unsettled state of mind, and increased his dislike to his profession. While wandering about in the south of Spain, he became acquainted, through some letters of introduction with which he had been provided, with a family of position of the name of De la Rosa. While staying with them he met with an accident which disabled him from travelling, and afforded him time and opportunity to flirt and sentimentalise with the beautiful Maria de la Rosa, who fell passionately in love with the handsome Englishman. Gerald's feelings were more on the surface, but he was much carried away by the circumstances; he felt that he would make a poor return for the hospitality that had been shown him if he only "loved and rode away."

He was enough irritated by the compulsion that his father had put upon him to feel glad to act independently; while the natural opposition of Don Guzman de la Rosa to his daughter's marriage with a foreigner, stirred Gerald to more ardour than Maria's dark eyes had already awakened. Her birth, at any rate, was all that could be desired, her religion ought not to be an objection in one so good and pious, and the nationality of his younger son's wife could be of no consequence to old Mr Lester. Don Guzman was not a zealous Catholic, and he yielded at length to his daughter's entreaties; the young Englishman's small independence seeming, in the eyes of the frugal Spaniard, a sufficient fortune.

Gerald Lester and Maria de la Rosa were married at Gibraltar, the difficulties of a legal marriage between a Protestant and a Roman Catholic being almost insurmountable on Spanish territory. In Gibraltar they lived for some time; but the marriage was not a happy one. Maria was a mere ignorant child, with all her notions irreconcilably at war with her husband's; and Gerald, who had his ideals, was very unhappy.

After some months, the sudden illness of his elder brother summoned him home, and while he was absent his child was born unexpectedly, and his young wife died. He learnt almost at once that he was his father's heir, and that a son was born to him. It seemed no moment for making such a disclosure. His grief for his brother sheltered the shock and surprise of the death of the poor young wife, and he satisfied his conscience by writing to the English clergyman who had solemnised his marriage, and desiring that he should baptise the boy according to the rites of the English Church. As this stipulation had been made at the marriage, Don Guzman allowed the order to be carried into effect. But as no desire was expressed by the father as to a name, it was christened Alvaro Guzman—the Spanish grandfather omitting the Gerald, which he felt had been an ill-omened name to his daughter.

Gerald himself, meanwhile, was almost ready to forget the little Alvar's existence. He was ashamed of his foolish marriage, and remorseful at its secrecy and disobedience; the new life opened to him by his brother's death was exceedingly congenial. Why could not those unhappy months be as if they had never been!

The child was of course an unfamiliar idea to him, and except with an occasional pang he hardly realised its existence; when the thought was forced on him, he regarded it with aversion.

Three months had not, however, passed since his wife's death, when he became acquainted with a Miss Cheriton, a young lady of good family and some fortune. She was not very pretty; but she was full of intelligence and refinement, and she was very good. Perhaps the force of contrast was half the attraction. When his father urged him to pay his addresses to Miss Cheriton, he felt how willingly he would have done so, but an awkward disclosure lay between them. With all his faults he could not be so dishonourable as to marry her, without telling her that his heir was already born.

But the friendship between them, so different from anything that he had ever known before, grew and strengthened, till at last one evening he told her all the story. He had married foolishly and secretly, as far as his relations were concerned; his wife was dead and had left a little son. That was the story. Must it be for ever a bar between them? Fanny Cheriton listened, though she was a merry, quick-tongued girl, in silence. Then she said that he must tell his father the whole truth, and must acknowledge the child; he ought to come home and be brought up as an Englishman.

"Who is to bring it up?" asked Gerald.

"I will," said Fanny simply, amid fierce blushes, as she saw what her answer implied.

Thus supported, Gerald would indeed have been a coward had he shrunk from the communication; but it was a great blow to his father, who, however, was a stronger man than his son; and having been satisfied that all was fair and legal, and that Alvaro Guzman Lester was really his lawful heir, and next to Gerald in the entail, said shortly,—

"Fetch him home, and make an Englishman of him if you can. What's done can't be undone."

But when Gerald arrived at Seville, where Don Guzman lived, and where little Alvar had been taken, he found that by a strange coincidence the child had at once become of importance to his relations on both sides. By the death of Don Guzman's son, Alvar had become his heir, and when Gerald expressed a desire to take him home, he was met by great reluctance, and by a declaration that the child was so delicate that a removal to a northern climate would certainly kill him. Perhaps Gerald's consciousness that he would not regard the poor little fellow's death as a misfortune, made him afraid to insist in the face of this argument. At any rate he returned without the child. Don Guzman's indifferentism in religion allowed him to consent that Alvar should, when he grew old enough, be taught the English language and the Anglican faith, and even showed how this might be managed by means of an English clergyman residing at Seville for his health; so that he was left with a sort of understanding that his mother's family were to have the charge of him for the present.

Miss Cheriton was much disappointed.

"Every year will make it harder," she said, and she resolved to use all her influence on Alvar's behalf. But her father-in-law's death soon after her marriage deprived her of his powerful aid, and, though his will carefully assured the succession to his son's eldest son, she could not contend with her husband's distaste and the Spanish relations' determination not to give up the child. She had no other troubles. Her husband shared her views as to the duties and responsibilities of his station, and they did much for the good of those around them.

In spite of some harshness, Gerald was a good landlord and a good magistrate, and the most loving of fathers to the fair rosy boy who was now born to them. He never cared quite so much for the younger ones, but "Cherry" was his delight and pride, so pretty, so clever, and so apt at riding his little pony, or learning to fire a gun, and so fond of his father! If Alvar could but have been forgotten!

But Mrs Lester was wise and far-seeing, and she would not allow Cheriton to forget. She talked to him about Alvar; she made him say his prayers for "my eldest brother away in Spain;" and she even caused him once to write a little letter expressing his wish to see his big brother, and to show him his pony and his dogs. Perhaps Alvar's education was less advanced, for there only arrived a message of love from him in one of the rare letters that Don Guzman indited to Mr Lester.

Cherry was rather a thoughtful child; his mother had succeeded in impressing his imagination, and he thought and talked a good deal about Alvar. One attempt was made to bring the child to England; but, when he reached France, he fell ill, and his grandfather hurried him back again, assuring his father that it was impossible he could live in a northern climate. Mr Lester was too ready to believe this.

Soon after Cheriton went to school, Mrs Lester died suddenly, and her loss was greater than even Cheriton in his passion of childish grief could guess. Grief sharpened Mr Lester's temper, and the loss of his wife's influence narrowed his mind and character. His mother, who lived with him, and took care of the four children, did not urge on him the need for Alvar's return. It ceased to be under discussion, and the intercourse grew less and less.

Cherry, in his school life, naturally forgot for the time to think much about him, and at home he had a thousand interests, some shared with his father, some of his own. For Cheriton and Jack inherited their mother's talent, and as they grew up, had their minds full of many things out of their father's ken. When Cherry was twenty-one, his birthday was celebrated with various festivities. He was very popular, and the tenants drank his health. Nature had given him a ready tongue, and the speech he made was much beyond the usual run of boyish eloquence. And as he concluded, thanking them for their kindness, he paused, and with a deep flush, added, "And I wish my eldest brother, who is now in Spain, was here too, that we might know him, and that you might drink his health as well as mine."

An English Squire | 19

"Cheriton, why did you say that?" said his father afterwards.

"Father, I thought they would forget Alvar's existence, and—I was afraid of forgetting it myself."

As Cheriton spoke, it occurred to Mr Lester with new distinctness that he was really doing his second son a wrong, by allowing him to take for the time a place which could not be his permanently. This boy, with his ready tongue, his bright wit, and the look in his face that his father loved, was not his heir; was it well for him to act as if he were so? With a sudden resolution he wrote his eldest son a letter, requesting him to pay him a visit, and make his brothers' acquaintance.

Alvar, perhaps hurt at the long neglect, refused to do so, giving as a reason his grandmother's serious illness, and his father gladly let the matter drop. Cheriton was disappointed, and asked to be allowed to spend his next long vacation in Spain, and to see his brother. Mr Lester, mindful of his own experiences, refused decidedly; and two years more had passed without any serious renewal of the subject (though Alvar's grandmother died in a few months), when Mr Lester, while hunting, had a dangerous accident, and though he escaped comparatively unhurt, the thought would obtrude itself, "A little more, and my boys must have welcomed as the head of the family an absolutely unknown foreigner." Under the influence of this feeling he wrote again to Alvar in a different strain, and received a different answer. Alvar agreed to come, and pledged himself to remain in England for a year, so as to have ample opportunity of becoming acquainted with his relations, and with the sort of life to which he was born as an English gentleman.

Chapter Three
A Mother of Heroes

"And the old grandmother sat in the chimney corner and spun."

Alvar Lester was coming home; but his image was so complete a blank to his brothers, that they could form no idea as to how it would become them to receive him. Jack, after lingering a little longer by the hall fire, observed that he could get nearly two hours' reading before dinner, and went off to his usual occupations. Cheriton's studies were, to say the least, equally important, as he was to take his degree in the ensuing summer; but now he shook his head.

"I can't fiddle while Rome is burning. There's too much to think of, and I'm tired with skating. I shall go and see what granny has to say about it."

But when he was left alone, he still stood leaning against the mantelpiece. The Lesters were not a family who took things easily, and perhaps there was not one of them who shrank from the thought of the strange brother as much as he who had so persistently urged his return. Not all his excellent arguments could cure his own distaste to the foreigner. He was shy too, and could not tell how to be affectionate to a stranger, and yet he valued the tie of relationship highly, and could not carelessly ignore it. And he knew that he was jealous of the very rights of eldership on which he had just been insisting. Which of those things that he most valued were his own, and which belonged to the eldest son and heir of Oakby? What duties and pleasures must he give up to the newcomer? He did not think that any of their friends would cease to wish to see him at their houses, even if they included Alvar in their invitations.

Certainly he had a much more powerful voice than his brothers in the management of the stable, and indeed of all the estate; but he held this privilege only by his father's will; and probably Alvar would ride very badly, if at all. No—that sentiment was worthy of Bob himself! Certainly he could not understand English farming, if he were only half as ignorant of foreign countries as the clever English undergraduate, who did not feel quite sure if he had ever heard of any animals in Spain but bulls and goats, and could have sworn to nothing but grapes as a vegetable product of the peninsula. Nor could any stranger enter into the wants and welfare of his father's tenants, nor be expected to understand the schemes for the amusement and improvement of the neighbourhood, with which Cheriton was in the habit of concerning himself.

How could Alvar be secretary of a cricket club, or captain of a volunteer corps? No more than he could know each volunteer and cricketer, or be known by them, with the experience and interest of a life-time. "They wouldn't hear of him," thought Cherry. He was too young, and his father was too young, for his thoughts to move easily forward to the time when Alvar was to be the master; it was simply as elder brother that he regarded him. "He ought to carve, and sit at the bottom of the table when my father's away!" And having come to this magnificent result of so much meditation, he laughed and shook himself, the ludicrous side of his perplexities striking him like a gleam of sunlight as he came to the wise resolution of letting things settle themselves as they came, and ran upstairs to his grandmother.

The ground-floor of Oakby Hall consisted of the hall, before mentioned, on one side of which opened a billiard-room, and on the other a large, long library, containing a number of old books in old editions, in which Mr Lester took a kind of pride, though he rarely disturbed them in their places. There were some pictures, dark, dingy, but bearing honoured names, and much respected by the family as "old masters," though Cheriton had once got into a great scrape by declaring that he had lived all his life in doubt as to whether a certain one in a corner was a portrait or a landscape, until, one exceptionally sunny day, he discovered it to be a fruit and flower piece.

The room was panelled with dark oak and fitted up with heavy carved furniture, and curtains, which, whatever their original tint, were now "harmonious" with the fading of more than one generation. Three small, deeply-recessed windows looked out to the front, and at the end of the long room opposite the door was a large one facing westward, with thick mullions and a broad, low-cushioned window-seat. This window gave its character to the room, for through its narrow casements miles and miles of moor and fell were visible; a wide, wild landscape, marked by no conspicuous peaks, and brightened by no expanse of water, yet with infinite variety in its cold, dark northern colouring, and grandeur and freedom in its apparently limitless extent.

Here was the place to watch sunset and moonrise, or to see the storms coming up or drifting away, and to hear them, too, howling and whistling round the house or dashing against the window-panes. The west window was one of the strong influences that moulded life at Oakby. This library was the Lesters' ordinary living room; but behind it was a smaller and more sheltered one, called Mr Lester's study, which he kept pretty much to himself.

The dining-room was at the other side of the house, behind the billiard-room, and had a view of a hill-side and fir-trees. It contained all the modern works of art in the house—a large picture of Mr Lester and his second wife, their children, horses, and dogs, all assembled at the front-door; and a very stiff pink and white, blue-eyed likeness of Cheriton in hunting costume, which had been taken when he came of age.

There was a fine old staircase with wooden wolves of inferior size, but equal ferocity, to their stone brethren without, adorning the corners of the balustrade, and above the library was the drawing-room, whither Cheriton now betook himself. It was a stiff, uninteresting room, but with an unmistakable air of stateliness and position, and though, like all the house, it lacked the living charm of living taste and arrangement, it possessed what even that cannot always give, and what is quite impossible to a new home without it—a certain air of rightness and appropriateness, as if the furniture had grown into its place. Still, the room, handsome as it was, and full of things which were choicer and more valuable than their owners knew, was uncomfortable, the chairs were high and the sofas were hard, and the yellow damask, with which they were covered, slippery; no one had a place of his own in it; the wild western view gave it an unhomely dreariness, hardly redeemed by an extra window looking south over the flower-garden, which in that bleak climate would have needed more fostering care than it ever obtained, to be very gay, even in summer. Now of course it was snowy and desolate.

Only in this winter weather would Mrs Lester have been found in her arm-chair in the drawing-room; but an attack of rheumatism had recently reminded her of her seventy years, and obliged her to remain in the house, at any rate till the frost was over. She had lived with her son ever since his second wife's death, and had kept his house, and in a manner presided over the education of his children; but though she was the only woman of the family, and an old woman and a grandmother, it was not from her that the boys looked for spoiling tenderness, nor were the softer and sweeter elements of the family life, few as they were, fostered by her influence.

She had handed down to her children, and still exhibited herself, their height and vigorous strength, and perhaps something of their beauty, though she was a darker and more aquiline-featured person than her son, who resembled his father. Whether the grandchildren inherited her clear, but narrow vision, her upright, but prejudiced mind, and her will, that went its way subject to no side lights or shadows, perhaps it was early days to tell.

She was an entirely unintellectual, unimaginative person; but within her experience, which was extremely limited—as she could hardly realise, the existence, much less the merits of natures unlike her own—she had a good deal of shrewd sense, and it was much easier to feel her strictures unjust than to prove them so.

She had a thorough knowledge of, and had all her life been accustomed to share in, the outdoor sports and occupations of country life, and very recently had been able to ride and drive with the skill of long practice. These had been the pleasures of her youth; but though she was rather an unfeminine woman, she had never been in any sense a fast one. She was altogether devoid of coquettish instincts, and though she had been a handsome girl, who had passed her life almost entirely among sporting men, and whose tongue was in consequence somewhat free, she had hardly left through the country-side the memory even of an old flirtation.

Within doors she had few occupations; but when her daughter-in-law's death rendered her presence at Oakby again necessary, she had taken the command of the children, and ruled them vigorously according to her lights. She wished to see them grow up after her ideal, and would have despised them utterly if they had gambled, drunk, or dissipated their property by extravagance. She would have thought very slightingly of them if their taste had been exclusively for an indoor or studious life, or if they had been awkward riders or bad shots, though she recognised the duty of "attention to their studies" in moderation, particularly on wet days.

She was tolerably satisfied with her grandsons, who had imbibed this view of life with the smell of the heather and the pines, but she was a little suspicious of the Cheriton blood, and of the talents of which she had succeeded in making Cherry and Jack half ashamed. Perhaps her granddaughter was her favourite, and she rejoiced in the girl's love for an outdoor life, and certainly did not discourage the outrageous idleness with which Nettie neglected the lessons she was supposed to learn of the governess at Oakby Rectory.

On the present occasion Cheriton found her in an unusually thoughtful mood. Her bright dark eyes were still so strong that she rarely used glasses; nor did she often give in to wearing a shawl; but her dress, which was scrupulously appropriate to her age and circumstances—handsome black silk, and soft white cap fastened under her chin—had an oddly inappropriate air on her tall, upright figure, and strong, marked features.

"Well, granny, so he's really coming," said Cheriton cheerfully, as he sat down opposite to her.

"Oh, your father's been here," said Mrs Lester. "We'll have to do with him for a year, I suppose."

"Oh, we'll get on with him somehow. I mean to strike up a friendship," returned Cherry boldly.

"You'll be very soft if you do. Your father and I, remember, know what these Spaniards are like; they're a bad lot—a bad lot."

"Well, my father ought to know—certainly! But you see he has told us so little about them."

"I have told my son that I think he couldn't have chosen a worse time to have him home—just when you lads are all growing up, and ready to learn all the tricks he can teach you."

"What tricks?" said Cheriton, feeling much insulted by the suggestion.

"D'ye think I'm going to teach you beforehand?"

"I assure you, granny," said Cheriton impressively, "that the tricks I see at Oxford are such that it would be impossible for Alvar to beat them."

"And what have you been up to now?" said his grandmother sharply.

"Why, granny, I really shouldn't like to tell you the half of them. But I'm quite accustomed to 'tricks,' a monkey couldn't be more used to them. There was that affair with the chapel door—"

"Oh, don't tell me your monkey tricks," said his grandmother, with half-humorous indignation. "I know what they lead to; they're bad enough. But your half-brother will smoke like a chimney and drink like a fish, and gamble before the lads on a Sunday. If those are your Oxford manners—"

"Really," said Cheriton seriously, "we have no reason to suppose that he will do anything of the kind; and if he did, the boys are very little in the mood to imitate him. I only hope they'll be decently civil to him." Mrs Lester was herself a much cooler and more imperturbable person than any of her descendants; but she was often the cause of irritation in others, from a calm persistency that ignored all arguments and refutation; and she was especially apt to come across Cheriton, whom she did not regard with the admiration due from a loving grandmother to a dutiful, handsome grandson.

"It's a great misfortune, as I always told my son it would be. You, Cherry, are fond of strangers and outlandish ways, so maybe he'll suit you."

"Well, granny, I hope he may, and we'll get you to come and light our pipes for us," said Cherry, keeping his temper. But the coaxing sweetness that made him the one non-conductor of quarrels in a sufficiently stormy household, was apparently lost, for Mrs Lester went on,—

"He'll suit the Seytons better than he'll suit us."

"There's nothing to say against the Seytons *now*," said Cheriton hotly; muttering under his breath, "I hate prejudice." Mr Lester's entrance interrupted the discussion, though a long story of a broken fence between his property and Mr Seyton's did not give it a smoother turn.

As Mr Seyton's fences had been in a disgraceful condition for at least as long as Cheriton could remember, he was well aware that the present grievance was only an outlet for a deeper-seated one, but his grandmother struck in,—

"Ah, Cheriton may see what it is to take to bad ways and bad connexions. I've been telling him his half-brother is likely enough to make friends with the Seytons, and bring their doings over here."

"With a couple of boys younger than Jack," cried Cheriton. "Any one would think, granny, that we had a deadly feud with the Seytons."

"I'll not hear the matter discussed," loudly interposed Mr Lester. "Hold your tongue, Cherry. Alvar will have to mind what he is about. I'm sick of the sound of his name. If he had a good English one of his own it would be something."

"Why hasn't he, then?" was on the tip of Cherry's tongue, but he suppressed it; and as his grandmother walked away, saying that it was time to dress for dinner, he got up and stood near his father.

"I say, dad, never mind; we'll get along somehow," he said.

The expression of passionate irritation passed out of Mr Lester's face, and was succeeded by a look of regretful affection as he put his hand on his favourite son's shoulder.

"I'd give half I'm worth, my boy, to undo it. It's a wrong to you, Cherry—a wrong. It gives me no pleasure to think of the place in his hands after I'm gone."

"Father," interposed Cheriton firmly, "the only wrong is in speaking of it so. It is no wrong to any of us. And you know," he added shyly and under his breath, "mamma would never let us think so."

Mr Lester was a person who would not endure a touch on his tenderest feelings. He had never mentioned the young wife, whose word had been his law, to the son whom he adored for her sake, and who influenced his violent yet impressionable nature by the inheritance of hers. That influence led him to listen to the words which he could not controvert; but he did not love his unknown son the better for the pain which this defence of him had cost him. Cheriton felt that he had ventured almost too far, and he turned off the subject after a pause, by saying quaintly,—

"I wonder what the fox thinks of it all."

"What d'ye mean?"

"Don't you remember that old lady who came to see granny once, and when Jack and I raved about a day's hunting, would say nothing but 'I wonder what the fox thinks of it all?' That was making the other side much too important, wasn't it?"

"Ah, you're ready with your jokes," said his father, not wishing to follow out the little fable, but with a daily sense of liking for the voice and smile with which it was uttered. "Come, I'll have a pipe with you before dinner."

Chapter Four
Strangers Yet!

"My mother came from Spain...
And I am Spanish in myself
And in my likings."

It was late on the afternoon of Christmas Eve. The hall at Oakby was full of branches of holly and ivy. Nettie, perched on the top of an oak cabinet, was sticking sprays into the frame of her grandfather's picture, and Jack and Bob were arranging, according to time-honoured custom, a great bunch of bright-berried holly over the mantelpiece, to do which in safety was a work unattainable by feminine petticoats.

"It's a great shame of Cherry not to come in time to help," said Nettie.

"They'll have got hold of him down at the church," said Jack. "There, that's first-rate."

"I say, Jack, do you know Virginia Seyton came home yesterday? Isn't it funny that they should have one too?"

"One what?"

"Why, a relation, a sister, when we've got a brother. I wonder—"

Suddenly Nettie stopped, as a crash of wheels sounded on the frosty gravel, and the front-door bell pealed loudly.

"Oh, Jack!" and Nettie jumped off the cabinet at one bound, six feet high though it was, and caught hold of the end of Jack's coat in a perfect agony of shyness. "Oh, let's run away!"

"Let go. I can't get down. Stand still and don't be silly," said Jack, gruffly, as he got off the steps, while the butler hurried forward and threw open the door. Nettie stood in the fire-light, her golden hair flying in the gust of wind, her hands together, like a wild thing at bay. Bob remained perched, half-way up the ladder, and Jack made a step or two forward.

A tall figure in a dark cloak, with bright crimson lining, and a large felt hat, stood in the doorway.

"Are you Cheriton?" he said eagerly, and with a strong foreign accent.

"No; he's out. I'm Jack. How d'ye do? We didn't know when you were coming," said Jack, in a tone from which embarrassment took every shade of cordiality. He put out his hand quickly, however, as the stranger made a movement as if possibly intending a more tender salutation. Alvar took it, then removed his hat, and advancing towards the speechless Nettie said,—

"This is my sister? May I not salute her?" and lightly touched her cheek with his lips. "I have thought of you, my sister," he said.

"Have you?" stammered Nettie, hanging down her head like a child. Bob remained motionless on his ladder, and Jack said,—

"Here's my father," as Mr Lester came hurriedly into the hall, nearly as much embarrassed as his children, and pale with an agitation which they did not share. Alvar turned round, and bowed low with a respectful grace that his brothers certainly could not have imitated.

Mr Lester came forward and held out his hand. It needed all his innate sense of good breeding to overcome the repulsion which the very idea of his strange son caused him. The sense of owing him amends for long-neglected duty, the knowledge how utterly out of place this foreigner must be as heir of Oakby, the feeling that by so recognising him he was wronging alike his forefathers and his other children, while he yet knew how much his whole life through he had wronged Alvar himself, came upon him with renewed force. Then as he heard such tones, and saw such a face as he had not seen for years, what rush of long past sentiment, what dead and buried love and hate came rushing over him with such agitating force, that in the effort to avoid a scene, and a display of feeling which, yielded to, might have smoothed the relations between them for ever, his greeting to his son was as cold as ice!

"How do you do, Alvar? I am glad to see you. We did not expect you so soon. You must have found your journey very cold."

"I did not delay. It was my wish to see my father," said Alvar, a little wistfully. "My father, I trust, will find me a dutiful son."

Here Bob giggled, and Jack nearly knocked him off the ladder with the nudge evoked by his greater sense of propriety.

"No doubt—no doubt," said Mr Lester. "I hope we shall understand each other, soon. Where's Cheriton? Jack, suppose you show—him—your brother, his room. Dinner at seven, you know. I daresay you're hungry."

"I did take a cup of coffee, but it was not good," said Alvar, as he followed Jack upstairs; and the latter, mortally afraid of a *tête-à-tête*, shut him into the bedroom prepared for him, and rushed downstairs to encounter Cheriton, who came hurrying in, thinking himself late for dinner.

"Cherry, he's come!"

"Oh, Cherry, he's so queer! He makes pretty speeches, and he bows!"

"He's a regular nigger, he's so black!"

"Oh, Cherry, it's *awful*!"

"What have you done with him? Where's the squire?" said Cherry, as soon as he could make himself heard.

"Oh, papa has seen him, and Jack's taken him into his room," said Nettie.

"He thought I was you," said Jack. Cheriton stood still for a moment, as shy as the rest, then, with an effort, he ran upstairs.

"It's only kind to go and say how d'ye do to a fellow," he thought, as he tapped at the bedroom door, and entered with outstretched hand, and blushing to the tips of his ears. "Oh, how d'ye do? I'm so sorry I was out of the way; they kept me to nail up the wreaths. I'm very glad to see you. Aren't you very cold?"

Probably the foreigner understood about half of this lucid and connected greeting; but something in the warmth of the tone made him come forward eagerly.

"You are then really my brother Cheriton? I thought it was again the other one."

"What, Jack? Yes, we're thought alike, I believe."

"I do not see that," said Alvar, contemplating him gravely; "but I have known you in my thoughts—always."

"I'm sure—we've all thought a great deal about you. But there's no one to help you. Have you got your things? I'll ring," nearly pulling down the bell-rope. "And, look here, I'll just dress and come back, and go down with you—shall I?" Cheriton's summons was rapidly answered, as curiosity inspired the servants as well as their masters; and leaving Alvar to make his toilet, he hastened upstairs. The three brothers slept in a long passage at the top of the house, over the drawing-room. As Cherry's step sounded, both his brothers' doors burst open simultaneously, and Jack and Bob, in various stages of dressing, at once ejaculated,—

"Well!"

"How can I tell? It's awfully late. I shall never be ready," and Cherry banged his own door, too much astounded by the new brother to stand a discussion on him.

As soon as he was ready he went down stairs, and found Alvar, rather to his relief, attired in correct evening costume.

"I suppose you haven't seen my grandmother yet?" he said.

"Your grandmother? I did not know there was a grandmother," said Alvar, in a much puzzled voice, which, together with the sense of how much his brother had to learn, nearly upset Cherry's gravity.

"My father's mother, you know. She lives with us," he said. "She is your grandmother too."

"Ah!" said Alvar, "I loved my grandmother much. This other one, she will be most venerable, I am sure."

"Come along then," said Cherry, unable to stand more conversation at present.

Mrs Lester, whatever her private opinions might be, had too much respect for the heir, for herself, and for the house of Lester, not to attire herself with unusual dignity, and to rise and advance to receive her grandson.

"How do you do, Alvar?" she said. "You have been a long time in coming to see us."

Alvar, after a moment's pause, as if doubtful what sort of salutation would be acceptable, bowed low and kissed her hand. Nettie laughed; but her grandmother drew herself up as if the act of homage was not altogether displeasing to her, and then looked keenly at the new grandson, who, as far as looks went, was no unworthy scion of the handsome Lesters.

He was as tall as his father, though of a different and slighter make, and stood with a sort of graceful stiffness, unlike the easy loose-limbed air of most young English gentlemen. He had a dark olive skin, and oval face; but his features were not unlike the prevailing family type; and though his hair was raven black, it grew and curled in the picturesque fashion of his father's, which Cheriton alone of the other sons inherited. But he had the splendid black liquid eyes, with blue whites, and slender arched eyebrows of his Spanish mother, and possessed a picturesque foreign beauty that seemed to group the fair-haired brothers into a commonplace herd. He had a grave, impassive face, and held his head up with an air suggestive of Spanish grandees.

It was very difficult to make conversation when they went in to dinner, the more so as Alvar evidently did not easily follow rapid English, and either he was bewildered by new impressions, or not very open to them, for he had not much to say about his journey. Cheriton, as he tried to talk as if there was no perplexing stranger present, could not help wondering whether all that was so strange to himself came with any familiarity to his father. Had he known what his son would be like? Could he touch any chord to which Alvar could find a response? Had eyes like those great rolling black ones ever looked love into his own? And if so, was it all forgotten, or was the remembrance distasteful?

"He was older than I am now," thought Cherry. "Surely the thoughts of to-day could never fade away entirely."

Mr Lester uttered no word that betrayed any knowledge of his son's country. He spoke less than usual, and after due inquiries for Alvar's relations, entirely on local matters; Alvar volunteered few remarks, but as the dessert appeared, he turned to Cherry, who sat beside him, and said,—

"Is it not now the custom to smoke?"

"Not at dinner," said Cherry hurriedly, as his father replied,—

"Certainly not," and all the bright blue eyes round the table stared at Alvar, who for the first time coloured, and said,—

"Pardon, I have transgressed."

"We'll go and have a pipe presently," said Cherry; and oh! how ardently he longed for that terrible evening to be over.

"It was a *horrid* Christmas Eve," muttered Nettie to Bob; and perhaps her father thought so too, for he rang the bell early for prayers.

"What is this?" said Alvar, looking puzzled, as a prayer-book was placed before him.

"We're going to have prayers," said Nettie, rather pertly. "Don't you?"

"Ah, it is a custom," said Alvar, and he took the book, and stood and knelt as they did, evidently matching for his cue.

When this ceremony was over, Bob and Nettie rushed off, evidently to escape saying good-night, and Cheriton invited the stranger to come and smoke with him, conducting him to a little smoking-room downstairs, which was only used for visitors, as the boys generally smoked in a room at the top of the house, into which Cherry knew Bob and Jack would greatly resent any intrusion. Mr Lester walked off with a general good-night. Alvar watched Cherry kiss his grandmother, but contented himself with a bow. Jack discreetly retired, and when Cheriton had ascertained that Alvar never smoked a pipe, but only a cigar or a cigarette, and had made him sit down by the fire, Alvar said,—

"My father is then a member of the clerical party?"

"I don't think I quite understand you," said Cherry.

"Your prayers—he is religious?"

"Oh, most people have prayers—I don't think we're more particular than others. My father and Mr Ellesmere, our rector, are friends, naturally," said Cherry, feeling it very difficult to explain himself.

"My grandfather," said Alvar, "is indifferent."

"But—you're a Protestant, aren't you?"

"Oh, yes. I have been so instructed. But I do not interest myself in the subject."

Cheriton had heard many odd things at Oxford said about religion, but never anything to equal the *naïveté* of this avowal. He was quite unprepared with a reply, and Alvar went on,—

"I shall of course conform. I am not an infidel; but I leave those things to your—clergy, do you not call them?"

"Well, some people would say you were right," said Cherry, thankful that Jack was not present to assert the inalienable right of private judgment.

"And politics?" said Alvar; "I know about your Tories and your Whigs. On which side do you range yourself?"

"Well, my father's a Tory and High Churchman, which I suppose is what you mean by belonging to the clerical party; and I—if all places were like this—I'd like things very well as they are. Jack, however, would tell you we were going fast to destruction."

"There are then dissensions among you?"

"Oh, he'll come round to something, I dare say. But our English politics must seem mere child's play to you."

"I have taken no part," said Alvar. "My grandfather would conform to anything for peace, and I, you know, my brother, am in Spain an Englishman—though a Spaniard here."

"I hope you'll be an Englishman soon."

"It is the same with marriage," said Alvar; "I have never betrothed myself, nor has my grandfather sought to marry me. He said I must see English ladies also. One does not always follow the heart in these matters," he concluded rather sentimentally.

"No one would ever dream of your following anything else," said Cherry, beginning gruffly, but half choked with amusement as he spoke.

"No? And you, you have not decided? Ah, you blush, my brother; I am indiscreet."

"I didn't blush—at least that's nothing. Turkey-cock was my nickname at school always," said Cherry hastily.

"I do not understand," said Alvar; and after Cherry had explained the nature and character of turkey-cocks, he said, "But I think that was not civil."

"Civil! It wasn't meant to be. English boys don't stand much upon civility. But," he added, as he knocked the ashes out of his pipe, "if we are rough, I hope you won't mind; the boys don't mean any harm by it. You'll soon get used to our ways, and—and we'll do our best to make you feel at home with us."

A sudden sense of pity for the lonely brother, a stranger in his father's house, softened Cheriton's face and voice as he spoke, though he felt himself to be promising a good deal.

Alvar looked at him with the curious, impassive, unembarrassed air that distinguished him. "You are not 'rough!'" he said! "you are my brother. I am told that here you do not embrace each other. I am an Englishman, I give you my hand."

Cheriton took the slender, oval-shaped hand, which yet closed on his more angular one, with a firm, vigorous grasp.

"All right," he said; "you'd better ask me if you don't know what to do. And now I think you must be tired. I'll show you your room. I hope you won't mind the cold much; I am sorry it's so frosty."

"Oh, the cold is absolutely detestable, but I am not tired," said Alvar briskly.

It was more than Cheriton could say, as he shut this perplexing brother into the best bedroom, which he could not associate with anything but a state visit. He felt oppressed with a sense of past and future responsibility, of distaste which he knew was mild compared to what every other member of his family would experience, of contempt, and kindliness and pity, and, running through all, the exceeding ludicrousness, from an Oakby point of view, of some of Alvar's remarks.

This latter ingredient in his perplexity was strengthened, when he got upstairs, by Jack, who, detecting his dispirited look, proceeded to encourage him by remarking solemnly,—

"Well, I consider it a great family misfortune. Dispositions and habits that are entirely incongruous can't be expected to agree."

"Do shut up, Jack; you're not writing an essay. Now I see where Alvar's turn for speechifying comes from; you get it somehow from the same stock! All I know is, it's too bad to be down on a fellow when he's cast on our hands like this. Now I am going to bed, I'm tired to death; and if we're late on Christmas morning, we shall never hear the last of it."

While the young brothers thus discussed this strange disturber of their accustomed life, their father's thoughts were still more perplexing. He had so long put aside the unwelcome thought of his eldest son that he felt inclined to regard his presence with incredulity. Surely this dark, stately stranger could have no concern with his beloved homestead with its surrounding moors and fells. This boy had never ridden by his side, nor taken his first shots from his gun, nor differed from him about the management of his estate.

Oakby, with all its duties and pleasures, had no connexion with him; and with Oakby Mr Lester had for many years felt himself to be wholly identified. But those dark eyes, those slow, soft accents, that air so strange to his sons, awoke memories of another self. He saw Cheriton's puzzled attempt at understanding the strange brother. But this strange son was *not* strange to him. He knew the very turns of expression that Alvar's imperfect English suggested. For the first time for years the Spanish idioms and Spanish words came back to his memory. He could have so talked as to set his son in accordance with his surroundings, he understood, to his own surprise, exactly where this very new shoe would pinch.

But these memories, though fresh and living, were utterly distasteful, and nothing that cost him pain awoke in Mr Lester's mind any answering tenderness. He was a man with a weak will, a careful conscience, and imperfectly controlled temper and affections.

He much preferred to do right than to do wrong, and he generally did do right; in this one crucial instance he had neglected and slurred over the right thing for years, and now he was not sufficiently accustomed to question himself to realise how far he could have made amends for past neglect, how far he could now make his son fit for the heirship of which he neither could nor would deprive him. No, Alvar was a painful sight to him, therefore he would continue to ignore him as far as possible. He stood in the beloved Cheriton's light, and therefore all the small difficulties that his incongruous presence caused would be left to Cheriton to set to rights, or not be set to rights at all.

It was pleasant, and it was not very difficult to Mr Lester, as he woke in the light of the Christmas dawn, to turn his mind from Alvar's presence to the many duties that the season demanded of him. The children all woke up curious and half-unfriendly. Cheriton wondered what Alvar was thinking of. But they none of them knew to what thoughts or feelings the pealing, crashing Christmas bells awoke the unknown heir.

"Nay, you'll know no more what he's after than if he was yonder picture," said the grandmother in answer to some remarks, and as Cheriton heard him coming down stairs he felt that this was exactly the state of the case.

Chapter Five
The Seytons of Elderthwaite

"All things here are out of joint."

In the midst of a waste of unswept snow across the hill behind Oakby Hall, there was a large old house, originally of something the same square and substantial type, but of more ambitious architecture, for there were turrets at the four corners, overgrown and almost borne down by enormous bushes of ancestral ivy; while the great gates leading to the stables were of fanciful and beautiful ironwork, now broken and falling into decay. Great tree-trunks lay here and there on undulating slopes, the shrubberies flung wild branches over the low stone wall dividing them from the park, where a gate swung weakly on its hinges. There were few tall trees, but litre and there along the drive a solitary beech of great size and beauty suggested the course of an avenue once without its equal in the country round. An old man was feebly sweeping away the snow in front of the house, and a gentleman stood smoking a cigar on the steps—a slenderly-made man, with a delicate, melancholy face, and a pointed grey beard, dressed in a shabby shooting-coat. His eyes turned from the slow old sweeper, past the relics of the avenue, to a ruinous-looking lodge, the chimneys of which sent no smoke into the frosty air.

Mr Seyton of Elderthwaite was used to these signs of adversity, but to-day he was struck by them anew, for he was wondering how they would look in the eyes of a stranger. Oakby, with its strict laws, its rough humours, its ready-made life, would be a strange experience to its foreign heir. What would Elderthwaite, with ruined fortunes and blighted reputation be to a petted and prosperous girl, brought up by gentle, religious women, in all the proprieties and sociabilities of well-to-do country villa life? What would his daughter say to the home she had left as a child, and had never seen since?

The Seytons were a family of older standing in the county than the Lesters, and had once been of superior fortune. At present their condition was, and rightly, very different. The Lesters, with many shortcomings, had been men who, on the whole, had endeavoured to do their duty in their station, and had governed their tenants, brought up their children, attended to public business, and managed their own affairs in an honest and right-minded, if not always in a very enlightened fashion.

But the Seytons had had a bad name for generations. It is true that no tales of wild and picturesque wickedness were told of the present head of the house, such as had made his father's name a bye-word for harshness and violence, and for all manner of evil living; but the family traditions were strong against him; he inherited debt and a dishonoured name, and, alas! with them the tendencies and temptations that had brought them about. He had looked with bitter, injured eyes at the timber that was sold for his father's gaming debts; but many a noble tree fell to pay his own, before he married a girl, innocent, high-minded, and passionate-tempered.

It was a very unhappy marriage, and Mr Seyton never forgave his wife for her broken heart, nor himself for breaking it. When she died, her relations took away her daughter, pledging themselves to provide for her, if she were left undisturbed in their hands. The father had enough to do with his sons. The eldest, Roland, was a fine, handsome fellow, and began life with the sad disadvantage of being expected to go wrong. He got a commission, but during the short intervals that he spent at home, was personally unpopular.

In one of these he took a great fancy to Cheriton Lester during an interval between the latter's school and college life, and Cheriton being warned against him as a bad companion, stuck to him with equal perverseness and generosity. Roland was much the elder of the two, but Cherry's vigorous youth took the lead in the friendship, and gave it his own impress. It was ended by such a scandal in Elderthwaite village as those which had made the name of Roland Seyton's grandfather hated by all the country round, as one by whom no man's hearth was respected, and with whom no man's daughter was safe.

The discovery shocked Cheriton unspeakably; all the parties concerned were well known to him, and he felt that of such sins he could never think or speak lightly. But he would not join in loud or careless blame of his friend, who perhaps felt his truest pang of repentance at the boy's confused miserable face in the one parting interview allowed by Mr Lester before Roland joined his regiment, about to sail for India.

"You need not have been afraid, sir," Roland said, when accused of having set him a bad example; "I knew how to choose my confidant."

After Roland's departure, other tales to his discredit, and debts which it was impossible to pay, came to his father's ears, and these additional troubles helped to strengthen habits of self-indulgence already formed, which had made Mr Seyton a man old before his time, melancholy-faced and gentle-mannered, whom nobody respected and nobody disliked. But the two younger boys had a bad start in life, and seemed little likely to redeem the family fortunes.

It was not often that Mr Seyton thought of anything but the immediate dulness and discomfort of the hour, or of its small alleviations; but to-day these recollections pressed on him. He thought, too, of his shabby furniture, and his ill-conducted household; how unfit a home for his well-dowered daughter; how unlike both her aunt's house and the pleasant foreign tour which, since her aunt's death, she had been enjoying.

"Papa, papa!" cried a bright voice behind him, "Good morning," then as he turned round, the newly-arrived daughter exclaimed, throwing her arms round his neck, "Oh, how nice it is to say 'Good morning, papa!'"

She was a fair creature enough, a true Seyton, with slender frame and pointed chin, creamy complexion and rich brown hair, but the large, round eyes, tender, intense, and full of life, were her mother's, though clear and untroubled as the mother's had never been.

"So you are glad to come home, Virginia?" said her father, rather sadly.

"Yes, papa, I am just delighted. I always made stories about home when I was at Littleton. I was very happy, you know, with dear Aunt Mary and all my friends; but it was so *uninteresting* not to know more of my very nearest relations."

"You will find it very different, my dear, from what you are accustomed to. This is a dull place."

"Oh, papa, I think it is so silly to be dull! I shall be quite ready to like anything you wish," said Virginia warmly.

"My dear, you shall take your own way. It would be hard at least if I could not give you that," said Mr Seyton, looking at her as if he did not quite know what to do with this gaily-dressed, frank-spoken daughter. "Now let us come to breakfast."

"I am afraid I am late," said Virginia; "but it is never easy to be in time after a journey."

"You are punctual for this house, my dear; we take such things easy. But your aunt is down, you see, in your honour." As Mr Seyton spoke they came into the dining-room, a long, low room, with treasures of curious carving round its oak-panels, hardly visible in its imperfect light.

A lady sat pouring out the tea. She had the delicate features and peculiar complexion of her family, but her eyes, instead of being like Mr Seyton's, vague and sad, were sharp and sarcastic; she had more play of feature, and, though she looked fully her age, had the air of having been a beauty.

Miss Seyton had once been engaged to be married, but her engagement had been broken off in one of the storms of discreditable trouble that had overwhelmed her father and brothers, no one knew exactly how or why. She had never married, and had lived ever since with her brother, not always without scandal and remark. Still her presence had kept Elderthwaite on the visiting-list of the county, and made it possible for her niece to live there.

In spite of her sharp, eager eyes, she had an indescribable laziness and nonchalance of manner, and poured out the tea as if it was an effort beyond her. The boys' places remained vacant. There was a little talk at breakfast-time, but it did not flow easily. Virginia would have had plenty to say, but she had a sense that what she did say caused her aunt inward surprise or amusement, and she began to feel shy.

When the meal was over, Mr Seyton sauntered away slowly, and Virginia said, "Do we sit in the drawing-room in the morning, Aunt Julia?"

"Yes, as often as not," said Miss Seyton. "You are welcome to arrange all such matters for yourself. Girls have ways of their own."

"I don't want to have any strange or uncomfortable ways, auntie," said Virginia; "I want to feel quite at home, and to be useful."

"Useful!" said Miss Seyton. "What's your notion of being useful?"

She did not speak unkindly, but with a curious sort of inward amusement, as if the notions of the bright-eyed girl were an odd study to her.

"I'm afraid I haven't very clear notions. I want to make it cheerful for papa—Aunt Mary always said he wasn't strong or well; and perhaps the boys want things done for them; my friends' brothers always did," said Virginia a little pathetically.

"There's one thing, my dear, I wish you to understand at once. I shall never interfere with you; but I don't mean to abdicate in your favour. I keep house—whatever house is kept—and you'd better shut your eyes and ears to it. It isn't work for you."

"Oh, Aunt Julia!" said Virginia distressed, "I would not think of such a thing. It is your place."

"No, my dear, it's not; but I mean to stick to it," interposed Miss Seyton.

"And I know nothing about housekeeping, I'm afraid. I should be very extravagant."

"Like a true Seyton. So much for that, then. And now another thing. Don't you ever give your brothers so much as a half-sovereign secretly. You have money, and they know it, and it's scarce here. Mind what I say."

A kind of puzzled sense of something that she did not understand crossed Virginia's face.

"I would rather give them things than money," she said. "Of course papa lets them have what is right."

"Of course," said Miss Seyton, with the same perplexing expression of indescribable amusement.

A good joke had for years been the solace, a bitter sarcasm the natural outlet, of a life which certainly had been neither prosperous nor happy in itself, nor glorified by any martyrdom of self-denial.

Miss Seyton was full of malice, both in the French and English acceptations of the word. She loved fun, and she could not see without bitterness the young, unworn creature beside her. To astonish Virginia offered an almost irresistible temptation to both these tendencies. Her evident unconsciousness of the life that lay before her, was at once so funny, and such a cruel satire on them all.

"So you built castles in the air about your relations?" she said, with an odd longing to knock some of these castles down.

"Sometimes," said Virginia; "then Ruth told me about you; and two years ago she and I met Cheriton Lester and his cousin Rupert in London, and I used to talk to them, Cheriton made me wish to come home very much."

"Why?" said Miss Seyton shortly.

"He used to tell her about the place, and he made me remember much better what it was like."

"Cheriton will have to play second fiddle. The eldest brother is coming back from Spain."

"Ah, I remember, he told us how much he wished it. Oh, and he told me Uncle James 'wasn't half a bad fellow.' I suppose that was a boy's way of saying he was very nice indeed. Perhaps I can help him, too, in the village. I like school-teaching, and I suppose there aren't many young ladies in Elderthwaite?"

"You little innocent!" exclaimed Miss Seyton. Then, moving away, she said, in the same wicked undertone, "Well, you had better ask him."

Virginia remained standing by the fire. She felt ruffled, for she knew herself to be laughed at, and not having the clue to her aunt's meaning, she fancied that her free and easy mention of Cheriton had elicited the remark; and being a young lady of decided opinions and somewhat warm temper, made up her mind silently, but with energy, that she would never like her Aunt Julia, never! She had been taken away from home when only eleven years old, and since then had only occasionally seen her father and her brothers. Her cousin Ruth, who had frequently stayed at Elderthwaite, had never bestowed on her much definite information; and perhaps the season in London and the renewal of her childish acquaintance with Cheriton Lester had done more than anything else to revive old impressions.

She had been most carefully brought up by her aunt, Lady Hampton, with every advantage of education and influence. Companions and books were all carefully chosen, and her aunt hoped to see her married before there was any chance of her returning to Elderthwaite. But such was the dread of the reckless, defiant, Seyton nature, that her very precautions defeated their wishes.

Virginia never was allowed to be intimate with any young man but Cheriton, who at the time of their meeting was a mere boy, and with thoughts turned in another direction; and though Virginia was sufficiently susceptible, with a nature at once impetuous and dependent, she came home at one-and-twenty, never yet having seen her ideal in flesh and blood.

"Duties enough, and little cares," had filled her girlhood, and delightful girl friendships and girl reverences had occupied her heart; while her time had been filled by her studies, the cheerful gaieties of a lively neighbourhood, and by the innumerable claims of a church and parish completely organised and vigorously worked.

Lady Hampton was one of the Ladies Bountiful of Littleton; and Virginia had taught in the schools, made tea at the treats, worked at church decorations, and made herself useful and important in all the ways usual to a clever, warm-hearted girl under such influences. And with the same passionate fervour of nature, and the same necessity to her life of an approving conscience, which had made her mother's heart beat itself to death against the bars of her unsatisfying home, Virginia's nature had flowed on in perfect tune with her surroundings; till, when she was nearly twenty, came the great grief of her kind aunt's death, leaving her heiress to a moderate fortune. By the terms of the will she was to travel under carefully selected guardianship till she was of age, and then to choose whether she would go home to her father, or have a home made for her at Littleton.

Virginia chose promptly, and then, in the delicate, indefinite language of those who fear to do harm by every word, was warned of difficulties.

Much would be painful to her, much would be strange; her home was not like anything she had been used to. She listened and looked sad, and understood nothing of what they meant to imply; and thus ready to admire, but with only one type in her mind of what was admirable; full of love, but with none of the blinding softening memories that make love easy, she came to a home where admiration was impossible, and love would demand either ignorant indifference to any high ideal, or a rare and perfect charity, alike unknown to a high-minded intolerant girl.

Chapter Six
Virginia

"A sense of mystery her spirit daunted."

The vicar of Elderthwaite was Mr Seyton's youngest brother. There had been one between them, the father of the Ruth mentioned in the last chapter, but he had married well, and died early, leaving this one girl, who lived with her grandmother, and paid occasional visits to Elderthwaite.

James Seyton had been the wildest of the three, and had taken orders to pay his debts by means of the family living, the revenues of which he had never fully enjoyed. He had never married, and his life—though just kept in bounds by the times in which he lived, so that he did not get tipsy in the Seyton Arms, nor openly scandalise a parish with so low a standard of right as Elderthwaite—was a thoroughly self-indulgent one. He read the service once on Sundays, and administered the Communion three times a year, while the delay and neglect of funerals, marriages, and baptisms were the scandal of every parish round. He rarely visited his flock; and yet the vicar was not wholly an unpopular man. He was good-natured, and though he drank freely and sometimes swore loudly, he had a certain amount of secular intercourse with his parishioners of a not unneighbourly kind.

The pressure of poverty made Mr Seyton a hard landlord, and between oppression and neglect the inhabitants of the picturesque tumbledown village were a bad lot, and neither squire nor parson did much to make them better. But their vicar now and then did put before the worst offenders the consequences of an evil life in language plain enough to reach their understanding; and he had a word and a laugh for most of them.

Mr Lester was frequently heard to inveigh against Parson Seyton's shortcomings, and seriously, as well he might, regretted the state of Elderthwaite parish; but Mr Seyton doctored all his horses and dogs when they were ill, and was, "after all, an old neighbour and a gentleman." He taught Cherry to catch rats, and took him out otter-hunting, and there was the oddest friendship between them, which Cherry, when a boy, had once exemplified in the following manner:—

The Bishop had paid an unexpected visit at. Oakby, and Cheriton following in the wake, while his father and Mr Ellesmere were showing off their new schools, heard him express his intention of going on to Elderthwaite; upon which Cherry ran full speed across the fields, found Parson Seyton shooting rabbits, decidedly in shooting-costume, gave him timely warning, and, with his own hands so tidied, dusted, and furbished up the wretched old church, that its vicar, entering into the spirit of the thing, fell to with a will, astonished the lazy blind old sexton, and produced such a result as might pass muster in a necessarily lenient north-country diocese.

Cherry then diffidently produced one of his father's white ties which he had put in his pocket, "thinking you mightn't have one clean," and as the old vicar, with a shout of laughter, arrayed himself in it, he said, —

"Ay, ay, my lad, between this and the glass of port I'll give his lordship (he won't better that in any parish), we'll push through."

And so they did.

Parson Seyton was a man, if an erring one; but the mischief with his young nephews was that they seemed to have no force or energy even for being naughty, and as they grew up their scrapes were all those of idle self-indulgence, save when the hereditary passion for gambling broke out in Dick, the elder of the two, as had been the case lately, causing his removal from the tutor with whom he had been placed. Like their father, they had not strong health, and they had little taste for field sports, and none for books; they lay in bed half the day, lounged about the stables, and quarrelled with each other. But then their father had nothing to do, read little but the paper, and drank a great deal more wine than was good for him.

Their uncle had conferred on them in his time the inestimable advantage of one or two good thrashings, and had scant patience with a kind of evil to which his burly figure, jolly red face, and hearty reckless temper had never been inclined.

Virginia had thought a good deal about her uncle, and was not unprepared to find him very far removed from the clerical ideal to which she was accustomed. Perhaps the notion of bringing a little enlightenment to so "old-fashioned" a place was neither absent nor unwelcome, as she thought of offering to teach the choir, and wondered who was feminine head of the parish.

"I daresay Uncle James has some nice old housekeeper," she thought, "who trots after the poor people, and takes them jelly, and perhaps teaches the children sewing. There must be a great many people here who remember mamma. I hope they will like me. It will be a much more real thing trying to be helpful here than at Littleton, where there were six people for each bit of work."

Virginia, finding that her brothers did not appear, began to revive her childish recollections by going over the house. It was very large and rambling, with long unused passages, with all the rooms shut up. Windows overgrown with interlacing ivy, panels from which the paint dropped at a touch, queer little turret chambers, with rickety staircases leading up to them, seemed hardly objectionable to Virginia, who liked the romance of the old forlorn house, and had not yet tried living in it. Yet it was not romantic, for Elderthwaite was not ruinous, only very dirty and out of repair; and perhaps the untidy housemaid, whom Virginia had encountered, was really more in accordance with its condition than the white lady or armed spectre that she gaily thought ought to walk those lonely passages. Her own young smiling face, and warm ruby-coloured dress, was in more startling contrast than either. So apparently thought her brother Dick as he ran up against her on the stairs.

"Hallo, Virginia!" he exclaimed in astonished accents. "What are you doing up here?"

"Trying to remember my way about. Don't we keep any ghosts, Dick? I'm sure they would find these dark corners exactly suited to them."

"Better ask old Kitty; she'll tell you all about them. Good-bye, I'm off," and Dick clattered downstairs, rather to Virginia's disappointment, for she had thought the night before that his delicate, handsome face was more prepossessing than the pale stout one of Harry who now joined her.

"Where is Dick going?" she asked.

"Don't know, I'm sure," said Harry. "Do you want to know all the old stories?"

"Yes! can you tell me?"

"Do you see that room there?" said Harry, with eyes that twinkled like his aunt's; "old grandfather Seyton was an old rip, you know, if ever there was one, and he and his friends used to make such a row you heard them over at Oakby. *His* brother was parson then, and bless you! Uncle Jem's a bishop to him. Well, he'd got a dozen men dining here, and they all got as drunk as owls, dead drunk every one of them, and the servants put them to bed up in this gallery. One of them was in the room next grandfather's, that room there, and he was found dead the next morning. Fact, I assure you."

"What a horrid story!" said Virginia, looking shocked.

"I'll tell you another. Grandfather and his brother played awfully high, that's how the avenue was cut down; and when they could get no one else they played with each other, and one night they quarrelled and seized each other by the throats, and they both would have been strangled, only grandmamma rushed in in her nightgown screaming, and parted them; but the parson had the marks on his throat for ever."

"Harry! you naughty boy!" exclaimed Virginia, laughing. "You are inventing all these frightful stories. I don't believe them."

"They're as true as gospel," said Harry, looking at her bright, incredulous eyes. "There's another about the parson—how he came through the park at sunrise. That's not a pretty story to tell you, though."

"I had much rather hear something about the parson, as you call him, nowadays. Come downstairs, it's so cold here, and answer all my questions."

"Oh, the parson's a jolly old card," said Harry, following her. "He's just mad with Dick because he won't hunt. He's been in at the death at every meet round, and don't he swear when any one rides over the dogs, that's all!"

Virginia began to think Elderthwaite must be very old-fashioned indeed.

"Doesn't Dick like hunting?" she said. "No, Dick takes after the governor. It's cards that'll send him to the devil, and the first Seyton he'll be that's not worth having, says Uncle James."

Harry talked in a low, solemn voice, with the same odd twinkle in his eyes, and it was very difficult to say whether it was wicked mischief, or a sort of shameless *naïveté*, that made him so communicative.

Virginia still strongly suspected him of a desire to astonish her; but his last speech gave her a strange new pang, and she turned away to safer subjects.

"I suppose the Lester boys are friends of yours?"

"Well, that's as may be. We're such a bad lot, you see, that Bob's never allowed to come here. There was a row once, and old Lester, a humbugging chap, just interfered. Jack's such a confounded prig he wouldn't touch us with a pair of tongs."

"And Cheriton, of course, is too old for you."

"Cherry! oh, he isn't a bad fellow. I go over to Oakby sometimes when he's there. But it's a slow place, and old Lester keeps them very tight. And then he's always humbugging after his schools and things. Writing to my father about the state of the village. As if it was his affair!" said Harry, in a tone of virtuous indignation.

"Doesn't papa approve of education?" said Virginia.

"Bless you, he don't trouble his head about it. Why should he? Teach a lot of poaching vagabonds to read and write!"

"But Uncle James—"

"Oh, Uncle James," said Harry, with a spice of mimicry, "he likes his glass of grog and his ferrets too well to put himself out of the way. By Jove, here's Aunt Julia! I shall be off before I'm asked what has become of Dick."

Virginia sat still where he had left her. She only half believed him, and strange to say there was something so comical in his manner that she was rather attracted by its cool sauciness. But she was frightened and perplexed. What sort of a world was this into which she had come? Those stories, even if true, happened a long time ago; Harry must be in joke about Dick, and everything was different nowadays.

It was true. The golden age, if such an expression can be permitted, of Seyton wickedness had passed away; and these were smaller times, times of neglect, mismanagement, and low poor living, the dreary dregs of a cup long since drained. Nobody could quote Mr Seyton as a monster of wickedness, because he dawdled away his time over his sherry, and knew no excitement but an occasional game of cards at not very high stakes. There was many another youth in Westmoreland who gambled and played billiards in low company like Dick, and some ladies perhaps who found all their excitement in the memory of other times, and troubled themselves as little over any question of conscience as Miss Seyton.

But it was not all at once that this absence of all that makes life worth living could be apparent, and Virginia found her first confirmation of Harry's words as she walked through the village on Christmas morning, and noted the wild, untidy look of the people, and the wretched state of their houses, and observed the sullen look of their faces as her father passed. Dick did not appear at all; Harry audibly "supposed the governor was going to church because Virginia was there," and certainly church-going did not appear to be a fashion of the village.

Neither her childish recollections, nor Harry's remarks, had prepared her, as they came into the small, ivy-grown church, for broken floors, cracked windows, and damp fustiness; still less for the very scantiest of congregations, and a rustling silence where responses should have been. Her uncle read the service rapidly, with the broad northern accent now strange to her ears. The old clerk trotted about whenever his services were not required, and did a little sweeping. Her uncle paused as he began the Litany, and called to him in a loud and cheerful voice to shut the door.

Virginia peeped out between the faded green-baize curtains that, hanging round the great square pew, represented to her every Church principle she had been taught to condemn; and found her view obstructed by a large cobweb. Harry poked at the spider, and Virginia recalling her own attention from her despairing visions of having no better church than this, perceived that her father was leaning idly back in his corner. All her standards of right and wrong seemed confused and shocked; so much so that, at the moment, she hardly distinguished the pain of finding herself left alone after the sermon, and seeing her father turn away, from her horror at her uncle's dirty surplice, and the dreary degradation of the whole place. When the parson came after her after service, and loudly told her she was the prettiest lass he'd seen for long enough, kissing her under the church porch, she still felt as if the typical bad parish priest of her imagination had come to life, and behold he was her own uncle!

Since this comprehensible form of evil was so plain to her eyes, what terrible secrets might not lurk behind it! Virginia felt as if she would never be light-hearted again.

Chapter Seven
Fire and Snow

"A northern Christmas, such as painters love.
* * * * *

Red sun, blue sky, white snow, and pearled ice,
Keen ringing air which sets the blood on fire."

Christmas is no doubt, theoretically, the right season for relations who have been long parted to meet, and there was an ideal appropriateness in the long absent heir appearing at Oakby for the first time on Christmas Day. But practically it would have been better for Alvar if he had come home at any other time of the year. In the first place the frost continued with unabated severity, and precluded every outdoor amusement but skating, in which Alvar of course had no skill, and which he did not seem at all willing to learn. Besides, the season brought an amount of local and parish business which Mr Lester attended to vigorously in person, but the existence of which Alvar never seemed to realise. His grandmother's charities he understood, and was rather amused at seeing the old women come to fetch their blankets and cloaks; but what could he have to do with any of these people?

Tenants' dinners and choir-suppers might form a good opportunity for introducing him to his neighbours; and Cheriton, who was the life and soul of such festivities, tried to put him forward; but he only made magnificent silent bows, and comported himself much as his brother Jack had done, when in an access of gruff shyness and democratic ardour he had called the Christmas feasts "relics of feudalism," and had shown his advanced notions of the union of classes by never speaking a word to any one.

Between the newcomer and his father there was an impassable distance. Alvar never failed in courtesy; but Cheriton's quick eyes soon perceived that he resented deeply the long neglect; saw too that the sight of him was a pain and distress to his father, sharpened his temper, and produced constant rubs; though he was careful to do everything that the proper introduction of his son demanded of him. A grand ball was organised in his honour, and also a stiff and ponderous dinner-party at which Alvar was to be introduced to the county magnates.

Special invitations were also sent to him by their various neighbours, and he created quite an excitement in the dull country neighbourhood. Mr Lester only half liked being congratulated on his son's charming foreign manners; but still, as a novelty, Alvar had great attractions, and in society never seemed shy or at a loss. Mr Lester's brother-in-law, Judge Cheriton, invited the stranger to pay him a visit when the season had a little advanced, and to let him see a little London society; for which attention Mr Lester, who hated London, was very grateful, as Alvar's grandfather had Spanish friends there, and it would have been too intolerable for the heir of Oakby to have appeared there under auspices which, however distinguished, Mr Lester thought suitable only to a political refugee or a music master.

He had, when he had ceased to pay for Alvar's English tutor, made him an allowance which had been magnificent in Spain, and greatly added to Alvar's consideration there, and he now increased this to what he considered a sufficient sum for his eldest son's dignity. In short he did everything but overcome his personal distaste to him; he never willingly spoke to him, and the very sight of him was an irritation to him. He got less too than usual of Cheriton's company; their walks, and talks, and consultations were curtailed by Alvar's requirements. Indeed Cherry was pulled in many different directions, and he ended by sacrificing all the reading that was to have been got through during the vacation. For the home life was very difficult, and the more they saw of the stranger the less they liked him.

"He's not of our sort," said Bob, as if that settled the matter, not perceiving that his slowness to receive impressions, and difficulty in accommodating himself to a new life, might spring as much from his Lester blood as from his Spanish breeding.

"He might try and *look* like an Englishman," growled Jack.

"When you go to Spain, we shall see you in a *sombrero* dancing under the orange-trees to a pair of castanets," retorted Cheriton. "*We* should all be so ready at foreign languages and so accommodating, shouldn't we?"

Alvar's individuality was not to be ignored, though unfortunately it was very distasteful to his kindred. He was so dignified, so terribly polite they were half afraid of him, and as the awe wore off, they wanted to quarrel with him. He announced that he loved riding, and seemed to know something of horses; he played billiards much too well to be a pleasant opponent to his father, he sang much too quaintly and prettily for his family to appreciate, and he played the guitar! Even Cheriton wished it had been a fiddle. He hated going to walk, smoked incessantly, and was indifferent to every one except Cheriton, to whom he deferred in everything.

Poor Cheriton! "Among the blind, the one-eyed is king," and his sentiments were amazingly liberal for Oakby; but he was very young and deeply attached to his home and his surroundings, too tender-hearted not to be touched at Alvar's preference, imaginative enough to realise his position, and yet repelled and put out of countenance by his peculiarities. To be tenderly addressed as "my brother," "mi caro," "mi Cheriton," "Cherito mio," to be deferred to on all occasions, and even told in the hearing of Jack and Bob "that his eyes when he laughed were the colour of the Mediterranean on a sunny day," was, as he said, "so out-facing, that it made him feel a perfect fool," especially when his brothers echoed it at every turn.

Yet he put up with it. It was so hard on the poor fellow if no one was kind to him! So hard, he added to himself, to be an unloved and unloving son.

Perhaps, after all, Alvar's essential strangeness prevented Cheriton from feeling himself put aside.

Cheriton was very popular at school and at college. He had strong, intellectual ambitions, and though of less powerful mind than Jack, had attained to much graceful scholarship and possessed much command of language. He hoped to take honours, to go to the bar, and distinguish himself there under his uncle, Judge Cheriton's, auspices. He had too a further and a sweeter hope, hitherto confided to no one.

But it was a certain "genius for loving" that really distinguished him from his fellows—really made him every one's friend. He did not seek out his poorer neighbours so much from a sense of duty, as because his heart went out to every one belonging to Oakby, nay, every animal, every bit of ground—nothing was a trouble that conduced to the welfare of the place. This loving-kindness was a natural gift; but Cheriton made good use of it. He had high principles, and deep within his soul, struggling with the temptations of this ardent nature, were the pure aspirations and the capability of fervent piety which have made saints—responsibilities with which he was born.

But all this fire and force did not make tolerance easy; he was full of instinctive prejudices, and perhaps his greatest aids in his dealings with his new brother were his joyous unchecked spirits and the keen sense of the ludicrous that enabled him to laugh at himself as well as at other people.

Some little time after Alvar's arrival there was a deep fall of snow, and while the pond was being swept for skating, the young Lesters, with Harry Seyton and the children from the rectory, who had come up for the purpose, proceeded to erect a snow man of gigantic proportions in front of the house.

"What a fright you have made of him!" said Cheriton, coming up with Alvar as they finished; "he has no nose and no expression."

"Well, come and do his nose, then; it keeps on coming off," said Nettie, who was standing on a bench to put the finishing touches.

Cherry was nothing loath, and was soon engaged in moulding the snowy countenance with the skill of long practice, while Alvar, with his great crimson-lined cloak wrapped about him, stood looking on.

"Give him a good *lumpy* nose, that won't melt," said Cherry. "There, he's lovely! got an old pipe for him?"

As he spoke a great snowball came stinging against his face, and in a moment, to the astonishment of Alvar, the whole party set on Cherry, and a wild bout of snowballing ensued.

"No, no, that's not fair! I can't fight you all," shouted Cherry; "and you've got all your snowballs ready made. Give me the girls, and then— Come on."

"Oh, yes, yes; we'll be on Cherry's side," cried Nettie.

It was a picturesque scene enough—the pale blue sky overhead, the dazzling snow under foot, the little girls in their scarlet cloaks or petticoats, their long hair flying as they darted in and out, the great boys struggling, wrestling, knocking each other about with small mercy. No one threw a snowball at Alvar; perhaps they had forgotten him, as he stood silently watching them as if they were a troop of Berserkers, till the contest terminated in a tremendous struggle between Cheriton and Jack, who were, of course, much the biggest of the party. Cherry was getting decidedly the worst of it, and either tripped in the rough snow or was thrown down into it by Jack, when suddenly Alvar threw off his cloak, stepped forward, and seizing Jack by the shoulders, pulled him back with sudden irresistible force.

"By Jove!" was all that Jack could utter.

"What on earth did you do that for?" ejaculated Cherry as soon as he gained his breath and his feet.

"He might have hurt you, my brother," said Alvar, who looked flushed, and for once excited. "And besides, I am stronger than either of you. I could struggle with you both."

"Hurt me? Suppose he had?" said Cherry disdainfully. "But, Jack— Jack, I do believe you're getting too many for me at last."

"That is what you call athletics," said Alvar, who looked unusually bright.

"Yes; wrestling is a regular north-country game, and the fellows about here have taught us all the tricks of it. Come, Jack, let us show him a bout."

The two brothers pulled off their coats, and set to with a will; and after a long struggle, and with considerable difficulty, Cheriton succeeded in throwing Jack.

"There, I've done it once more!" he said breathlessly, "and I don't suppose I shall ever do it again. You're getting much stronger than I am, and of course you're heavier."

"Let me try to throw you down," said Alvar eagerly.

"Nay, Jack may have first turn; but it's fair to tell you there's a great deal of knack in it."

Alvar, however, was man instead of boy; he was quite as tall as Jack, and however he might have learnt to exercise his muscles, his grasp was like steel; and though Jack's superior skill triumphed in the end, Alvar rose up cool and smiling, and Jack panted out, in half-unwilling admiration, —

"You'd beat us all with a little training."

"Ah yes; that is because I am an Englishman," said Alvar complacently. "But I bear no malice, Jack. It is in sport."

"Of course," said Jack. "Now, Cherry, you try."

"It's hardly fair in a biting frost," said Cherry; "nobody can have any wind. However, here's for the honour of Westmoreland."

The younger ones gathered round in an admiring circle, and Cheriton, who did not like to be beaten, put forth all the strength and skill of which he was master. But he was the more slightly made, and had met his match, and to the extreme chagrin of his brothers and Nettie, sustained an entire defeat.

"Well, I never thought you would throw *him*," said Jack, in a tone of deep disappointment.

"Ah," said Alvar, "they always called me the strong Englishman."

"Papa was the strongest man in Westmoreland," said Nettie.

"Then," said Alvar, "so far I have proved myself his son, and your brother. I would not skate with you, for I should look like a fool; but I knew you could not easily throw me down, since that is your sport. But, my brother, I have hurt you."

"No," said Cheriton getting up, "only knocked all the wind out of me, and made *me* look like a fool! Never mind, we shall understand each other all the better. Come upstairs, and we will show you some of the cups and things we have won in boat-races and athletics."

This was a clever stroke of Cheriton's; he wanted to make Alvar free of the premises, and had not yet found a good excuse. So, leaving the younger ones to finish their snowballing, he and Jack conducted Alvar up to the top of the house, where, at the end of the passage where they slept, was a curious low room, with a long, low window, looking west, above the west window of the drawing-room, and occupying nearly one side of the room, almost like the windows of the hand-loom weavers in the West Riding.

There was a low seat underneath, broad enough to lie on, but furnished with very dilapidated cushions. There was a turning-lathe in the room, and a cupboard for guns, and sundry cases of stuffed birds, one table covered with tools, glue-pots, and messes of all descriptions; and another, it is but justice to add, supplied with ink, pens, and paper, and various formidable-looking books, for here the boys did their reading. There was a great, old-fashioned grate with a blazing fire in it, and very incongruous ornaments above it—a stuffed dormouse, Nettie's property—she maintained a footing in the room by favour—various pipes, two china dogs, white, with brown spots on them, presented to Cherry in infancy by his nurse, and a wooden owl carved by their cousin Rupert—a cousin in the second degree, who had been much with them owing to his father's early death. On one side of the room were arranged on a sort of sideboard the cups and tankards which were the trophies of the brothers' prowess, and these were now each pointed out to Alvar, and the circumstances of their acquisition described. Cheriton's were fewer in proportion, and chiefly for leaping and hurdle-racing; and Jack explained that Cherry's forte was cricket, and that, since he had once knocked himself up at school by a tremendous flat-race, their father had greatly objected to his going into training.

"Oh, it's not that," said Cherry; "he would not care now; but I really haven't time. I must grind pretty hard from now to midsummer."

"There is one thing I have read of," said Alvar, "in English newspapers. It is a race of boats on the Thames between Oxford and Cambridge."

"Oh, yes, you must go and see it. That's Jack's ambition—to be one of the crew."

"Ah, but you see there's no river at R—, and that's so unlucky," said Jack seriously.

And so what with explanations and questions the ice melted a little. Alvar looked smiling and beneficent; he did not seem at all ashamed of his own ignorance; and Jack evidently regarded him with a new respect.

Cheriton also contrived that the Seytons, with the vicar of Oakby, Mr Ellesmere and his wife, should be asked to dinner; and as the vicar had some general conversation, some information about Spain was elicited from Alvar, who, moreover, was pleased to find himself in ladies' society, and was evidently at ease in it; while Virginia, in exchange for the pleasant talk that seemed to come out of her old life, could tell Cheriton that her cousin Ruth was coming to stay with her, and could confide in him that home was still a little strange.

"Well, strangers *are* strange," said Cherry. "*We* are shaking down, but the number of tempers lost in the process might be advertised for 'as of no value except to the owners,' if to them. Only the home-made article, you understand—"

"Dear me," said Virginia, "I should as soon think of losing my temper with the Cid. Aren't you afraid of him?"

Cheriton made an irresistibly ludicrous face.

"Don't tell," he said, "but I think we are; and yet, you know, we think 'yon soothern chap,' as old Bates called him, must be 'a bit of a softy' after all."

"Oh, Cherry, that is how you talked yourself when we were children," exclaimed Virginia impulsively. "Do you know I *feel* I was born here, when I hear the broad Westmoreland. I never forgot it."

"Nay, I'm glad you don't say I talk so now," said Cherry. "They tell me at Oxford that my tongue always betrays me when I am excited. But here comes Alvar; now make him fall in love with Westmoreland. Alvar, Miss Seyton *has* been abroad, so *she* is not quite a benighted savage."

"My brother Cheriton is not a savage," said Alvar, smiling, as Cherry moved away. "He is the kindest and most beautiful person I have ever seen."

"Yes, he is very kind. But I hope, Mr Lester, that you do not think us *all* savages, with that one exception."

"In future I can never think so," said Alvar, with a bow. "These boys are savage certainly—very savage, but I do not care."

"It is strange, is it not," said Virginia, rather timidly, "to have to make acquaintance with one's own father?"

"Of my father I say nothing," said Alvar, with a sudden air of hauteur, that made the impulsive Virginia blush, and feel as if she had taken a liberty with him, till he added, with a smile, "Miss Seyton, too, I hear, is a stranger."

"Yes, I have been away ever since I was a little girl, and—and I had forgotten my relations."

"I have not known mine," said Alvar; "Cheriton wrote to me once a little letter. I have it now, and since then I have loved him. I do not know the rest, and they wish I was not here."

"But don't you think," said Virginia earnestly, "that we—that you will soon feel more at home with them?"

"Oh, I do not know," said Alvar, with a shrug. "It is cold, and I am so dull that I could die. They understand no thing. And in Spain I was the chief; I could do what I wished. Here I must follow and obey. My name even is different. I do not know 'Mr Lester.' I am 'Don Alvar.' Will you not call me so?"

"But that would be so very strange to me," said Virginia, parrying this request. "Every one will call you Mr Lester. How tall Nettie is grown. Do you not think her very pretty?"

"Oh, she is pink, and white, and blue, and yellow; but she is like a little boy. There is not in her eyes the attraction, the coquetry, which I admire," said Alvar, pointing his remark with a glance at his companion's lucid, beaming, interested eyes, in which however there was little conscious coquetry.

"I am sorry to hear you admire coquettes," was too obvious an answer to be resisted.

"Nay, it is the privilege of beauty," said Alvar.

Virginia, like many impulsive people, was apt to recollect with a cold chill conversations by which at the time she had been entirely carried away. But on looking back at this one she liked it. Alvar's dignity and grace of manner made his trifling compliments both flattering and respectful. His feelings, too, she thought, were evidently deep and tender; and how she pitied him for his solitary condition!

Chapter Eight
A Day of Rest

"Gaily the troubadour touched his guitar."

On the third Sunday morning after Alvar's arrival, Mr Lester came down as usual at the sound of the gong, and as he glanced round the dining-room missed his two elder sons.

Prayers were over and breakfast had begun before Alvar entered.

"Ah pardon," he said, bowing to his grandmother; "I did not know it was late."

"I make a point of being punctual on Sunday," said Mr Lester, in a tone of incipient displeasure.

"Cheriton is late too," said Alvar.

"No," said Jack, "he's gone to Church."

"All, then *we* do not go to-day," said Alvar, with an air of relief so comical that even the solemn Jack could hardly stand it.

"Oh, yes, we do," he said, "this is extra."

"Cheriton," said Mr Lester, "is very attentive to his religious duties."

"I suppose he'll have breakfast at the Vicarage," said Nettie, as Alvar raised his eyebrows and gave a little shrug.

It was a gesture habitual to him, and was not intended to express contempt either for religion or for Cheriton, but only a want of comprehension of the affair; but it annoyed Mr Lester and called his attention to the fact that Alvar had appeared in a black velvet coat of a peculiar foreign cut, the sight of which he disliked on a week-day, and considered intolerable when it was contrasted with the spruce neatness of the rest of the party. He could not very well attack Alvar on the subject, but he sharply reproved Bob for cutting hunches of bread when no one wanted them, and found fault with the coffee. And then, apparently *à propos* of nothing, he began to make a little speech about the importance of example in a country place, and the influence of trifles.

"And I can assure *every one* present," he concluded emphatically, "that there is no need to look far for an example of the evil effects of neglect in these particulars."

"Elderthwaite?" whispered Nettie to Jack.

"Ay," said Mrs Lester, "young people should show respect to Sunday morning. It is what in my father's house was always insisted on. Your grandfather, too, used to say that he liked his dogs even to know Sunday."

"It is strange to me," said Alvar coolly.

"It will be well that you should give yourself the pains to become accustomed to it," said his father curtly.

It was the first time that the stately stranger had been addressed in such a tone, and he looked up with a flash of the eye that startled the younger ones.

"Sir, it is by your will I am a stranger here," he said, with evident displeasure.

"Stranger or no, my regulations must be respected," said Mr Lester, his colour rising.

Alvar rose from his seat and proved his claim at any rate to the family temper by bowing to his grandmother and marching out of the room.

"Highty tighty!" said the grandmother. "Here's a spirt of temper for you!"

"Intolerable insolence!" exclaimed Mr Lester. "Under my roof he must submit to what I please to say to him."

"It's just what I told ye, Gerald; a foreigner's ways are what we cannot do with," said Mrs Lester.

"Of course," blurted out Jack, with the laudable desire of mending matters; "of course he is a foreigner. How can you expect him to be anything else? And father never said it was his coat."

"His coat?" said Mr Lester. "It is his temper to which I object. When he came I told him that I expected Sunday to be observed in my house, and he agreed."

"But he did not understand that you thought that coat improper on Sunday," said Jack with persevering justice.

"I am not in the habit of being obscure," said Mr Lester, as he rose from the table, while Jack thought he would give Alvar a little good advice.

Cherry was too soft; he was equally impartial, and would be more plain spoken. But as he approached the library he heard an ominous tinkling, and entering, beheld Alvar, still in the objectionable coat, beginning to play on the still more objectionable guitar, an air which Jack did not think sounded like a hymn tune.

Jack really intended to mend matters, but his manner was unfortunate, and in the tone he would have used to a disobedient fag he remarked, as he stood bolt upright beside his brother,—

"I say, Alvar, I think you'd better not play on that thing this morning."

"There is no reason for you to tell me what to do," said Alvar quietly.

"It's not, you know," said Jack, "that *I* think there's any harm in it. *My* views are very liberal. I only think it's a frivolous and unmanly sort of instrument; but the governor won't like it, and there'll be no end of a row."

"You have not a musical soul," said Alvar loftily, for he had had time to cool down somewhat.

"*Certainly* not," said the liberal Jack, with unnecessary energy and a tone of disgust; "but that's not the question. It's not the custom here to play *that sort of thing on a thing like that* on a Sunday morning. Ask Cherry."

"Would it vex my brother?" asked Alvar.

"If you mean Cheriton, it certainly would. He hates a row."

"A row?" said the puzzled Alvar, "that is a noise—my guitar?"

"Oh, hang it! no, a quarrel," began Jack, when suddenly—

"Sir, I consider this an act of defiance; I beg I may see that instrument put away at once," and Mr Lester's voice took the threatening sound that made his anger always appear so much worse than it really was. "I will have the proprieties of my house observed, and no example of this kind set to your younger brothers."

Alvar had taken Jack's interference with cool contempt, but now he started up with a look of such passion as fairly subdued Jack into a hasty—

"Oh come, come, I say, now—don't!" Alvar controlled himself suddenly and entirely.

"Sir, I obey my father's commands. I will say good morning," and taking up his guitar went up to his own room, from which he did not emerge at church time, and as no one ventured to call him they set off without him. Among themselves they might quarrel and make it up again many times a day, but Alvar's feelings were evidently more serious.

It was occasionally Cheriton's practice to sing in the choir, more for the popularity of his example than for his voice, which was indifferent. Alvar had been greatly puzzled at his doing so, and had then told him that "in that white robe he looked like the picture of an angel," a remark which so discomfited Cherry that he had further perplexed his unlucky brother by saying,—"*Pray* don't say such a thing to the others, I should never hear the last of it. You'd better say I look like an ass at once."

He did not therefore see anything of his family till he met them after the service, when Jack attacked him.

"What induced you to go out this morning? Everything has gone utterly wrong, and I shouldn't wonder if we should find Alvar gone back to Spain."

"Why, what's the matter?"

"Alvar came down late in that ridiculous coat and then played the guitar. And if ever you saw a fellow in a passion! He likes his own way."

"Was father angry?"

"I should just think so, I don't expect they'll speak."

This was a pleasant prospect. Cheriton saw that his father's brow was cloudy, and as he went upstairs his grandmother called him into her room.

"Cheriton," she said mysteriously, as she sat down and untied her bonnet, "Jack has told you of your brother's behaviour, and it's my belief there's a clue to it, and I hope you'll take warning, for I sometimes think ye've a hankering after that way yourself."

"What way, grandmamma? I never play the guitar on a Sunday morning."

"Nay, but there's more behind. It's well known how Sunday is profaned in Popish countries. I've heard they keep the shops open in France. Your brother has been brought up among Papists, and it would be a sad thing for your father's son to give all this property into the hands of the priests."

"Dear me, granny, what a frightful suggestion. But I'm sure Alvar has no Romish sympathies. He has no turn for anything of the kind, and I should think the Roman Church was very unattractive in Spain."

"Ay, but they're very deep."

"Well," said Cherry, "if Alvar is a Jesuit in disguise, as you say, and rather a dissipated person, as my father seems to think, and has such an appalling temper as Jack describes, we're in a bad way. I think I'll go and see for myself."

When Cherry entered Alvar's room he found this alarming compound of qualities sitting by the fire looking forlorn and lonely. "Why, Alvar, what's all this about?"

"Ah, my brother," said Alvar, "you were absent and all has been wrong. My father is offended with me. I know not why. He insulted me."

"Oh, nonsense! we never talk about being insulted. My father's a little hasty, but he means nothing by it. What did you do that annoyed him?"

"I played my guitar and Jack scolded me. No one shall do so but you."

"I daresay Jack made an ass of himself—he often does; but he is a thorough good fellow at bottom. You know we do get up in our best clothes on Sunday."

"I can do that," said Alvar, "but your Sunday I do not understand. You tell me I may not play at cards or at billiards; you do not dance nor go to the theatre. What good does it do? I would go to church, though it is tiresome, and I shudder at the singing. It is a mark, doubtless, of my father's politics; but at home—well, I can smoke, if that is better?"

Driven back to first principles, Cheriton hardly knew what to say. "Of course," he answered. "I have often heard the matter discussed, and I don't pretend to say that at Oxford the best of us are as particular as we might be. But in a country place like this, carelessness would do infinite harm. And, on the whole, I shouldn't like the rule to be otherwise."

Alvar sighed, and made no answer.

"But," continued Cherry, "I think no one has a right to impose rules on you. I wouldn't bring out the guitar in the morning—it looks rather odd, you know—nor wear that coat. But we're not so very strict; there are always newspapers about, and novels, and, as you say, you can smoke or talk, or play the piano—I'm sure no one would know what the tune was—or write letters. Really, it might be worse, you know."

Perhaps Cherry's coaxing voice and eyes were more effectual than his arguments; any way, Alvar said, "Well, I will offer my hand to my father, if he will take it."

"Oh, no; pray don't make a scene about it. There's the gong. Put on your other coat, and come down. We *do* eat our dinner on Sunday, and I'm awfully hungry."

Whether Mr Lester accepted the coat as a flag of truce, or whether he did not wish to provoke a contest with an unknown adversary, nothing more was said; but Alvar's evil star was in the ascendant, and he was destined to run counter to his family in a more unpardonable way.

He had no sympathy whatever with the love for animals, which was perhaps the softest side of his rough kindred. All the English Lesters were imbued with that devotion to live creatures which is ingrain with some natures. No trouble was too great to take for them. Bob and Nettie got up in the morning and went out in all weathers to feed their ferrets, or their jackdaws, or whatever pet was young, sick, or troublesome. Cheriton's great Saint Bernard, Rolla, ranked somewhere very near Jack in his affections, and had been taught, trained, beaten, and petted, till he loved his master with untiring devotion. Mrs Lester had her chickens and turkeys, Mr Lester his prize cattle and his horses, some of the latter old and well-tried friends.

It must be admitted that Oakby was a trying place for people devoid of this sentiment. Every one had a dog, more or less valuable, and jackdaws and magpies have their drawbacks as members of a family. Alvar openly said that he had never seen anybody make pets of dumb animals, and that he could not understand doing so; and though he took no notice of them, Rolla and an old pointer of Mr Lester's, called Rose, had already been thrashed for growling at him.

On this particular Sunday afternoon, the bright cold weather clouded over and promised a thaw. Alvar preferred dulness to the weather out-of-doors, and Cheriton accompanied his father on the Sunday stroll, which included all the beasts on the premises, and generally ended in visits to the old keeper and coachman, who thought it the height of religious advantage to bear the squire read a chapter.

Mr Lester was aware that he had been impatient with his son, and that Alvar could not be expected to be imbued with an instinctive knowledge of those forms of religion with which his father had been inspired by his young brilliant wife, when "Fanny" had taught him to restore his church and build his schools in a fuller fashion than had satisfied his father, and made him believe that his position demanded of himself and his family a personal participation in all good works—some control of them he naturally desired.

He was, as Mr Ellesmere said, with a little shrug, when forced to yield a point, "a model squire," conscientious and open-handed, but unpersuadable. Perhaps the clear-eyed, wide-souled Fanny might have allowed more readily for the necessary changes of twenty years. Certainly she would better have appreciated a newcomer's difficulties; while poor Mr Lester felt that Fanny's ideal was invaded, and not by Fanny's son. It spoilt his walk with Cheriton, and made him reply sharply to the latter's attempts at agreeable conversation. Cheriton at length left him at the old gamekeeper's; and while Mr Lester's irritable accents were softened into kindly inquiries for the old father, now pensioned off, he chatted to the son, at present in command, who had been taking care of a terrier puppy for him.

Finding that Buffer, so called from his prevailing colour, was looking strong and lively, Cheriton thought it would be as well to accustom him to society, and took him back to the house. He could not help wondering what would become of Alvar when he was left alone at Oakby. Another fortnight would hardly be sufficient to give him any comfortable, independent habits; how could he endure such deadly dulness as the life there would bring him? That fortnight would be lively enough, and there would be his cousin, Rupert Lester, for an additional companion, and another Miss Seyton, more attractive than Virginia, for an occasional excitement. If Alvar was so fascinating a person to young ladies, would he—would she—? An indefinite haze of questions pervaded Cheriton's mind, and as he reckoned over the county beauties whom he could introduce to Alvar, and whom he would surely admire more than just the one particular beauty who had first occurred to his thoughts, he reached the house. He found his brothers and Nettie alone in the library, Alvar sitting apart in the window, and looking out at the stormy sky.

"Hallo!" said Jack, "so you have brought Buffer up. Well, he has grown a nice little chap."

"Yes, I thought it was time he should begin his education. Nice head, hasn't he? He is just like old Peggy."

"Yes, he'll be a very good dog some day."

"Set him down," said Bob; "let's have a look at him."

"Little darling!" said Nettie, enthusiastically.

Buffer was duly examined, and then, as Cherry turned to the fire to warm himself, observing that it was colder than ever, began to play about the room, while they entered on a discussion of the merits of all his relations up to their dim recollection of his great-grandmother.

Buffer made himself much at home, poked about the room, and at last crossed over to Alvar, who had sat on, unheeding his entrance. Buffer gave his trousers a gentle pull. Alvar shook him off. Here was another tiresome little beast; then, just as Cherry crossed over to the window in search of him, he made a dart at Alvar's foot and bit it sharply. Alvar sprang up with a few vehement Spanish words, gave the little dog a rough kick, and then dashed it away from him with a gesture of fierce annoyance. Buffer uttered a howl of pain.

"I say, that's too rough," exclaimed Cherry, snatching up the puppy, which cried and moaned.

"But it bit me!" said Alvar, angrily.

"I believe you have killed him," said Cheriton.

"You cruel coward," cried Nettie, bursting into a storm of tears.

Alvar stood facing all the four, their blue eyes flashing scorn and indignation; but, angry as they were, they were too practical to waste time in reproaches. Jack brought a light, and Bob, whose skill in such matters equalled his literary incapacity, felt Buffer's limbs scientifically.

"No ribs broken," he said; "he's bruised, though, poor little beggar! Ah! he has put his shoulder out. Now, Cherry, if your hand's going to shake, give him to Jack. I'll pull it in again."

"I can hold him steady," said Alvar, in a low voice.

"No, thank you," said Cherry, curtly, as Jack put a hand to steady his hold, and the operation was performed amid piteous shrieks from Buffer. Alvar had the sense to watch them in silence. What had he done? A kick and a blow to any domestic animal was common enough in Spain. And now he had roused all this righteous indignation, and, far worse, offended Cherry, and seen his distress at the little animal's suffering, and at its cause. Buffer was no sooner laid in Nettie's arms to be cossetted and comforted, than he seized Cherry's hand.

"Ah, my brother! I did not know the little dog was yours. I would not touch him—"

"What difference does that make?" said Cherry, shaking him off and walking away.

"I shall keep *my* dog out of his way," said Bob, contemptuously.

"I suppose Spaniards are savages," said Jack, in a tone of deadly indignation.

"He'd better play a thousand guitars than hurt a poor little innocent puppy!" said Nettie, half sobbing.

Alvar stood looking mournfully before him; his anger had died out; he looked almost ready to cry with perplexity.

Cheriton turned round. "I won't have a fuss made," he said. "Take Buffer upstairs to my room, and don't say a word to any one. It can't be helped."

"I know *who* I shall never say a word to," said Nettie; but she obeyed, followed by Jack and Bob. Alvar detained Cheriton.

"Oh, my brother, forgive me. I would have broken my own arm sooner than see your eyes look at me thus. It is with us a word and a blow. I will never strike any little beast again—never."

He looked so wretched that Cheriton answered reluctantly, "I don't mean to say any more about it."

"But you are angry still?"

"No, I'm not angry. I suppose you feel differently. I hate to see anything suffer."

"And I to see you suffer, my brother."

"I? nonsense! I tell you that's nothing to do with it. There, let it drop. I shall say no more."

He escaped, unable further to satisfy his brother, and went upstairs, where Buffer had been put to bed comfortably.

"Did you ever know such a nasty trick in your life?" said Jack, as they left the twins to watch the invalid's slumbers.

"Oh!" said Cherry, turning into his room, "it's all hopeless and miserable. We shall never come to any good—never!"

"Oh, come, come now, Cherry," said Jack, for once assuming the office of consoler. "Buffer'll do well enough; don't be so despairing."

Cheriton had much the brighter and serener nature of the two; but he was subject to fits of reaction, when Jack's cooler temperament held its own.

"It's not Buffer," he said, "it's Alvar! How can one ever have any brotherly feeling for a fellow like that? He's as different as a Red Indian!"

"It would be very odd and unnatural if you had much brotherly feeling for him," said Jack. "Why do you trouble yourself about him?"

"But he does seem to have taken a sort of fancy to me, and the poor fellow's a stranger!"

"You're a great deal too soft about him. Of course he likes you, when you're always looking him up. Don't be superstitious about it—he's only our half-brother; and don't go down to tea looking like that, or you'll have the governor asking what's the matter with you."

"Remember, I'll not have a word said about it," said Cheriton emphatically.

Nothing was said publicly about it, but Alvar was made to feel himself in disgrace, and endeavoured to re-ingratiate himself with Cherry with a simplicity that was irresistible. He asked humbly after Buffer's health, and finally presented him with a silver chain for a collar.

When Buffer began to limp about on three legs, his tawny countenance looking out above the silver engraved heart that clasped the collar with the sentimental leer peculiar to puppyhood, the effect was sufficiently ludicrous; but he forgave Alvar sooner than his brothers did, and perhaps grateful for his finery, became rather fond of him.

Chapter Nine
Ruth

"She has two eyes so soft and brown."

There was a little oak-panelled bedroom at Elderthwaite, which had been called Ruth's ever since, as a curly-haired, brown-skinned child, the little orphan cousin had come from her grandmother's in London and paid a long visit in the North some five or six years before the winter's day on which she now occupied it, when she came to be present at the Lesters' ball. She was a nut-brown maid still, with rough, curly hair and great dark eyes, with curly, upturned lashes—eyes that were like Virginia's in shape, colour, and fervour, but which glanced and gleamed and melted after a fashion wholly their own. She was slender and small, and though with no wonderful beauty of feature or perfection of form, whether she sat or stood she made a picture; all colours that she wore became her, all scenes set off her peculiar grace. Now, her brown velvet dress, her rusty hair against the dark oak shutter, as she sat crouched up in the window-seat, were a perfect "symphony in brown."

Ruth Seyton was an orphan, and lived with her grandmother, Lady Charlton, a gentle, worldly old lady, whose great object was to see her well married, and to steer her course safely through all the dangers that might affect the course of a well-endowed and very attractive girl. The scorn which Ruth felt for the shallow feelings and worldly notions with which she was expected to enter on the question of her own future was justifiable enough, and led to a violent reaction and to a fervour of false romance. Ruth had found her hero and formulated her view of life, and the hero was Rupert Lester, whom she was about to meet at the ball given in Alvar's honour, and between whom and herself lay the memory of something more than a flirtation.

The theory was, that the hero once found, the grand passion once experienced, was its own justification, itself the proof of depth of character and worth of heart. A girl who paused to consider her lover's character or her friends' disapproval, when she had once given her heart away, was a weak and cold-natured creature in her opinion. She knew that many difficulties lay between her and Rupert Lester, and she gloried in the thought of how they should be overcome, rejoiced in her own discrimination, which could see the difference between this real passion and the worldly motives of some of her other admirers, or the boyish fancy of Cheriton Lester, who talked to her about his brothers and his occupations, and had room in his heart, so it seemed to her, for a thousand lesser loves. Ruth believed that she despised flirtation; but there could be no harm in being pleasant to a boy she had known all her life and whose attentions just now were so convenient. Besides, Cheriton was really very like his cousin Rupert, very like the photograph which she now hid away as Virginia came in search of her.

The two cousins had been a great deal together at intervals and were fond of each other, and Virginia knew something about Rupert; but Ruth knew better than to give her full confidence on the subject.

"Well," she said, as her cousin entered, "and how does the world go with you? Do you see much of the Lesters?"

"Yes; while the frost lasted I used to go down to the ice with the boys, and we met there. Cheriton comes over here sometimes, and once he brought his brother."

"What, the Spaniard? How *do* they manage? Is he very queer?"

"Oh, no! Of course he is very unlike the others. Cherry gets on very well with him. I believe Mr Lester does not wish the boys to come here much," added Virginia, abruptly.

"Well, it wasn't approved of in Roland's time," said Ruth.

"Were we always bad company?" said Virginia. "I have had a great deal to learn. Why did you never make me understand better what Elderthwaite was like?"

"But, Queenie," said Ruth cautiously, using a pet name of Virginia's girlhood, "surely you *were* told how tumbledown the place was, and how stupid and behindhand everything would be. Poor dear Uncle James ought to have lived fifty years since."

"I don't believe that parish priests taught their people nothing but to catch rats fifty years since," said Virginia, with a touch of the family bitterness in her voice. "Is it because papa is poor that the men-servants get tipsy, and Dick and Harry are always after them? Oh, Ruth," suddenly softening, "I ought not to have said it, but the boys aren't brought up well; and if you *saw* how wretched the people in the village are—and they look so wicked."

"Yes," said Ruth, as Virginia's tears silenced her, "but you know we Seytons *are* a bad lot. We're born, they say, with a drop of bad blood in us. Look at Aunt Julia, *she* was driven desperate and ran away—small blame to her—when her lover's father forbade the match; but they caught and stopped her. After that she never cared what she did, and just lived by making fun of things."

Virginia shuddered. Could her lazy, sarcastic aunt have ever known the thrillings and yearnings which were beating in her own heart now?

"There is not much fun in it," she said. "No. As for Dick, I don't think much of him. Poor old Roland was worth a dozen of him. I don't care what people *do* as long as they *are* something. But Dick has no fine feelings."

"Ruth," said Virginia, "I think I was not taught better for nothing. I am sure papa is very unhappy; he thinks how wrong everything is. Poor papa! Grandpapa was such a bad father for him. I cannot make friends with Dick, and Harry will go back to school. Indoors I have nothing to do; but I am going to ask Uncle James, and then if I go to the cottages and get the children together a little, perhaps it may be better than nothing. Old nurse says they all grow up bad. Poor things, how can they help it!"

"Well, Queenie," said Ruth dubiously, "I don't think the people are very fit for you to go to. I don't think Uncle Seyton would like it."

"I should not be afraid of them," said Virginia. "It would be doing something for papa, and doing good besides."

To think of her father as an involuntary victim to the faults of others was the one refuge of Virginia's heart; his graceful, melancholy gentleness had caught her fancy, and she was filled with a pity which, however strange from a child to a father, vibrated in every tender string of her nature. On the other hand, all her notions of right were outraged by the more obvious evils prevailing at Elderthwaite, and she went through in those first weeks a variety of emotions, for which action seemed the only cure. She felt as if the sins of generations lay on her father's shoulders, and she wanted to pull them on to her own—wanted to stand in the deadly breach with the little weapon that her small experience had put into her hand. She wanted to teach a few poor children, a thing that might only be a pleasant occupation or the most commonplace of duties. But it was turning her face right round on the smooth slope the Seytons were treading, and trying to make a step up hill.

Ruth did not think that first step would be easy, and would have liked to see Virginia go downstairs in a somewhat less desperate humour, to find her uncle chatting to Miss Seyton in the drawing-room.

"Ha, ha, Miss Ruth! Come North just in time to make a conquest of the fine Frenchman at Oakby."

"I thought he was a Spaniard, uncle," said Ruth.

"Eh, pretty much of a muchness, aren't they? I've got a card for a grand ball to go and see him. Ha, ha! I'd sooner see him with a red coat on at Ashrigg meet next Thursday."

"But you must go to the ball, uncle, and dance with me," said Ruth.

"That's a bargain," said the jolly parson, striking his hands together. "Any dance I like?"

"To be sure."

"Ah, mind you look out, then. When you're sitting quiet with the Frenchman you'll see your old uncle round the corner."

"I never dance with any one who doesn't know the *trois temps*, uncle."

"Bless my soul! My favourite dance is the hornpipe, or old Sir Roger— kiss the girls as you pop under. That's an old parson's privilege, you know."

All this time Virginia had been standing apart, working up her courage, and now, regardless of the unities of conversation, and with a now-or-never feeling, she began, her fresh young voice trembling and her colour rising high.

"Uncle James, if you please. I wanted to tell you I shall be very glad to do anything to help you, if you will allow me."

"Help me, my dear? Teach me the *troy tong*, or whatever Ruth calls it?"

"To help you in the parish, uncle."

"Parish? Ha, ha! Do they have the pretty girls to read prayers in the grand Ritualistic places nowadays?"

"I thought I might perhaps teach some of the children," faltered poor Virginia through her uncle's peal of laughter.

"Teach? We don't have many newfangled notions here, my dear. Do your wool-work, and dance your *troy tong*, and mind your own business."

"I have always been accustomed to do something useful," said Virginia, gaining courage from indignation.

"Now look here, Virginia," said Parson Seyton emphatically. "Don't you go putting your finger into a pie you know nothing of. There's not a cottage in the place fit for a young lady to set her foot in. There's a vast deal too much of young women's meddling in these days; and as for Elderthwaite, there's an old Methody, as they call him, who groans away to the soberer folks, and comforts their hearts in his own fashion. What could a chit of a lass like you do for them? Go and captivate the Frenchman with your round eyes—you've a grand pair of them—and give me a kiss."

Parson Seyton put out his hand and drew her towards him.

"But, uncle," she stammered, yielding to the kiss in such utter confusion of mind that she hardly knew what she was doing—"But, uncle, do you *like* that Methodist to—to attract the people?"

"Bless your heart, child, people must have their religion their own way. They'd stare to hear *me* convicting them of their sins. 'What's the parson done with his own?' they'd ask. But it comforts them like blankets and broth, and it's little they get of either," with a side glance at his sister; "so I take good care to keep out of the way. I told Cherry Lester I should go and hear him some Sunday afternoon. 'Hope it would do you good, parson,' says he, coolly. Eh, he's a fine lad. What a confounded fool old Lester must think himself to have this foreign fellow ready to step into his place."

"Are you and Cheriton as great friends as ever, uncle?" asked Ruth.

"Friends! Oh, he's like Virginia here. Wants to teach me a lesson now and then. Got me over last year to their grand meeting of clergy and laity for educational purposes, and there I was up on the platform with the best of them."

"Did you make a speech, uncle?" asked Ruth.

"I did, my lass, I did! When they had quarrelled and disputed, and couldn't by any means agree, some one asked my opinion, and I said, 'My lord,'—Lord — was there, you know,—'and my reverend brethren, having no knowledge whatever of the subject, I have no opinion to give.' And old Thorold—he comes from the other side of the county, mind you,— remarked that 'Mr Seyton's old-fashioned wisdom might find followers with advantage.' Ha—ha—you should have seen Cherry's blue eyes down below on the benches when I gave him a wink! 'Old-fashioned wisdom,' Miss Virginia; don't you despise it."

"Hallo, uncle!" shouted Harry, putting his head in, "here's a fellow come tearing up to say the wedding's waited an hour, and if the parson isn't quick they'll do without him."

"Bless my soul, I forgot all about 'em. Coming—coming—and I'll give 'em a couple of rabbits for the wedding dinner. Virginia'll never ask me to marry her, that's certain." And off strode the parson, while poor Virginia, scandalised and perplexed as she was, was fain, like every one else, to laugh at him.

Chapter Ten
The Old Parson

"He gave not of that text a pulled hen
That saith that hunters ben not holy men."

Perhaps no amount of angry opposition to her wishes could so have perplexed Virginia as her uncle's *nonchalance,* which, whether cynical or genial, seemed to remove him from the ranks of responsible beings, and to make him a law unto himself. When we read of young high-souled martyrs, we are apt to fancy that their way was plain before them; that however hard to their flesh, it was at least clear to their spirit; that Agnes or Cecilia, however much afflicted by the wickedness of their adversaries, were never perplexed by anything in them that was perhaps not wicked. Virginia Seyton was full of desires as pure, wishes as warm to lead the higher life, was capable of as much "enthusiasm of humanity" as any maiden who defied torture and death; but she was confronted by a kind of difficulty that made her feel like a naughty girl; the means to fulfil her purpose were open to so much objection that she could hardly hold firmly to the end in view. It may seem a very old difficulty, but it came upon her as a startling surprise that so much evil could be permitted by those who were not altogether devoid of good. For she was inclined to be sorry for this jolly, genial uncle, and not to wish to vex him; while yet his every practice and sentiment was such as she had been rightly taught to disapprove.

Anxious for a chance of settling her confused ideas, she slipped away by herself, and went out into the muddy lanes, heedless of a fast-falling shower.

The thaw had set in rapidly, and rich tints of brown, green, and yellow succeeded to the cold whiteness of the snow on moor and hill-side. A thaw, when the snow has fairly gone, even in the depth of winter, has a certain likeness to spring; the violent, buffeting wind was warm and soft, and the sky, instead of one pale sheet of blue, showed every variety of wild rain-cloud and driven mist.

Virginia plunged on through the mud with a perplexity in her soul as blinding as the tears that rose and confused the landscape already half-blotted out by wreaths of mountain mist. Suddenly, as she turned a corner, something bounced up against her, nearly knocking her down, and a voice exclaimed,—

"Down, Rolla! How dare you, sir! Oh, dear me, how sorry I am! that great brute has covered you with mud;" and Cheriton Lester, very muddy himself, and holding by the neck an object hardly recognisable as Buffer, appeared before her.

"I was very muddy before," said Virginia. "Why, what has happened to the puppy?"

"He fell into the ditch. Nettie will wash him; it's her favourite amusement. I was coming up here to ask after a young fellow I know, who works at this farm; he hasn't been going on very well lately."

"I suppose you know every one in Oakby," said Virginia, abruptly.

"Pretty well," answered Cherry. "I couldn't help doing so."

"I should like to know the people in Elderthwaite," said Virginia.

"It would be a very good thing for some of them if you did."

"Ah!" she said, suddenly, "but Uncle James will not let me do so."

"Ah!" said Cherry, with an inflection in his voice that Virginia did not understand. Then he added quickly, "What did you want to do?"

"I wanted," said Virginia, moved, she hardly knew why, to confidence as they walked on side by side, "to go to the cottages sometimes, and perhaps teach some of the children. Don't you think it would be right?"

"I think it would hardly do for you to go about at haphazard among the cottagers."

"But why? I am used to poor people," said Virginia.

Her sentences were short, because she was afraid of letting her voice tremble; but she looked at him earnestly, and how could he tell her that many of the people whom she wished to benefit owed her family grudges deep enough to make her unwelcome within their walls, how betray to her that the revelations they might make to her would affect her relations to her own family more than she could hope to affect their lives in return. But Cheriton was never deaf to other people's troubles, and he answered with great gentleness—

"Because we're a rough set up here in the North, and they would scarcely understand your kind motives. But the children—I wish you could get hold of them! I do wish something could be done for them. What did the old parson say to you?"

"He said he didn't approve of education."

"Oh, that's no matter at all! I declare I think I see how you might do it, and we'll make the parson hunt up a class for you himself! What! you don't believe me? You will see. Could you go down to the vicarage on Sunday mornings?"

"Oh, yes! but Uncle James—"

"Oh, I'll make him come round. They might send over some benches from Oakby, and the children would do very well in the vicarage hall."

"But, Cheriton," exclaimed the astonished Virginia, "you can't *know* what my uncle said about it!"

"He said, 'Eh, they're a bad lot. No use meddling with them,' didn't he?" said Cheriton, in the very tone of the old parson.

"Something like it."

"Never mind. He would like to see them a better lot in his heart, as well as you or I would."

"Ruth says he is really very kind," said Virginia; "and I think he means to be."

"Ah, yes, your cousin knows all our odd ways, you know. She is with you?"

"Yes, she came yesterday."

"Ah! she knows that he *is* a very kind old boy. He loves every stone in Elderthwaite, and you would be surprised to find how fond some of the people are of him. Now I'll go and see him, and come and tell you what he says. May I?"

"To be sure," said Virginia, "and perhaps then Aunt Julia will not object."

"Oh, no, not to this plan," said Cherry. He called Rolla, and went in search of the parson.

Cherry liked management; it was partly the inheritance of his father's desire for influence, and partly his tender and genial nature, which made him take so much interest in people as to enjoy having a finger in every pie. As he walked along, he contrived every detail of his plan.

Jack was wont to observe that Elderthwaite was a blot on the face of the earth, and a disgrace to any system, ecclesiastical or political, that rendered it possible. But then Jack was much devoted to his young house-master, and wrote essays for his benefit, one of which was entitled, "On the Evils inherent in every existing Form of Government," so that he felt it consistent to be critical. Cheriton had a soft spot in his heart for a long existing form of anything.

He soon arrived at the vicarage, a picturesque old house, built half of stone and half of black and white plaster. It was large, with great overgrown stables and farm-buildings, all much out of repair. Cheriton found the parson sitting in the old oak dining-room before a blazing fire, smoking his pipe. Some remains of luncheon were on the table, and the parson was evidently enjoying a glass of something hot after it. Cheriton entered with little ceremony.

"How d'ye do, Parson?" he said.

"Ha, Cherry! how d'ye do, my lad? Sit down and have some lunch. What d'ye take? there's a glass of port in the sideboard."

"Thanks, I'd rather have a glass of beer and some Stilton," said Cherry, seating himself.

As he spoke, a little bit of an old woman came in with some cold pheasant and a jug of beer, which she placed before him. She was wrinkled up almost to nothing, but her steps were active enough, and she had lived with Parson Seyton all his life.

"Ay, Deborah knows your tastes. And what do you want of me?"

"I want to give you a lecture, Parson," said Cherry coolly.

"The deuce you do? Out with it, then."

"Virginia has been telling me that you will not let her teach the little kids on a Sunday."

"Bless my soul, Cheriton! d'ye think I'm going to let the girl run all over the place and hear tales of her father and brothers, and may be of myself into the bargain?"

"No," said Cherry; "but you ought to be very much obliged to her, Parson. It's a shame to see those little ruffians. Now you're going to call on half-a-dozen decentish people and tell them to send their children down here of a Sunday morning at ten o'clock. Virginia will teach them in the hall. I'll get them to send over a couple of forms from Oakby. Don't let her begin with above a dozen, and don't have any big boys at first. Deborah might give them a bit of cake now and again to make the lessons go down. What do you say?"

"I say you're the coolest hand in Westmoreland, and enough to wile the flounders out of the frith!" said the old parson, as Cherry peeped at him over his shoulder to see the effect of his words.

"What are we coming to?"

"A model school, perhaps."

"And a model parson. Eh, Cherry, these enlightened days can't do with the old lot much longer."

"Oh, you're moving with the times," said Cherry, as he came and stood with his back to the fire, looking down at the parson as he filled his pipe, and smiling at him. Perhaps no other being in the world could have got Parson Seyton to consent to such an innovation, but he loved Cheriton Lester, who little knew how much self-respect the allegiance of his high-principled, promising youth was worth to the queer old sporting parson. One atom of pretence or of priggishness in a well-conducted correct young man would have been of all things odious to him, but the shrewd old man believed in Cheriton to the backbone, and of all the admiration and affection that the popular young man had won perhaps none did him so much credit as the love that made him a sort of good angel to rough Parson Seyton.

"You got my best dog out of me when I gave you Rolla," he said, "so I suppose you'll have your own way now."

"And it'll turn out quite as well as Rolla," said Cherry rather illogically.

Parson Seyton set about fulfilling his promise after a manner of his own.

He rapped with his dog-whip at a cottage door and thus addressed the mother:—

"Eh, Betty, there's a grand new start in Elderthwaite. Here's Miss Virginia going to turn all the children into first-rate scholars. Wash them up and send them over to my house on Sunday morning, and I'll give a penny to the cleanest, and a licking to any one that doesn't mind his manners."

If Parson Seyton had been a school-board visitor he could hardly have put the matter more plainly, and on the whole could hardly have adopted language more likely to be effectual.

Chapter Eleven
Alvar Confidential

"He talked of daggers and of darts,
Of passions and of pains."

The rain had ceased, and long pale rays of sunshine were streaming through the mist as Cheriton made his way through a very dilapidated turnstile and across a footpath much in need of drainage towards Elderthwaite House. As he came up through the overgrown shrubberies he saw in front of him a small fur-clothed figure, and his colour deepened and his heart beat faster as he recognised Ruth. He had been thinking that he should see her ever since his promise to Virginia, but he had not expected to meet her out-of-doors on so wet a day, and he had hardly a word to say as he lifted his hat and came up to her. She was less discomposed, perhaps less astonished.

"Ah! how do you do?" she said. "Do you know when I saw some one coming I hoped it might be your new brother. I am *so* curious to see him."

"He is not a bit like any of us," said Cherry.

"No? That would be a change, for all you Lesters are so exactly alike."

Ruth had a way of saying saucy things in a soft serious voice, with grave eyes just ready to laugh. Cheriton and she had had many a passage of arms together, and now he rallied his forces and answered,—

"Being new, of course he'll be charming. Rupert and Jack and I will know all our partners are longing for him. But as he can only dance with one young lady at a time, in the intervals I shall hope—I am much improved in my waltzing—just to get a turn."

"Really improved—at last?" said Ruth; then suddenly changing to sympathy—"But isn't it very strange for you all? How do you get on? How do *you* like him?"

"Oh, he isn't half a bad fellow, and we're excellent friends."

"That's very good of you. Now I have such a bad disposition that if I were in your place I should be half mad with jealousy."

Cheriton laughed incredulously.

"I daresay you would stroke us all down the right way. Rupert says he feels as if he were lighting his cigar in a powder-magazine. But they get on very well, and Grace and Mary Cheriton think him perfectly charming."

"I think I shall come to the ball in a mantilla. But have you done anything for poor Virginia?"

"Oh, yes; the old parson only wanted a little explanation," said Cherry, quite carelessly enough to encourage Ruth in adding earnestly,—

"It is *so* good of her to want to help these poor people. Queenie is like a girl in a book. I really think she likes disagreeable duties."

"I am sure you, who can sympathise with Virginia and yet know all the troubles, will be able to make it smooth for her. I wish you would."

"Ah, but I am not nearly so good as Virginia," said Ruth—a perfectly true statement, which she herself believed. Whether she expected Cheriton to believe it was a different matter.

Alvar had no excuse now for finding Oakby dull; the house was full of people, Lady Cheriton and her daughters were enchanted with his music, and he brightened up considerably and was off Cheriton's mind, so that nothing spoilt the radiance of enjoyment that transfigured all the commonplace gaiety into a fairy dream. The younger ones found the times less good. Jack was shy and bored by fine people, Bob hated his dress clothes, Nettie was teased by Rupert, who varied between treating her as a Tomboy and flattering her as an incipient beauty, and thought her grandmother's restrictions to white muslin and blue ribbons hard. But Mrs Lester had no notion of letting her forestall her career as a county beauty.

When Cheriton came back from Elderthwaite he found the whole party by the hall fire in the full tide of discussion and chatter, Nettie on the rug with Buffer in her arms complaining of the white muslin.

"Sha'n't I look horrid, Rupert?"

"Frightful; but as you'll be sure to bring Buffer into the ball-room he'd tear anything more magnificent."

"I sha'n't bring in Buffer! Rupert, what an idea! He'll be shut up, poor darling! But at least I may turn up my hair, and I shall. I'm quite tall enough."

"Turn your hair up? Don't you do anything of the sort, Nettie. Little girls are fashionable, and yellow manes and muslin frocks will carry the day against wreaths and silk dresses. You let your hair alone, and then people will know it's all real by-and-by."

"Well, I'd much rather turn it up," said Nettie simply.

"Well, perhaps I would," said Rupert. "Fellows might say you let it down on purpose."

Rupert conveyed a great deal of admiration of the golden locks in his tone, but Nettie, though vain enough, was insensible to veiled flattery.

"Plait it up, Nettie," said Cherry briefly.

"If anybody thought I did such a nasty, mean, affected thing as that I'd never speak to him again. *Never*! I'd cut it all off sooner," cried Nettie.

"Young ladies' hair does come down sometimes," said Rupert; "when it's long enough."

"Mine *never* shall," said Nettie emphatically.

"Don't do it yourself, then," said Cherry.

"If Nettie ever takes to horrid, affected, flirting ways," said Jack, who had joined the party, "I for one shall have nothing more to say to her."

"You don't admire flirts, Jack?" said Rupert.

"I don't approve of them," said Jack crossly.

"Oh, come, come, now, Jack, that's very severe."

"Poor Jack!" said Cherry; "he speaks from personal experience. There was that heartless girl last summer, who, after hours of serious conversation with him, went off to play croquet with Tom Hubbard, and gave him a moss-rose-bud. Poor Jack! it was a blow; he can't recover from it! It has affected all his views of life, you see."

"Poor fellow!" said Rupert, as Jack forcibly stopped Cherry's mouth; "I'd no notion it was a personal matter. Will she be at the ball?"

"No; you see, we avoided asking her."

"Cherry!" interposed the disgusted Jack, "how can you go on in this way! It's all his humbug, Rupert."

This serious denial produced, of course, shouts of laughter—in the midst of which Alvar entered and joined himself to the group round the fire as they waited for the arrival of some friends of Cheriton's.

"And what have you been about?" asked Cherry.

"I have been singing with your cousins. Ah, it is pleasant when there are those who like music!"

"You found all these fellows awful savages, didn't you?" said Rupert.

Alvar turned his great dark eyes on Cheriton with the same sort of expression with which Rolla was wont to watch him.

"Ah, no," he said; "my brother is not a savage. But I do like young ladies."

"But I thought," said Rupert, "that in Spain young ladies were always under a duenna, so that there was no chance of an afternoon over the piano?"

"But I assure you Miladi Cheriton was present," said Alvar seriously.

"Oh, that alters the question!" said Rupert. "But come, now, we have been hearing Jack's views—let us have your confessions. Is the duenna *always* there, Alvar?"

"Here is my sister," said Alvar, with the oddest sort of simplicity, and yet with a tone that conveyed a sort of reproach to Rupert and—for the first time—of proprietorship in Nettie.

Rupert burst into a shout of laughter: "My dear fellow, what are you going to tell us?"

"She is a young girl; surely even here you do not say everything to her?" said Alvar, looking perplexed.

"By Jove, no!" said Rupert; "not exactly."

"Since Nettie is here, we should not have asked you to tell us anything we did not wish her to hear," said Cheriton, with a sense of annoyance that Alvar should be laughed at.

"*You* did not ask me," said Alvar quietly.

At this moment Bob called Nettie so emphatically, that she was obliged unwillingly to go away.

"Now then, Alvar," said Rupert, "now for it. We won't be shocked. Tell us how you work the duennas."

"It would not have been well to explain that to Nettie," said Alvar seriously.

"Why not?" said Jack, suddenly boiling up. "Do you think *she* would ever cheat or want a duenna? English girls can always be trusted!"

"*Can* they?" said Rupert. "Shut up, Jack; you don't understand. We only want you to tell us how you do in Spain. *Affaires du coeur*—you know, Alvar."

Alvar looked round with an air half-shrewd, half-sentimental; while Cheriton listened a little seriously. He knew very little of Alvar's former life; perhaps because he had been too reticent to ask him questions; perhaps because Alvar found himself in the presence of a standard higher than he was accustomed to. Anyway, Nettie might have heard his present revelations.

"There was a time," he said, sighing, "when I did not intend to come to England—when I had sworn to be for ever a Spaniard. Ah, my cousin, if you had seen my Luisa, you would not have wondered. I sang under her window; I went to mass that I might gaze on her."

"Did you now? Foreign customs!" interposed Rupert; while Cherry laughed, though he felt they were hardly treating Alvar fairly.

"I knew not how to speak to her. She was never alone; and it was whispered that she was already betrothed. But one day she dropped her fan."

"No, no—surely?" said Cherry.

"I seized it, I kissed it, I held it to my heart," said Alvar, evidently enjoying the narration, "and I returned it. There were looks between us— then words. Ah, I lived in her smiles. We met, we exchanged vows, and I was happy!"

Rupert listened to this speech with amusement, which he could hardly stifle. It was inexpressibly ludicrous to Cheriton; but the fun was lost in the wonder whether Alvar meant what he said. This was neither like the joking sentiment nor the pretended indifference of an Englishman's reference to such passages in his life; yet the memory evidently cost Alvar no pain. Jack sat, looking totally disgusted.

"At last," Alvar went on, "we were discovered. Ah, and then my grandfather was enraged, and her parents, they refused their consent, since she was betrothed already. I am an Englishman, and I do not weep when I am grieved, but my heart was a stone. I despaired."

"She must have been a horrid little flirt not to tell you she was engaged," said Jack.

"She did not know it till we had met," said Alvar.

"What awful tyranny!"

"Ah, and she was your only love!" sighed Rupert.

"No," said Alvar simply, "I have loved others; but she was the most beautiful. But I submitted, and now I forget her!"

"Hm—the truest wisdom," said Rupert.

Cherry was growing angry. He did not think that Rupert had any business to make fun of Alvar, and he was in a rage with Alvar for making himself ridiculous. That Alvar should tell a true love-tale with sentimental satisfaction to an admiring audience, or sigh over a flirtation which ought to have been a good joke, was equally distasteful to him. He burst out suddenly, with all his Lester bluntness, and in a tone which Alvar had hitherto heard only from Jack, —

"If you fellows are not all tired of talking such intolerable nonsense, I am. It's too bad of you," with a sharp look at Rupert. "I don't see that it's any affair of ours."

"You're not sympathetic," said Rupert, as he moved away; for he was quite familiar enough with his cousins for such giving and taking.

Chapter Twelve
The Oakby Ball

"She went to the ball, and she danced with the handsome
prince."

That week of gaiety, so unusual to Oakby, was fraught with great
results. The dim and beautiful dream of the future which had grown with
Cheriton Lester's growth became a definite purpose. Ruth Seyton was his
first love, almost his first fancy. Whatever other sentiments and flirtations
had come across him, had been as light as air; he had loved Ruth ever
since he had taught her to ride, and since she had tried to teach him to
dance. He had always found her ready to talk to him of the thoughts and
aspirations which found no sympathy at home, and still more ready to tease
him about them. She was part of the dear and sacred home affections, the
long accustomed life which held so powerful a sway over him, and she was
besides a wonderful and beautiful thing, peculiar to himself, and belonging
to none of the others.

He had not seen her since the season when he had met her in town with
Virginia; he did not know very much really about her, but she was kind
and gracious to him, and he walked about in a dream of bliss which made
every commonplace duty and gaiety delightful. Ruth was mixed up in it all,
it was all in her honour; and though Cheriton's memory at this time was
not to be depended on, he had spirits for any amount of the hard work of
preparation, and a laugh for every disagreeable.

He regarded his tongue as tied till after he had taken his degree in the
summer—he hoped with credit; after which his prospects at the bar with
Judge Cheriton's interest, were somewhat less obscure than those of most
young men. He had inherited some small fortune from his mother, and
though he could not consider himself a brilliant match for Miss Seyton, he
would then feel himself justified in putting his claims forward. Many spoke
with admiration of the entire absence of jealousy which made him take the
second place so easily; but Cheriton hardly deserved the praise, he had no
room in his mind to think of himself at all.

His cousin Rupert was a more recent acquaintance of Ruth's, though
matters had gone much further between them. His attentions had not been

encouraged by her grandmother, as, though his fortune was far superior to anything Cheriton possessed, his affairs were supposed to be considerably involved, and this was so far true, that it would have been very inconvenient to him to lay them open to inquiry at present. He hoped, however, in the course of a few months to be able so to arrange them, as to make it possible to apply to Ruth Seyton's guardians for their consent.

Rupert was a lively, pleasant fellow, with a considerable regard for his Oakby cousins, though he had never considered it necessary to regulate his life by the Oakby standard, or concerned himself greatly with its main principles. His life in the army had of course been quite apart from Cheriton's at school and college, and the latter did not care to realise how far the elder cousin, once a model in his eyes, had grown away from him. Nor did he regard him as a rival.

Ruth gave smiles and dances to himself, and he little guessed that while he did his duty joyously in other directions, looking forward to his next word with her, she had given his cousin a distinct promise, and engaged to keep it secret till such time as he chose to ask for her openly. Perhaps Rupert could not be expected to scruple at such a step, when he knew how entirely Ruth had managed her affairs for herself in all her intercourse with him.

And as for Ruth she rejoiced in the chance of making a sacrifice to prove her love; and whether the sacrifice was of other people's feelings, her own ease and comfort, or of any little trifling scruples of conscience, ought, she considered, to be equally unimportant. "Love must still be lord of all," but the love that loves honour more was in her eyes weak and unworthy. Faults in the hero only proved the strength of his manhood; faults in herself were all condoned by her love.

Ruth was clever enough to put into words the inspiring principles of a great many books that she read, and a great deal of talk that she heard, and vehement enough to act up to it. Rupert, who had no desire to be at all unlike other people, had little notion of the glamour of enthusiasm with which Ruth plighted him her troth at Oakby.

The Lesters had expended much abuse on the morning of their ball on the blackness of the oak-panels, which no amount of wax candles would overcome but what was lost in gaiety was gained in picturesqueness, and the Oakby ball, with its handsome hosts and its distinguished company, was long quoted as the prettiest in the neighbourhood. Perhaps it owed no little of its charm to the one in whose honour it was given. Alvar in society was neither silent nor languid; he was a splendid dancer, and played the host with a foreign grace that enchanted the ladies, old and young. At the dinner-party the night before he had been silent and stately, evidently fearing to commit himself before the country gentlemen and county grandees, who were such strange specimens of humanity to him; but with their daughters it was different, and those were happy maidens who danced with the stranger. He was of course duly instructed whom he was thus to honour, but he found time to exercise his own choice, and Virginia was conscious that he paid her marked attention.

Why waste more words? She had found her fate, and softened with home troubles, attracted by the superiority of the Lesters, and dazzled with the charm of a manner and appearance never seen before, yet suiting all her girlish dreams of heroic perfection, she was giving her heart away to the last man whose previous training or present character was likely really to accord with her own.

Though she had never been an acknowledged beauty, she could often look beautiful, and the subtle excitement of half-conscious triumph was not wanting to complete the charm.

"There never had been such a pleasant ball," said Cheriton the next morning, as he was forced to hurry away to Oxford without a chance of discussing its delights.

"It is indeed possible to dance in England," said Alvar.

"I think we made it out very well," said Rupert, with a smile under his moustaches.

"There are balls—and balls," said Ruth to her cousin. "You don't always have black oak, or black Spanish eyes, eh, Queenie? or some other things?"

And Virginia blushed and said nothing.

Nettie, after all, had rejoiced in the partners of which her white frock and plaited hair had not defrauded her (she never should forgive her hair for coming down in Rupert's very sight in the last waltz). Jack had not been so miserable as he expected; and Alvar found that it was possible to enjoy life in England, and that the position awaiting him there was not to be despised, even in the face of parting from his beloved Cheriton.

Rupert by no means considered Alvar as an amusing companion, nor Oakby in the dull season an amusing place, but it suited him now to spend his leave there, and suited him also to be intimate at Elderthwaite. Consequently he encouraged Alvar to make excuses for going there, and certainly in finding some interests to supply Cheriton's place. He cultivated Dick Seyton, who was of an age to appreciate a grown-up man's attentions, so that altogether there was more intercourse between the two houses than had taken place since the days of Roland.

Ruth was paying a long visit at Elderthwaite. One of her aunts—her grandmother's youngest and favourite child—was in bad health, and Lady Charlton was glad to spend some time with her and to be free from the necessity of chaperoning her granddaughter. The arrangement suited Ruth exactly. She could make Elderthwaite her head-quarters, pay several visits among friends in the north, and find opportunities of meeting Rupert, whose regiment was stationed at York, and who was consequently within reach of many north-country gaieties.

For the present no gaieties were needed by either to enliven the wintry woods of Elderthwaite; they were as fairy land to the little brown maiden who, among their bare stems and withered ferns found, as she believed, the very flower of life, and had no memory for the bewitching smiles, the soft, half-sentimental laughter, the many dances, and the preference hardly disguised which were the food of Cheriton's memory, and gave him an object which lightened every uncongenial task. These little wiles had effectually prevented every one from guessing the real state of the case. Rupert's difficulty was that he never could be sure how far Alvar was unsuspicious. There was a certain blankness in his way of receiving remarks, calculated to prevent suspicion, which might proceed from entire innocence, or from secret observation which he did not choose to betray. But he was always willing to accompany Rupert to Elderthwaite, and in Cheriton's absence found Virginia by far his most congenial companion.

The amount of confidence already existing between Ruth and her cousin really rendered the latter unsuspicious, and ready to further intercourse with Rupert, believing Ruth to be in a doubtful state of mind, half encouraging, and half avoiding his attentions. And Ruth was very cautious; she never allowed Rupert to monopolise her during his ostensible visits, and if any one at Elderthwaite guessed at their stolen interviews, it was certainly not Virginia.

The scheme of the Sunday class had answered pretty well. Virginia knew how to teach, and though her pupils were rough, the novelty of her grace and gentleness made some impression on them.

The parson did not interfere with her, and it never occurred to her that he was within hearing, till one Sunday, as she tried to tell them the simplest facts in language sufficiently plain to be understood, and sufficiently striking to be interesting, and felt, by the noise on the back benches, that she was entirely failing to do so, a head appeared at the dining-room door, and a stentorian voice exclaimed,—

"Bless my soul, you young ruffians; is this the way to behave to Miss Seyton? If any lad can't show respect to a lady in my house, out he'll go, and, by George he won't come in again."

This unwonted address produced an astonished silence; but it frightened the teacher so much more than her class, that her only resource was to call on the more advanced ones with great solemnity "to say their hymn to the vicar."

Parson Seyton straightened himself up, and listened in silence to —

"There is a green hill far away," stumbled through in the broadest Westmoreland; and when it was over, remarked, —

"Very pretty verses. Lads and lasses, keep your feet still and attend to Miss Seyton, and — *mind* — I can hear ye," a piece of information with which Virginia at any rate could well have dispensed.

But she was getting used to her rough uncle, and was grateful to Cheriton for the advice that he had given her, and so she told Alvar one day when they were all walking down to the vicarage, with the ostensible purpose of showing Nettie some enormous mastiff puppies, the pride of the vicar's heart.

In the absence of her own brothers Nettie found Dick Seyton an amusing companion, "soft" though he might be; she began by daring him to jump over ditches as well as she could, and ended by finding that he roused in her unsuspected powers of repartee. Nettie found the Miss Ellesmeres dull companions; they were a great deal cleverer than she was, and expected her to read story books, and care about the people in them. Rupert and Dick found that her ignorance made her none the less amusing, and took care to tell her so.

So everything combined to make intercourse easy; and this was not the first walk that the six young people had taken together.

"Your brother," said Virginia to Alvar, "was very kind to me. I should never have got on so well but for his advice."

"My brother is always kind," said Alvar, his eyes lighting up. "I cannot tell you how well I love him."

"I am sure you do," said Virginia heartily, though unable to help smiling.

"But in what was it that he helped you?" asked Alvar.

Virginia explained how he had persuaded her uncle to agree to her wishes about teaching the children.

"To teach the ignorant?" said Alvar. "Ah, that is the work of a saint!"

"Oh, no! I like doing it. It is nothing but what many girls can do much better."

"Ah, this country is strange. In Spain the young ladies remain at home. They go nowhere but to mass. If my sister were in Spain she would not jump over the ditches, nor run after the dogs," glancing at Nettie, who was inciting Rolla to run for a piece of stick.

"Do you think us very shocking?" said Virginia demurely.

"Nay," said Alvar. "These are your customs, and I am happy since they permit me the honour of walking by your side, and talking with you. You, like my brother, are kind to the stranger."

"But you must leave off calling yourself a stranger. You too *are* English; can you not feel yourself so?"

"Yes, I am an Englishman," said Alvar. "See, if I stay here, I have money and honour. My father speaks to me of a 'position in the county.' That is to be a great man as I understand it. Nor are there parties here to throw down one person, and then another. In Spain, though not less noble, we are poor, and all things change quickly, and I shall not stay always here in Oakby. I am going to London, and I see that I can make for myself a life that pleases me."

"Yet you love Spain best?"

"I love Spain," said Alvar, "the sunshine and the country; but I am no Spaniard. No, I stayed away from England because it was my belief that my father did not love me. I was wrong. I have a right to be here; it was my right to come here long ago, and my right I will not give up!"

He drew himself up with an indescribable air of *hauteur* for a moment, then with sudden softness, —

"And who was it that saw that right and longed for me to come, who opened his heart to me? It was Cheriton, my brother. He has explained much to me, and says if I learn to love England it will make him happy. And I will love it for his sake."

"I hope so; soon you will not find it so dull."

"Nay, it is not now so dull. Have I not the happiness of your sympathy? Could I be dull to-day?" said Alvar, with his winning grace.

Virginia blushed, and her great eyes drooped, unready with a reply.

"And there is your cousin," she said, shyly; "he is a companion; don't you think him like Cheriton?"

"Yes, a little; but Cheriton is like an angel, though he will not have me say so; but Rupert, he has the devil in his face. But I like him—he is a nice fellow—very nice," said Alvar, the bit of English idiom sounding oddly in his foreign tones.

Virginia laughed, spite of herself.

"Ah, I make you laugh," said Alvar. "I wish I had attended more to my English lessons; but there was a time when it was not my intention to come to England, and I did not study. I am not like Cheriton and Jack, I do not love to study. It is very pleasant to smoke, and to do nothing; but I see it is not the custom here, and it is better, I think, to be like my brother."

"Some people are rather fond of smoking and doing nothing even in England."

"It is a different sort of doing nothing. I hear my father or Cheriton rebuke Bob for doing nothing; but then he is out of doors with some little animal in a bag—his ferret, I think it is called—to catch the rats; or he runs and gets hot; that is what he calls doing nothing."

There was a sort of *bonhommie* in Alvar's way of describing himself and his surroundings, and a charm in his manner which, added to a pair of eyes full of fire and expression, and a great deal of implied admiration for herself, produced no small effect on Virginia.

She saw that he was affectionate and ready to recognise the good in his brothers, and she knew that he had been deprived of his due share of home affection. She did not doubt that he was willing himself to do and to be all that he admired; and then—he was not boyish and blunt like his brothers, nor so full of mischief as Cheriton, nor with that indescribable want of something that made her wonder at Rupert's charm in the eyes of Ruth; she had never seen any one like him.

She glanced up in his face with eyes that all unconsciously expressed her thoughts, and as he turned to her with a smile they came up to the vicarage garden, at the gate of which stood Parson Seyton talking to Mr Lester, who was on horseback beside him.

"Ha, squire," said the parson, "Monsieur Alvar is a dangerous fellow among the lasses. Black eyes and foreign ways have made havoc with hearts all the world over."

Mr Lester looked towards the approaching group. Virginia's delicate face, shy and eager under drooping feathers, and the tall, slender Alvar, wearing his now scrupulously English morning suit with a grace that gave it a picturesque appropriateness, were in front. Ruth and Rupert lingered a little, and Nettie came running up from behind, with Rolla after her, and Dick Seyton lazily calling on her to stop. Mr Lester looked at his son, and a new idea struck him.

"I wish Alvar to make acquaintances," he said. "Nothing but English society can accustom him to his new life."

Here Alvar saw them, and raised his hat as he came up.

"Have you had a pleasant walk, Alvar?" said his father, less stiffly than usual.

"It has been altogether pleasant, sir," said Alvar, "since Miss Seyton has been my companion."

Virginia blushed, and went up to her uncle with a hasty question about the puppies that Nettie was to see, and no one exchanged a remark on the subject; but that night as they were smoking, Rupert rallied Alvar a little on the impression he was making.

Alvar did not misunderstand him; he looked at him straight.

"I had thought," he said, "that it was here the custom to talk with freedom to young ladies. I see it is your practice, my cousin."

"Yes, yes. Besides, I'm an old friend, you see. Of course it is the custom; but consequences sometimes result from it—pity if they didn't."

"But it may be," said Alvar, "that as my father's son, it is expected that I should marry if it should be agreeable to my father?"

"Possibly," said Rupert, unable to resist trying experiments. "Fellows with expectations have to be careful, you know."

"I thank you," said Alvar. "But I do not mistake a lady who has been kind to me, or I should be a coxcomb. Good-night, my cousin."

"Good-night," said Rupert, feeling somewhat baffled, and a little angry; for, after all, he had been perfectly right.

Chapter Thirteen
Two Sides of a Question

"Love me and leave me not."

The hill that lay between Oakby and Elderthwaite was partly covered by a thick plantation of larches, through which passed a narrow footpath. In the summer, when the short turf under the trees was dry and sweet, when the blue sky peeped through the wide-spreading branches, and rare green ferns and blue harebells nestled in the low stone walls, the larch wood was a favourite resort; but in the winter, when the moorland winds were bleak and cold rather than fresh and free, when the fir-trees moaned and howled dismally instead of responding like harps to the breezes, before, in that northern region, one "rosy plumelet tufted the larch," or one lamb was seen out on the fell side, it was a dreary spot enough.

All the more undisturbed had it been, and therefore all the more suitable for the secret meetings of Rupert and Ruth. Matters had not always run smooth between them. An unacknowledged tie needs faith and self-restraint if it is to sit easily; and at their very last parting Rupert expressed enough jealousy at the remembrance of Cheriton's attentions to make Ruth furious at the implied doubt of her faith, forgetting that *she* was miserable if he played with Nettie, or talked for ten minutes to Virginia.

Rupert insisted that "Cherry meant mischief." Ruth vehemently asserted "that it wasn't in him to mean;" and after something that came perilously near a quarrel, she broke into a flood of tears, and they parted with renewed protestations of inviolable constancy, and amid hopes of chance meetings in the course of the spring.

Ruth fled away through the copses to Elderthwaite feeling as if life would be utterly blank and dark till their next meeting; and Rupert strolled homeward, thinking much of Ruth, and not best pleased to meet his uncle coming back from one of his farms, and evidently inclined to be sociable; for Rupert, as compared with Alvar, had an agreeable familiarity.

Mr Lester, though he had held as little personal intercourse with Alvar as the circumstances of the case permitted, had hardly ceased, since he came home, to think of his future, and that with a conscientious effort at justice and kindness. He still felt a personal distaste to Alvar, which ruffled his temper, and often made him less than civil to him; but none the less did he wish his eldest son's career to be creditable and fortunate, nor desire to see him adapt himself to the pursuits likely to be required of him. He made a few attempts to instruct him and interest him in the county politics, the requirements of the estate, and the necessities of the parish; but Alvar, it must be confessed, was very provoking. He was always courteous, but he never exerted his mind to take in anything that was strange to him, and would say, with a shrug of his shoulders and a smile, "Ah, these are the things that I do not understand;" or, as he picked up the current expressions, "It is not in my line to interest myself for the people," with a *naïveté* that refused to recognise any duty one way or the other. In short, he was quite as impervious as his brothers to anything "out of his line," and, like Mr Lester himself, thought that what he did not understand was immaterial.

Mr Lester was in despair; but when he saw Alvar and Virginia together, and noticed their mutual attraction, it occurred to him that an English wife would be the one remedy for Alvar's shortcomings; and he also reflected, with some pride in his knowledge of foreign customs, that Alvar would probably require parental sanction before presuming to pay his addresses to any lady.

As for Virginia, though she was of Seyton blood, all her training had been away from her family; her fortune was not inconsiderable, and she herself, enthusiastic, refined, and high-minded, was exactly the type of woman in which Mr Lester believed. Besides, since he could not make Alvar other than the heir of Oakby, his one wish was that his grandchildren at least should be English. He was very reluctant that Alvar should return to Spain, and at the same time hardly wished him to be a permanent inmate of Oakby. It had been arranged that Alvar should pay a short visit to the Cheritons before Easter, when he would see what London was like, go to see Cherry at Oxford, and having thus enlarged his experiences, would return to Oakby for Easter and the early part of the summer.

After Cheriton had taken his degree, he too would enjoy a taste of the season, and Alvar might go to town again if he liked; while in August Alvar must be introduced to the grouse, and might also see the fine scenery of the Scotch and English lakes. These were plans in which Alvar could find nothing to complain of; but they would be greatly improved in his father's eyes if they could end in a suitable and happy marriage; for he saw that Alvar could not remain idle at Oakby for long, and had the firmest conviction that he would get into mischief, if he set up for himself in London. His mind, when he met Rupert, was full of the subject, and with a view to obtaining a side light or two if possible, he asked him casually what he thought of his cousin Alvar, and how they got on together.

"I don't think he is half a bad fellow," said Rupert, "a little stiff and foreign, of course, but a very good sort in my opinion."

This was well meant on Rupert's part, for he did not personally *like* Alvar, but he had tact enough to see the necessity of harmony, and family feeling enough to wish to produce it.

"Of course," said Mr Lester, "you can understand that I have been anxious about his coming here among the boys."

"I don't think he'll do them any harm, sir."

"No; and except Cherry, they don't take to him very warmly; but I hope we may see him settle into an Englishman in time. A good wife now —"

"Is a very good thing, uncle," said Rupert, with a conscious laugh.

"Yes, Rupert, in a year or two's time you'll be looking out for yourself."

Rupert liked his uncle, as he had always called him, and, for a moment, was half-inclined to confide in him; but he knew that Mr Lester's good offices would be so exceedingly energetic, and would involve such thorough openness on his own part, that though his marriage to Ruth might possibly be expedited by them, he could not face the reproofs by which they would be accompanied.

So he laughed, and shook his head, saying, "Excellent advice for Alvar, sir; and see, there he comes."

Alvar approached his father with a bow; but was about to join Rupert, as he turned off by another path, when Mr Lester detained him.

"I should like a word or two with you," he said, as they walked on. "I think—it appears to me that you are beginning to feel more at home with us than at first."

"Yes, sir, I know better how to suit myself to you."

"I am uncommonly glad of it. But what I meant to say was—you don't find yourself so dull as at first?" said Mr Lester rather awkwardly.

"It is a little dull," said Alvar, "but I can well endure it."

This was not precisely the answer which Mr Lester had expected; but after a pause, he went on, —

"It would be hard to blame you because you do not take kindly to interests and occupations that are so new to you. I do not feel, Alvar, that I have the same right to dictate your way of life as I should have, if I had earlier assumed the charge of you; but I would remind you that since one day you must be master here, it will be for your own happiness to—to accustom yourself to the life required of you."

"My brother ought to be the squire," said Alvar.

"That is impossible. It is not a matter of choice; but it would cause me great unhappiness if I thought my successor would either be constantly absent or—or indifferent to the welfare of the people about him."

"You would wish me," said Alvar, "to live in England, and to marry an English lady."

"Why, yes—yes. Not of course that I would wish to put any restraint on your inclinations, or even to suggest any line of conduct; but it had occurred to me that—in short, that you find Elderthwaite attractive, and I wished to tell you that such a choice would have my entire approval."

Mr Lester's florid face coloured with a sense of embarrassment; he was never at his ease with his son, whereas Alvar only looked considerate, and said thoughtfully,—"Miss Seyton is a charming young lady."

"Very much so, indeed," said the squire; "and a very good girl."

Alvar walked on in silence. Probably the idea was not strange to him; but his father could not trace the workings of his mind, and a sense of intense impatience possessed him with this strange creature whose interests he was bound to consult, but whose nature he could not fathom. Suddenly Alvar stopped.

"My father, I have chosen. This is my country, and Miss Seyton—if she will—shall be my wife."

"Well, Alvar, I'm very glad to hear it," said his father, "very glad indeed, and I'm sure Cheriton will be delighted. Don't, however, act in a hurry; I'll leave you to think it over. I see James Wilson, and I want to speak to him."

And Mr Lester called to one of the keepers who was coming across the park, while Alvar went on towards the house.

Chapter Fourteen
Virginia's choice

"Things that I know not of, belike to thee are dear."

There was the shadow of such a thought on the blushing face of Virginia Seyton as she sat in a great chair in the old drawing-room at Elderthwaite and listened to the wooing of Alvar Lester. She held a bouquet on her lap, and he stood, bending forward, and addressing: her in language that was checked by no embarrassment, and with a simplicity of purpose which had sought no disguise. Alvar had reflected on his father's hints over many a cigarette, he had thought to himself that he was resolved to be an Englishman, that Miss Seyton was charming and attractive beyond all other ladies, it was well that he should marry, and he would be faithful, courteous, and kind.

Assuredly he was prepared to love her, she made England pleasant to him, and he had no strong ties to the turbulent life of Spain, from which his peculiar circumstances and his natural indolence had alike held him aloof. He had no thought of giving less than was Virginia's due, it was a simple matter to him enough, and he had come away that morning, with no false shame as to his intentions, with a flower in his coat and flowers in his hand, and had demanded Miss Seyton's permission to see her niece, heedless how far both households might guess at the matter in hand.

With his dark, manly grace, and tender accents, he was the picture of a lover, as she, with her creamy skin rose-tinted, and her fervent eyes cast down, seemed the very type of a maiden wooed, and by a favoured suitor. But if the hearts of this graceful and well-matched pair beat to the same time, the notes for each had very different force, and the experiences and the requirements of each had been, and must be, utterly unlike those of the other.

Alvar recognised this, in its obvious outer fact, when he began, —

"I have a great disadvantage," he said, "since I do not know how best to please an English lady when I pay her my addresses. Yet I am bold, for I come to-day to ask you to forget I am a stranger, and to help me to become truly an Englishman. Of all ladies, you are to me the most beautiful, the most beloved. Can you grant my wish—my prayer? Can I have the happiness to please you—Virginia?"

Virginia's heart beat so fast that she could not speak, the large eyes flashed up for a moment into his, then dropped as the tears dimmed them.

"Ah! do I make you shed tears?" cried Alvar. "How shall I tell you how I will be your slave? *Mi doña, mi reyna!*—nay, I must find English words to say you are the queen of my life!" and he knelt on one knee beside her, and took her hand.

Perhaps it was all the more enchanting that it was unlike a modern English girl's ideal of a likely lover.

"Please don't do that," said Virginia, controlling her emotion with a great effort. "I want to say something, if you would sit down."

With ready tact Alvar rose at once, and drew a chair near her.

"It is my privilege to listen," he said.

"It is that I am afraid I must be very different from the girls whom you have known. My ways, my thoughts, you might not like them; you might wish me to be different from myself—or I might not understand you," she added very timidly.

"In asking a lady to be my wife, I think of no other woman," said Alvar. "In my eyes you are all that is charming."

"This would not have occurred to me," said Virginia; "but since I came home I have not been very happy, because it is so hard to accommodate oneself to people who think of everything differently from oneself. If that was so with us—with you—"

"My thoughts shall be your thoughts," said Alvar. "You shall teach me to be what you wish—what my brother is. I know well," and he rose to his feet again and stood before her, "I am not clever, I do not know how to do those things the English admire; my face, my speech, is strange. Is that my fault; is it my fault that my father has hated and shunned his son? Miss Seyton, I can but offer you myself. If I displease you—"

Alvar paused. Virginia had been pleading against herself, and before his powerful attraction her misgivings melted away. She rose too, and came a step towards him.

"I will trust you," she said; and Alvar, more moved than he could himself have anticipated, poured forth a torrent of loving words and vows to be, and to do all she could wish. But he did not know, he did not understand, what she asked of him, or what he promised.

"But we must be our *true* selves to each other," she said afterwards, as they stood together, when he had won her to tell him that his foreign face and tones were not displeasing to her—not at all. No, she did not wish that he was more like his brothers.

"I will be always your true lover and your slave," said Alvar, kissing the hand that she had laid on his. "And now must I not present myself to your father? He will not, I hope, think the foreigner too presuming."

"There is papa," said Virginia, glancing out of the window; "he is walking on the terrace. Look, you can go out by this glass door." And leaving Alvar to encounter this far from formidable interview, she ran away up to the little oak room in search of her cousin.

There were tears in Ruth's great velvety eyes as she turned to meet her, but she was smiling, too, and even while she held out her arms to Virginia, she thought—"What, jealous of the smooth course of *her* little childish love! I would not give up one atom of what I feel for all the easy consent and prosperity in the world." But none the less was she interested and sympathetic as she listened to the outpourings of Virginia's first excitement, and to the recital of feelings that were like, and yet unlike, her own.

"You see, Ruthie, I could not help caring about him, he was so gentle and kind, and he never seemed angry with the others for misunderstanding him. But then I thought that our lives had been so wide apart that he *might* be quite different from what he seemed; and one has always heard, too, that foreigners pay compliments, and don't mean what they say."

"I should have despised you, Queenie, if you had thrown over the man you love because he was half a foreigner."

"Oh, no, not for *that*. But I didn't—I hadn't begun to—like him very much *then*, you see, Ruth. And if he had not been good—"

"And how have you satisfied yourself that he is what you call 'good' now?" said Ruth curiously.

"Of course," replied Virginia, "it is not as if he had been brought up in England. He cannot have the same notions. But then he cannot talk enough of Cherry's goodness, and seemed so grateful because he was kind to him. Cherry *is* a very good, kind sort of fellow of course; but don't you think there is something beautiful in the humility that makes so much of a little kindness, and recognises good qualities so ungrudgingly?"

Ruth laughed a little. Perhaps she thought Alvar's "bonny black eyes" had something to do with the force of these arguments.

"Since you love each other," she said, "that is a proof that you are intended for each other. What does it matter 'what he is like,' as you say?"

"But 'what he is like' made all the difference in the first instance, I suppose?" said Virginia.

"Perhaps," said Ruth, with a little shrug. "But now you have once chosen, Virginia, *nothing* ought to make you change, not if he were ever so wicked—not if he were a murderer!"

"Ruth," exclaimed Virginia, "how can you be so absurd! A murderer!"

"A murderer, a gambler, or a—well, I'm not quite sure about a thief," said Ruth, cooling down a little; and then the girls both laughed, and Virginia sank into a dreamy silence. She did not even yet know the story of her mother's married life, or she could not have laughed at the thought of a gambler for her husband; but she did know enough of her family history to give definiteness to the natural desire of a high-principled girl to find perfection in her lover. Virginia's nature inclined to hero-worship; reverence was a necessary part to her of a happy love. She had thought often to herself that she would never marry a man of whose good principles she was not satisfied. And since Alvar's offer had not entirely taken her by surprise—his gallantry having been tenderer than he knew—she had considered the point with an effort at impartiality, and had justified the conclusion to which her heart pointed by Alvar's admiration for the brother, whom, in Virginia's opinion, he idealised considerably. Of course, if she had chosen wisely, it was instinct, and not knowledge, that led her aright. She knew absolutely nothing of Alvar; and just as from insufficient grounds she now gave him credit for many virtues, it might be that, when the differing natures jarred, a little failure, a little defectiveness, might make her judgment cruelly hard, at whatever cost to her own happiness.

It might come to a struggle between the girl's ideal and the woman's love—and in such a struggle compromises and forgivenesses and new knowledge on either side would lead to final comprehension and peace. But it comes sometimes to a fight between heart and soul, between the higher self and the love that seems stronger than self. To this extremity Alvar Lester was not likely to drive any woman; but impatience and inexperience sometimes mistake the one contest for the other. Virginia would have something to bear, he much to learn, before mutual criticism ceased, as they became indeed part of each other's existence, before Virginia's flutter of startled joy subsided into unquestioning content.

"You talk, Ruthie," exclaimed Virginia, after a little more confidential chatter, "but you cannot make up your own mind. You cannot decide whether you will have poor Captain Lester."

"Hark! hark!" cried Ruth, "they are calling you! Every one is not so lucky as you." And as Virginia obeyed her father's summons, and she was left alone, she pulled out the locket that contained Rupert's portrait, kissed it passionately, and exclaimed, half-aloud,—

"Not make up my mind! Do *I* doubt and hesitate? What do I care 'what you are like,' my darling? I love you with all my heart and soul! I love you—I love you! What would life be without love?"

The congratulations of Virginia's family on the occasion were characteristic. Her father had but a nominal consent to give. Virginia was of age, and besides, the trustees of her fortune could not of course take any exception to such an engagement; but he rejoiced exceedingly, as at the first good and happy thing that had happened in his family for long enough.

"And so you have got a husband, though you are a Seyton?" said her aunt. "Well, Roland's a long way off, and I don't suppose Dick and Harry can create scandal enough to put an end to it before next October."

"But you'll give me a kiss, auntie?" said Virginia; and in the warmth of her embrace she tried to show the sympathy for that long past wrong which she never would have dared to utter.

Miss Seyton was silent for a moment, and patted her soft hair; then suddenly, with an expression indescribably *malin* and elfish, she said, "And all those poor little neglected children, whose souls you were going to save, what will become of them when you are married? Do you think your uncle will teach them himself?"

"And I shouldn't be surprised if he did, Aunt Julia," interposed Ruth briskly, "now Virginia has shown him the way." Parson Seyton's remark was somewhat to the same effect, though made in a more genial spirit.

"Well, my lass, so you've caught the Frenchman? Why didn't you set your cap at Cherry? He's worth a dozen of him."

"Cherry didn't set his cap at me, uncle," said Virginia, laughing.

"And all the little lads and lasses? Ha, ha, I must set about learning the catechism myself. What's to be done, my queen?—what's to be done? Send away Monsieur Alvar; we can't do without you." Virginia had not forgotten the children; but as her marriage was not to take place till the late autumn, there was no immediate question of her leaving them.

Mr Lester thought that it would be far better that Alvar should see something of England before his marriage, and Alvar acquiesced readily in his father's wish; and he very shortly left Oakby for London, after receiving congratulations from his brothers, in which astonishment was the prevailing ingredient, though Cheriton softened his surprise with many expressions of satisfaction.

He was glad that Alvar had chosen an English wife; still more glad that he had no disposition to choose Ruth.

Chapter Fifteen
A Bit of the Blarney

"With him there rode his sone, a younge squire,
A lovyere and a lusty bachelere."

In that year Easter fell very late, and it was nearly the end of April before the Lesters gathered together once more at Oakby. Alvar and Virginia had hardly had time to grow accustomed to their new relations to each other before the former went to London, where he perhaps adapted himself more easily to his surroundings than he would have done in the presence of his father and brothers. He found that all English people did not regard life precisely from the Oakby point of view; that Lady Cheriton greatly regretted that Nettie was such a tomboy, and almost feared that Bob would never be fit for polite society.

He was introduced to people who thought his music enchanting and his foreign manners charming; he was allowed to be on cousinly terms with the Miss Cheritons, and was an object of exciting interest to every young lady who met him. Under these circumstances he was very well content, and despatched graceful and tender letters to Virginia, which often had an amusing *naïveté* in their details of his impressions of English life. He also sent her various offerings, ornaments, sweetmeats, and flowers, always prettily chosen, and commended to her notice by some pleasant bit of tender flattery. His engagement was of course generally known, but his soft words and softer looks, though too universal to be delusive, were doubtless none the less attractive from the fact that his foreign breeding offered a constant cause and excuse for them.

Virginia, on her side, it need hardly be said, wrote him many letters, full of thoughts, feelings, and hopes, and sometimes requests for his opinion on any subject that interested her. Alvar's replies were so charming, so flattering, and so tender, that she hardly found out that they were in no sense *answers* to her own.

He made a very great point of going to Oxford, and was full of excitement at the prospect of meeting "my brother" again. Cheriton, however, had lost some time by his idle Christmas vacation, and was forced to work very hard to make up for it. He had always too many interests in life to make it easy to concentrate all his efforts in one direction; but now the ambition and love of distinction that were a constant stimulus to the idle Lester nature in himself and Jack were fairly alight.

Cheriton cared for success in itself; he was too sweet-natural to *resent* failure, and conscientious enough to know that his love of triumph might be a snare to him, but each object in its turn seemed to him intensely desirable. He could not feel, and even prevailing fashion made it difficult for him to affect, indifference. Besides, he wanted to appear in the light of a young man likely to succeed in life before Ruth's relations. So he wrote that he hoped Alvar would not think it unkind if he asked him to pay him only a short visit; and Alvar was half consoled by hearing the Judge speak in high terms of his nephew as a brilliant young man and likely to do them all credit.

"Ah," said Alvar, "I fear I should have done my name no credit if I, like my brother, had gone to Oxford."

"You are an eldest son, my dear fellow, and I don't doubt that you would have kept up the family traditions," said Judge Cheriton drily.

So Alvar went for one day to Oxford, where he showed an overpowering delight at seeing Cherry again, and a reprehensible preference for pouring out to him his various experiences, to inspecting chapels and halls. He greeted Buffer respectfully, and taxed Cheriton with overworking himself. He looked pale, he said, and thin—not as he did at Oakby.

Cherry only laughed at him, but insisted emphatically that he should say no word at home of any such impression, as perhaps he should stay up and read during the Easter vacation.

"But what shall I do," said Alvar, "when the boys, who do not like me, come home, and you are not there?"

"You—why, you will be all day at Elderthwaite."

"I shall never forget my brother who was kind to me first," said Alvar earnestly.

Alvar finished up his London career by going to see the Boat Race, where he was exceedingly particular to appear in Oxford colours, and felt as if the triumph of the dark blue was Cherry's own.

Easter week brought unwontedly soft airs and blue skies to Oakby, and, after all, Cheriton himself for a few days' holiday. Every one rejoiced at the sight of him, though Jack promptly told him that he was very foolish to waste time by coming, and when Cherry owned that he wanted a little rest, grudgingly admitted that he might be wise to take it; then seized upon him, first to discuss with him the work he himself was doing with a view to a scholarship for which he meant to compete at Midsummer; then demanded an immediate settlement, from Cherry's point of view, of several important and obscure philosophical questions; and finally confided to him a long history of Bob's scrapes and deficiencies during the past term.

He was so low in the school—he got in with such a bad lot—he ought to leave school and go to a tutor's. He, Jack, had told him he was going straight to the bad, but had done no good. Would Cherry give him a good blowing-up? Then Mr Lester, having had a letter from the headmaster, wanted to consult him on this very point, as well as to tell him all the story of Alvar's courtship and his own diplomatic behaviour. Also to regret that Alvar would not take the trouble to understand the details of English law as applied to local matters; could not see why Mr Lester, as a magistrate, was prevented from transporting a poacher for life, or why, as an owner of land, he thought it necessary to be so particular as to the character of his tenants. Then an attempt at peacemaking with and for Bob, which resulted in little more than a persistent growl "that Jack was an awful duffer."

Altogether the family did not seem in a restful state. Mrs Lester was very indignant because Mrs Ellesmere had observed that Nettie was growing too tall a girl to go about so much by herself. "Who was there that did not know Nettie in all the country-side?" While Bob and Nettie themselves, who usually hung together in everything, especially when either was in trouble, had an inexplicable quarrel, which made neither of them pleasant company for their elders.

Then Mr Lester's affairs came forward again in the shape of a dispute with one of his chief farmers about a certain gate which had been planted in the wrong place, involving a question of boundaries and rights of way, and engaging Mr Lester in a difference of opinion with a new neighbour, "a Radical fellow from Sheffield," whom Mr Lester would neither have injured nor been intimate with for the world. Alvar had the misfortune to observe that "he thought it was not worth while to be so distressed about the post of a gate," an indifference even more provoking than the misplaced ardour of Jack, who had taken upon himself to examine the matter, and believing his father mistaken, thought it necessary to say so, which might have been passed over as a piece of youthful folly, if there had not been a frightful suspicion that Mr Ellesmere was of the same opinion.

Cherry had heard enough of the "post of a gate" by the time he had read half-a-dozen letters of polite indignation, and listened to an hour's explanation from his father of the grounds of the dispute, after which he was requested to form an independent opinion on the subject.

"Well, father," he said, looking askance at a plan of the scene of action which Mr Lester had drawn for his benefit, "it seems that the removal of this gate has mixed up Ashrigg, Oakby, and Elderthwaite to such a degree that we sha'n't know who is living in which. Of course Alvar *can't* see any boundaries between Oakby and Elderthwaite just now. How should he? His imagination leaps over them at once. But I *don't* think it will 'precipitate the downfall of the landed gentry,' Jack, whichever way it is settled." And having thus succeeded in making his father and Alvar laugh, and Jack remark "that he never could see the use of making a joke of everything," he asked Mr Lester to come and show him the fatal spot. Couldn't they ride over and look at it?

"And I have never seen you yet," said Alvar reproachfully, when Mr Lester had acceded to this arrangement.

"But you are going to Elderthwaite? I will come and meet you there. And, look here, the weather is so fine I am sure we might all join forces and make an excursion somewhere. Wouldn't that be blissful?"

"Ah, you make sport of me!" said Alvar; but he promised to propose the plan at Elderthwaite.

So Cheriton and his father rode through the bright spring lanes together, like Chaucer's knight and squire, with the larks singing in the furrows, and the blue sky overhead, the sunshine full of promise and joy, even in the wild, bleak country, whose time of perfection never came till the purple heather clothed the bare moorlands and the summer months had had time to chase away all thought of the long, dreary winter. Every breath of the air of the hill-side was like new life to Cherry.

"It is so delightful to be at home," he said; "it's impossible to be very angry about 'the post of a gate.'"

Perhaps this happy humour contributed no small share towards the harmonious ending of the scene which Cherry described quaintly enough when he presented himself at Elderthwaite in the afternoon. How on arriving at the scene of action they had found Farmer Fleming and the fellow from Sheffield both engaged in discussing the point; how Mr Wilson had expressed *his* readiness to put up two gates if that would settle the matter, but he could not be dictated to on his own land; how Mr Fleming's view of the matter seemed to consist in a constant statement of the fact that he had been the squire's tenant all his life, and his father before him; how the squire had remarked that Mr Fleming's father, he was sure, would have known well that those four feet of land were common land, and half in Oakby and half in Ashrigg parish, Elderthwaite bordering them on the south, and that he, as Lord of the Manor, could not allow them to be enclosed; Mr Wilson had purchased certain manorial rights in Ashrigg parish; they certainly extended over the two feet on his own side of the lane.

Then Cherry had remembered Mr Wilson's son at Oxford, and knew that last year he had taken a first. He had met him at breakfast; was he coming down soon? This had created a diversion; and while the squire and his tenant were at it hammer and tongs, Cherry had received several invitations, had warmly applauded Mr Wilson's remark that he did not wish to be unpleasant to old inhabitants on first coming into the county, and the squire, having got his own way with the farmer, an amicable arrangement was arrived at; while Cherry went to see Mrs Fleming's dairy, "because he remembered how she used to give him such beautiful new milk."

"Oh, Cherry, you have more than a bit of the blarney," said Ruth. "Haven't you a drop of Irish blood somewhere?"

"*No* more than Jack," said Cherry, who was perhaps a little pleased at his diplomacy. "I like to smooth things down, unless, to be sure, one is angry oneself."

"You are always the peacemaker," said Alvar.

"Ah, not always, I am afraid! But now I want all the blarney I can muster to persuade you that it is warm enough to go and spend the day at Black Tarn. We might go by train from Hazelby to Blackrigg; have lunch at the inn there, and go up to Black Tarn by the Otter's Glen. I asked Mr and Mrs Ellesmere, and they will come with us"—to Virginia—"I assure you Alvar agrees."

"You are wasting your blarney," said Virginia smiling, "for we had agreed to go before you came. It will be very cold up at Black Tarn, but that will not signify if we take plenty of wraps."

Such a genuine piece of natural and innocent amusement was quite a novelty at Elderthwaite, and the boys were delighted. The party agreed to meet at Hazelby station, and go by train some ten or twelve miles towards the mountains on the outskirts of which Black Tarn lay. There was a train in the evening by which they could return, and no one left at home was to be anxious about them until they saw them coming back.

Chapter Sixteen
The Otter's Glen

"An empty sky, a world of heather,
Purple of foxglove, yellow of broom,
We two among them, wading together,
Stepping out honey, treading perfume."

There was hardly a lonelier spot in all the country round than the little Black Tarn. The hill in which it lay possessed neither the rocky grandeur nor the fertile beauty of the neighbouring mountains; it was covered with grass and bog, not a tree relieved its desolateness, no grey rocks pushed their picturesque heads through the soil and gave variety to its shape. The approach to the little lake was defended by great beds of reeds and rushes, its waters were shallow, and later in the year full of weeds and water-lilies. But there was a fine view of the heathery backs of some of the more important mountains, and the stream that rushed down the Otter's Glen was broad and clear, and had been the scene of many an exciting chase in grey misty mornings.

To-day the sun was bright and strong, the fresh mountain wind intensely exhilarating, and the whole party were in the highest spirits and ready to enjoy every incident of their excursion. They had had their lunch, as proposed, at the little wayside inn, where the Lesters were well known and always welcome, and had then set off on their three-miles walk to the tarn in scattered groups, all at their own pace and with different views of the distances they meant to effect.

A large division, headed by Mr Ellesmere, had started off at a brisk pace, intending to get to the top of the hill and see half over the country, but stragglers began to drop behind.

Mrs Ellesmere thought the tarn would be enough for herself and her younger children; every one dropped off from Alvar and Virginia, and left them to their own devices, while Cherry set himself to persuade Ruth that the best thing to do was to follow the stream, step by step, along its winding course, heedless of the end.

He could hardly believe in his own good luck as the voices of the others died away in the distance, and Ruth put her hand into his to be helped along the slippery stepping-stones planted here and there on the marshy path-way.

Whatever was missing for Ruth in the perfection of the day's pleasure, her great dark eyes were bright and soft, and a little flush on her brown cheeks gave her an additional beauty. She wore a small closely-fitting hat with a red plume in it, and a tight dark dress; and thus, with her hand in his, and her bewitching eyes raised to his face, her image recurred to him in after days.

He had been laughing, and talking, and managing the expedition, but now alone with her he fell silent, and there was that in his face as he looked down at her that frightened Ruth a little.

During these past months he had grown less "boyish," and it crossed Ruth's mind to wonder if he had had any special purpose in getting her to himself.

"And have you been working very hard?" she said, smiling at him.

"Pretty well," answered Cherry. "I shall be glad when it's all over."

"Won't they ring all the bells at Oakby?"

Cherry laughed.

"I hope they won't have occasion to toll them," he said; "it seems sometimes much more likely."

"Ah! that is because you get out of spirits. And after all, who cares except a lot of stupid old tutors?"

"I don't suppose you—any one, would care much."

"Why," said Ruth dexterously; "who judges a man by the result of an examination? that would be very unfair."

"Then," said Cherry shyly, "if I come to grief I shall go to you for—for consolation. You won't despise me?"

"Oh, Cherry! I am sure when one knows life one sees that after all those tests are rather childish. *I* should not think less of you if you made a mistake." Perhaps it was characteristic of Cheriton that he felt more than ever resolved to attain success, and he answered,—

"You ought to think less of me if I did not do my best to avoid mistakes."

"Now that is worthy of Jack, of whom I am becoming quite afraid. I care for my friends because—well, because I care for them, and what they do makes no difference."

"That," said Cherry, "is the sort of backing up that would make a man able to endure failure till success came. But still one must wish to bring home the spoils!"

There was a dangerous intensity in Cheriton's accent, and Ruth laughed gaily.

"Of course, men are always so ambitious. Well, I believe in your spoils, Cherry, but don't work *too* hard for them. Don Alvar told Virginia you would knock yourself up."

"Oh, Alvar! Hard work is a great puzzle to him. No fear of my working too hard, I get stupefied too quickly, otherwise I should not be here now; but I can't grudge what is so—so delightful. Take care, that is a very slippery stone. Won't you give me your hand? There, that's a safe one."

Ruth was not a great adept at scrambling independently, but she knew how to be helped with wonderful grace and gratitude. Nor was a solitary ramble with Cheriton at all an unnatural thing. He had helped her up in many a difficult place in their boy-and-girl days, and teased her by pretending that he would not help her down; but now she felt that in more senses than one she was treading on slippery ground, and guided the conversation on to the safer topic of Alvar and Virginia.

"Weren't you very much surprised," said Cheriton, "when that came about?"

"Well, you know," said Ruth, "Virginia is rather transparent. I couldn't help guessing that she was interested in your brother. She is so romantic, too, and he is such a cavalier."

"I suppose *you* always study common sense," said Cherry, who preferred greatly to talk about Ruth herself than to discuss Virginia.

"I have my own ideas of romance," said Ruth; "but I think I have outgrown the notion that every one ought to look like a hero."

"And what is your idea of romance?" asked Cherry, gratified by this remark.

"Self-devotion," said Ruth briefly, giving up everything for the one object. "That's true romance."

"Self-sacrifice?" said Cherry. "That is too hard work to be romantic about."

"Not for any one—anything one loved," said Ruth very low, but with flushing cheeks.

"Then," said Cheriton, "there would be no other self left to sacrifice."

Ruth was startled. Rupert had never so answered her thoughts, had never given her quite such a look.

Cherry paused and turned round towards her with a desperate impulse urging him to speak, her face shining with enthusiasm giving him sudden courage.

"Ah!" exclaimed Ruth, springing across on to a very unsteady stone, "you are getting too serious! I declare, there's a white butterfly, the first for the year. And look—oh, look, Cherry, isn't that bit of gorse pretty against the sky? It's too bad to discuss abstract questions at a picnic on a spring day."

Cheriton stood still for a moment. He heard the rush of the water, he saw the shine of the sun, his eyes followed the butterfly as it fluttered up to the bit of yellow gorse, he could see Ruth smiling and graceful, beckoning to him to follow her; the glamour and dazzle had passed, and the day was like any other fine day now.

"I did not mean to discuss *abstract* questions," he said, with a touch of offence.

"Ah! but you were getting very deep! Come, don't be cross, Cherry; you look exactly like Jack at this minute, and *you* can't make your eyebrows meet, so don't try."

"Poor Jack, you are very hard on him," said Cherry, recovering himself. "Will you have a bit of the gorse for your hat, if I cut all the prickles off?"

"If you cut all the prickles off, what will you leave?" said Ruth.

They had a very charming walk after this, and were much more merry and talkative than at first. There was a sense of being baffled deep down in Cherry's heart, but if the rest was surface work it was very enchanting, and they dawdled and chattered till the time slipped away, and they saw their party in the distance coming back from the tarn.

"Oh, let us run," said Ruth, "and get into the road before them."

"Come," said Cherry, holding out his hand, and they ran across the short turf, the sweet, keen air blowing in their faces, a sort of excitement urging Ruth, who was a lazy little thing usually, to this childish proceeding.

They came running down into the road just as the whole party came back from the tarn, crying out on them for their laziness.

"We have been looking for you," said Virginia, whose hat was daintily wreathed with stag moss. "Alvar and I tried to find you."

"Oh, yes, you were miserable without us of course," said Cherry. "Hallo, Rupert! where on earth did you spring from?"

"I came over for a ball at the Molyneuxes; they have taken Blackrigg Hall, you know. I must get back by the first thing to-morrow. I heard of your picnic from some of the people about, and came to see if I could fall in with you."

"You are just in time to come back with us to the inn," said Mr Ellesmere; "we shall have no more than time to get a cup of tea and be off for the train."

"I thought you would not come," whispered Ruth to Rupert as they all walked back together.

"So it seemed; what were you doing with Cherry?" said Rupert sharply.

Ruth looked at him with reproach in her eyes, but they had no chance then of obtaining private words. Rupert looked savage, but directed his efforts to sitting next her in the omnibus which was to convey most of the party to the station.

"Don't spoil these few minutes," whispered Ruth imploringly as she looked up in his displeased face. "Could I let people guess how I was longing for you? I thought you would have been here sooner."

"Cherry is always to the fore," said Rupert with an amount of ill-temper for which Ruth could not quite account. She felt profoundly miserable, so wretched that she could hardly keep the tears out of her eyes. She had looked forward for the last day or two to this poor little meeting as such a light in the darkness, and now some one spoke to Rupert and some one else to herself. There was no chance of making it up—if they were to part so! Oh, it was hard! Virginia could say as much as she liked to *her* lover. Then Ruth saw that Alvar was not in the omnibus, nor Cheriton either, and hoped that the latter fact might assuage Rupert's jealousy. Perhaps he felt ashamed of it, for as they neared Blackrigg she felt his hand clasp hers, and he whispered, "Forgive me."

In the meanwhile Cheriton, having lingered a moment to make payments and final arrangements, was left for the "trap," a very nondescript vehicle, which had brought Bob and Jack from the station. To his surprise he found that Alvar instead of one of the younger ones was his companion.

"Why, how's this?" he said.

"I thought that I would wait for you. Is it not my turn?" said Alvar, who sometimes liked to claim an equality with the others.

"I'm afraid you'll get wet," said Cherry; "they've all the plaids, and it is going to rain. These mountain showers come up so quickly."

"I do not mind the rain," said Alvar. Cheriton, however, mindful of Alvar's short experience of the cold, driving rain of the country, made him put a dilapidated rug that was in the carriage over his shoulders, and drove on as fast as he could, through mist and wind, till about half-way to Blackrigg there was a great jolt,—off came the wheel of the trap, which turned over, and they were both thrown out on to the high bank beside the road.

Cherry felt Alvar's arm round him before he had time to get up, and heard him speaking fast in Spanish, and then, "You are not hurt, my brother?"

"Oh, no—no. Nor you? That's all right; but we're in a nice fix. No getting to Blackrigg to-night. Here's the wheel off."

The bank was soft and muddy; and they were quite unhurt, and after a minute, Cherry hailed a man passing by, and asked him to take the horse back to the inn, proposing to Alvar to try to catch the train at Stonybeach, an intermediate station, to which he knew a short cut.

"Can you make a ran for it?" he said.

"Yes—oh, yes, I can run," said Alvar. "This is an adventure."

It was such a run across country as reminded Cheriton of his days of paper-chases, and was probably a new experience to Alvar, who remarked breathlessly, as they neared the station,—

"I can run—when it is necessary; but I do not understand your races for amusement."

Cheriton made no answer, as they entered the station and found that after all a neighbouring market had delayed the train, and that they had still some minutes to wait.

"That's too bad," said Cherry, as strength and breath fairly failed him, and he sat hastily down on a bench, to his own surprise and annoyance, completely exhausted.

"All! you are too tired!" exclaimed Alvar, coming to him; and with a kindness and presence of mind for which few had given him credit, he made Cherry rest, and got the porter to fetch some water for him (the little roadside station afforded nothing else), till after a few minutes of dizzy faintness and breathlessness, Cherry began to revive into a state of indignation with himself, and gratitude to his brother, the expression of which sentiments Alvar silenced.

"Hush! I will not have you talk yet! You must rest till the train comes. Lean back against me. No—you have not made a confounded fool of yourself, when you could not help it."

"I suppose the fall shook me," said Cherry, presently. "Hark! there is the train. Now, Alvar, don't you say a word of this. I am all right now."

He stood up as the train came creeping and groaning into the station, and Jack made signs to them out of the window. The train was crowded, and the rest of the party were farther back. Jack exclaimed at their appearance, and while they were explaining their adventure, Alvar got some wine for Cheriton out of a hamper that had been brought for the luncheon.

"Why, Alvar, you are more than half a doctor," said Cherry, as he took it. "I'm all right again now."

Jack scanned him a little anxiously. "You had no business to be knocked up," he said briefly. "You should not have tried to run when you were so out of condition."

"If I am a doctor, Jack," said Alvar, "I will not have my patient scolded. He is better now, are you not, *Cherito mio*? And we are not fit to see the ladies. See, I am covered with mud," and Alvar endeavoured to brush the mud off his hat, and to make his wet clothes look a little less disreputable.

Cherry put a great coat on, as a measure both of prudence and respectability. He had been desperately desirous of catching the train for the sake of a few more words with Ruth; for on the next day he was obliged to return to Oxford. They were all to part at Hazelby, where their respective carriages awaited them.

Ruth had forgotten his very existence as he hurried up to her in the crowded station; for Rupert had been forced to go on by the train. She remembered now that her walk with him had made Rupert angry, and hardly able to control her voice to speak at all, she wished him a cold, hasty good-night, and sprang into the carriage without giving him time for a word.

Cheriton was both angry and miserable; he stood back silently, while Alvar put Virginia into the carriage, and excused himself gaily for his muddy coat. Dick Seyton ran up at the last minute, and the Lesters set out on their six-miles drive in an open break, under waterproofs and umbrellas, through the pouring rain. The twins disputed under their breath, and Jack lectured Cheriton on the amount of exercise necessary during a period of hard reading.

Cherry, for once, answered him sharply, and Alvar, as was usually the case when his *Geschwistern* quarrelled, wondered silently, both how they could be so un-courteous to each other, and how they could excite themselves so much about nothing. But there had been something in the manner of his kindness and attention that dwelt pleasantly in Cheriton's memory of a day which for many reasons he had afterwards cause to look back upon with pain.

Chapter Seventeen
Rifts

"It is the little rift within the lover's lute."

In the June following the expedition to Black Tarn, some great festivities were held in honour of the coming of age of a young nobleman, who possessed a large property about fifteen miles from Oakby.

His father, the late Lord Milford, had been a friend of Mr Lester, and the young man himself was at school for a time with his sons. The event being also of importance in the county, old Mrs Lester broke through her usual home-staying habits, and took Ruth and Virginia Seyton for a three days' visit to Milford Hall.

It was right for Virginia to be seen in her own county before her marriage; it was years since her father and aunt had been present at such a gathering, and Alvar and his father were of course among the guests. Cheriton was passing, or had passed, his examination; but he had decided not to come home until he knew his fate; and in studying the papers every morning, in the hope of seeing the Class Lists long before they could possibly be printed, Mr Lester and Alvar found at last a subject on which they could thoroughly sympathise, though Mr Lester frequently remarked that there was never any knowing how those matters would be managed; he did not expect much, while Alvar suffered from no misgivings at all.

Rupert and some of his brother officers were among the guests; the entertainments were of the most brilliant description, and the weather perfect.

Ruth was well known and popular. True, she distinguished herself neither in archery nor any other outdoor sport; she was not even a very great dancer; but she could talk, and look, and smile as if her companion's words were the one thing interesting to her; hence her success. And Rupert was there, and in the dark alleys and lonely shrubberies of the great gardens at Milford, opportunities for *tête-à-têtes* were not wanting. Ruth, conscious of her becoming dress of the soft, warm maize that suited her brown skin, with amusement and admiration to froth her cup of pleasure, and Rupert's exciting presence to spice it and make it worth the drinking, might seem to be enjoying the most brilliant outcome of young-lady life. Sparkle and colour, feeling and passion, she would have chosen as her greatest good. Theoretically she would have willingly embraced the pains and penalties which they might bring in their train. Yet Ruth on the sunny lawns and stately paths of Milford was profoundly and violently miserable, full of anger and despair.

The terms on which she stood with Rupert were such as could only be endurable with the most perfect trust on both sides. Where it was necessary to feign neglect, it was sometimes a strain to believe in the real devotion. Neither Ruth nor Rupert were people whose manners precluded the possibility of a mistake, and, as has been seen, Rupert was not proof against jealousy. The strength of Ruth's own passion made her more trustful of his, but at the same time she demanded more from him, and he failed to fulfil her ideal of an ardent lover. He appeared to her to be too cautious, to miss opportunities, and be his necessity for secrecy what it might, she *could* not bear to see him attentive to others—to another, rather.

There was a young Lady Alice, in her first season, a charming childish beauty, after whom it was the fashion to run, and who found it agreeable enough to torment her many admirers, and provoke the aunt who chaperoned her, by flirting with the handsome Captain Lester, who, on his side, knew well enough that she meant nothing serious; and, while he was true in his heart to Ruth, was vain enough to be flattered by the preference of a beauty, and of a lady, moreover, of rank and distinction. It showed every one that he was a man of the world, and a very agreeable fellow.

Perhaps matters might have mended if Mrs Lester, who thought modern manners much too free, and drew a sharp distinction between the simplicity of her own straightforward, unwatched girlhood and the coquetries of a ball-room, and who, moreover, disapproved of Ruth, had not looked so very sharply after her, that private interviews were rendered difficult, and Ruth was growing too angry to seek one.

She had not sat by him at dinner; they were separated at the great concert that had been given on the day of their arrival; and on the next, which was one long *fête*, ending in a ball, they only caught a few hasty words with each other; and it appeared to her excited fancy that he was for ever at Lady Alice's side. In the evening she would not dance with him, crowding her card with names, laughed, talked, flirted, and was wretched. It was not till after supper that he pursued her into the last of a long vista of conservatories, where a very youthful partner had conducted her to smell the stephanotis, and claim the next dance as his own.

The warm, scented air, the distant music, the soft, dim mingling of lamp and moonlight, through which strange, rare flowers gleamed out from their dark foliage, formed such a background as Ruth's vivid fancy, fed by many a tale and poem, had often painted, to scenes that should satisfy her in their tenderness and intensity. Among the wild fir-woods of Oakby, here and there, at odd times and by unexpected chances, she had known blissful moments, every one of which was before her now as she set her mouth hard, and looked at Rupert with eyes full both of love and anger.

Rupert was excited and eager, conscious of having given cause of offence, and a little off his head with the flattery he had received. He failed to read the meaning of her face, and turned to her eagerly.

"At last, my child! Mrs Lester is a perfect dragon!"

"I don't think it has been Mrs Lester's fault."

"It has been none of mine," said Rupert. "Your fine, yellow dress escaped me at every turn, and I could not get away from the people. I have had to work hard for my fun, and arrange dozens of things."

"I daresay it is very pleasant to be so popular," said Ruth, detecting the little boast, which in a cooler moment would have passed unnoticed. There was a sort of airiness in Rupert's manner, inexpressibly irritating when she wanted every assurance of the passion which she was so often obliged to take upon trust.

"Come, Ruthie, that's not fair. What is a poor fellow to do? I have been horribly down in the mouth since we parted; it takes so long to get one's affairs to rights. Your guardians would bow me out of the house pretty quickly if I applied to them now. Can you trust me a little longer, my darling? I'm living on twopence a day to bring things round."

"And did the gloves Lady Alice won from you, come out of the twopence?" said Ruth, unable to control her anger, sarcastic because such a storm of tears was pending.

Rupert's quick temper took fire in a moment.

"If you have so little confidence in me, Ruth, as to be angry at such a trifle," he said hotly, "it is impossible—You make me feel that I ask more of you than you can give."

"Yes," said Ruth, "I cannot give such confidence. When it is months since I have seen you—weeks since I heard from you. I *cannot* see you devoted to—to another, when you cannot find a moment for me. If *you* can bear it—"

"You are very unreasonable, Ruth. I thought that you were generous before all other women, and patient. You speak as if you doubted my honour."

"If it comes to talking of *honour*," cried Ruth, "if you need *that* to bind you, you are free. I will not hold you one hour by your honour!"

"Nor I you to a trial of generosity, which it seems you cannot bear."

If Rupert had not been first *tête montée*, and then very angry, he would not have made this remark.

"Generosity!" cried Ruth. "No. If honour and generosity are required between us, I'll make no claim on them. Let it all be over—we'll part. Yes, we'll part, and then you need deny yourself nothing—nothing for my sake."

"It might be best—if you look on it in this way."

There was a silence. Rupert pulled his moustaches sharply; his face was pale; in that hot moment he felt he might be well quit of Ruth's unreasonable jealousy and suspicion. Ruth sat quite still; she would have yielded at a word, perhaps—in a minute more she might even have made the first advance to a reconciliation. But as the dance ended the conservatory filled with people. They were joined by two or three couples, and a young lady, an old acquaintance of Rupert's, exclaimed, with sufficient forwardness,—

"Oh, Captain Lester, what do you think we were discussing? People say that you are engaged to be married. Is it true—do tell me?"

"No," said Rupert shortly. "I am not engaged to be married, nor likely to be."

He laughed bitterly as he spoke, and perhaps under the circumstances could hardly have avoided some sort of denial; but the directness of this one, and the tone in which it was spoken, seemed to seal Ruth's fate. She said afterwards that she went mad at that moment, and certainly she lost the soft self-possession that was one of her chief charms, grew daring and defiant, and said and did things that others remembered long after she had recovered from the wild excitement that prompted them. The sacredness of ungovernable feeling was an article of her faith, and she was quite as miserable as she ever thought true love would demand of any one. But the poor child, as she sat on the floor in her own room that night, with her face hidden on a chair, did not think at all that she was "having an experience," nor going through the second volume of the story, in the beginning of which she had so gloried; she only felt that she was utterly and inconceivably wretched, and angry beyond expression. Rupert did not care for her, or only cared in a commonplace fashion. There was nothing left in life for her. Evidently he had been glad to find in the quarrel an excuse for an escape.

Ruth's hot displeasure culminated when she came down to breakfast the next morning, and found that every one was regretting the departure of the officers from York, who had been obliged to take leave early that morning. They would be a great loss at the tenants' ball that night.

"Father, my father," suddenly exclaimed Alvar Lester, coming into the room with a newspaper in his hand. "See, it is here, 'Gerald Cheriton Lester.' And he is first. I said so. Ah! I rejoice!"

Alvar's eager voice and excited face attracted general attention, as he put the paper into his father's hand, and pointed over his shoulder. There was a chorus of congratulation, while Mr Lester's blue eyes looked as bright as his son's black ones, as he hummed and ha'd, coughed two or three times, and said, with as little exultation as he could manage to show, "That he was glad Cheriton had worked hard and done his best. He was a good lad, and had never given any trouble. Now, they could have him at home for a bit."

"Ah! that will be *jolly*," said Alvar. "But he will have come home, through last night, and we shall not be there."

"Send a telegram to meet him, and ask him to come over," said young Lord Milford. "He always was a capital fellow, and I shall be delighted to see him."

"And I hope, Milford," said the young lord's mother, "that you will take example by your friend."

"Don't you build on any such hopes, mother, but I'll go and see about getting him over here at once."

Mrs Lester was moved to encomiums on Cherry's studies and steadiness; and more than one of those present remarked with admiration the unselfish pleasure taken by the elder brother in the success of his universally popular junior.

Virginia Seyton watched her betrothed a little wistfully. Ruth's was not the only love story that was running its course through these early summer months, and Virginia's heart was not quite at ease. If "what Rupert was like," had come upon Ruth with a sudden blow, "what Alvar was like," was still something of a problem to Virginia. He was attractive to her beyond measure, he occupied every corner of her heart; it was joy to her to be near him; his gentle, chivalrous courtship gave her unimaginable delight. She could remember every glance of his eyes, every touch of his hand; but—But what? Alvar was at once too obtuse and too proud ever to assume a character that did not belong to him. He did not think it worth while to acquire or profess new sentiments; perhaps he never even perceived that they were desired. He was, spite of his courteous tongue, as absolutely candid a person as his brother Jack. He was not a bit worse than he seemed, neither was he much better. He behaved very well in his difficult life, and regulated his conduct by certain maxims of honour and courtesy; but, in the sense in which Virginia understood the word, he had no principles at all. It was with a curious mixture of sensations that, when, *à propos* of some scrape of Dick's, she had timidly alluded to the gambling that had brought such distress on her family, Virginia heard him answer,—

"Ah, they have had much ill-fortune," without a spark apparently of righteous indignation.

Nor could she help perceiving that he scarcely ever occupied himself with anything more useful than a cigar. "My father is always busy," he would say complacently, as he sat idle; but he did not point any popular moral; for idleness made him neither ill-humoured nor mischievous.

Virginia loved him well enough to set all her will on the side of making allowances. When he saw her scrupulous and earnest in fulfilling her religious duties, he would kiss her hand and say, "My queen is as holy as a saint," and he conformed sufficiently to the Oakby standard to satisfy her conscience, if not his own, never uttering a word that could offend her. But, as he had told Cheriton, "he did not interest himself in these matters," and she knew it.

Perhaps Virginia, diffident as to her knowledge of masculine standards and modes of expression, might never have realised even thus much to herself, but for the instinctive sense of another shortcoming in her lover, which she would not admit, and which she hated herself for even imagining. It came, by a strange turn of fate, both to her and to Ruth, to feel that the love they gave was not returned in its fulness. With what a passion of despair and jealousy Ruth had resented the discovery has been seen.

To Virginia it brought a disheartening sense of her own demerit, a doubt of the truth of her own impressions, vexation at her own want of trustfulness, shame and self-blame, because she could not help knowing that Alvar missed sometimes the chance of a word or an interview when *she* would have secured it, because she felt that he did not care as she cared. But then, temperaments differ; some people were reserved; perhaps she was exacting, and her cheek had flushed and her eyes sparkled with joy when Alvar praised the dresses she had taken such pains to choose for the Milford *fêtes*, and when he paid her all the *attention* due from an affianced lover.

She had no cause to feel neglected, while Ruth was chafing at the sight of Rupert's flirtations. And when the news came of Cheriton's success, was she not proud of Alvar's generous delight? Yes, but *she* had never stirred his passive content to such pleasure; he had never been in such high spirits for her! Ah! how hatefully selfish she was to think of it!

The two girls exchanged no confidences. Ruth's heart was too sore, and Virginia's too loyal for a word; but as they consulted over their dresses, and speculated whether Cheriton would arrive in time for the tenants' dance that night, each wondered what the other would say to the secret thoughts of her heart.

Chapter Eighteen
Red Sunrise

"O happy world!" thought Pelleas, "all me seems
Are happy—I the happiest of them all."

On that same hot summer night, when Ruth and Rupert were first making each other miserable, and then finding out separately that they were very miserable themselves, Cheriton, with hope and joy in his heart, was speeding home to Oakby. With hope and joy, for Ruth had made up for her cold farewell, by making some little excuse for writing to him, and asking him to get her a picture of the Arms of the Colleges, a commission which, it is needless to say, he found time to execute.

This pleasure had helped him through his hard work, for he was excitable enough to have felt the last few weeks of effort and suspense a severe strain, and had not brought quite his usual health and strength to bear on them; for he had caught a bad cold with the race in the rain at Black Tarn, and had never given himself a chance of getting rid of it. However, it was all over now, he thought, his mind was relieved, and the prospect of home with its leisure and its occupations had never seemed so delightful to him. For his love for Ruth did not shut out the thought of all other affections, it rather cast a radiance over them, and made him more conscious of their sweetness.

It was a lovely summer morning, as the train came in to Ashrigg station, the wide landscape showed clear and fresh against the cloudless sky, the peculiar northern sharpness was in the air. It was sweet to Cherry's senses, and finding no conveyance so early at Ashrigg, he set off to walk home across the dewy fields, Buffer, enchanted at his release from durance vile, trotting and barking at his heels.

By various short cuts the walk was under three miles, and Cheriton soon found himself at the house, where he had time to get some breakfast, and to feel somewhat disappointed that no one was at home to hear his good news, for he felt too tired to go and seek for congratulations at the Vicarage, where Nettie was staying, or where he would have been at least equally certain of them, to the Lodge to which the old family nurse had migrated.

So he contented himself with greeting all the dogs, and with the delightful consciousness that he had no need to exert himself, till Lord Milford's telegram arrived, and the thought of so quickly greeting Ruth, and of finding her belonging as it were to his own party, and thus making a thousand opportunities for paying her attention, roused him from his fit of languor and fatigue, and he eagerly made his preparations, and started off in the middle of the bright June day, on his further travels.

The midsummer weather in that northern country had still much of the freshness and the delicacy of the spring. The trees were in their first bright green, the bluebells lingered in the woods, the birds sang songs of hopefulness to him. Milford was in a softer, more richly-wooded landscape than Oakby, and the gardens were splendid with early roses and flowering shrubs, the park still here and there white with hawthorn.

This was the children's day, a great school feast for all the parishes round, to be followed by a children's dance in the evening. Cheriton arrived in the midst of a grand tea in the park, and pausing to detect his relations, perceived Alvar looking even unusually tall, stately, and graceful, as he walked along a row of the very tiniest children, and filled their mugs with milk and water from a huge can. He looked up as he came to the end, and saw Cheriton's laughing eyes fixed full upon him.

"Ah! Cheriton!" he exclaimed, "you are here, and with all your honours! Welcome."

"Thanks; I knew you would be pleased. So you are making yourself useful. Where's my father?"

"In the tent with Lady Milford. I will show you."

Cheriton was inclined to think it a great bore to find his own people surrounded by strangers, and was ashamed of the congratulations which the circumstances of his arrival and the warm-heartedness of his hosts called forth. So he and his father hardly said a word to each other, though they experienced a great content in being together; perhaps a more uncommon ending to a university career than Cherry's honours, even had they been doubled.

"Come, Lester," said Lord Milford, "and make yourself useful. I know you are great at sack-races, and three-legged races, and such diversions."

"After being up all night? Well, as long as I am not expected to jump in a sack myself—" said Cheriton. "Come, Alvar, don't you want another can of milk and water?"

"Ah! you laugh at me," said Alvar contentedly. "I am too glad to see you to care. This *fête* is very pleasant. I am glad you came back in time for it."

"Yes; but I wish we were all at home," said Cheriton absently, and looking anxiously round him. He soon discovered Virginia, much in her element among a crowd of school-girls; and at length his eyes found the object of their search. A little apart on a bench sat Ruth in the most delicate of white muslins, gloves, fan, and ribbons, all in first-rate order, looking, with the fantastic fashion, and brilliant dashes of colour in her dress, like a figure on a fan. She gave a little start as she saw Cheriton's figure in the distance, and her flush of disappointment as he came nearer was at once noted by him, and—misinterpreted.

"So you have got your laurels?" she said softly, as she held out her hand, and looked up in his face. "I am glad."

"Then they are worth having?" said Cheriton.

It might have been a mere jesting answer, but Ruth did not so take it, nor did he intend that she should do so. He would have altered nothing in her greeting to him, it was a better meeting than he could have imagined. Afterwards, if Ruth had wished to discourage him, she would not have found it easy; he had but one purpose, and he set himself to fulfil it; hopeful through the charm of present bliss. It was not often that Cheriton's native skies were so cloudless, nor were these hot, full summer days at all typical of the home that he loved so well. But it was in such "blue unclouded weather," in such smiling midsummer beauty, that he pictured afterwards the wind-swept moors and hardy fir-woods of his north-country home. Nor did the memory of hot, glaring sunshine, of dust, and noise, and fatigue, cease to haunt Ruth for many a day to come.

She was one of those to whom excitement gives another and an intenser self. Of this she was dimly conscious, and when she had said that she could die for Rupert, she had perhaps not been far wrong. That extreme anger would urge her to a course almost equally desperate she had never guessed, but to give Rupert pain, to cause him chagrin and remorse, in short, to make him jealous and miserable as he had made her, she would have endured tortures.

When people are thus minded, in other words, when they are in a passion, life always helps them on. Whether by accident or by malice, she had heard plenty of gossip about Rupert; he had written no word of repentance; she knew that Lady Alice would shortly meet him again. Well, if *her* conduct was discussed between them, he should hear enough, both to hurt his provoking self-love, and to show that he did not suffer. And Cheriton offered the sort of strange counter-attraction often felt on such occasions to any one else than the object of anger.

She had always liked to "talk to Cherry," his love was flattering, and she instinctively knew that it was true. He was also a singularly attractive and lovable person, and in Ruth's sore-hearted rage she felt his charm. "It was nice to be with him—he did her good;" and if she could wound Rupert and please herself, the possible disappointment to Cheriton was not worth considering. But Ruth reckoned without her host. She neither allowed for Cheriton's ardour, nor for the effect that it would have on her; she did not know how definite her choice must be.

Cherry was not nearly so useful as his friend had expected; he was too tired to play games, and dancing, he said, gave him a pain in his side and made him cough, which was true, and would have been an equally good reason against wandering about in the shrubberies and distant paths with Ruth, where he incurred other dangers than night air and dewy grass. He was too happy to heed any of them. She listened, as Ruth knew how to listen, to his account of his Oxford life—his hopes and fears—his future prospects—and she was carried away, spite of herself, by the single-minded earnestness with which he spoke. He interested her, and she forgot herself for the moment as they strolled along; the yellow sunset dying in the distance, the first star shining over the great house behind them. Suddenly Cheriton turned and took her hand.

"Ruth," he said, "I have told you all this because it is so sweet to see you listen. I have something more to tell you now. I have a great many aims and ambitions—there's one dearer than the rest. I love my own people—my home—very much. I love you best, infinitely best. I always have loved you. Can you love me?"

"Oh, Cherry!" cried Ruth, in desperate self-defence, "don't say so! That sort of love is all a mistake. Keep to the other sort—it is a great deal better for you."

"Better!" exclaimed Cheriton. "One thing is best for me—to have you for my wife. Oh, Ruth, my darling! ever since I was a boy I have loved you. Can't you care a little for me? I think you can—I hope you can. *You* have always listened to me and understood me. I think you know me better than any one does!"

"I know—you *do* care," said Ruth, half to herself.

"It is my very life," he said, and as she, trembling, hardly able to stand, made a half movement towards—not away from him—he threw his arms round her and drew her close. "My darling!—oh, my darling! am I so happy?—ah! thank God! Thank God!"

Ruth burst into a passion of tears. Retreat was growing impossible; she hardly knew what she wished; anger, a sort of wild triumph, the difficulty of resisting this passionate pleading, the inconceivable joy of Cheriton's face and voice, added to the overstrained excitement of her previous feelings, completely overpowered her, till her sobs were uncontrollable, and with them came the strangest impulse to tell him all, the most incongruous confidence in the justice and sympathy of this passionate lover for the love and sorrows that would have wrecked his hopes. Ah! if she had but done so!

"Oh, what a fool I have been!" cried Cheriton, exceedingly distressed. "Oh, Ruth, my darling! I have frightened you. I'll be patient; I'll not say another word. See, here's a seat—sit down. I deserve that you should never speak to me again."

Ruth let him lead her to the bench, and endeavoured to collect her senses.

"I am not half good enough for you. You don't know what you want," she faltered.

"Oh, yes, I do. I know just what I want," said Cheriton softly and gently; but venturing to sit down beside her, and trying to reassure her by a little playfulness; "but I don't know how to ask for it. Alvar might have shown me the way."

"Oh, you know well enough," said Ruth, in a more natural tone, and in the few moments, while he sat watching her, her excitement cooled down, or rather hardened itself into shape. Her tears dried up, and she said,—

"What would your father say?"

"He will think me too happy! Will you forgive me for startling you, and give me my answer now?"

He was half smiling, as he timidly put out his hand again. She had given reason enough to hope for the answer he wanted, and suddenly there darted into her mind as an excuse, a reason, an explanation of all this conflict of impulses, of the wish to pique Rupert to avenge herself on the one side—to snatch something from life if she could not have all on the other—a thought—"When Rupert knows he has such a rival, if he loves me, he will not give me up." She yielded her hand to Cheriton's, and said quickly,—

"Only promise me one thing. I did not think of this—it is so sudden. I am going away to-morrow, to Mrs Grey's, for a fortnight. Promise not to tell any one—your father, your brothers, till I come back. Give me time to—to get used to it first."

"Of course," said Cheriton reluctantly, "that must be as you please. But I long to tell them of my great happiness. And my father will care so much about it. But of course I promise. But I may write to you?"

"No—no—then every one will find it out!" said Ruth, with recurring agitation. "You—you don't know how I feel about it."

"Well, I have gained too much to complain," said Cheriton, too loyal-hearted, and too inexperienced, for a single doubt. "But Ruth, *my* Ruth, one thing—give me one kiss to remember!"

"Go then—go! some one will find us!" cried Ruth, and startled by approaching footsteps, she rushed away from him; but the treacherous kiss was given, though she felt in a moment that she would almost have died to recall it. She had revenged herself; she hated herself; she already began to try to excuse herself.

A little later, while troops of gaily-dressed children were dancing in the lighted hall, and the outdoor guests were rapidly departing, Alvar was standing on the terrace, wondering what could have become of his brother. More than one person had remarked that he looked delicate and overworked; and Alvar felt anxious as he saw him come slowly up from the grounds towards him.

"Where have you been, Cherry?" he said. "Are you not well?"

Cheriton smiled rather dreamily.

"Oh, yes, quite well," he said. There was a far-away look of blissful, peaceful content in his eyes, as if it were indeed well with him; an expression of perfect, thankful happiness, as far removed from the ordinary state of this tolerably comfortable work-a-day world as one of great wretchedness and misery; and as remarkable. As Alvar looked at him, they heard the cry of a little child. Cheriton turned and saw trotting along the terrace in the dusk a very little boy, left behind by some of the schools now trooping out of the park. Cherry lifted him up in his arms and smiled kindly at him, trying to make out whom he belonged to, and the child clung to him, quite at ease with him. "Milford School; ah! I see their flag. Come, my lad, we'll go and find them. There, don't cry, nobody must cry to-night, of all nights in the year."

"When Lady Milford has been so kind," said Alvar, for the child's benefit.

"Ah! every one is kind!" said Cherry, with a little laugh, as he carried away the child, "and we must—say thank you."

BROTHERS

"There are none so dependent on the kindness of others as
those that are exuberantly kind themselves."

Chapter Nineteen
Life and Death

"As we descended, following hope,
There sat the shadow feared of man."

Perhaps it was well for the permanence of Cheriton's new-born happiness that he had but a very short glimpse of Ruth. The next morning, the Oakby party started early, that Mr Lester might arrive in time to attend a magistrate's meeting at Hazelby, while Ruth remained for the later train that was to take her on her separate visit. She would not give him a chance of seeing her alone, and one look, one clasp of the hand, and—"Remember your promise" was all the satisfaction he obtained from her. Yet he could hardly collect his thoughts to answer his father's many questions on their journey home, and trying to shout through the noise of the train made him cough so much that his grandmother scolded him for catching such a bad cold.

"Young men are so foolish," she said, but she did not look at all uneasy. *Her* grandchildren's illnesses were never serious; and all the Lesters thought any amount of discomfort preferable to "having a fuss made." Cherry hardly knew himself how ill he was feeling, as they reached home and the day went on; but he was so weary with bad nights and fatigue that it was a perpetual effort to remember that all his suspense of every sort was over, that the examination was passed, and that Ruth was his. He lay on the sofa trying to rest; but the cough disturbed him, and by dinner-time he was obliged to own himself beaten and to go to bed, saying that a night's rest would quite set him up again.

"Boys have no moderation," said Mr Lester, in a tone of annoyance. "It is well it is all over now. Cheriton might have taken quite as good a place without overworking himself in this way."

Alvar, not understanding that peculiarly English form of anxiety that shows itself in shortness of temper, thought this remark very unfeeling. Mrs Lester suggested some simple remedy for the cough; Cherry promised to try it, and was left to his "night's rest."

He woke in the early morning from a short, feverish sleep, to such pain and breathlessness and such a sense of serious illness as he had never experienced in his life, and, thoroughly frightened and bewildered, was trying to think how he could call any one, when his door was softly opened, and Alvar came in.

"I heard you cough so much," he said. "You cannot sleep. I am afraid you are ill."

"Very ill," said Cherry. "You must send some one for the doctor."

He was but just able to tell Alvar where to find the young groom who could ride into Hazelby to fetch him; and soon there was terrible alarm through all the prosperous household, as, roused one after another, they came to see what was amiss. Nettie fled, with her hands up to her ears, right out into the dewy garden, away from the house, afraid to hear what the doctor said of Cherry. Mr Lester gave vent to one outburst of rage with examiners, examination, and Oxford generally, then braced himself to wait in silence for tidings; as he had waited once before when his wife lay in mortal danger—would the verdict be the same now? Mrs Lester preserved her self-possession, sent for the keeper's wife, who was the best nurse at hand, and though sadly at a loss what remedies to suggest, sat down to watch her grandson, because it was her place to do so.

They were all too thankful for any help in the crisis to wonder that it was Alvar who held Cherry in an easier position, and soothed him with quiet tenderness.

When the doctor at length arrived, he pronounced that Cheriton was suffering from a violent attack of inflammation of the lungs. He was very ill; but his youth and previous good health were in his favour. Overwork and the neglected cold would doubtless account for it.

"Will it be over—in a fortnight?" said Cherry, suddenly.

"We'll hope so—we'll hope so," said the doctor. "You have only to do as you are told, you know. Now, have you a good nurse?" turning to Mrs Lester.

"Yes, we think Mrs Thornton very trustworthy—she was nursery-maid here before she married."

"There must be as few people about him as possible. No talking and no excitement."

"But—Alvar will stay?" said Cherry, wistfully. "Father, he came in the night—I want him."

"Hush, hush, my boy—yes, of course he will stay with you if you like," said Mr Lester, hastily.

"Of course," said Alvar, with a curious accent, half-proud, half-tender, as he laid his hand on Cheriton's.

The foreign brother was the last person whom Mr Adamson expected to see in such a capacity; but if he was inefficient, both he and his patient would probably soon discover it; he looked the most self-possessed of the party, and his manner soothed Cheriton. Mrs Thornton had plenty of practical experience to supply his inevitable ignorance. Cheriton was exceedingly ill; his strength did not hold out against the remedies as well as had been hoped, and he suffered so much as to be hardly ever clearly conscious.

"I was so happy!" he said several times with a sort of wonder, and his father felt that the words gave him another pang.

Mr Lester was threatened with the most terrible sorrow that could befall him, and no mitigation of the agony was possible to him. He thought that his best-loved son would die, and made up his mind to the worst, feeling hope impossible; but he made a conscientious effort at endurance, an effort sadly unsuccessful.

"Eh! my son," said his old mother, "he is a good lad, take that comfort."

And this reserved hint at the one real consolation was almost the only attempt at comforting each other that any of them made. No one tried to "make the best of it," to look at the hopeful side, or to find in any mutual tenderness a little lightening of the burden. They held apart from each other with a curious shyness, and as far as possible pursued their several businesses. Nettie went to her lessons, and refused to hear a word of sympathy from her friends, and when at last she could endure the agony no longer, ran away by herself into the woods and hid herself all day. Why should they kiss her and give her flowers—it did not cure Cherry, or make it less dreadful that another doctor was coming from Edinburgh, because Mr Adamson thought him so ill. But she did not want to see him, and had no instinct whatever to do anything for him. Speech was no relief to any of them; it was easier to conceal than to indulge their feelings; and Mr Lester went about silent and stern; Nettie attempted to comfort no one but the dogs; and her grandmother found no relief but in talking of Cherry's "folly in overworking himself" to Virginia, who came hurriedly at the first report that reached Elderthwaite. She was a rare visitor; it was characteristic of her relations with Alvar that a sort of shyness kept her away. She forgot to be shy, however, when Alvar came to speak to her for a moment, and sprang towards him.

"Oh! dear Alvar, this is terrible. I am so sorry for you. But you think he will be better."

"Yes, surely," said Alvar, as if no other view had occurred to him. "*Mi dona*, this is wrong that I should let you seek me; but I cannot leave him—he suffers so much—that cough is frightful."

"But he likes to have you with him?"

"Yes, I can lift him best, and I do not ask him how he is when he cannot speak," said Alvar, with the simplicity that was so like sarcasm. "Ah! it is not right to let you go back alone, *mi Reyna*—but I dare not stay."

"That does not matter; only take care of yourself," said Virginia, as Alvar kissed her hand and opened the door for her, and promised to let her have news every day.

But she went away tearful for more than Cheriton's danger. Alvar had never told her that it comforted him to see her; he did not care whether she came or not.

"Eh! my lass, what news have you?" said an anxious voice, and looking up, Virginia saw her uncle, looking unusually clerical for a week day, hanging about the path in front of her.

"Alvar thinks he will be better, he is very ill now," said Virginia; "they have sent for another doctor."

"Ah! that's bad! There's never been such another in all the country. Queenie, did I ever tell you how he kept up our credit with the bishop?"

And Parson Seyton, whose nature was very different from his neighbour's, spent a long hour in telling tales of Cherry's boyhood to his willing listener. "Eh!" he concluded, "and I meant to fetch him over to hear our fine singing, and see how spick and span we are now-a-days—new surplice and all! Eh! he wrote me a sermon once—when he was a little lad not twelve years old—and I'll swear it might have been preached with the best."

Although Virginia had said nothing and done little to mend matters at Elderthwaite, there had been a certain revival of the elements of respectability. A drunken old farmer had been succeeded by his son, who had been brought up and had married elsewhere. This young couple came to church, and Virginia had by chance made acquaintance with the bride. Her husband got himself made churchwarden—Elderthwaite was not enlightened enough for parochial contests, and Virginia having shyly intimated that want of means need not stand in the way, the windows were mended, and some yards of cocoa-nut matting appeared in the aisle. There had always been a little forlorn singing; young Mr and Mrs Clement were musical, and the Sunday children were collected in the week and taught to sing. The parson had been presented with the surplice, and as by this time he would have done most things to please his pretty niece, accepted it with some pride. Whether from the effect of these splendours, or from consideration for the fair attentive face that he never failed to see before him, the parson himself began to conduct the service with a slight regard to decency and order; and being with his Seyton sense of humour fully conscious of the improvement, and, with the simplicity that was like a grain of salt in his character, rather proud of it, had looked forward to Cherry's approbation.

"Eh!" he said, "I'd like to see him—I'd like to see him."

"He mustn't see any one," said Virginia; "they will hardly let his father go in."

"Well, it's a pity it's not the Frenchman. Eh! bless my soul, my darling, I forgot."

"Alvar is almost ready to think so too, uncle," said Virginia, hardly able to help laughing.

"If I could do anything that he would like—catch him some trout—" suggested the parson.

"Uncle," said Virginia timidly, "in church, when any one is sick or in trouble, they pray for them. They will mention Cherry's name at Oakby to-morrow. Could not we—"

"Ay, my lass, it would show a very proper respect," said the parson; "and the lad would like it too."

And of all the many hearty prayers that were sent up on that Sunday for Cheriton Lester's recovery, none were more sincere than rough Parson Seyton's.

The Edinburgh doctor could only tell them what they knew before, that though there was very great danger, the case was not hopeless. A few days must decide it. In the meantime he must not talk—he must not see any one who would cause the slightest agitation; and poor Mr Lester, whose self-control had suddenly broken down before the interview, was about to be peremptorily banished; but Cherry put out his hand and caught his father's, looking up in his face.

"Send for the boys," he said.

"Yes, but you know you mustn't see them, my boy—my dear boy."

"But Cherry will like to know they are here," said Alvar, in the steady voice that always seemed like a support.

"They shall come. What else—what is it, Cherry?" said Mr Lester, as his son still gazed at him wistfully.

"Nothing—not *yet*," whispered Cheriton. "Oh! I want to say so much, father! I am so glad Alvar came home!"

The words and the sort of smile with which they were spoken completely overpowered Mr Lester; but the doctor, who was still present, would not permit another word.

"You destroy his only chance," he said; and after that nothing would have induced Mr Lester to let Cheriton speak to him. That evening, however, when he was alone with Alvar, Cherry's confused thoughts cleared themselves a little. He had been told to be hopeful, and he did not feel himself to be dying! while with his whole heart he wished for life— the young bright life that was so full of love and joy, of which no outward trouble, no wearing anxiety, and no cold and selfish discontent had rendered him weary. Home and friends, the long lines of moorland that were shining in the sunset light, the hard work in the world behind and before him, the answering love of the woman whom he had chosen, were all beautiful and good to him; he felt no need of rest, no lack of joy.

He prayed for his life, not because he was afraid to die, but because he wished to live; and when, with a sort of awful, solemn curiosity, he tried to realise that death might be his portion, his thoughts, not quite under his own control, turned forcibly to those near to him. If he was to die, there were things he must say to his father, to Jack, to Alvar, a hundred messages to his friends in the village—they would let him see Mr Ellesmere then— when it did not matter how much he hurt himself by speaking; but one thing could not wait—

"Alvar, I *must* say something."

"Yes, I can hear," said Alvar, seeing the necessity, and leaning towards him.

"When there is no chance, you will tell me?"

"Yes."

"But I must tell you about—her—a secret."

"I will keep it. Some one you love?"

"It is Ruth; we are engaged. Does she know—this?"

Alvar's surprise was intense; but he answered quietly,—

"I suppose that Virginia will have told her."

"Let her know; it would be worse later. Write to her—you—when it is hopeless."

"Yes," said Alvar.

"My love—my one love! And say she must come and see me once more. She will—*I* would go anywhere."

"Hush, hush! my brother; I understand you. I am to find out if Virginia has written to her cousin; and if you are worse, I write and ask her if she will come. I will do it."

"Thanks. I can't thank you. God knows how I love her."

"Not one more word," said Alvar, steadily. "Now you must rest."

"I shall get better," said Cherry.

But as the pain grew fiercer, and his strength grew less, this security failed; and then it was well indeed for Cheriton that, be his desires what they might, he believed with all his warm heart that it was a loving Hand that had given him life both here and hereafter.

Time passed on, and Cheriton still lay in great danger and suffering. It was a sorrowful Sunday in Oakby when his name headed the list of sick persons who were prayed for in church. Every one could tell of some boyish prank, some merry saying, some act of kindness that he had done; and now that he was believed to be dying, be the facts what they might, there was a sort of sense that he had been deprived of his rights by his foreign brother.

"It had a deal better a' been yon black-bearded chap. What's he to us?" many a one muttered.

Alas! that the thought would intrude itself into the father's mind, spite of the gratitude he could not but feel!

But Alvar went on with his anxious watching, heeding no one but his brother. That Sunday was a day of great suffering and suspense, and all through the afternoon came lads from the outlying farms, children from the village, messengers from half the neighbourhood to hear the last report. Silence and quiet were still so forcibly insisted on, that even Mr Lester was advised by the doctor to keep out of his son's room; but Mr Ellesmere came up to the house at his request and waited, for all thought that the useless prohibition would soon be taken away; and in the meantime his presence was a support to the father and grandmother, the latter of whom, at least, could bear to hear Cheriton praised.

Towards evening, Alvar, who had scarcely stirred all day, was sent downstairs by Mr Adamson to get some food, and as he came into the dining-room, where the customary Sunday tea was laid on the table, he was greeted with a start of alarm. The two poor boys, tired, hungry, and frightened, had arrived but a few minutes before, and were standing about silent and awestruck.

Jack leant on the mantelpiece, with his lips shut as if they would never unclose again; Bob was staring out of the window; Nettie sat forlorn on one of a long row of chairs. Not one of them made an attempt to comfort or to speak to the others; they were almost as inaccessible in the sullen intensity of their grief as the two dogs, who, poor things! shared it, as they sat staring at Nettie, as dogs will when they do not comprehend the situation.

Alvar, with his olive face and grave dark eyes, looked, after all his fatigue, less changed than Jack, who was deadly pale, and hardly able to control his trembling.

"Ah! Jack," said Alvar, in his soft, slow tones, "he will be glad to hear that you are come!"

Jack did not speak at first, and Alvar, as silent as the rest, went up to the table and poured out some claret and took some bread.

"It's quite hopeless, I suppose?" said Jack, suddenly.

"No, do not say so!" said Alvar, half fiercely. "It is not so; but, oh, we fear it!" he added, in a voice of inexpressible melancholy.

Jack could not utter another word—he was half choking; but Nettie, unable to restrain herself any longer, began to cry piteously.

"Don't Nettie," said Bob, savagely.

"Ah!" said Alvar, "poor child, she is breaking her heart!" he went over to her, and took her in his arms and kissed her. "Poor little sister!" he said. "Ah! how we love him!"

The simple expression of the thought that was aching in the minds of all of them seemed to give a sort of relief. Nettie submitted to be caressed and soothed, and the boys came a little closer, and gave themselves the comfort of looking as wretched as they felt.

"Now I must eat some supper, for I dare not stay," said Alvar; "and you—you have been travelling—come and take some."

The poor boys began to find out how hungry they were, and Bob began to eat heartily; while the force of example made Jack take a few mouthfuls, till the vicar came into the room.

"Jack," he said quietly, "Cherry is so very anxious to see you that Mr Adamson gives leave for you to go for one moment. Not the twins—they must wait a little. Can you stand it?"

"Yes, sir," said Jack, though, great strong fellow as he was, his knees trembled.

"Then, Alvar, are you ready? Have you really eaten and rested? You had better take him in."

Jack stood for a moment beside the bed, without attempting a word, hardly able to see that Cherry smiled at him, till he felt the hot fingers clasp his with more strength than he had looked for, and his hand was put into Alvar's, while Cheriton held them both, and whispered, "Jack, you *will*—"

"Yes, Cherry, I will," said Jack, understanding him. "I will, always."

"There, that must be enough," said Alvar. "Jack is very good—he shall come again."

"Oh! don't send me quite away," whispered Jack, as they moved a little. "Let me stay outside. I could go errands—I'll not stir."

Alvar nodded, and Jack went out into the deserted gallery, where, of course, he and Bob were not to sleep at present. The old sitting-room was full of things required by the nurses, and Jack sat down on a little window-seat in the passage, which looked out towards the stables. He saw Bob and Nettie arm-in-arm, trying to distract their minds by visiting their pets, and his grandmother, too, coming slowly and heavily to look at her poultry. He had not seen his father, and dreaded the thought of the meeting. Idly he watched the ordinary movement of the servants, the inquirers coming and going, and he thought of the brother, best-loved of all and most loving—oh! if he could but hear Cherry laugh at him again!

Upstairs all was silent, save for poor Cheriton's painful cough and difficult breathing; and presently it seemed to Jack that the cough was less frequent, till, after an interval of stillness, the doctor came out. Jack's heart stood still. Was this the fatal summons?

"Your brother is asleep," said Mr Adamson. "I feel more hopeful. I am obliged to go, but I shall be here early. Every one who is not wanted had better go to bed."

He went downstairs as he spoke, but Jack remained where he was, thinking he might be at least useful in taking messages or calling people. He had never sat up all night before, and, anxious as he was, the hours were woefully long.

Once or twice his grandmother came to the head of the stairs, and Jack signalled that all was quiet. At last, over the stable clock, the dawn came creeping up; there was the solitary note of a bird, then a great twitter and the cawing of the rooks.

Jack put his head out of the window, and felt the fresh, sharp air blowing in his face. A cock crowed—would it wake Cherry? Some one touched him on the shoulder; he drew his head in, and Alvar stood by his side.

"He is much better," he said. "He has been so long asleep, and now the pain is less, and he can breathe—he is much better."

Jack was afraid to speak, but he gave Alvar's hand a great squeeze.

"Now, will you go and tell my father this? Ah, how he will rejoice! But do not let him come."

Jack sped downstairs and to his father's door, which opened at the sound of a footstep.

"Papa, he is better. Alvar says he will get well."

Half a dozen hasty questions and answers, then Mr Lester put Jack away from him and shut his door.

They could hardly believe that the relief was more than a respite, but the gleam of hope brightened as the day advanced. Cherry slept again, and woke, able to speak and say that he was better.

"And I must tell you, sir," said Mr Adamson, afterwards, "that it is in a great measure owing to your son's good nursing."

Mr Lester turned round to Alvar, who was beside him.

"I owe you a debt nothing can repay. I can never thank you for my boy's life," he said, warmly.

"Ah, do you *thank* me? You insult me!" cried Alvar, suddenly and fiercely. "Is he more to you than to me—my one friend—my brother— *Cherito mio!*" And, completely overcome, Alvar clasped his hands over his face and dashed out of the room.

Jack followed; but his admiration of Alvar's self-control was somewhat shaken by the sort of fury of indignation and emotion that seemed to stifle him, as he poured out a torrent of words, half Spanish, half English, walking about the room and shedding tears of excitement.

"I say," said Jack, "they won't let *you* go in to Cherry next, and then what will he do?"

Alvar subsided after a few moments, and said, simply and rather sadly,—

"It is that my father does not understand me. But no matter—Cherry is better—all is right now."

Chapter Twenty
Face to Face

"And with such words—a lie!—a lie!
She broke my heart and flung it by."

In the early days of August, after as long a delay as she could find excuse for, Ruth Seyton returned to Elderthwaite, knowing that Rupert was to come next week to Oakby for the grouse shooting, and that Cheriton was ready to claim her promise; for as she came on the very day of her arrival to a garden-party at Mrs Ellesmere's, she held in her pocket a letter written in defiance of her prohibition, urging her to let him speak to her again, and full of love and longing for her presence.

She knew that Rupert was coming, for the quarrel between them was at an end. Ruth had been very dull and desolate during her quiet visit to some old friends of her mother's, very much shocked at hearing from Virginia of Cherry's illness, and more self-reproachful for having let him linger in the damp shrubberies by her side than for the greater injury she had done him.

She wrote on the spur of the moment, and sent Alvar a kind message of sympathy; but every day her promise to Cheriton seemed more unreal, and when at last Rupert came, ashamed of the foolish dispute, and only wanting to laugh at and forget it, she yielded to his first word, and, though a little hurt to find how lightly he could regard a lover's quarrel, was too happy to forgive and be forgiven. But one thing she knew that he would not have forgiven, and that was her reception of Cheriton's offer, and though it had never entered into her theories of life to deceive the real lover, she let it pass unconfessed—nay, let Rupert suppose, though she did not put it in words, that she had discovered "Cheriton's folly" in time to put it aside.

That she must shortly meet them both, and in each other's presence, was the one thought in her mind, even while she heard from Virginia that Cherry was almost well again, and detected a touch of chagrin in her eager account of Alvar's clever and constant care. "No, she had not seen him yesterday, but they would all meet to-day."

Still it was startling, when the two girls came out into the garden of the rectory, to see in the sunshine Cheriton Lester with a mallet in his hand, looking tall and delicate, but with a face of eager greeting turned full on her own.

In another moment he held her hand in a close, tight grasp, as she dropped her eyes and hoped that he was better.

"Quite well now," said Cheriton, in a tone that Ruth fancied every one must interpret truly.

"That is, when he obeys orders," said another voice; and Ruth felt her heart stand still, for Rupert came up to Cheriton's side and held out his hand to her.

For the first time in her life she was sorry to see him. She could have screamed with the surprise, and her face betrayed an agitation that made Cheriton's heart leap, as he attributed it to her meeting with him after his dangerous illness.

"I am quite well," he repeated. "I am not going to give any more trouble, I hope, now."

Rupert looked unusually full of spirits. "Good news," he whispered to Ruth, with a smile of triumph. She could hardly smile back at him. Alvar now came up and spoke to them. He looked very grave; as Ruth fancied, reproachful.

Some one asked Ruth to play croquet, and she declined; then felt as if the game would have been a refuge. But she took what seemed the lesser risk, and walked away with Rupert; and Cheriton tried in vain for the opportunity of a word with her—she eluded him, he hardly knew how. The sense of suspicion and suspense which had been growing all through the later weeks of his recovery was coming to a point.

Ruth seemed like a mocking fairy, like some unreliable vision, as he saw her smiling and gracious—nay, answered occasional remarks from her—but could never meet her eyes, nor obtain from her one real response.

These perpetual, impalpable rebuffs raised such a tumult in Cheriton's mind that he restrained himself with a forcible effort from some desperate measure which should oblige her to listen to him, while all his native reticence and pride could hardly afford him self-control enough to play his part without discovery.

An equal sense of baffled discomfort pressed on Virginia. She had very seldom seen a cloud on Alvar's brow; he never committed such an act of discourtesy as to be out of temper in her presence; but to-day he looked so stern as to prompt her to say, timidly, "Has anything vexed you, Alvar?"

"How could I be vexed when you are here, queen of my heart?" said Alvar, turning to her with a smile. "See, will you come to get some strawberries—it is hot?"

"I would rather you told me when things trouble you," said Virginia.

"It is not for you, *mi doña*, to hear of things that are troubling," said Alvar, still rather abstractedly.

"Are you still anxious about Cherry?" she persisted.

"*Ay de mi*, yes; I am anxious about him," said Alvar, sharply; then changing, "but I am ungallant to show you my anxiety. That is not for you."

"Ah, how you misunderstand what I want!" she cried. "If I only knew what you feel, if you would talk to me about yourself! But it is like giving an Eastern lady fine dresses and sugar-plums."

The gentle Virginia was angry and agitated. All through Cheriton's illness she had felt herself kept at a distance by Alvar, known herself unable to comfort him, had suffered pangs that were like enough to jealousy, to intensify themselves by self-reproach. Yet she gloried in Alvar's devotion to his brother, in his skill and tenderness. Alvar did not perceive what she wanted, and, moreover, was of course unable to tell her the present cause of his annoyance, at the existence of which he did not wish her to guess.

"See now," he said, taking her hands and kissing them, "how I am discourteous; I am sulky, and I let you see it. Forgive me, forgive me, it shall be so no more. You shed tears; ah, my queen, they reproach me!"

Virginia yielded to his caresses and his kindness, and blamed herself. Some day, perhaps, in a quieter moment, she could show him that she wanted to share his troubles and not be protected from them. In the meantime his presence was almost enough.

Alvar, like some others of his name, was a person of slow perceptions, and was apt to be absorbed in one idea at a time. He did not guess that while he paid Virginia all the courtesy that he thought her due she longed for a far closer union of spirits. He was proud of being Cheriton's chief dependence during the tedious recovery that none of the others could bear to think incomplete, and to find that his tact and consideration made him a welcome companion when Jack's ponderous discussions were too great a fatigue. But he would not endure thanks, and after the outburst with which he had received his father's nobody proffered them. Not one of the others, full of anger with Ruth and of anxiety for Cheriton, could have abstained from fretting him with one word on the subject, as Alvar did all that afternoon and evening. But his mind was free to think of nothing else.

As for Ruth, the moment that should have been full of unalloyed bliss for her, the moment when Rupert told her that concealment was no longer necessary, was distracted by the terror of discovery.

Rupert had to tell her that the sale of a farm, effected on unusually advantageous terms, had made the declaration of his wishes possible to him, and he was now ready to present himself before her guardians and ask their consent to a regular engagement. Ruth was about to go back to her grandmother, and all might now be well. Ruth did not know how to be glad; she could not tell how deeply the Lesters might blame her. Her one hope was in Cheriton's generosity, and to him at least she must tell the whole truth.

"To-morrow I shall come and see you," he said gravely, as he wished her good-night, and she managed to give him an assenting glance, but he knew that she was treating him ill, and tormented himself with a thousand fancies—that his illness had changed him, that something during their separation had changed her. He said nothing, but the next day started alone for Elderthwaite.

It was a bright morning, with a clear blue sky. Cheriton passed into the wood and through the flickering shadows of the larches. He did not spend the time of his walk in forming any plans as to how he should meet Ruth; he set his mind on the one fact that a meeting was certain. But perhaps the brightness of the morning influenced his mood, for as he came out on to the bit of bare hill-side that divided the wood from the Elderthwaite property, a certain happiness of anticipation possessed him—circumstances might account for the discomfort of the preceding day, Ruth's eyes might once more meet his own, her voice once more tell him that she loved him.

The bit of fell was divided from Mr Seyton's plantation by a low stone wall, mossy, and overgrown with clumps of harebells and parsley fern, and half smothered by the tall brackens and brambles that grew on either side of it. Beyond were a few stunted, ill-grown oak-trees, with a wild undergrowth of hazel.

As Cheriton came across the soft, smooth turf of the hill-side, he became aware that some one was sitting on the wall beside the wide gap that led into the plantation, and he quickened his steps with a thrill of hope as he recognised Ruth. She stood up as he approached and waited for him, as he exclaimed eagerly,—

"This is too good of you!"

"Oh, no!" said Ruth, and began to cry.

Her eyes were red already, and with her curly hair less deftly arranged than usual, and her little black hat pushed back from her face, she had an air indescribably childish and forlorn.

Every thought of resentment passed from Cheriton's mind, he was by her side in a moment, entreating to be told of her trouble, and in his presence the telling of her story was so dreadful to her that perhaps nothing but the knowledge of Rupert's neighbourhood could have induced her to do it. Ruth hated to be in disgrace, and genuine as were her tears, she was not without a thought of prepossessing him in her favour. But she could not run the risk of Rupert's suddenly coming through the fir-wood.

"Please come this way," she said, breaking from him and skirting along inside the wall till they were out of sight of the pathway. Then she began, averting her face and plucking at the fern-leaves in the wall.

"I—I don't know how to tell you, but you are so good and kind and generous, so much—*much* better than I am—you won't be hard on me."

"It doesn't take much goodness to make me feel for your trouble," said Cheriton, tenderly. "Tell me, my love, and see if I am hard."

"Every one *is* hard on a girl who has been as foolish as I have."

Cheriton began to think that she was going to tell him of some undue encouragement given to some other lover in his absence or before her promise to him, and to believe that here was the explanation of all that had perplexed him.

"I shall never be offended when you tell me that I have no cause for offence," he said, putting his hand down on hers as she fingered the fern-leaves.

"*Indeed*, I would not have deceived you so long, but for your illness," said Ruth, a little more firmly.

"Deceived me! Dearest, don't use such hard words of yourself. Tell me what all this means. What fancy is this?"

"Will you promise—promise me to be generous and to forgive me? Oh, you may ruin all my life if you will," said Ruth, passionately.

"*I* ruin *your* life! ah, you little know! When my life was given back to me, I was glad because it belonged to you," said Cheriton, faltering in his earnestness.

"Then oh! Cherry, Cherry," cried Ruth, suddenly turning on him and clasping her hands, "then give me back my foolish promise—forget it altogether—let us be friends as we were when I was a little girl. Oh, Cherry, forgive me—I cannot—cannot do it!"

"What can you mean?" said Cheriton, slowly, and with so little evidence of surprise that Ruth took courage to go on.

"Cherry!" she repeated, as if clinging to the name that marked her old relation to him; "Cherry, a long time ago—last spring, I was engaged to some one else—to your cousin; but it suited him—us—to say nothing of it at first. And oh! I was jealous and foolish, and we quarrelled, and I was in a passion, and thought to show him I didn't care. And you came that day at Milford, and I knew how good you were, and you begged so hard I couldn't resist you—you gave me no time. And then very soon he came back, and I knew I had made a mistake. I would have told you at once, indeed I would, but for your illness. How could I then?"

Cheriton stood looking at her, and while she spoke, his astonished gaze grew stern and piercing, till she shrank from him and turned away. Then he said, with a sort of incredulous amazement, with which rising anger contended,—

"Then you *never* meant what you said? When you told me that you loved me, it was false—you did not mean to give yourself to me? You kissed me to deceive me?"

"Oh, Cheriton!" sobbed Ruth, covering her face, "don't—don't put it like that. I was very—very foolish—very wicked, but it was not all plain in that way. Won't you forgive me? I was so very unhappy! I thought you were always kind—"

"Kind!" ejaculated Cheriton. "There is only one way of putting it! Which is your lover, to which of us are you promised, to Rupert or to me?"

Anger, scorn, and a pain as yet hardly felt, intensified Cheriton's accent. She had expected him to plead for himself, to bemoan his loss, and instead she shrank and quailed before his judgment of her deceit. His last words awoke a spark of defiance, and suddenly, desperately, she faced him and said, clearly,—

"To Rupert."

Cheriton put his hand back and leant against the wall. He was beginning to feel the force of the blow. After a moment he raised his head, and looked at her again, with a face now pale and mournful.

"Oh, Ruth, is it indeed so? Have I nothing to hope—nothing even to *remember*? Did you *never* mean it—never?"

"I was so angry—so miserable that I was mad," faltered Ruth. "I thought *he* was false to *me*."

"So you took me in to make up for it?" said Cheriton roughly, his indignation again gaining ground. "Well, I should thank you for at last undeceiving me!"

He turned as if to go; but Ruth sobbed out, "I know it was very wrong, indeed I am sorry for you. I can never, never be happy, if you don't forgive me."

"What can you mean by forgiving?" said Cheriton bitterly. "I wish I had died before I knew this! You have deceived me and made a fool of me, while I thought you—I thought you—"

"Then," cried Ruth, stung by the change of feeling his words implied, "you can tell them all about it if you will, and ruin me!"

"What!" exclaimed Cheriton, starting upright. "Is *that* what you can think possible? Is *that* why you are crying? You may be perfectly *happy*! The promise you had the prudence to exact has been unbroken. No! when I thought that I was dying, I told Alvar that *you* might be spared any shock. Neither he nor I are likely to speak of it further. I had better wish you good-morning."

It was Cheriton whose love had been scorned, whose hopes had all been dashed to the ground in the last half-hour, and who had received a blow that had changed the world for him; but it had come in such a form that the injured self-respect struggled for self-preservation. The first effect on his clear, upright nature was incredulous anger, a sense of resistance, of shame and scorn, that, all-contending and half-suppressed, made him terrible to Ruth, whose self-deceit had expected quite another reception of her words. She had shrunk from the idea of giving him pain, had dreaded the confession of her own misdeeds; but she had indemnified her conscience to herself for ill-treating Cheriton by a sort of unnatural and unreal admiration of what she called his goodness; which seemed to her to render self-abnegation natural, if not easy, to him.

She, with her passionate feelings, her warm heart, might be forgiven for error; but he, since he was high-principled and religious, would surely make it easier for her, would stand in an ideal relation to her and tell her that "her happiness was dearer than his own."

"Good" people were capable of that sort of self-sacrificing devotion. She thought, as many do, that Cheriton's battle was less hard to fight, because he had hitherto had the strength to win it. Poor boy, it had come to the forlorn hope now! He only knew that he must not turn and fly.

As Ruth looked up at him all tear-stained and deprecatory, his mood changed.

"Oh, Ruth, Ruth—Ruth!" he cried, as he turned away, "and I loved you so!"

But he left her without a touch of the hand; without a parting, without a pardon. No other relations could replace for him those she had destroyed. Ruth watched him hurry across the fell and into the fir-wood, and then, as she sank down among the ferns and gave way to a final burst of misery, she thought to herself, "Oh, Rupert, Rupert, what I have endured for your sake!"

Chapter Twenty One
In the Thick of the Fight

"Oh, that 'twere I had been false—not she!"

In the meantime the unconscious Rupert was strolling up and down in front of the house waiting for his uncle to come out, and intending to take him into his confidence and ask for his good offices with Ruth's guardians. It was well for her that he had no suspicion of what was passing; for little as she guessed it, he would have greatly resented her treachery towards Cheriton as well as towards himself. But Rupert was in high spirits, and when Mr Lester joined him, he told his tale with the best grace that he could. His uncle was pleased with the news, and questioned him pretty closely upon all its details, shook his head over the previous difficulties which Rupert admitted, told him that he was quite right to be open with him, congratulated him when he owned to having met with success with the lady herself, and, pleased with being consulted, threw himself heart and soul into the matter.

As they came up towards the back of the house, they met Alvar, who, rather hastily, asked if they had seen Cheriton.

"He went to take a walk. I am afraid he will be tired," he explained.

"Eh, Alvar, you're too fidgety," said his father good-humouredly. "There's Cheriton, looking at the puppies."

Alvar looked, and beheld a group gathered in the doorway of a great barn, the figures standing out clear in the sunshine against the dark shadow behind. Nettie was standing in the centre with her arms apparently full of whining little puppies; the mother, a handsome retriever, was yelping and whining near. Buffer was barking and dancing in a state of frantic jealousy beside her. Bob and Jack were disputing over the merits of the puppies. Dick Seyton, with a cigar in his mouth, was leaning lazily against the barn door, while Cheriton, looking, to Alvar's anxious eyes, startlingly pale, was standing near.

"But say, Cherry, say," urged Nettie, "which of them are to be kept? Don't you think this is the best of all?"

"That," interrupted Bob, "that one will never be worth anything. Look, Cherry, this one's head—"

"Bob, what are you about here at this time in the morning?" said his father. "I told you I must have some work done these holidays. Be off with you at once."

"Cherry said yesterday he would come and help me," growled Bob.

"*I* want him," said Mr Lester. "Got a piece of news for you, Cherry. No secret, Rupert, I suppose?"

"I'll tell Cherry presently," said Rupert, thinking the audience large and embarrassing.

Cheriton started, and the unseeing look went out of his eyes, and for one moment he looked at Rupert as if he could have knocked him down. Then the reflection of his own look on Alvar's face brought back the instinct of concealment, the self-respect that held its own, while all their voices sounded strange and confused, and he could not tell how often his father had spoken to him or how long ago.

"I think I can guess your news," he said. "But I must go in. Come back to the house with me, Rupert."

He spoke rather slowly, but much in his usual manner. Rupert was aware that the news might not be altogether pleasant to him; but he had the tact to turn away with him at once; while Alvar watched them in utter surprise, the wildest surmises floating through his mind. But what Cherry wanted was to hear whether Rupert would confirm what Ruth had told him; somehow he could not feel sure if it were true.

"How long have you been engaged?" he said; "that was what you were going to tell me, wasn't it?"

"My uncle is frightfully indiscreet," said Rupert, with a conscious laugh. "Nothing has been settled yet with the authorities; but we have understood each other for some time. She—she's one in a thousand, and I don't deserve my luck."

Rupert was very nervous; he had always thought that Cheriton had a boyish fancy for Ruth, though he was far from imagining its extent, and he was divided between a sense of triumph over him and a most real desire not to let the triumph be apparent, or to give him unnecessary pain. Being successful, he could afford to be generous, and talked on fast lest Cherry should say something for which he might afterwards be sorry.

"I suppose we haven't kept our secret so well as we thought," he said, laughing, "as you guessed it so quickly. All last spring I was afraid of Alvar's observations."

"Did Alvar know? He might have—he might—?" Cheriton stopped abruptly, conscious only of passion hitherto unknown. He never marvelled afterwards at tales of sudden wild revenge. In that first hour of bitter wrong he could have killed Rupert, had a weapon been in his hand, have challenged him to a deadly duel, had such a thought been instinctive to his generation. Rupert did not look at him, or the wrath in his eyes must have betrayed him. He longed to revenge himself, to tell Rupert all; even his sense of honour shook and faltered in the storm. "She promised *me!* She kissed *me!*" The words seemed to sound in his ears, something within held them back from his lips. Another moment, and Alvar touched his arm.

"Come in, Cherito, the wind is cold," he said. "Come in with me."

Rupert, glad to close the interview, little as he guessed how it might have ended, turned away, saying, with a half-laugh, "I must go and check Uncle Gerrald's communications; they are *too* premature."

Then Cheriton felt himself tremble from head to foot; he knew that Alvar was talking, uttering words of vehement sympathy, but he could not tell what they were.

"You came in time—you came in time to save me!" said Cheriton wildly, as his senses began to recover their balance. He turned away his face for a few moments, then spoke collectedly.

"Thank you. That is all over now! You see I'm not strong yet. You will not see me like this again. The one thing is to prevent any one from guessing, above all my father."

"But, my brother, how can you—you cannot conceal from all that you suffer?" said Alvar, dismayed.

"Cannot I? I *will*," said Cheriton, with his mouth set, while his hands still trembled.

"Why? *You* have done no wrong," said Alvar. "Are you the first who has been deceived by a faithless woman? She is but a woman, my brother; there are others. You feel now that you could stab your rival to revenge yourself. Ah, that will pass; she's only a woman. Heavens! I tore my hair. I wept. I told all my friends of my despair; it was the sooner over. You will find others."

"We usually keep our disappointments to ourselves," said Cheriton coldly. "I could not forgive any betrayal. Now I'll go in by myself. I'll come down to lunch. As you say, I'm not the first fellow who has been made a fool of."

"What will he do?" thought Alvar as he reluctantly left him. "He would forgive his rival sooner than himself. They pretend to feel nothing, my brothers, that gives them much trouble. If I were to tell a falsehood to please them, they would despise me; but Cherito will tell many falsehoods to hide that he grieves."

Cheriton gathered himself up enough to hide his rage and grief, hardly enough in any way to struggle with them, and the suffering was as uncontrollable and as exhausting as the pain and fever of his late illness. It shut out even more completely the remembrance of anything but his own sensations. And it was all so bitter—he felt the injury so keenly—he had not yet power to feel the loss. He kept up well, however, and during the next two or three days his father saw nothing amiss; while Alvar, though anxious about his health, regarded the misery as a phase that must have its way. But Nettie declared that Cherry was cross, and Jack, who had lately acquired the habit of noticing him, felt that he was not himself. It was difficult to define; but it seemed to him as if his brother never looked, spoke or acted exactly as might have been expected. Things seemed to pass him by.

The twelfth of August proving hopelessly wet and wild, even Mr Lester could not think his joining the shooting party allowable, and Cheriton expressed a proper amount of disappointment; but Jack recollected that when they had all been speculating on the weather the night before, Cherry had hardly turned his head to look at it. He would not let Alvar stay at home with him, and felt glad to be free from observation.

In the meantime matters had not gone much more pleasantly at Elderthwaite. Ruth was in such dread of discovery that even in Rupert's presence she could not be at ease. Her conscience reproached her, and she was by no means sure that Rupert was quite unsuspicious, for he talked a good deal about his cousin, and once said that he thought him much changed by his illness. Neither was she happy with Virginia, towards whom a certain amount of confidence was necessary, as she could not lead her to suppose that all had been freshly settled with Rupert; and Virginia, who was usually reticent and shy, questioned her closely as to Rupert's behaviour and modes of action. Indeed she marvelled at her cousin's ignorance, for Alvar seemed to her to imply displeasure in every look. He came seldom to Elderthwaite, and, when there, scarcely spoke of Cherry. Ruth could only hurry her return to her grandmother, which was to take place in a few days; but an Oakby dinner-party, in honour of the engagement, could not be avoided. Ruth dared not have a head-ache or a cold, and in a tremor most unlike her usual self she prepared to meet her two lovers face to face. If Cheriton had any mercy for her, or any feeling for himself, he would avoid her. How little she had once thought ever to be afraid of Cherry! But he was there, with a flower in his coat, and plenty of conversation, apparently on very good terms with Rupert, and facing the greeting with entire composure. He even ate his dinner; he sat, not opposite Ruth, but low down on the other side of the table, while she had Alvar for her neighbour—a very silent one, as Virginia, on his other side, remarked with a sigh. It would have been natural for her to talk to Rupert, who sat on the other side of her, but she felt Cheriton's eyes on her in all their peculiar intenseness of expression. Ruth was very sensitive, and they seemed to mesmerise her; she grew absolutely pale, and she knew that Rupert saw it. How could Cheriton be so cruel!

Her white face and drooping lip flashed the same thought to Cheriton himself. What a coward he was thus to revenge himself! He turned his head away with a sudden rush of softening feeling. Disappointed love and jealousy had, she told him, driven her mad—what were they making of him? At least it was more manly to let her alone.

"Cheriton, I want a word with you," said Rupert, turning into the smoking-room when the party was over. "Of course, you have a right to refuse to answer me, but—I can't but observe your manner. Do you consider yourself in any way aggrieved by my engagement?"

It did not occur to Cheriton that, if Rupert had had full trust in Ruth, he would never have put such a question. He was conscious of such unusual feelings that he knew not how far he stood self-betrayed in manner. Rupert was his cousin, almost as intimate as a brother, and he could not resent the question quite as if it had come from a stranger. It could have been answered by a short negative, leaving the sting that had prompted it where it had been before. Full of passion and resentment as Cheriton still was, he could not *now* have broken his word and deliberately betrayed the girl who had betrayed him.

He was silent for a minute; still another part was open. At last he looked up at Rupert and said,—

"I made her an offer—she has refused me. Don't mind my way—there's an end of it."

"Cherry, you're a good fellow, a real good fellow—thank you!" said Rupert warmly. "I'm sorry, with all my heart."

"Don't think about me," repeated Cheriton rather stiffly. "But I'll say good-night."

He was so obviously putting a great force on himself that Rupert, feeling that he could not be the one to offer sympathy, would not detain him; but as he gave his hand a hearty squeeze, Cherry, with another great effort, said,—

"I *do* wish her—happiness," then turned away and hurried upstairs.

Chapter Twenty Two
Struggling

"And my faith is torn to a thousand scraps,
And my heart feels ice while my words breathe flame."

It was a wild, wet morning, some days after the Oakby dinner-party. Summer weather was apt in those regions to be invaded in August by something very like autumn; bits of brown and yellow appeared here and there among the green, and fires became essential. To-day the mist was driving past the windows of the boys' sitting-room, blotting out the view, till the wind rent it apart and showed dim sweeps of distant moor.

Bob Lester was sitting at the table, with his eyes fixed, *not* on the exceedingly inky copy of Virgil before him, but on the window, as he remarked dolefully,—

"Birds are wild enough already, without all this wind to make them worse."

Jack was writing at the other end of the table; Nettie, with an old waterproof cloak on, was kneeling on the window-seat, watching the weather, with Buffer, apparently similarly occupied, by her side; and Cheriton, with considerable sharpness of manner, was endeavouring to drive the Latin lesson into Bob's head.

For Bob was under discipline. Such a bad report of him had come from school as to idleness, troublesomeness, and general misbehaviour, that his father, after a private interview, the nature of which Bob did not disclose, had ordered a certain amount of work to be done every day, to be taken back to school, and had forbidden a gun or a fishing-rod to be touched till this was accomplished. Cherry in the early days of his convalescence, had received Bob's growls on the subject, and had offered to help him, as Jack's efforts as a tutor were not found to answer, and had actually coaxed a certain amount of information into him. Lately, however, the lessons had not gone off so well. Cheriton had made a great point of them, and held Bob as if in a vice by the force of his will; but he was sarcastic instead of playful, and contemptuous instead of encouraging, and now lost patience, laying down his book and speaking in a cutting, incisive tone that made Bob start—and stare.

"We have all got aims in life, I suppose; I wish we were all as likely to succeed in them as you are, Bob."

"I haven't got an aim in life," said Bob, turning round as if affronted.

"No? I thought your aim was to be the greatest dunce in the county. It's well to know one's own line, and do a thing *well* while one's about it. A low aim's a mistake in all things."

Jack laid down his pen, and stared hard at Cheriton. Bob waited unconscious, expecting the smile and twinkle that took the sting out of all Cherry's mischief, but none came.

"Come now, you needn't be down on a fellow in that way," he said, angrily. "My line mayn't be yours, but I'll—I'll stick to it one day."

"I just observed that you were sticking to it now, heart and soul. Let all your wits lie fallow; with the skill and energy you are showing at present, you may get to the level of a ploughboy in time."

"I say, Cherry," said Jack, "that's a little strong."

Bob shut the book with a bang and stood up.

"I'm not going to stand that," he said; and Cheriton recollected himself and coloured. "I beg your pardon, Bob," he said. "It was too bad. I—I was only joking. Will you go on now?"

"No," said Bob. "I won't be made game of."

"You tire Cherry to death," said Jack. "No wonder he loses patience."

"*I* didn't ask him to do it," said Bob. "Nettie, where are you going?"

"Out," said Nettie, briefly.

"Then I'm going too," said Bob, following her; while Cheriton wearily threw himself down on the cushions in the window-seat and in his turn stared out at the mist. Jack sat and watched him. He had never uttered a word even to Alvar, but he was full of anxiety. What was the matter with Cherry?

He was lively enough at meal-times and with his father and grandmother; he had resumed all his usual habits, except that the bad weather had prevented him from going out shooting. He had laughed at Alvar for being over-anxious about him, and had taken a great deal of unnecessary trouble about sundry village matters and affairs at home. He had talked what Alvar called "philosophy" to Jack with unusual seriousness; and yet Jack, with whom perhaps he was least on his guard, missed something. And then Mrs Ellesmere had remarked that she did not like to see Cheriton with such a pink colour and such black circles round his eyes, and had warned her husband not to let him fatigue himself on some walk they were taking. Surely Cherry coughed oftener, and was more easily tired, than he had been ten days ago.

Jack could bear it no longer, and began, severely—

"Cherry, you shouldn't worry yourself with Bob. It's too much for you."

"Not generally," said Cheriton. "I'm tired to-day."

"What's the matter with you, Cherry?" said Jack, coming nearer.

"The matter?" said Cherry, sitting up, and laughing more in his usual way. "What should be the matter? Are you taking a leaf out of Alvar's book? Of course, one isn't very strong after such an illness, and I don't sleep always. I shall go away, I think, soon, and then I shall be right enough."

"Where will you go to? Let me go with you. Or must it be Alvar?"

"Oh, I shall be best alone. Don't worry, Jack. I'm no worse, really."

Poor Cheriton! His efforts at concealment, made half in pride, and half in consideration, were not very successful.

As he lay awake through the long nights, Ruth's woeful look and appealing eyes haunted him, and as he remembered their parting, his own bitter scorn came back on him with a pang, partly, no doubt, because she was still irresistible to him, but partly, also, because he knew that *he* had felt the temptation under which *she* had fallen. She had treated him shamefully; and she declared that her excuse was, if excuse it could be called, that she had been driven so frantic by her misjudgment of Rupert, that anything seemed legitimate that would give him pain. She had transgressed every code of womanly honour, and had cost Cheriton pain beyond expression by obeying a sudden impulse of mortified passion. Any sort of revenge on her by Cheriton was at least as incompatible with any standard of social obligation, no extra high principle was needed to condemn it; to take such a blow and be silent over it seemed a mere matter of course. Cheriton was very high-principled, he had conquered in his time strong temptations; moreover, he was more than commonly loving and tender, and yet he felt that there had been more than one moment when he might have committed this utter baseness. He forgot for a moment that he *had* conquered, that strength, however unconscious, had come to him from his former struggles, and had held him back; he felt that if this were possible to him, he was safe from nothing. He shuddered as he thought of his interview with Rupert, and his first prayer since the blow turned into a thanksgiving.

But any thought of his own conduct was soon swept away by the rush of regret and pain. She *had* failed him, however unworthy he might be to judge her; and as he remembered the many sweet and enchanting moments that had led up to his final disappointment, he could not but feel that she had deliberately deceived him. And yet—and yet—as he recalled her face at the dinner-table, he knew that he would have come back to her at a word; he felt as if life was worth nothing without her, as if father and brothers, home, interests, and ambitions had all lost their charm. Cheriton retained enough command over himself to resolve to make head against this state of mingled regret and bitterness; he could not yet bring himself to accept it with any sort of submission; his feelings of gratitude and joy at his returning strength seemed almost as if they had been sent in mockery to make disappointment more cruel. But this thought brought its own remedy. His life had been given back to him, not surely only that he might endure this fierce trial— something would come out of the furnace. And when he remembered what his well-being was to his father, the resolution of self-conquest was made in something else than pride. "God help me. I'll learn my lesson!" he thought; and he dimly felt that that lesson meant more than putting a bold face on things, or even than a surface recovery of spirits, of the probability of which last he was of course then no judge. It meant whether this bitter trial was to leave him more or less of a man than it found him—more of a Christian if he would not be less of a man.

It must not be supposed that Cheriton at this time attained with any permanence to such convictions—he worked his way to them at intervals; but, after all, most of his sleepless hours were spent in a hopeless involuntary recall of his past happiness. Ruth haunted him as if she had been a spirit, and of course the over-fatigue produced by the effort to force his mind into its usual channels affected his health, and made him still less able to fight against his troubles.

He was very reluctant to confess himself beaten, and began to talk to Jack with would-be eagerness about going to London and beginning his reading for the bar. His name had been entered at the Temple, most of his "dinners" were eaten, and he had never intended his time of waiting for a brief to be an idle one. Presently his father called him, and he started up and went downstairs, while Jack went back to his writing with divided attention, and dim suspicions of the truth gaining ground.

Meanwhile Cheriton found himself called to a conference in the study.

All the arrangements for Alvar's marriage had been deferred through Cheriton's illness, and Mr Lester felt it somewhat strange that he should be the first person who saw the need of recommencing them. He told Alvar that he wished to speak to him, and made a sort of apology to him for Cheriton's presence by saying that he wished him to hear the money arrangements which he thought fit to make.

"I am sure, Alvar," said Mr Lester, formally, "you have shown great unselfishness in putting your own affairs so completely on one side during your brother's illness; but now there is no longer any reason for deferring the consideration of your marriage, and I should be glad to know what plans you may have formed for the future."

"It is your wish, sir, that I should be married—soon?" said Alvar, coolly and deferentially.

"Why—October was mentioned from the first, wasn't it?" said Mr Lester, with a sort of taken-aback manner that made Cheriton smile.

"Yes," said Alvar. "If that is your desire, and Mr Seyton approves, I should wish it."

"Why—why—haven't you settled it all with Virginia?"

"I did not think one should trouble a lady with those matters, nor did I wish to marry while my brother might need me."

"That was very good of you; but I hope by that time to be in London," said Cherry, decidedly, and with a look, conveying caution.

Alvar was silent for a moment, and then said, with what Cheriton called his princely air,—

"I shall then marry in October, and I will take my wife to visit my friends and my—other country."

"Why, yes; that would be very proper, no doubt; and I think you once told me that you wished to take a house in London."

"That would be good luck for me," said Cherry, by way of encouragement.

"Yes," said Alvar, "I wish it to be so."

Mr Lester then entered into an explanation of the means which he was prepared to place at Alvar's disposal, talked of house rent and of Virginia's fortune, and said a few words on the amount of his own means, and what he meant to do for the younger ones. Nettie was provided for by her mother's fortune, a smaller proportion of which would be inherited by the sons also at their father's death. "But," as Mr Lester concluded, "of course they all know that in the main they must look to their own exertions."

"Of course," said Cheriton.

Alvar looked very much surprised.

"The boys," he said, "yes; but I thought, my father, you would wish that Cheriton should be rich."

"Alvar," said Mr Lester, rising and speaking with real dignity, "you misunderstand me. In such matters I can make no distinctions between my sons. Cheriton and his brothers stand exactly on the same footing. As for you, you will have to represent the old name, and keep the old place on its proper level. I shall not stint you of the means of doing so with ease and dignity."

Alvar cast down his eyes, and a curious look as of a sort of oppression passed over his face.

"That will be an obligation to me," he said, gravely. "You are most—honourable to me, my father."

"Not at all," said Mr Lester. "I should not think of acting otherwise. Well—now you had better be off to Elderthwaite and settle all your affairs."

Alvar left the room, and Mr Lester burst out,—

"I declare, there's something about that fellow that makes me feel as if I were a schoolboy!" Then, a little ashamed of the admission, he went on, "I like to see more ardour in a lad when his marriage is in question. Why, Rupert lived at Elderthwaite, while he was here!"

"We must make allowance for the difference of manners," said Cherry. "Alvar is very good to me. But, father, I don't think I shall be strong enough to shoot this month; it would be foolish to catch another cold; so I thought I should like a little trip somewhere soon—just a change before I settle down to work again."

"Why, yes," said Mr Lester; "of course, if you wish, though we haven't had much good of you since you came home, my boy. Where do you want to go?"

"I don't know—to Paris, perhaps," said Cherry, on the spur of the moment. "Huntingford and Donaldson both asked me to join them this summer; so I shouldn't interfere with Alvar. Then, afterwards I can make all my arrangements for London."

"Well, yes," said Mr Lester, reluctantly; "if you can't shoot, there's no use, of course, in your going to Milford or Ashrigg."

"Jack can go; it's time he went about a little, and he will be a better shot than I am soon. And when I come back, I'll be ready for anything."

Cherry's energy was quite natural enough to deceive his father, especially as he kept out of sight during this interview; but when he went away from the study, his heart suddenly failed him, and he felt as if he never should have the courage to set about carrying out the plans on which he had just been insisting.

Chapter Twenty Three
Misgivings

"I looked for that which is not, nor can be."

A few days before Alvar's interview with his father, Rupert had left Oakby to make his personal application to Ruth Seyton's guardians, backed up by a letter from Mr Lester, and by her own communication to her grandmother. Of course, nothing could be said of the six months of mutual understanding, and this concealment weighed lightly enough on Ruth's conscience. She vexed Virginia by her reserve on all the details of her engagement, but what really troubled her was her parting interview with Rupert, as they were alone together in the garden at Elderthwaite.

This had once been laid out in the Italian style, with fountains, statues, and vases, stiff, neat paths, and little beds cut in the smooth turf and full of gay colour. Of all kinds of gardening, this kind can least bear neglect, and at Elderthwaite a few occasional turns with the scythe and a sprinkling of weedy-looking flowers did not suffice to make it a pleasant resort.

Ruth sat on the pedestal of a broken nymph by the side of a dried-up fountain. This garden was supposed to be "kept up," so some flaring yellow nasturtiums and other inexpensive flowers filled the little beds round. It was a dull day, and the weather was chilly, and Ruth in her crimson shawl looked by far the most cheerful object in the garden. Rupert had stuck some of the nasturtiums in her hat, and they suited her dark hair and warm, clear skin. After a great deal of talk, entirely satisfactory to both, Rupert said, lightly,—

"By the way, I thought I would take Master Cherry to task for his manner to you the other night."

"Cherry—his manner—what do you mean?" stammered Ruth, with changing colour.

"Well, I was rather sorry I had said anything about it, but he was very frank, poor boy, and told me you had refused him."

"I—I did not think you would have asked him such a question," said Ruth, hardly knowing what she said in the agony of fear, relief, and shame.

"Oh, well, we're almost like brothers, you know, and I was not going to have him make such great eyes at you for nothing. What had he to reproach you with?"

The words were more an exclamation than a question, but they terrified Ruth, and she pressed coaxingly up to Rupert, and said with a good deal of agitation,—"Oh, I am very sorry—very; but—but of course I couldn't tell of him—could I? And he is so impetuous and so set on his own way! But I don't want you to be angry with him, poor boy, or—or with me, for, oh! my darling, we mustn't quarrel again, or it would kill me!"

"Is she afraid I shall find out how much encouragement she gave him?" said Rupert in his teasing way.

"Oh! he didn't want much *encouragement*," said Ruth. "But there, never mind, he'll soon forget all about me. Did you think no one ever liked me but you?"

Rupert's rejoinder was cut short by the appearance of Virginia, and Ruth ran towards her, for once glad to leave Rupert. She tried to persuade herself that she had told him no direct falsehood, but the memory of her two interviews with Cheriton lay heavy on her soul.

She knew that she had sinned against her own article of faith, her love for Rupert; and her perfect pride and glory in its perfection was marred. She had fallen below her own standard; she could no longer feel that she acted out her own ideal. Ruth was a girl capable of an ideal, though she had not set up a lofty one. Perhaps every one has some standard, however poor, and the crucial test of character may be whether we pull it down to suit our failures, or no. Ruth at this time was earnestly endeavouring to do so, but it did not come easy to her, and by way of set-off she occupied herself with being exceedingly kind to Virginia, whom she was beginning to consider injured, and in whom she recognised an unexpected warmth of resentment. Not that Virginia ever uttered a complaint of Alvar, but she avoided his name in so marked a manner, and looked so unhappy, that she was self-betrayed.

They were sitting together in the drawing-room on the day of Alvar's interview with Mr Lester. It was a dreary, un-homelike-looking room on that wet, cloudy day, but Ruth, spite of misgivings, had a bright prosperous air as she sat writing to Rupert, curls, ribbons, and ornaments all in order, the deep red bands on her summer dress giving it a cheerful air even on a wet day.

Virginia was sitting in the window doing nothing; she was pale, and her white dress with its elaborate flouncings had seen more than one wearing.

She did not look expectant of a lover. Ruth watched her for a little while, and then said, slyly,—

> "He cometh not, she said,
> She said I am aweary, aweary;
> I would that I were dead!"

"Ruth! how can you?" exclaimed Virginia, indignantly. "Who would expect anybody on such a wet day as this? Of course I don't?"

"Queenie!" said Ruth, springing up and kneeling down beside her, "I don't like to see you look so miserable. If Don Alvar is a lukewarm lover, he's not good enough for my Queenie, and he shan't have her. There!"

"You have no right to say such a thing, Ruth. I may be silly and foolish, but I won't hear any one find fault with him, not even you!"

"Bravo, Queenie! but I wasn't going to find fault with him exactly. I daresay he thinks it is all right enough, only—only that's not *my* idea of a lover! Give him a little pull up, Queenie; scold him—if you can."

Virginia coloured, trembled, and scarcely refrained from tears.

"You make me reproach myself, Ruth," she said, "for being so silly and exacting. It ought to please me that Alvar is so good and kind, and that at last his people have found him out. It *does*—"

"Look!" exclaimed Ruth, pointing out of window. "Who comes there? And your gown is crumpled, and your necktie is faded, and you're not fit to be seen! Run—run and adorn yourself!"

But Virginia hardly heard her, she was too eager to see Alvar for any delay, and, hurrying to the garden-door, she opened it, while Ruth recollected the awkwardness of an interview with Alvar and fled. But he was far too punctilious to come into the drawing-room with his wet coat, hat, and umbrella, and he waved his hand to Virginia and went round to the front door, where, in the hall, he met Ruth, and acknowledged her as he passed with a stately bow that nearly annihilated her.

Virginia had meant to be distant and reproachful, but her resolutions always melted in Alvar's presence; he was so delightful to her that she forgot all her previous vexations. Demonstrative she never could be to him, but she contrived to say,—

"It *is* a long time since you were here, dear Alvar."

"Ah, yes," he said, "*mi dona*, too long indeed; but we have had people in the house, and Cherry is not strong enough to entertain them."

"How is he?" asked Virginia, feeling, as she always did, as if rebuked for selfishness.

"Pretty well; this rain is bad for him; he may not go out," said Alvar, who did not wish to represent Cheriton as specially unwell just then. "But see, *mi querida*, I have been talking to my father, and he gives me courage to speak of the future." And then in the most deferential manner Alvar unfolded his plans, ending by saying, —

"And will you come with me to Seville that I may show my English bride to my countrymen, and teach them what flowers grow in England?"

"I would rather go to Spain than *anywhere* else," said Virginia, all misgivings gone. "I hope they will — like me."

"Ah," said Alvar, smiling, "there is no fear. They would not like those boys — but you — they would worship!"

Virginia laughed gaily, and he continued presently, touching the bow on her dress, — "But this ribbon — it is not a pretty colour. I am rude, but I do not like it."

"Oh, Alvar, I am very sorry. Ruth said I ought to change it. I thought you would not come, and I didn't care for my ribbons. I *do* not care — except when you see me."

There was a break in her voice as she looked at Alvar with eyes full of pathetic appeal for a response to the love she gave him.

Alvar smiled tenderly.

"We will soon change it," he said, and, opening the glass door again, he picked two crimson roses that climbed over it, shook the rain-drops carefully from their petals, and then fastened them into Virginia's hair and dress. "There!" he said, "that is the royal colour, the colour for my queen. See, I must have a share of it. Give me the rosebud."

Virginia stood for a moment with her eyes cast down. She could have thrown herself into Alvar's arms, and poured forth her feelings with a fervour of expression that might have startled him, but the doubt and timidity which she had never lost towards him restrained her; she put the rose into his coat and was happy. The sun came out through the clouds, they strolled through the garden together, and Alvar talked to her about Spain, his stately old grandfather, his many cousins, and all the surroundings of his old life.

When he left her at length, and she ran indoors to Ruth, she was another creature from the pale, lifeless girl who had watched the rain-clouds in the morning.

Alvar, too, went home well pleased with his morning, and ready to make himself agreeable, and as he came through the larch wood into the park, he suddenly encountered the twins.

Nettie was standing with her back to a tree, a very shabby-looking book under her arm. She was scarlet, and almost sobbing with indignation. Bob was opposite to her, evidently having got the upper hand in their dispute. He was talking in a downright decisive voice, and ended with,—

"And so I tell you, I won't have it."

"I don't care."

"If you do it again, I'll tell Cherry."

"Well, tell him, then! I'll tell him myself. *He* would do just the same, I know he would."

"Then why do you get up in the morning and go out—?"

Here Bob caught sight of Alvar and stopped short.

"What is the matter with you two? Why do you dispute?" said Alvar, good-naturedly.

"Nothing," said Bob, shortly; "I was only talking to Nettie."

"We were only talking," said Nettie; and they walked away together, with a manifest determination to exclude Alvar from a share even in their quarrels. Interfering between the twins, Cheriton had once said, was like interfering between husband and wife; the peacemaker got the worst of it.

Apparently Cheriton was experiencing this truth, for when Alvar came in, he heard sounds of lively discussion in the library. His father was speaking in aloud, clear voice, and with his Westmoreland tones strongly marked, a sure sign that he was in a passion. Jack was standing very upright, looking impatient and important. Cherry sat listening, but with an irritated movement of the fingers, and a flush of annoyance on his face. It had been a rough time lately at Oakby, and Mr Lester was just anxious enough about Cheriton to be ready to find fault with him.

"No, Cheriton," he was saying, as Alvar entered, "I'll not hear a word of the kind. It's a fine result of your influence over the lads if it's to lead to this sort of mischief. Warn them! I forbid it positively. You have made too much of these boys, letting them write to you at Oxford. Much good their writing does them, and lending them books beyond them. No, I'll do my duty by my tenants in every way—education and all; but there's a limit."

"But, father," said Cherry, "I can't make it out. Of course, if Wilson has seen the young Flemings in the copses, I'm very sorry; but anyhow, it would be better to try to talk to them."

"No, I'll not have it done. Wilson has orders to watch to-night, and if they're caught, over to Hazelby they shall go, and no begging off for them."

"Oh, father," said Cherry, starting up; "do let me go and see them this afternoon. I haven't been near them since I was ill, and I'm sure I can find out the truth of it. It's ruin to a lad to get into a row with the keepers, and they are capital fellows. Just let me try."

"What is the matter?" asked Alvar.

"Why," said his father, "some young fellows that Cheriton has a special fancy for, have been poaching in my copses!"

"Why, they deserve hanging for it!" said Alvar.

"Hanging!" cried Jack. "The evils of the Game Laws—"

"Oh, nonsense, Jack. Put that in your 'Essay on the Evils of all Sorts of Governments,'" said Cherry; then turning to the squire, "But they are not poachers, father."

"I will not be interfered with. You take too much on yourself," said Mr Lester; then, seeing Cheriton look first blankly amazed, then angry, and finally hurt beyond measure, he suddenly softened.

"Well, you can go and see them if you wish. Don't vex yourself, my lad; you make too much of it. But you're looking better than you did yesterday."

"Oh, my head ached yesterday," said Cherry brightly; but he looked up at his father with a sudden pang and sense of ingratitude. Why could he care so little for anything, so little for the Flemings, even while he argued in their behalf? He lingered a little, talking to his father, while Jack returned to his essay "On the Evils Inherent in every Existing Form of Government;" and then set off on his walk to the Flemings' farm. He ought to care for lads to whom he had taught their cricket and their catechism, and who were much of an age with himself and his brothers, and often thought to resemble them, being equally big, fair, and strong. He talked and sympathised till the story of certain wrongs was confided to him by the younger one—how a certain "she" had nearly driven him to bad courses, but "she warn't worth going to the bad for."

Cherry looked at the lad's serene and ruddy face, and felt as if he might get a lesson.

Did all his culture and his principle and refinement only sap his powers of endurance?

"You're a brave fellow, Willie," he said, putting out his hand. "I wish— well, don't let me hear of your getting into trouble, or going with those poaching fellows."

"No, sir, not for her, nor for any lass. But—there's the old parson."

Cherry got up from the wall of the field where he had been sitting, and went to meet him.

"Ha, Cherry, my lad, glad to see you out again," said Parson Seyton, coming cheerily over the furrows. "Good-day t'ye, Willie; turnips look well."

Young Fleming touched his hat, and after a word or two, Cheriton asked Mr Seyton if he were going Oakby way, as they might walk together; and, with a farewell to Fleming, they started down the hill.

"If I hadn't found you here, I should have been inclined to poach on Ellesmere's manor, and give young Willie a word of advice," said Mr Seyton.

"I know. He has been getting in with the Ryders and Fowlers, and my father heard an exaggerated story about him and Ned being seen in our copses at night. I think that the Flemings are above taking to poaching; but Willie has been in a bad way."

"Hope your father'll catch some of my fellows; do 'em good," said the parson. "If he caught my nephew Dick, and shut him up for a bit, the place might be all the better. Hangs about all day, just like his father. He's after something, and I can't make out what."

"Sometimes I see him about with Bob."

"With Bob? Ha! you look about you, Cherry," said the parson, mysteriously. "My eyes are sharp. I knew when Miss Ruth and Captain Rupert had their little meetings; but then, I knew better than spoil sport."

"You knew more than most," said Cherry.

"Ay, and look here, Cherry," said the parson, stopping and looking full at him. "There's another thing I can see, and that is, when a man's in earnest and when he isn't; and when all's smooth and sweet to a girl, and when she looks this way and that for something that's wanting."

"I have nothing to do with my cousin's engagement," said Cherry, bewildered.

"Nay—nay, it's not your cousin. I don't believe in foreigners, Cherry; and Master Alvar isn't what I call a lover for a pretty girl that worships the ground he treads on. If he wants her money, why, a gentleman should keep up appearances at least."

Cheriton looked very much affronted.

"I don't know if you are aware," he said, "that my brother's marriage has just been fixed to take place in October; he was at Elderthwaite to-day.

And for the rest, Alvar is very unselfish, and I have taken up a great deal of his time."

The parson looked at him with an odd sort of twinkle. "Ay, *ay*; I know all about that," he said; "but we old fellows know what we're about. Well, I turn off here; so good day to you, and mind my words." Cheriton walked on, somewhat ruffled and disturbed. He knew the old parson would not have spoken as he had without some reason; and it crossed his mind that Bob must be engaged in some undesirable amusements with Dick; but if so, what could he do? It was instinctive with Cheriton to try to do something when any difficulty was brought before him. Unselfish, loving, and, like all influential people, fond of influence, he had surrounded himself by calls on his energies and his interest. And now these surroundings were all unchanged, while he was changed utterly. The relations of son, brother, neighbour, friend, which he had filled so thoroughly, remained; and the feelings due to each seemed to have all died away, killed by the blow that had come upon him. He had never lived to himself, nor realised his life apart from the other lives in which it was bound up, or from his school, his college, and, most of all, his home; and now, with this great loss and pain, he suddenly found that he had a self behind it all—a self, fearfully strong, utterly absorbing; all the proportions of life were changed to him. Nothing seemed to matter but the chance of rest and relief. The plans he made had no heart in them; he felt as if the labour necessary for success in life was impossible, the success itself indifferent. His tastes were pure; the many temptations of life had been fairly met and conquered by him; but each one now seemed to look him in the face from a new point of view, and with new force. Soul as well as heart is risked in such an injury as Ruth had done him, and the more finely balanced perhaps the more easily overthrown. He did not cease to resist; but it was chiefly against the increasing weakness and languor which were sure in the end to prove irresistible to him.

Chapter Twenty Four
A Crisis

"I will take a year out of my life and story."

One chilly morning, a week or so after these events, Virginia was sitting in the drawing-room, with a heap of patterns in her lap. She was choosing her wedding gown, and as she laid the glistening bits of silk and satin on the table before her, she sighed at the thought that there was no one to help her, no one to take an interest in her choice. Ruth was gone, and Virginia missed her sorely, feeling as if the loneliness, the uncongeniality of her home would be intolerable but for the thought of the release so soon coming. She felt that, though her little efforts in the village had had some reward, within doors she had never felt naturalised, never been able to produce any impression. Her father never showed her nearly as much affection as her uncle did, and she could not know how much this was owing to a sense of his own deficiencies towards her. He was exceedingly irritable, too, and difficult to deal with, discontented wholly with life; while Miss Seyton's sarcastic tongue always seemed to pierce the weak places in Virginia's armour, and when she was inclined to be cheerful, her talk implied such alien views of life and duty that she made Virginia wretched.

Dick had been offered some appointment in London, provided that he could pass a decent examination next spring, but his sister could not perceive that he made much preparation for it. She also began to suspect that he and Nettie Lester were more together than was good, and to wish for an opportunity of hinting as much to Cheriton, whom she instinctively felt to be the best depositary of such a vague suspicion.

But Cheriton was much less well again; he had been obliged to give up going to Paris, and the whole family were suffering anxiety on his account, more trying, perhaps, though less openly acknowledged, than that caused by his actual illness. Virginia was not quite the girl to deal successfully with her home troubles. Ruth, who did not care a bit whether she could respect her relations or not, had made herself more agreeable to them; while Virginia was timid and miserable, afraid of being unfilial, and yet perpetually conscious of defects. Of course, if she could have felt that Alvar had really comprehended her troubles, they would have weighed more lightly; but though his tenderness always made her forget them for a time, she never had the sense of taking counsel with him.

Now, as she turned over her patterns, her first thought was which he would prefer, and as her aunt came in and with irresistible feminine attraction began to examine them, Virginia said,—

"I shall wait till Alvar comes, and ask him whether he would like me to have silk or satin."

"He will tell you that you look enchanting in either. That will be a pretty compliment, and save the trouble of a choice."

"Oh, no," said Virginia, "Alvar has a great deal of taste, and he likes some of my dresses much better than others. I wonder if Cherry is better to-day."

"Probably, as I see his most devoted brother coming up the garden."

Virginia's face flushed into ecstasy in a moment. She sprang to the garden-door, scattering her patterns on the floor; while her aunt looked after her, and muttered more softly than usual as she left the room, "Poor little thing!"

Alvar looked very grave as he came towards her, as if he hardly saw the slender figure in its fluttering delicate dress, or noticed the eager eyes and smiling lips; but, as usual, he smiled when he came up the steps, and seemed to put aside his previous thoughts, and to adopt the courteous manner which made Virginia feel herself held at a distance.

For once, she was more full of her own affairs than of his. "Look," she said, picking up her silks, "do you see these? Which do you like best?"

Alvar twisted the patterns over his fingers as he stood in the window and did not at once answer.

"How is Cherry?" she said. "Is he better to-day?"

"Perhaps—a little," said Alvar. "But the doctors have seen him again, and they say that he must not stay here—that he must go abroad for all the winter."

"Do they?" said Virginia; "that looks very serious."

"Ah yes," said Alvar a little impatiently, "but my father—they all talk as if it would kill him to go; he will get well away from these bitter winds—and—and the businesses that are too much for him."

"Yes," said Virginia slowly, perceiving that Alvar did not quite understand how startling a sound being ordered abroad had to English ears after such an illness as Cheriton's. "What does he say himself about it?"

"He dreads it very much; but we will go to Seville, and then he *must* find it pleasant."

Virginia started; she changed colour, and her heart began to beat very fast.

"*Mi querida!*" said Alvar, taking her hand. "I feel that I—affront you—I do not know how to ask you to let me go; but how can I send my brother away without me? For his sake I expose myself perhaps to blame from your father—"

"I don't quite understand," said Virginia, withdrawing a little, and speaking with unusual clearness. "Did Cherry ask you to go with him?"

"Ah, no. He refused and said it must not be. But he told Jack that he hated the thought of going to Mentone or any such place alone. My father is too unhappy about him to be his companion, and Jack must go to Oxford. So, when I told him how the wish of my heart was to show him my Spanish home, he owned that he should like to see it. The climate will not cure him if he is dull and miserable."

"Certainly you must *go* with him," said Virginia steadily, though she felt half suffocated.

"Ah, *mi reyna!*" cried Alvar, his brow clearing; "you see my trouble. Without your approval I could not *go!*"

Virginia turned round and fixed her eyes on Alvar with a look never seen before under their soft fringes. The sharp agony of personal loss and disappointment, the feeling, horrible to the gentle modest girl, that the loss and the disappointment reserved all their sting for *her*, the outward necessity of the proposal, and the inward knowledge that Alvar wronged her by his feeling, though not by his act, drove her to bay at last. She would have *shared* in any sacrifice, but she instinctively knew that Alvar was making none. The vague dissatisfactions, the dim misunderstandings, the unacknowledged jealousies of many months, all rushed at once into the light. Her love was too passionate to be patient, and her self-control broke down at last.

"Yes," she said, "of course you must go with your brother. I see that. I admit it quite. But—Alvar—that's not all. I have seen for a long time that our engagement was a tie to you—it was a mistake. I don't blame you—you did not understand—but it is better to end it. I release you—you are free!"

"*Señorita!*" cried Alvar, flashing up, "I have given no one the right to doubt my honour. You mistake me."

"No," said Virginia, "I do not mistake. I know—I know you mean rightly—I ought not to wonder if you don't—if you don't—" she broke off faltering and trembling, humiliated by the sense that she had not been able to win him.

But Alvar's pride had taken fire. "I am at your service," he said proudly, "since you mistake my request."

"I will not hold you back one day," she answered. "Nor do I blame you. Don't mistake *me*. You have done all for me that you could; but our ideas are different, and I feel convinced we should only go on making each other unhappy. It is better to part."

"Since it is your wish to have it so," said Alvar in a tone of deep offence, but with a curious pang at his heart. "I was your true lover, and I would never have caused you grief. But since I did not satisfy you, I withdraw. I force myself on no lady."

"Indeed—indeed," faltered Virginia, "I do not blame you; it is perhaps my fault, that—that we have so often mistaken each other."

"It is that to you—as to my father I am a stranger," said Alvar. "I will go—it is as you wish."

He took up his hat, paused, made her a formal bow, and went out. Virginia sprang after him; but he did not look back. She felt herself cruel, exacting, selfish, and yet she *knew* that her causes of complaint were just. She had sent him away from her, and she would never see him again. As he passed out of sight, she ran down the steps, whether after him or away from the house, she hardly knew. The trailing overgrown roses caught in her dress and held her back. She turned, and all the desolation of the untrimmed garden and unpainted house seemed to overwhelm her spirit. The wind came up in long, dismal rustles, the sky was grey and cold. As she paused, she saw her aunt's still graceful figure in its shabby dress cross the lawn, her face with its fair outline and hard, bitter look turned towards her.

"*She* lost *her* lover!" thought Virginia, and her own future flashed upon her like a dreadful vision. She turned and fled up to her own room, where every other thought was destroyed by the sense of loss and misery. It was in the middle of the afternoon that she was startled out of her trance of wretchedness by a call in her aunt's voice, "Virginia, Virginia! Come here, I want you particularly."

Virginia obeyed passively. She might as well tell her aunt of the morning's interview then as put it off longer. As she came into the drawing-room, Miss Seyton left it by another door, and she found herself alone with Cheriton Lester.

"Thank you for coming down," he said, eagerly. "I want to explain; I think there has been a great mistake."

"No, I think not," said Virginia, rather faintly.

"But let me tell you. It is all my fault indeed. Alvar must not be punished for my selfishness. You know, I got a fresh cold somehow, and my cough was bad again, so my father was frightened and sent for the doctors, and they ordered me away for the winter. I must not go to London now, they say—"

"Indeed, Cherry, I am *very* sorry," faltered Virginia, as the cough stopped him.

"No, but let me tell you. This was a great shock to me. I want to get to work—and then—my poor father! It seemed to knock me down altogether, and foolishly, I let Jack see it, and said that I hated the notion of any of those regular invalid places, and that going there would do me no good. And then Alvar came and asked me if I should not like to see his friends and Seville, and I said, 'Yes, if I must go anywhere,' and he tried in his kind way to make the idea seem pleasant to me, and my father caught at it because he thought I might like it. I shall never forgive myself for making such a fuss! But of course to-day—now I am in my right senses—I should not think of such a thing. If Alvar goes with me, even to Seville, and stays for a few weeks, then, if I am better, he can come home, and I shall not mind staying there alone, and at Christmas Jack might come to me, or my father—it can easily be managed. In short, Virginia," he added, with an attempt at his usual playfulness, "I want you to understand that I made a complete fool of myself yesterday, and that that's the whole of it."

"Did Alvar ask you to come and tell me this?"

"No," said Cheriton, "he was hurt by your misunderstanding him, he does not know I am here. Jack drove me over. But I shall not agree to any other arrangement than what I have told you, unless," he added slowly, "things should go badly, and then I *know* you would have patience."

"Oh, Cherry," said Virginia, struggling with her tears, "I hope you don't think me so selfish as to wish to prevent Alvar from going with you. It is not *that*."

"But what is it, then? Can you tell me?" said Cherry gently, and sitting down by her side.

"I have no one to ask," she said; "but you will think me wrong, and yet—"

"I know too well how difficult it is to be right in matters of feeling, if you once begin to analyse them," said Cherry sadly.

The gentleness of his voice and the kind look of his eyes gave her courage, and she said, very low, —

"I think I should not make Alvar happy, because he does not care for me. Please understand that he has done all he could; he is very *kind* to me, but he does not care for me."

"You know, Virginia," said Cherry eagerly, "Alvar has different ways from ours. Indeed, he *is* loving—"

"He loves *you*," said Virginia quickly; then, blushing scarlet, she added, "oh, Cherry, I think it is beautiful the way he is grateful to you, and thinks so much of you. Please, please, don't think I would have it otherwise."

"I have far more cause to be grateful to him."

"Yes! I like to think that. But Cherry, when you were ill, he didn't care for me to comfort him, it was no rest to him to come and see me. He never tells me his troubles. It isn't as Ruth and Rupert love each other. If I say anything, he turns it aside. It will not make him unhappy to give me up."

"It made him exceedingly angry," said. Cheriton, too clear-sighted not to acquiesce in the truth of Virginia's words, though he was unwilling to own as much.

"I don't think," said Virginia, "that I should bear that feeling patiently. Things are very miserable any way, but I think Alvar will be happier without me. It has not turned out well."

She spoke in a low tone of complete depression, evidently uttering convictions that had been long formed, gently and humbly, but with an undercurrent of firmness.

"I will tell Alvar what you say," he said. "I quite see what you mean, but perhaps he will be able to show you that you have misinterpreted him."

"No," said Virginia, with decision, "do not let him try."

As she spoke, there was a tap at the door, and Jack opened it.

"Cherry," he said, "it is so late; are you ready?"

"One minute, Jack," said Cheriton, "I am coming. Virginia," he added, taking her hands in his with sudden earnestness, "Alvar will love you enough some day. I am sure of it."

Cheriton hardly knew what put the words into his mouth; but they chimed in Virginia's heart for many a weary day, lighted up by the bright, brave smile which had accompanied them.

Chapter Twenty Five
Farewell

"O near ones, dear ones! you in whose right hands
Our own rests calm, whose faithful hearts all day,
Wide open, wait till back from distant lands
Thought, the tired traveller, wends his homeward way."

"Of course, since Miss Seyton insists, and you say you wish it, I come home for my marriage in October," said Alvar.

"You don't understand," replied Cheriton vehemently, "and you are unfair to Virginia. She is as kind as she can be. Go and show her that you really care for her as she deserves, and it will all come right. If anything could make matters worse for me, it would be to think I had been the excuse for a break between you!"

Alvar was standing in the library window, leaning back against the shutter. He looked perfectly unmoved and impervious to argument, his mouth shut firm and his eyebrows a little contracted. Cheriton, on the other hand, half lying on the window-seat, was flushed and eager as if he had been pleading for himself, not for another.

"No," said Alvar obstinately. "Miss Seyton has dismissed me. She tells me that I do not content her. Well, then, I will go."

"Why make yourself wretched for a mere misunderstanding?"

"I? I shall not be wretched. I hope I can take my dismissal from a lady. She finds that I do not suit her, so I withdraw," said Alvar in a tone of indescribable haughtiness.

"Perhaps she knows best," said Cherry, "and is right in thinking you indifferent to her."

"No—but I will be so soon," said Alvar coolly.

"It is no good to *say* so," said Cherry; then, starting up, he came and put his hand on Alvar's arm. "Don't do this thing," he said imploringly, "you don't know what it will cost you."

The two faces clear against the sky were a contrast for a painter; Alvar's with its rich dark colouring, and calm impassive look just a little sullen, and

Cheriton's delicate, sharpened outlines, the eyes all on fire and the colour varying with excitement.

Perhaps the two natures sympathised as little as the faces. Alvar's look softened, however, as he put Cherry back on the cushions.

"Lie still," he said; "why do you care so much? You will be as ill as you were yesterday. If I had known it, you should not have gone to Elderthwaite."

"But," said Cherry, more quietly, "I felt sure that there had been a misunderstanding. It was my fault. Of course I like best to have you with me; but I could not consent to any indefinite putting off of your marriage. My father would not agree to it either. And that is not quite the point. Show Virginia that she is your first thought, and everything can be put right."

Alvar stood silent for a minute, then said suddenly and emphatically,—

"No. I have not the honour of pleasing her as I am. I can change for no one. Do not grieve, *Cherito mio*, I shall forget all when I show you Seville, and I will teach you to forget too. I take the best of my English home with me when I take my brother."

He took Cheriton's hands in his as he spoke, with a gesture, half playful, half tender. The response was cruelly disappointing. Cherry withdrew a little and said, in a tone of extreme coldness,—

"In that case Virginia is perfectly right. I quite understand her meaning. But it will be a great vexation to my father that your engagement should be broken for such a cause."

"My father cannot complain. I have obeyed him," said Alvar. "But I shall go and tell him that the proposals he so honourably made me will be unnecessary." He went away as he spoke, and Jack, who had been listening silently, exclaimed,—

"By Jove! he doesn't know what he's in for now?"

"Oh," cried Cherry, "it is intolerable! If they had married, she would never have found out his coolness! It is most unlucky."

"Well," said Jack, "I don't know. Alvar worships you, and has ways that suit you, yet you can't understand each other. Alvar is altogether different from us. He is outside our planetary system, and always will be. I'd like my wife to belong to the same species as myself."

"But the occasion is so annoying," said Cherry. "Why must they order me off in this way—or why couldn't I have held my tongue about it? Oh, Alvar is the wise man after all."

"You'll get well," said Jack gruffly.

"Well, I'll try. But—" he paused; but the thought in his mind was that the home ties had regained their power now that he believed himself likely to leave them for ever.

"Cherry," said Jack, turning his back, and hunting in a bookshelf, "I know all about it."

"Do you, Jack?"

"Yes. You ought to go away; but do you mind going alone with Alvar? Let me come."

"Well, Jack," said Cheriton, after a pause, "if you know, I can tell you how it is. I've had a hard time, and I think I should like to be quiet. But it is right to give oneself a chance, and as for Alvar, I am not at all afraid of going alone with him. You know what a good nurse he is. If I want you, you will come to me."

"Yes," muttered Jack.

"But I don't want father to guess at what the doctors call 'mental anxiety,' nor to talk hopelessly to him. You must comfort him. I'm afraid a great deal will be thrown on you, my boy."

Jack did not answer; and Cheriton, divining his feelings, made an effort, and said cheerfully,—

"Of course, one is no judge oneself in such cases. I am quite willing to go now, and I shall look forward to seeing you at Christmas. You must write and give me your impressions of Oxford."

"Oh yes," said Jack, consoled; "and perhaps Alvar will pick up a Spanish lady, and then we should be all right again." Cherry smiled and shook his head, feeling that he could not wish to dispose of Alvar in so unceremonious a fashion. He was angry with him now, and felt how wide a gulf lay between their points of view; yet he had grown to be very dependent on him, and was keenly conscious of all his unselfish devotion. He saw, too, that it would not do to talk freely even to Jack, since it frightened him and made him miserable, and resolved to keep all his confusing feelings to himself—feelings that seemed to tear him to pieces while he was utterly weary of them all.

He was afraid that he had been hard on Alvar, and still more afraid of how his father would take the revelation; but he had long to wait before the study door was flung open, and Alvar walked in, with his head up, and his face crimson. He was passing through without heeding his brothers, but Cherry's call checked him, and he came up to the window.

"*Mi querido*, this will do you harm," he said gently; "you excite yourself too much."

"But tell me—"

"Yes, I will tell you. But we will go upstairs; you must rest."

But as he spoke, his father came out of the study, and coming up to them, said, in a tone of strong indignation,—

"I wish to know, Cheriton, how long you have been aware of a state of feeling on your brother's part which places me in a situation of which I am thoroughly ashamed; whether you were aware that, as appears from his own confession, *my* son has done Miss Seyton the disrespect of engaging himself to her as a matter of expediency, and not of affection."

"Sir," said Alvar firmly, "your displeasure is for me alone. I will not allow my brother to be questioned; he is not strong enough to bear it."

"No, Alvar, it won't hurt me. Father, I don't think you understand. If they find that they cannot satisfy each other, it is better to part. Neither would act dishonourably by the other."

"There is no use in talking," said Alvar hotly. "At my father's wish I gave myself to Miss Seyton as I am. Well, she rejects me; there is an end of it. I can change for no one. I am myself. Well, I do not please any of you, but I do not ask you to change yourselves, nor will I." His words sounded like a mere defiance to his father, but as Cheriton heard them, he felt their force. Why should they all expect Alvar to conform to their standard instead of trying to understand his?

"Be that as it may," said Mr Lester, "you have found an unworthy pretext. I am far from ungrateful for all your kindness to Cheriton, but it was fair on none of us to take the opportunity of his going abroad to put off your marriage. If you had had the manliness to say at once that your engagement was distasteful to you, we should have known how to act."

"I will not stay—I will not hear myself so insulted!" cried Alvar, with a sudden fury of passion, that flared high above his father's angry displeasure, startling both the brothers into an attempt to interfere.

"Father is mistaken," cried Jack; while Cheriton began to say,—

"Come into the study, father; I think I can explain—" when his words were stopped by a violent fit of coughing. Agitated and over-fatigued as he was, he could not check it, and the alarm was more effectual than any explanations could have been in silencing the quarrel.

Alvar sprang to his side in a moment, and sent Jack for remedies; while Mr Lester forgot everything but the one great anxiety and distress.

The doctors had given a strong enough warning against the possible consequences of such excitement to make them all feel self-reproachful at having caused it; and the next words exchanged between the disputants were an entreaty from Mr Lester to know if Alvar was alarmed, a gentle reassurance on Alvar's part, and a request, at once complied with, that his father would move out of sight, lest Cherry should attempt to renew the discussion.

It never was renewed. When Cherry recovered, he was too much exhausted to try to speak, or to think of Alvar in any light but of the one who knew best what was comfortable to him, and once more everything seemed indifferent to Mr Lester beside the approaching parting. But though a quarrel was averted, there was much discomfort. Mrs Lester took her son's view decidedly, and treated Alvar like a culprit, the only voice raised in his favour being Bob's, who observed unexpectedly "that he thought Alvar was quite right to do as he chose." Mr Lester had an interview with Mr Seyton, and probably made more than the *amende* expected from him, for the next day he received a note from Virginia:—

"Dear Mr Lester,—As I find from my father that you do not entirely understand the circumstances which have led to the breach of my engagement, I think it is due to your son to tell you that it was entirely my own doing, and that I have no cause of complaint against him. We parted, because I believe we are unsuited to each other, not because he in any way displeased me; certainly not because he very rightly wished to go abroad with Cheriton. I hope you will forgive me for saying this, and believe me,—

"Yours very sincerely,—

"Virginia Seyton."

Well meant as poor Virginia's letter was, it may be doubted whether it much enlightened Mr Lester as to the point in question; but he showed it to Alvar, who read it with a deep blush, and said,—

"She is, as ever, generous—but—I am a stranger to her still."

Meanwhile, all the arrangements for the journey were being made. Cheriton received a warm invitation from Seville, and it was agreed, at his earnest request, that his father should remain behind at Oakby, but that Jack should go with him to Southampton, whence they were to go to Gibraltar by P and O steamer, the easiest way, it was thought, of making the journey. In London, Cheriton was to see a celebrated physician.

He went bravely and considerately through all the trying leave-takings and arrangements, taxing his strength to the uttermost, in the desire to leave nothing undone for any one. He put aside with a strong hand, that inner self which yet he could not conquer, with its passionate yearning, its bitter disappointment, its abiding sense of wrong; but it was there still, and gave at times the strangest sense of unreality, even to the pain of the partings, which was true pain nevertheless though he seemed to feel it through the others, rather than through himself. Perhaps the vehement Lester temperament was not a very sanguine one, for though they were told to be hopeful, they were all full of fear, and Cheriton himself hardly looked forward to a return, or, indeed, to anything but possible rest from the strain of making the best of himself, for he suffered very much, while all the vivid and appropriate sensations with which he had once looked out on life and death had died away.

He could hardly have borne it all but for Alvar's constant care and watchfulness, and for the ease given by his apparent absence of feeling, and for the soothing of his tender gentle ways, and yet though he clung to him with ever-increasing gratitude and affection, there was a curious sense of being apart from him.

Alvar, though he had too much tact to fret Cherry by opposition, had no sympathy with the innumerable interests, for each one of which he wished to provide, and thought his parting interviews with the young Flemings and with many another waste of strength and spirits. Cherry had also to go through a trying conversation with old Parson Seyton, who, between anger on Virginia's account and grief on Cheriton's, was difficult to deal with, entirely refusing to see Alvar, and more than disposed to quarrel with Cherry for going abroad with him. Even Mr Ellesmere regarded Alvar's conduct with considerable disapproval, though he would not mar his relations with Cherry by a word.

Alvar said nothing and made no explanations, but he was exceedingly impatient of the strain on Cherry's fortitude and cheerfulness, not seeing what the memory of this sad time might one day be to them all, and least of all appreciating the value of that last Sunday's church-going and Communion, which, much as it tried both their feelings and their shy reserve, not one of the others, even Bob, would for worlds have omitted. Yet, when many an old servant and neighbour made a point that day of following the example of the squire and his children, Mr Ellesmere thought the scene no small testimony to the value of the lives, which, however faulty and imperfect, had been led, though at different levels, with a constant sense of responsibility towards man and of looking upwards to God. Yes, and as something to give thanks for, even while his heart swelled at the thought that the best-loved of those tall fair-faced youths might never kneel in Oakby Church again.

That same Sunday evening, Mr Lester was sitting alone in the library in the dusk, sad enough at heart, when Cherry came slowly in behind him, and leaned over the back of his chair.

"Father," he said, "I've been thinking, and I want to tell you something before I go."

"What is it, my boy?—don't stand—here, sit here."

He pulled another chair towards his own as he spoke, and Cherry sat down, and said,—

"Father, I think I had rather you knew as much as I ought to tell you; I don't want to have any secret between us."

"Well, my boy?"

"And, besides, I heard you say that, if you could have found any reason for my being worse, you would be less anxious about me. Well, it is not a reason exactly, but I suppose it made me careless. I—I've had a great trouble lately—a—a disappointment. It's over now—but it cost me a good deal at the time. I can't tell you any more about it; but I thought—after all—I had rather you knew—*now!*"

Mr Lester did not ask a single question.

"I never guessed this," he said, in a tone of surprise; then, after a pause, "Well, my dear boy, it's a great relief to my mind."

Cherry nearly laughed, though his heart was full enough.

"You need never imagine that it will turn up again," he said, decidedly.

"Ah, well, Cherry, we've all had disappointments," said Mr Lester, more cheerfully than he had spoken for some time; "and I'm glad there's something to account for your looks lately. You weren't strong enough for vexations. You'll shake them off with the change of scene. But, my lad, don't go and make a fool of yourself in the reaction."

Cherry was sufficiently acquainted with his father's history to guess at the drift of this warning; but he only shook his head and smiled, and then there was a long silence. Cherry leaned against the arm of his father's chair, and, after a long-forgotten childish fashion, began to finger the seals on his watch-chain.

"These are the first things I remember," he said.

Mr Lester passed his arm round him, as when he had been a slim boy, standing by his side; and though no other word was spoken, and in the darkness there were tears on both their faces, Cherry felt that after such a drawing together, this worst of all the partings was easier to bear.

Seville

"Wo die Citronen blühn."

Chapter Twenty Six
Fighting the Dragon

"Does the road wind uphill all the way?
Yes, to the very end."

"So, papa, here we are, off at last! I can hardly believe it, and nothing left behind! Isn't it delightful? Such lovely weather and so many people! I wish we were going to India right away! I wonder how many of those people are good sailors."

"A very small proportion, my dear, in all probability."

"How I do like to look at people and imagine histories for them! And you cannot start for India without a sort of story; can you? As for you and me, *we're* just going to enjoy ourselves!"

The speaker looked capable of enjoying herself and all around her. She was a girl of eighteen or nineteen, dressed in a tightly-fitting dark blue dress with a little black felt hat, very becoming to her small, slender shape, and dark glowing complexion. She had pretty features and very white teeth, which showed a little in her frequent smiles; dark hazel eyes, bright, clear, and penetrating; and curly wavy hair, as black as an English girl's can be. She had quick, decided movements, a clear, firm voice, and the sweetest laugh possible.

Among all the anxious, hurried, fidgety people on the deck she looked perfectly happy and at her ease—not careless, for a variety of small packages were neatly piled up beside her, but entirely content; for was not the desire of her heart in process of fulfilment? Ever since Elizabeth Stanforth, always appropriately called Gipsy, had been a little girl, she had delighted in sharing her father's expeditions when the great London artist sought new ideas, new models, or a cessation from ideas and models, in the enjoyment of natural beauty. These expeditions had not hitherto been long or frequent, for Gipsy was the eldest of seven, and holiday trips away from the old house at Kensington were generally made in company with her mother and the children, with occasional divergences of Mr Stanforth's. Gipsy, too, was but newly released from the thraldom of lessons and classes, though a week once at the Lakes, and another in Cornwall, had shown Mr Stanforth that she possessed various requisites for a good traveller—a great capacity for enjoyment and a great incapacity for being bored, good health, a good appetite, and a good temper.

Therefore, when a long-cherished wish of Mr Stanforth's own was put in practice, and he set out for a three months' tour in search of the picturesque in Southern Spain, he took Gipsy with him, and this warm, sunshiny September morning found them on the deck of a P and O steamer, just about to leave Southampton on its way to Gibraltar.

They had arrived on board early, and were now watching the approach of their fellow-passengers, the farewells and last words passing between them and their friends: Gipsy simply delighted with the novelty of the scene, and her father watching it with a peculiarly acute and kindly gaze of accurate observation.

Mr Stanforth, with his slender figure and dark beard, looked young enough to be sometimes mistaken for his daughter's elder brother; she resembled him in colouring and feature, but keen and sweet as her bright eyes were, they had not looked out long enough on life to have acquired the thoughtful sympathetic expression that gave to her father's face an unusual charm—a look that seemed to tell of an insight that reached beyond the artist's observation of form and colour, or even of obvious character, and penetrated the very thoughts of the heart, not merely to note but to understand them. Perhaps this was why Mr Stanforth's portraits were thought such good likenesses, and why his original designs never wanted for character and expression.

He was not thinking purposely of anything but his holiday and his daughter, but the blue sky and bright sunshine of this unusually summer-like September helped his sense of enjoyment, and every face as it passed before him interested or amused him from the bright, fresh-faced schoolgirl just "finished," and looking forward through a few parting tears to incalculable possibilities in her unknown life, to the climate-worn official who had been bored during his leave at home, yet was far from regarding India as a paradise. Brides blushing and smiling, mothers with eyes and hearts sad for the children left at home, young lads with the world before them—the deck offered specimens of all these. Some were surrounded by groups of friends, but most of the sadder partings had been got over elsewhere, and the passengers were coming on board with a sense of relief, and minds chiefly full of their luggage and their state-rooms, their places at the table, and their chairs for the deck.

As Mr Stanforth's eye travelled over the various groups he observed two young men sitting close together on one of the benches at a little distance. The one nearest to him sat with his face turned away towards his companion, a tall, powerful lad, with fair hair, and features of an unusually fine and regular type, now pale and half sullen with a pain evidently almost beyond endurance. The other's hand lay on his knee, and he seemed to be speaking, for the boy nodded and murmured a word or two occasionally. "That's a bad parting," thought the artist; "I wonder which is the traveller."

"Look, papa," said Gipsy, "there's a model for you! Isn't that an uncommon face?" She pointed out to him a tall, dark young man, with a peculiar oval face of olive tinting, who stood close to them making inquiries of some officials. "There's a distinguished foreigner for you," she said.

"Yes, a foreigner of course; a very fine fellow."

Something restrained the kindly-natured artist from drawing his daughter's attention to the parting moments that were evidently so painful; but the "distinguished foreigner," as the last minutes approached, drew near to the pair and touched the lad on the shoulder. He started up; the other rose also and turned round, showing a face like enough in type to suggest the closest kinship, but white, thin, telling a tale of sickness as well as of present suffering. They grasped each other's hands. Mr Stanforth involuntarily turned his eyes away, and in a moment the lad pushed through the crowd, evidently unseeing and unheeding, passed close by them and knocked over all Gipsy's bags, shawls, and bundles, pushed on, never knowing what he had done, and turning, gave one last look at his brother, who met it with a beaming, resolute smile, and a wave of the hand.

The olive-faced foreigner who had followed, saw the accident, and made a gesture of apology, then bid the boy farewell with clasped hands and some rapidly-uttered sentences, watching him over the side, and, coming back to the Stanforths, hastily replaced the fallen articles.

"Pardon," he said, "my brother could not see."

"Don't mention it; no harm done," said Mr Stanforth kindly, as the young man moved away, other groups came up and separated them, and he was seen no more till dinner-time, when he appeared, but without his companion.

In the intervals of making acquaintance with her fellow-passengers and of beginning the letter which was to tell her mother of *every* event of their tour, Gipsy Stanforth speculated as to how the "distinguished foreigner" came to call such an unmistakable Englishman his brother.

The three days that the Lesters had spent in London had been trying and fatiguing. Judge Cheriton and his wife had come up from the country to their town house on purpose to receive them, but the very kindness and interest which had prompted them to inquire into all the causes of Cheriton's illness, and to question the prudence of some of the home measures had fretted both Cheriton and Jack, the latter being a little disposed to resent any interference. But the right of the Cheritons to a share in their nephews' affairs had always been admitted, and Mr Lester, little as he felt himself able to bear the further strain, would hardly have let them go to London without him, but for his brother-in-law's assurance that they should not start till every arrangement had been made. The judge was surprised at the confidence reposed in Alvar, and though he had too much sense to try to shake it, had caused Mr Lester to insist that they should be accompanied by a servant experienced in travelling and in illness, instead of the Oakby lad at first chosen—an arrangement which Cheriton secretly much disliked, though he acquiesced in it as sparing his father anxiety.

Judge Cheriton also undertook to give Mr Lester a full report of the physician's opinion, which was not, on the whole, discouraging. He said that though the illness had left manifest traces, and that he considered Cheriton in a critical state, there was nothing to prevent entire recovery, of which the winter abroad offered the best chance; and if he wished to go to Southern Spain, Spain it might be, as rest and change were as much needed as climate. There was no use in thinking of any profession or occupation till the next summer. Some overstrain had resulted in a complete break-down, and the cough was part of the mischief. Fatigue, cold, and anxiety were all equally to be avoided, but as there was no predisposition to any form of chest disease in the family, they might look forward hopefully.

This verdict entirely consoled Alvar, who, indeed, had never looked much beyond the present, and brightened the anxious hearts at Oakby, especially when accompanied by a note from Cherry himself, which he had made Jack read to "see if it was cheerful enough."

He and Jack clung to each other closely during those last few days, and till they parted, Cheriton never ceased to be the one to uphold and to cheer; but when Jack was out of sight, he broke down utterly, and while Alvar was beginning to make acquaintance with the Stanforths, Cheriton lay fighting hard with all the suffering which he had so long held at bay. He was not passive, though Alvar thought him so, as he lay still and silent, unwilling to speak or be spoken to. He was struggling actively, strenuously, with all the force of a strong will against a passionate and rebellious nature. He was sufficiently experienced in self-control, and unselfish enough to have succeeded in behaving well and courageously under his various troubles. But Cherry's notions of self-conquest aimed higher and went deeper. He would be master of his own inmost soul, as well as of his outward actions. His eyes were pure enough to see as in a vision what was implied in saying honestly, "Thy Will be done," and clear enough to know that he could not say it; while, on the other hand, there was scarcely any form of wrath and bitterness to which memory did not tempt him. Why must he suffer in so many ways? Perhaps the moments of softer yearning for the lost love of his boyhood, sad as they were, were the least painful part of his suffering. The loss of health and strength, and of the power of substituting some other aim in life for those earlier and sweeter hopes, came as a separate, but to so active a person, an exceeding trial, while he was separated from all the lesser interests which had the power of custom over him, a power in his case unusually strong; yet in these he felt lay the hope of salvation, at least from those intermittent waves of utter despondency which made all alike worthless and blank. Cheriton had all his life tried to choose the better part, to follow his own higher nature, and seek what was lovely and of good report, had all his life looked upward. Had he not done so, these present temptations would have attacked him on a far lower level, or, set apart as he was just now from all outward action, he would more probably not have recognised that he had a battle to fight at all. But to Cheriton it was given to see the issues of the battle that has been fought by all true saints, and perhaps by some sinners; and his chief mistake now was that he was young enough to think that, like the typical dragon fights of the old world, it could be won by one great struggle. This was his inner life, of which no one knew anything, save perhaps Jack, who was like-minded enough to guess something of it.

Alvar only saw that he was weak and weary, and suffering from a great reaction of mind and body. He was a very judicious companion, however, and after a day or two of repose succeeded in coaxing Cherry on to the deck; where the fresh air sent him to sleep on the cushions that Alvar had arranged for him, more quietly than for some time past.

When he opened his eyes, and began to look about him, it was with a refreshing sense of life and circumstances apart from himself and his perplexities. The blue sky, the dancing waves, the groups of people moving about, the unfamiliar sights and sounds amused him. He looked round for his brother, and presently discovered him sitting at a little distance, smoking his unfailing cigarette, and looking both comfortable and picturesque in the soft felt hat, which, though not especially unlike other people's, always had on him the effect of a costume. He was talking to a young lady, with an air of considerable animation and intimacy. She was knitting a gay-striped sock, the bright pins twinkling with the rapid movement of her fingers, and she laughed often, a particularly gay, musical laugh.

Alvar glanced round, and seeing that Cherry was awake, sprang up and came over to him.

"Ah, you have had quite a long sleep," he said.

"Have I? I feel all the better for it. This is very comfortable. And pray who is the young lady with the knitting-needles?"

"Why, that is Miss Stanforth. Did I not tell you how kind they have been? You see, Jack nearly knocked her down, and so we made acquaintance; and just now I was teaching her some Spanish."

"Did Jack create a favourable impression by that mode of introduction?"

"Why, yes," said Alvar, delighted at hearing the shadow of a joke from Cherry; "for I explained how it was that he was in trouble, and they were interested at hearing of you. Now you must have some breakfast, and then perhaps you would like to see them."

"Oh, no," said Cherry, "I don't feel up to talking; but I am glad you have some one to amuse you."

However, Cherry began to be amused himself by watching his brother. He felt the relief of having nothing to do and no one to think of, and as he lay looking on, was surprised at perceiving how sociable the stiff, reserved Alvar appeared to be, how many little politenesses he performed, and how gay and light-hearted he looked. Evidently Mr and Miss Stanforth were the most attractive party, though Alvar seemed on speaking terms with every one; and at last Cherry, seeing that he wished it, begged that Mr Stanforth would come and speak to him, and their new acquaintance, having the tact to see that he was shy in his character of invalid, came and sat down beside him, and talked cheerfully on indifferent topics.

"And where are you bound for," he asked presently, "when you reach Gibraltar?"

"For Seville," said Cheriton; "Don Guzman de la Rosa, my brother's grandfather, lives there at this time of the year. He has a country place, too, I believe, for the summer. But Alvar thinks the journey would be too much for me yet. I hope not; he must want to be with his friends."

"My daughter and I," said Mr Stanforth, "have some friends at Gibraltar, and they have recommended us to join them at a place on the coast, San José, I think they called it. Afterwards our dream has been to spend some weeks at Seville. Can you tell us anything of ways and means there, for we are trusting entirely to fate and a guide-book?"

"I'm afraid," said Cherry, smiling, "that I am trusting with equally implicit faith in Alvar. I haven't asked many questions. Alvar, can you tell Mr Stanforth what he must do, and how he must manage in Seville?"

"All I know is at his service," said Alvar, sitting down at Cherry's feet; "but he will, I hope, visit my grandfather, who will be honoured by his coming. My aunt, too, and my cousins would be proud to show Miss Stanforth Seville."

"Oh, papa," exclaimed Gipsy impetuously, catching these words as she approached, "to know some Spaniards. Then we should really see the country." She broke off, blushing; and Alvar, springing up, offered her a seat, and introduced her to his brother, while Mr Stanforth said, —

"Thank you, we could not refuse such a kind offer; but I want to make Seville my head-quarters, and make excursions from thence. What sort of inns have you? Are they pleasant for ladies?"

"Papa, you know we settled that I was not going to be a lady."

"Did we, my dear? I was not a party to that arrangement. You are not *quite* a gipsy yet, you know."

"There are inns," said Alvar, "but the best plan is to take a flat in what we call a '*Casa de pupillos*,' a *pension*, I suppose. I know one. Dona Catalina, who keeps it, is an excellent lady, most devout, and she once received an English family, so she knows better how you like to eat and drink."

"I don't mean to eat and drink anything that is not Spanish," said Gipsy, laughing.

"Indeed," said Alvar, "you will not often find anything that is English. I sometimes fear that my brother will not like that."

"You have a lively remembrance of being asked to eat oat-cake and porridge, and drink what we call sherry," said Cheriton.

"But I will not expect that you shall like things that are strange to you, *querido*," said Alvar, a speech that revealed a little of the family history to Mr Stanforth's sharp eyes; while Gipsy said earnestly, —

"Oh, the strangeness is what I expect to enjoy."

A good deal more information of different kinds followed, and Cherry wondered at this own ignorance of Alvar's former surroundings.

"Why, I did not know that your cousins lived with you," he said.

"I did not speak much of Seville to *you*," said Alvar, with ever so slight an emphasis, the first reminder he had ever given that there had been one to whom he could talk freely.

"We were all too much occupied with teaching you about Westmoreland, and lately I think I have been too stupid to care. But you must give me some Spanish lessons soon."

"Have you been long in England?" said Mr Stanforth to Alvar.

"I came at Christmas. Ah, how cold it was! The boys and Nettie laughed at me because I did not like it. They ran out into the snow without their hats that I might feel ashamed of sitting by the fire," said Alvar quaintly.

"Ah, we were a set of terrible young Philistines!" said Cheriton. "Do you remember the snow man and the wrestling?"

"I wish you could wrestle with me now, my brother," said Alvar affectionately.

"That must be the effect of Spanish sunshine, instead of Westmoreland snow; and in the meantime we must not tire you with talking," said Mr Stanforth, perceiving that Cherry hardly liked the allusion. "Come, Gipsy, isn't it time for one of the innumerable meals we have on board ship?"

"Oh, papa, I am sure you are always ready for them," said Gipsy, following him.

Mr Stanforth, on discovering more clearly the whereabouts of Oakby, recollected having visited Ashrigg some years ago, when engaged on a portrait of some member of Sir John Hubbard's family. He perceived with some amusement that Alvar attached no ideas to his name or to his profession; and Cherry had scarcely realised either, so that when the next morning Mr Stanforth came up to speak to him, with a sketch-book in his hand, he said, quite simply,—

"I see you have been drawing; may I look?"

"If you will not think I have taken a great liberty," said Mr Stanforth, giving him the book.

Cheriton laughed and exclaimed at one or two exquisitely outlined likenesses of their fellow-passengers, hitting off their peculiarities with a touch, then admired a little bit of blue sky and dancing wave, with a pair of sea-gulls hanging white and soft in the midst, while under were written the lines,—

> "As though life's only call and care
> Were graceful motion."

"How lovely!" he said; "how wonderfully well you do it! Ah, that is Alvar—yes, you have caught that grave, graceful look exactly. Alvar is just like a walking picture; he can't be awkward."

"I am afraid I have not been so successful with Alvar's brother; but the contrast was irresistible," said Mr Stanforth, as Cherry turned another page, and saw a sketch of himself lying on the deck, and Alvar, leaning over him, and pointing out something in the distance.

"That is just Alvar's look."

"You are a much more difficult subject than your brother," said Mr Stanforth.

"I? I don't think I'm fit to sit for my picture. We tried in London to get a photograph taken; but it made me look worse than I am, so we did not send it home."

"You must let me try again. As an artist I may be forgiven for rejoicing in the chance of studying such a likeness beneath such a contrast as there is between you two. See, your faces are in the same mould; it is the colour, and still more the character, that differs."

"I think that may be true of more than our faces," said Cherry thoughtfully; "but I see what you mean, at least when I think of Jack, and we were alike when I was well. I will show you."

Here Cheriton caught sight of the name on the first page of the book, "Raymond Stanforth," looked at the drawings, and then at his new friend's face with a rush of comprehension.

"How stupid I have been!" he exclaimed, colouring. "I beg your pardon. Of course I ought to have guessed who it was at once. Pray don't think I am so ignorant as not to know your pictures. And I have been presuming to praise your sketches."

Mr Stanforth laughed kindly.

"You must not leave off doing so now we have found each other out. Don't imagine that appreciation is not always pleasant."

"You have a great many admirers at Oxford," said Cheriton, a little stiffly and shyly. "Some of the fellows prided themselves immensely on their appreciation of all sorts of modern art; but I'm afraid I don't know very much about it."

"You employed your time, your brother tells me, to better purpose?"

"I don't know. I thought so then. And it seemed more worth while to get a ride or pull on the river. I don't see what a fellow wants in his room but an armchair and a place for his books, and a good fire. One had better be out of doors when one isn't working. I don't care to have my rooms like a lady's drawing-room. But of course," he added apologetically, "I always like to go to the Academy and see the pictures."

Mr Stanforth looked very much amused, but he was interested too. It is not uncommon in youth that considerable powers of mind may be exercised so entirely in one line, as to leave many fields of intelligence completely blank, and there were many points on which Cheriton simply accepted the code of his home, which, put into plain language, was, that study was study, and recreation out-of-door exercise of different kinds, intellectual amusements being regarded with suspicion. But there was much more than the boyish "Philistinism" of this last speech written on the face of the speaker, and Mr Stanforth felt inclined to draw it out.

"What did you say you were going to show me?" he said.

"I wanted you to see the rest of us!" said Cherry. "Where is Alvar? He would get my photograph case."

Alvar was near at hand, talking to Gipsy Stanforth and to some other ladies, and he soon brought Cheriton a little leather case which contained a long row of handsome Lesters, and ended with the favourite dogs and horses, and a view of the front door at Oakby, with Nettie holding Buffer on the back of one of the stone wolves.

"There is a ready-made picture," said Mr Stanforth.

"My brother loves that little animal," said Alvar smiling, "he would like his picture better than that of any of us."

"I am sure some of our dogs are worth painting," said Cherry, "but Alvar does not appreciate Buffer's style."

And so, brightened by the fresh companionship and new scenes, the days slipped by, till Cheriton wished their sameness could continue for ever.

Chapter Twenty Seven
San José

"The lizard, with his shadow on the stone,
Rests like a shadow, and the cicala sleeps,
The purple flowers droop."

At Gibraltar the new acquaintances parted, and Mr Stanforth and his daughter went at once to join their friends at San José, with many hopes expressed of soon meeting at Seville; whither Cheriton, unwilling to detain Alvar from his friends, wished to go immediately. Mr Stanforth's holiday was not an idle one. Every walk he took, every change of light and shade was a feast of new colour and form for him, to be perpetuated by sketches more or less elaborate, and the enjoyment of which was intense. But the pair of dissimilar brothers had afforded him interest of another kind, and it was with real pleasure that he thought of a renewal of the intercourse with them, which came about sooner than he had expected.

His friends, the Westons, were a brother and two sisters, lively people approaching middle age. Mr Weston had a government appointment in Gibraltar, and his sisters lived with him. They were enterprising, cultivated women, and very fond of Gipsy Stanforth; who possessed that power of quick sympathetic interest which of all things makes a delightful companion. She was always finding "bits" and "effects" for her father, or suggesting subjects for his pencil; and she was almost equally pleased to hunt for flowers for the botanical Miss Weston, and to look out words in the dictionary for the literary one, who was translating a set of Spanish tales.

À *propos* of these, she related with much interest their acquaintance on board ship, describing the two Lesters with a *naïveté* that amused her friends, and prompted Miss Weston to say,—

"You seem to have been very fortunate in your travelling companions, Gipsy."

"Yes, we were. And it will be such an advantage to know a native family at Seville. That sounds as if they were heathens; but I declare that *is* Don Alvar, buying oranges! Oh, I am so glad to see you! So you have come here after all."

"Yes. Cheriton was so ill at Gibraltar that it was plain that he could not bear the journey to Seville. It is cooler here, and he is a little better; but he can do nothing yet, and I am very unhappy. I do not know what to write to my father about him."

"Oh, I am sorry," said Gipsy warmly. "He seemed better on board. And this place is so lovely."

"Yes," said Alvar simply. "I could feel as if I was in heaven in the sunshine, and when I hear the voices of my home; but when he suffers, it darkens all. But I must go back to him."

"Papa will come and see you," said Gipsy; "and this is Miss Weston, with whom we are staying. Good-bye. I think your brother will be better when he has had a rest."

Gipsy's cheerful sympathy brightened Alvar, who had expected that Spanish sunshine would make a miraculous cure; but Cherry's cough had been worse since they came on shore, and his spirits had failed unaccountably just when Alvar had expected him to recover them.

Alvar had all along declared that it would be better to go by a Cadiz packet and thence by rail to Seville; but Mr Lester believed in Peninsular and Oriental steamers, and in the English doctors and hotels of Gibraltar. But there the heat and glare were hateful to Cheriton, the servant they had brought proved more of a hindrance than a help, and Alvar thought himself fortunate in obtaining leave from some Gibraltar acquaintances to use their house at San José for a month, after which Cheriton might be better able to encounter the strangers whom he really dreaded more than the travelling. Certainly if change was what Cherry had needed he had obtained it thoroughly. Nothing could well have been more unlike Oakby than San José, and when Cheriton had had a little rest, had been teased by Mr Stanforth for comparing the marble-paved *patio* of the house to the Alhambra at the Crystal Palace, and, moved by the fortunate sympathy that had enabled him to "take a fancy" to the kindly artist, had confided to him that he was very homesick, and longed for Jack, though he did not like Alvar to know it, he brightened up and grew rather stronger. He was soon able to sit on the beach and try to learn Spanish, insisting on understanding the construction of the language, and asking questions sometimes rather puzzling to his tutor; while Gipsy set up a rivalry with him as to the number of words and phrases to be acquired in a day, in which she generally beat him hollow. Nor had he any real want of appreciation of the new and beautiful world around him, and Mr Stanforth helped him to enjoy it. Life would be very dull but for the involuntary inclinations to acquaintance and friendship that brighten its ordinary course, and "fancies" are more often things to be thankful for than to put aside. This one roused Cheriton from the dulness that accompanies sorrow and sickness, and enabled him to turn at any rate the surface of his mind to fresh interests.

Mr Stanforth, on the other hand, whose sympathy had been quickened by the practice of a most kindly life, found much to interest him in the bright, tender nature, evidently struggling under so heavy a cloud, and did not wonder at the affection with which the young man was obviously regarded—an affection made pathetic by the sad possibilities that were but too apparent.

Gipsy was on very friendly terms with both the brothers, and was a new specimen of girlhood for them. She was quite as clever and as well educated as either Ruth or Virginia, and had been in the habit of living with much more widely cultivated people—people who talked, and had something to talk about, so that she had a great deal to say; while there was a quaint matter-of-factness about her too, and she talked art as simply as she would have talked dress; and while she was very much interested in the two young men, she never troubled herself at all about her relations towards them. She scolded Cherry for walking too far, and discoursed on the suitability of his appearance for artistic purposes with equal simplicity; fetched and carried for him, and triumphed over his deficiencies in Spanish. She received Alvar's courtesies and compliments with the greatest delight, and proceeded to return them in kind, till she actually rendered him almost free and easy, and he talked so much of her that Cheriton grew half-frightened, unknowing that his own remark, that he wished Nettie could know so nice a girl as Miss Stanforth, had inspired Alvar with the notion that Ruth might find a successor in La Zingara, as he called her. But Gipsy was perfectly unconscious, and was moreover carefully watched over by her father and her friends. By the end of the month Cheriton was able to undertake the journey to Seville, and the Stanforths proposed to start at the same time, but to go by a different route, which enabled them to see more of the country.

"But," said Gipsy, one evening when they were all together on the beach, "we *must* get to Seville in time for a bull-fight, and Don Alvar says there are none in the winter."

"But, Miss Stanforth," said Cherry, "*you* surely would not go to a bull-fight?"

"Wouldn't you?" said Gipsy mischievously.

"Well, yes—for once I think I should."

"You would not like it, Cherito," said Alvar.

"Don't you?" echoed Cherry, with a glance at Gipsy.

"Oh, yes; it is grand! When the bull makes a rush one holds the breath, and then—it is a shout!"

"I suppose it is a wonderful spectacle," said Mr Stanforth. "I hope to have a chance, but I think Gipsy will have to take it on trust."

"Jack desired me not to encourage them," said Cherry, "but I must own to a great curiosity about it."

"But I shall not let you go," said Alvar; "it would tire you far too much; and besides you are too tender-hearted. My brothers," he added to Mr Stanforth, "cannot bear to see anything hurt, unless they hurt it themselves; then they do not mind."

"Of course," said Cherry, "there is an essential difference between incurring danger, or at least fatigue and exertion yourself, and sitting by to see other people incur it. I have no doubt it is a barbarous sort of thing, and there is something dreadful in the idea of a lady being present at it; but it would be stupid, I think, to come away without seeing anything so characteristic."

"The Spanish ladies do not mind it, nor I," said Alvar, "any more than you mind killing your foxes, or your fish; but it is different for foreigners. They do not like to see the horses, though they are mostly worthless ones, torn in pieces. You would be ill, *querido*, you might faint."

"Nonsense," said Cherry. "I might hate it, but I should not be so soft as that."

"You do not know," said Alvar, evidently not disposed to yield. "Some day," with a glance at Gipsy, "I will tell you. You shot the old horse yourself for fear the coachman should hurt him—but it made you cry; and if a dog whines it grieves you."

"Old Star that I learnt to ride on!" said Cherry indignantly. "What has that to do with it?"

"And besides," resumed Alvar, perhaps a little wickedly, "bull-fights are usually on Sunday, and are quite as bad as billiards or the guitar, which you say in England are wrong."

"These are frightful imputations on you, Cheriton," said Mr Stanforth: "a tender heart and too strict a sense of duty. No wonder you are obstinate. But if what I have read be true, a bull-fight is a hard pull on our insular nerves sometimes, and I doubt if you are in condition for one."

"I don't want to see a bull-ring at Oakby," said Cherry; "but Alvar is mistaken if he thinks I should mind it more than other people do. There is enough of a sporting element, I suppose, to keep one from dwelling on the details."

"I see, Mr Lester," said Gipsy, "that you don't believe in the rights of women."

"No, Miss Stanforth, I certainly don't. I believe in my right to protect them from what is unpleasant."

"But not to give them their own way! Papa, don't look at me like that. *I* don't want to go and see horses killed on a Sunday, if Mr Lester does. But a bull-fight—the national sport of Spain—and the matadors who are so courageous—ah! it makes such a difference the way things are put."

"You must learn to look at the essentials, my dear. But now shall we have a last stroll to the point to see the sunset?"

"You need not tell Granny if I *do go* to the bull-fight," whispered Cherry, as Alvar helped him up, and gave him his arm across the rough shingles.

Chapter Twenty Eight
Seville

"Golden fruit fresh plucked and ripe."

"And now, my brother, you see Seville. At last I can show you my beautiful city!"

"Why—why, you never said it was like *this*!"

The Lesters had finally settled to go to Cadiz by sea, and thence by rail to Seville, again breaking their journey at Xeres. The Stanforths were making the journey across country; but Cheriton was not equal to long days on horseback, nor to risking the accommodations or no accommodations of the *ventas* and *posadas* (taverns and inns) where they might have to stop. He was quite ready, however, to be excited and patriotic as they passed through the famous waters of Trafalgar, and curious to taste sherry at Xeres, where it proved exceedingly bad. They arrived at Seville in the afternoon, and were driving from the station when Alvar interrupted Cherry's astonished contemplation of the scene with the foregoing remark.

"Ah, it pleases you!" he said in a tone of satisfaction, as they passed under the Alcazar, the Moorish palace, with its wonderful relics of a bygone faith and power—the great cathedral, said to be "a religion in itself"—and saw the gay tints of the painted buildings, the picturesque turn of the streets, the infinite variety of colour and costume, and over all the pure blue of the sky and the glorious intensity of Southern sunlight.

Cheriton had no words to express his admiration, and only repeated,—

"You never told me that it was like this."

"You did not understand," said Alvar; "and perhaps I did not know."

He did not show any emotion, but his face smoothed out into an expression of satisfaction and well-being, and he smiled with a little air of triumph at Cherry's ecstasies. This was what he had belonging to himself in the background all the time, when his relations had thought him so ignorant and inexperienced, and Alvar, like all the Lesters, valued himself on his own belongings.

They drove up to the door of a large house, painted in various colours, and with gaily-striped blinds and balconies; while through the ornamental iron gates they caught glimpses of the *patio*, gay with flowers.

Cheriton thought of the winter's night, the blazing fire, the shy, stiff greetings that had formed Alvar's first glimpse of Oakby. The great gates were opened, and as they came in a tall old man came forward, into whose arms Alvar threw himself with some vehement Spanish words of greeting; then, in a moment, he turned and drew Cheriton forward, saying, still in Spanish, —

"My grandfather, this is my dear brother."

Don Guzman de la Rosa bowed profoundly, and then shook hands with Cheriton, who contrived to understand his greeting and inquiry after his health, and to utter a few words in reply, feeling more shy than he had ever done in his life; but then he was at fault.

"My grandfather says you are like what our father was when he came here; that is true, is it not? And now come in."

Don Guzman showed the way into an inner room, which seemed dark after the brilliant *patio*, and was furnished much like an ordinary drawing-room; and here Cheriton was introduced to Dona Luisa Aviego, a middle-aged lady, Don Guzman's niece, and to two exceedingly pretty young girls, and a little girl, her daughters. He felt surprised at seeing them all in French fashions. Here also was their brother, Don Manoel, a tall, dark, solemn-looking young man, who exactly fulfilled Cheriton's idea of a Spaniard, and enabled him to understand Dona Luisa's remark that Alvar had grown into an Englishman. The old grandfather was like a picture of Don Quixote, a very ideal of chivalry, which character a life of prudent, careful indifferentism entirely belied.

Alvar would not let Cherry stay to talk, telling him that he must rest before dinner, which was at five, and soon took him upstairs into a very comfortable bedroom, looking out on a pretty garden, and opening into another belonging to himself.

Cheriton laughed and submitted, but the novelty and beauty had taken his impressionable nature by storm and carried him quite out of himself. When left alone, he had leisure for the surprising thought that his father had gone through all these experiences without their apparently leaving any trace except one of distaste and aversion; next, to wonder whether it was Alvar's fault or their own that they had remained so ignorant of Alvar's country; and lastly, that spite of the similarity of colouring to his Spanish kindred and something in the carriage, Alvar *did* look like a Lester and an Englishman after all.

Cherry had got used by this time in some degree to the Spanish eatables, and as he liked the universal chocolate and was as little fanciful as any one so much out of health could be, he got on as well as his bad appetite would let him, with the *ollas* and *gazpachos* spite of their garlic, and at any rate he liked omelettes and the bread, which was excellent. Their servant, Robertson, had, however, regarded everything Spanish with such horror, and had proved of so little use and so disagreeable, that Cheriton finally cut the knot by sending him back to Gibraltar, where he hoped to find a homeward-bound family, Alvar being certain that there would be sufficient attendance at his grandfather's.

Conversation at dinner was difficult. They all understood a little English, which was rather more available than Cheriton's Spanish, and Don Manoel spoke tolerably fluent French, to which, as Cheriton had in his time earned several French prizes, he *ought* to have been able to respond more readily than was perhaps the case. Cheriton did not mind seeing grapes and melons eaten after soup, though he thought the taste an odd one, but he could not quite reconcile himself to the universal smoking after the first course in the presence of the ladies. The young ones were very silent, though they cast speaking glances at him with their great languishing eyes; till after dinner the little girl, whom Cherry thought the softest and prettiest thing he had ever seen, produced a great blushing and tittering by whispering a question, which, while apparently reproving, Dona Carmen was evidently encouraging her to repeat to Alvar, who sat on her other side.

Alvar laughed and shook his head.

"No, Dolores; I think there is not one like him," he said, adding to Cherry—"She wants to know if all Englishmen are like you—white and golden like the saints in the cathedral. It is true, she means the painted statues."

"I am pale, because I have been ill," said Cherry, in his best Spanish, and holding out his hand. "Little one, will you make friends? What shall I say to her, Alvar?"

But Dolores, with an ineffable expression of demure coquetry, retreated upon her sister, and would not accept his attentions, though she peeped at him under her long eye-lashes directly he turned away.

The family met at eleven for a sort of *déjeuner à la fourchette*, but every one had chocolate in their own rooms at any hour they pleased, with bread or sponge-cake, which they called *pan del Rey*. Alvar brought some on the next morning to Cheriton and while he was drinking it proceeded to enlighten him a little on the family affairs and habits.

"I perceive that the prayer-bell does not ring at half-past eight," said Cherry smiling.

"No, the ladies all go to church every morning. In the country my grandfather is up early, and Manoel too, but here I cannot say—we meet at eleven. It is usual to write letters or transact business in the morning on account of the heat."

"Does Don Manoel—is that what I ought to call him?—live here? Has he anything to do?"

Alvar then explained that Manoel had no regular occupation, having a little money of his own. He smoked and played cards, and went to the casino, "that is what you call a club." Moreover he was a very good Catholic, and though he had not openly joined the Carlist party—the Royalists as Alvar called them—he was thought to have a leaning towards them: but Don Guzman never allowed politics to be discussed in his house—neither politics nor religion.

"Is he a 'good Catholic,' too?" asked Cherry.

Alvar shrugged his shoulders.

"He conforms," he said. "You understand that I am English. I have no part in these matters, otherwise at times my grandfather might have suffered for allowing me to be brought up as a Protestant; but I was taught to see that they did not concern me. But, *querido*, you must not talk and 'discuss' as you do with Jack at home, or you might make a quarrel."

"No, I understand that. But if I were you I should not like to be supposed to be an outsider."

"In both countries?" said Alvar. "No; but you see I had been taught that I was an Englishman."

"Yet your grandfather would not let you come to England when you were a boy."

"My grandfather," said Alvar, "hates the priests. He would rather have me for his heir, though I am a heretic, than Manoel. That is true, though he would not say so. Look, he has seen many changes in this country, one is as bad as the other; he would rather be quiet and let things pass. So would I."

"The Vicar of Bray," murmured Cherry. "That creed is born of despair," he said aloud. "I should be miserable to think so of any country."

"Yes?" said Alvar, with a sort of unmoved inquiry in his tone. "You have convictions. In England they are not difficult. But, besides, my grandmother loved me very much, and not only was she religious like all women, she was what you call good. She would not part with me, and I loved *her*."

Alvar paused and put his hand across his eyes, with more emotion than he often showed.

"She thought," he continued, "that I should perhaps become a Catholic if I married a *Sevillana*, and that my father's neglect would make me altogether a De la Rosa. Forgive me, Cherito, it is not quite to be forgotten."

"I think it was very likely to be the case," said Cheriton.

"No, it was not the part for my father's son, nor for an Englishman, nor did my grandfather wish it. I am no Catholic—never!"

"I suppose your tutor was—was a strong Protestant?" said Cheriton, rather surprised at the first religious conviction he had ever heard from Alvar's lips.

"Well, I do not think you would have approved of him nor my father if he had known. He, what is it you say?—did no duty—and I do not think he was much like your Mr Ellesmere. He told me that he was paid 'to put the English doctrines into me and teach me to speak English;' and he would say, 'Remember it is your part to be a Protestant because you are an English gentleman.'"

"But," said Cherry, "when you came to England you must surely have seen that we did not look on it in that way?"

"I did not much attend to your words on it," said Alvar. "As you know, what my father required of me I did, and I saw that English gentlemen thought much of their churches and their priests—or at least, that my father did so. I conformed, but I had not expected that in England, too, I should be a *foreigner*—a stranger. And I would not be other than my real self."

"I'm afraid we were very unkind to you."

"You? Never!" said Alvar.

"But why did you never tell me all this before? I should have understood you so much better."

"I did not think of it till I considered what would seem strange to you here—what you would not comprehend easily."

Cheriton remained silent. That Alvar had all his life considered himself so entirely as a Lester and an Englishman was a new light to him, and he could fully appreciate the check of finding himself regarded by the Lesters as an alien, for he knew that even he himself had never ceased so to look upon Alvar.

"We understand each other now," he said affectionately. "I am glad you have told me this. But, Alvar, though 'convictions' may seem to you easy in England, you would make a great mistake if you imagined that the religion of such a man as my father was for the sake of what you call conformity, and that it did not influence his life."

"No," said Alvar, "I did not think so of my father and you. I did not comprehend at first, but I see now that—it interests you."

"Never doubt that," said Cheriton earnestly. "You have seen all my failures, but never doubt that is the one thing 'interesting,' the one thing to—to give one another chance."

He paused as a look of unspeakable enthusiastic conviction passed over his face; then blushed intensely, and was silent. Like most young men, whatever their views, he was in the habit of talking a good deal of "theology," and could have rectified Alvar's hazy notions with ease; but personal experiences in such discussions were generally left on one side.

Alvar did not follow him; but perhaps that look made more impression than a great many arguments on the status of religion in England.

"Don't imagine I underrate your difficulties, or my own, or any one's," Cherry added hurriedly.

"I have no difficulties," said Alvar simply; "I believe you—always— Now, do not talk any longer—rest before you get up."

Cheriton now perceived that the sort of separation that had been pursued with regard to Alvar accounted for much of his indolence and indifference. He recognised how deeply his pride had been wounded by his kindred's cold reception, and he in a measure understood the sort of loyalty, half-proud, half-faithful, that held him to his own. He found that Alvar had never written a word of complaint of his family home to Seville; he perceived that as time went on he dropped nothing that he had acquired in England, either of dress or speech, attended the English service at the Consulate regularly, even if Cheriton was unable to go, and preferred to be called Mr Lester. Cheriton saw that he intended no one to think that his English residence had been a failure.

But there was one phase of this feeling of which even Cheriton had no suspicion. Alvar did not forget that one thing had belonged to him in England, to which Spain offered no parallel. He refused to answer any questions from his grandfather as to his engagement or its breach. He had not been brought up to think that romantic passion was a necessary accompaniment of a marriage engagement, but rather as a thing to be got through first; and it had been with a very quiet appreciation that he had given his hand away at his father's request. And when Virginia was once his, he was thoroughly contented with her, her rejection had wounded him exceedingly, and now he missed her confiding sweetness increasingly, he felt that a good thing was gone from him, and he would not now have attempted to console Cheriton as he had done at Oakby. But he never spoke of his feelings, and as Cheriton could not think that he had acted rightly by Virginia, the subject was never mentioned between them.

Chapter Twenty Nine
El Toro

"The ungentle sport that oft invites
The Spanish maid and cheers the Spanish swain."

One of Alvar's first occupations was to find a lodging for the Stanforths, and for one of the Miss Westons, whom they brought with them, and he succeeded in obtaining a flat in a *casa de pupillos* or *pension*, not far from the De la Rosa's, in a picturesque street, with a pleasant shady sitting-room, where Mr Stanforth could paint. There was a delightful landlady, Señora Catalina, who went to mass with the greatest regularity every morning, but afterwards was ready to spend any part of the day in escorting the ladies wherever they wished to go, only objecting to Gipsy's dislike to allow her dress to trail on the pavement, a point on which neither could convince the other, Spanish ladies considering the looping of the dress improper, and Gipsy not being able to reconcile herself to the normal condition of the pavements of Seville. Mr Stanforth, however, frequently accompanied them, and they did a vast amount of sight-seeing, in which they were joined by the two Lesters so far as Cheriton's strength would permit; and as sketching often made Mr Stanforth stationary, Cherry liked to sit by him, enjoying a great deal of discursive talk on things in general, and entering with vivid interest into the novelty and beauty around. Cherry asked a great many more questions about Moorish remains, and ecclesiastical customs, than Alvar was at all able to answer; and as his Spanish improved, endeavoured to pick the brains of every one with whom he came in contact; was so intelligent and so inquisitive about the arrangement of the different churches, that old Padre Tomè, the ladies' confessor, looked upon him as a possible convert, and though solemnly warned by Alvar never to talk politics with any one, could not always resist teasing him by hovering round the subject. He got on very well with Don Guzman, and listened to a great deal of prosing about the best way of breeding young bulls for the ring, and about all the varieties of game to be found on the old gentleman's country estate, and soon perceived that he had considerably underrated the sporting capacities of the peninsula. He was not a favourite with Don Manoel, who suspected himself of being laughed at; and though Dona Luisa was very kind to him, he was hardly allowed to exchange a word with the young ladies, and to his great amusement perceived that he was considered likely to follow his father's example, and make love to them. Little Dolores, however, was less in bondage to propriety, and became very fond of him, making vain endeavours to pronounce "Cherry," and teaching him a great deal of Spanish. Miss Weston, who was a hearty enthusiastic woman, with rather an overpowering amount of conversation, approved of what she called his spirit of inquiry, and was possibly not insensible to his good looks and winning manners. He did not now shrink from home letters, and indeed spent more time than Alvar thought good for him in replying to Jack's voluminous disquisitions on his first weeks of Oxford. Alvar thought that he had entirely recovered his spirits, and indeed Cheriton was one whose "mind had a thousand eyes," and they let in a good deal of surface light, though he was himself well aware of colder, darker depths whose sun had set for ever, and which could only be reached by the slowly penetrating rays of a far intenser light. Though no word of direct confidence ever passed between him and Mr Stanforth, the latter knew perfectly well that mental as well as physical change had been sought in the sunny south. His health improved considerably, though with many ups and downs, he felt fairly well, and did not attempt to try the extent of his powers.

He was very anxious not to be a restraint on Alvar's intercourse with his friends or on his natural occupations; but except that he sometimes went to evening parties which Cheriton avoided, Alvar generally preferred escorting Gipsy and Miss Weston to the tops of all the buildings which Mr Stanforth sketched from below, or into every corner of the Alcazar, and every chapel of the cathedral, both of which places had a wonderful charm for Cheriton.

Miss Stanforth was allowed to make friends with Alvar's cousins. Carmen and Isabel. She had once gone to a fancy ball, dressed in a mantilla, and had been told that she looked "very Spanish," with her dark eyes and hair; a delusion from which she awoke the first time she saw her new friends dressed for church (they did not wear mantillas often on secular occasions); and great was their amusement at Gipsy's vain endeavour to give exactly the becoming twist to the black lace, and to flirt her fan in the approved style. Gipsy was a bit of a mimic, but she could not satisfy herself or them.

"It is of no use, Miss Stanforth," said Cheriton, when she complained to him of her difficulties. "Alvar does not like walking out with me in an 'Ulster' when the wind is cold, so he endeavoured to teach me to wear one of those marvellous cloaks which they all throw about their shoulders; but I can only get it over my head, and under my feet, and everywhere that it ought not to be."

"Well," said Alvar, "you would not let me go to Hazelby in my cloak; you said that the little boys would laugh at me."

"But a great coat," said Cherry, "is a rational kind of garment that can't look odd anywhere."

"That is as you think," said Alvar; "but I do not care what you wear, if you like it. You will not certainly look like a Spaniard even in the cloak."

"A great coat," said Mr Stanforth, "is one of those graceful garments which have commended themselves to all ages. I do not know what early tradition was followed by the inventors of Noah's Arks in the case of that patriarch—"

"Now, Mr Stanforth, that is too hard," interrupted Cherry. "At least it has pockets."

"So many," said Alvar, "that what you want is always in another one."

"Alvar, that cloak is your one weakness. You clung to it in England, and you put it on the moment you landed in Spain."

"Cheriton thinks it is a seal-skin," said Mr Stanforth smiling.

"Seal-skin," said Alvar. "No, it is cloth and silk."

"Did you never hear of the fisherman who married a mermaid, and she lived happily on shore till she fell in with a seal-skin; when she put it on, and, forgetting her husband and children, jumped into the sea, and never came up any more?"

"Ah, no!" said Alvar. "It is only that I want Cherry to be comfortable while he is down among the fishes."

"I will take to it some day, for the sake of astonishing Jack," said Cherry. "But, Alvar, those friends of yours last night were very much interested in my travelling coat, and asked me if it was a Paris fashion. They put it on, and I tried to get Don Manoel into it; but he thought it was a heretical sort of affair."

"Cherry, if you laugh at Manoel, he will think you insult him. He hates Englishmen, and our father especially. He was angry because you gave the jessamine to Isabel—and—we are polite here to each other; but if there is what you call a row, it is worse than when every one is sulky all at once at Oakby."

Cherry looked as if the temptation to provoke this new experience was nearly irresistible; but Alvar continued to Mr Stanforth,—

"I am glad that Cherito should laugh once more as he used to do; but my cousin does not understand."

"My dear Alvar, I will content myself with laughing at you; you always understand a joke, don't you?"

"I do not care if I understand or no. When I see you laughing," said Alvar simply, "that is good."

Something in this speech so touched Cheriton that his laughter softened away into a very doubtful smile, and he changed the subject; but he tried afterwards to propitiate Don Manoel by the most courteous treatment. The Spaniard did not respond, and he perceived that contending elements were discordant in Seville as well as in England.

Carmen and Isabel found novelty less distasteful. It is true that they thought Gipsy's free intercourse with their cousin Alvar and with the English stranger shocking; but they preferred them to any other subject of conversation, and Isabel in particular made quite a romance of the incident of the Cape Jessamine, and how Don Cherito had looked at her when he gave it to her.

"But why shouldn't he pick a bit of jessamine for you, if you couldn't reach it for yourself?" asked Gipsy.

"Oh, Manoel said it was an attention."

"Oh dear no," said Gipsy, rather cruelly, "we shouldn't think anything of it in England. Don Manoel needn't be afraid."

"Oh, but Manoel is terrible. He swore before Don Cherito came that he would poniard us if we, like our Aunt Maria, listened to a heretic, a stranger. For Don Giraldo was a wild wicked Englishman, but beautiful in the extreme; they have no religion, and no morals."

"Isabel!"

"Ah, I tell you what Manoel says. He came, he pretended an accident, and then Dona Maria married him. Now, he says it is the same with Don Cherito. An illness—"

"Any one can see that Cheriton Lester is really ill, at any rate."

"Well—Manoel was angry with my grandfather for letting him come, and he has told Alvar that it should be death before such a marriage. Alvar told him he knew nothing of his English brother, who loved an English lady. But Manoel says that what happened once might again happen."

"Isabel," said her sister, "it is wrong to talk of this. If Zingara repeats it, there will be a quarrel."

"I shall not repeat it," said Gipsy; "but it is all nonsense, I assure you."

"Ah," said Isabel, "Manoel knows not. He knows not that I love one whom I have seen at mass, though I know not his name. But with my fan I can show him—"

"Isabel!" again said the grave Carmen; while Gipsy, who was far too well bred and well brought up to have made signs in church with anything, thought that "mass" and "a signal with a fan" sounded interesting, and that what would have been highly unladylike at home was rather romantic in Seville.

On their side, Carmen and Isabel thought Gipsy hardly used in being kept away from the bull-fights, though she was too loyal to her nationality to express any wish to see them.

Don Manoel was a great lover of the ring, and as certain young bulls from Don Guzman's estate were to be brought forward at the last *corrida* of the season, there was a great desire that the Englishmen should be present. Mr Stanforth intended to avail himself of the chance of seeing such a spectacle, and Cheriton, Don Guzman said, might see one contest, and go away before the other bulls were brought forward, if he found the fatigue too much for him. They would get seats on the shady side of the bull-ring, the great amphitheatre said to be capable of holding ten thousand spectators.

Cheriton, who went against Alvar's wish, did not stay for the end, and Mr Stanforth went to see if he had repented of the rather perverse desire to prove himself capable of enduring the spectacle. He found him, still full of excitement, resting on a sofa in the *patio*; while Alvar sat near him, smoking, and looking cool and bored, as if the bull-fight had been a croquet party.

Mr Stanforth's entrance was rather inopportune, for Cherry was still too full of his impressions not to talk of them, and, in answer to Mr Stanforth's question, said eagerly,—

"Oh, the heat has tired me—that is nothing. But it made one feel like a fiend. I felt all the fascination of it—even the horror had a dreadful sort of attraction. I could not have come away if Alvar had not pulled me out when I was too dizzy to resist him."

"Very unwholesome fascination," said Mr Stanforth.

"Unwholesome! I should think so! It is abominable that such things should be. I tell Alvar that in his place I never would encourage an appeal to the worst passions of human nature."

"Well, you would go, *mi caro*. I told you you would not like it," said Alvar coolly.

"You should set an example of indignation!"

"I? I do not care what they do to amuse themselves. It does not interest me, as much, I think, as it did you, my brother."

"No," said Cherry slowly, "I understand a good many things by this. I should be as bad as any of them. But when a country encourages and allows such 'amusements,' when women look on and like it, one cannot wonder at Spanish cruelties. It appeals to everything that is bad in one."

"You insult my country and your hosts! Don Cherito, such language is unpardonable!" exclaimed an unexpected voice; and Don Manoel came suddenly forward from one of the curtained doorways, close at hand. "What right have you, señor, to speak of our ancient customs in terms like these?"

"I beg your pardon," said Cheriton, after a moment's pause of amazement, "if I have said anything to annoy you; but—I was not aware that you were present. I was speaking to my brother."

"Would you insinuate that I disguised my presence?" cried the Spaniard, with real rage in his tones, and a determination to show it.

Then Alvar fired up with the sudden passion that had always startled his English kindred.

"How dare you so address my brother! He shall say what he chooses!"

"He shall not—nor you either! You call yourself Spaniard—Andaluz— you claim rights in Seville, and listen with complacence to the cowardly scruples—"

Here Alvar broke in with much too rapid Spanish for the Englishmen to follow, interrupted as it was by Manoel's rejoinder, and by furious gestures as if the disputants were going to fly at each other's throats, while Mr Stanforth's mild attempts at interposing with—"Come—come now; what nonsense! What is all this about?" were entirely unheard.

Meanwhile, Cheriton's previous excitement cooled down completely. He got up from the sofa, and stepped between them, laying his hand on Alvar's arm.

"Excuse me, Alvar," he said, in his slow, careful Spanish, "this seems to be my affair. Señor Don Manoel, will you have the goodness to tell me why you are offended with me?"

"He called you a coward—you, my brother!"

"My dear fellow, be quiet, don't be an ass." (This in English for Alvar's benefit.) "Would you tell me what has provoked you?"

"Señor Don Cherito," said Manoel, forced to answer civilly by Cheriton's coolness—"first, did you mean to insinuate that I listened to your conversation with my cousin?"

"By no means," said Cherry. "I merely meant to say that I had not seen you."

"Then I ask you, señor, to repeat or to withdraw the remarks you made about the bull-fight," said Don Manoel, with the air of delivering an ultimatum.

"He will not withdraw them!" cried Alvar. "He is no coward!"

"I hope," said Cheriton, "I did nothing to offend. Were I in Don Manoel's place I should feel, I am sure, as he does. I, too, am attached to the customs of my country. It is no doubt difficult for a stranger to judge. If I said the sport was cruel, I did not for a moment mean to imply that—that—those who see it must be cruel. Excuse my bad Spanish. I cannot express myself, but—pray let us shake hands."

He smiled, and held out his hand.

"Well, señor, you are Don Guzman de la Rosa's guest. If this is meant for an apology—"

"For having offended you—yes. Being Don Guzman's guest, I could not quarrel with his nephew."

"I accept, the apology," said Don Manoel, with much solemnity, and accepting Cherry's hand.

"But," said Alvar, "you applied an expression to my brother."

"Oh, nonsense, Alvar; you know we never think of 'expressions' when we are angry; and I'm not aware of having had any opportunity of showing either cowardice or courage."

"H'm," said Mr Stanforth, in English, "a tolerably cool head, I think."

Don Manoel, who appeared to have made up his mind to be magnanimous, remarked that his expression had been used too hastily to a stranger; but that a true Spaniard would look on any scene with equanimity. Cherry's lip curved a little, as if he thought this a doubtful advantage; but he answered with a laugh,—

"I *am* a stranger, señor; and besides, I was fatigued."

"Ah," said Manoel, "that amounts to an entire excuse. The expression is withdrawn."

And with a profound bow to Cheriton, he went away, and Cherry burst out laughing.

"What in the world did all that mean?" he said. "Did I really offend his national pride by turning sick at the dying horses?"

"That is not all," said Alvar hurriedly; "he hates the English and us all; he would like to kill me."

"Ah, ha, Alvar, it is my turn to talk about 'excitement' now."

"Well, I do not understand you. When you came home you could not be still; you seemed crazy. And now, when any gentleman would be enraged, you laugh."

"Oh, I hate quarrels. And besides," shrugging his shoulders, "why in the world should I care for such mock-heroics as that?"

"Ah, Cherry," said Mr Stanforth, "there spoke the very essence of English scorn."

Cheriton coloured.

"True," he said, candidly, "Don Manoel had a right to be angry with me, after all. But I don't mean it. I dare say he isn't half a bad fellow."

"Ah, you are coughing. You will be tired out; and I am sure that you will not sleep," said Alvar. "Come, you shall not talk any more about anything."

"Very wise advice," said Mr Stanforth, "especially as Gipsy has persuaded the whole party to come to-morrow to see my sketches, and drink English 'afternoon tea.' So rest now in preparation."

Cheriton paid for his day's work by a bad night and much weariness. Don Manoel made very polite inquiries after him; but there was something in the atmosphere that, to quote Alvar, Cherry "did not understand."

Chapter Thirty
Nettie at Bay

"A child, and vain."

After the departure of the travellers, a period of exceeding flatness and dulness settled down on Oakby and its neighbourhood. The weather was dismal, one or two other neighbouring families were away, and no one thought it worth while to do anything. Jack had refused a congenial invitation, and conscientiously stayed at home "to make it cheerful," until he went up to Oxford; but, though he was too well conducted and successful not to be a satisfactory son, he and his father were not congenial, and never could think of anything to say to each other. He had outgrown companionship with Bob, and did not now get on very well with him; while Nettie was never sociable with any one but her twin. Mrs Lester, though very attentive to her son's dinners and other comforts, did not trouble herself much about the boys, and moreover did not possess the comfortable characteristic common to most elderly ladies—of being often to be found in one place. As Jack expressed it to himself, "no one was ever anywhere;" and prone as he was to look on the dark side of things, the thought that this was what home would be without Cherry, was perpetually before his mind. He did not like to go to Elderthwaite, and saw nothing of its inhabitants till one misty day early in October, as he was walking through the lanes with Rolla and Buffer at his heels, he came suddenly upon Virginia, leaning over a stile, and looking, not at the view, for there was none, but at the mist and the distant rain. Her figure, in its long waterproof cloak, under an arch of brown and yellow hazel boughs, had an indescribably forlorn aspect; but Jack, awkward fellow, was conscious of nothing but a sense of embarrassment and doubt what to say. She started and coloured up, but with greater self-possession spoke to him, and held out her hand.

"How d'ye do?" said Jack. "Down, Buffer, you're all over mud."

"Oh, never mind, I don't care, dear little fellow!" exclaimed Virginia, who would have hugged Buffer, mud and all, but for very shame. "I did not know you were at home, Jack."

"Yes, but I'm going to Oxford next week."

"And—and you have good accounts of Cherry?"

"Yes, pretty good, better than at first. He says that he looks better, and does not cough so much, and he likes it,—so he says, at least," replied Jack, who, conceiving that propriety precluded the mention of Alvar's name, found his personal pronouns puzzling.

"I am *very* glad," said Virginia softly.

"Yes, I suppose they are at Seville by this time; they stayed at San José till Cherry was stronger. Al—he—they thought it best."

"Your eldest brother would be very careful of him, I am sure," said Virginia, with a gentle dignity that reassured Jack, though she blushed deeply.

"Yes," he said more freely, "and they have made some friends; Mr Stanforth, the artist, you know, and his daughter; they're very nice people, and they have been learning Spanish together. He writes in *very* good spirits," concluded Jack viciously, and referring to Cherry, though poor Virginia's imagination supplied another antecedent.

"I am glad to hear it," she said. "*I* met that Miss Stanforth once. She was a pretty, dark-eyed child then. Good-bye, Jack, I am going soon to stay with my cousin Ruth."

"Good-bye," said Jack, with a scowl which she could not account for. "I hope you'll enjoy yourself."

"Good-bye; good-bye, Buffer."

Jack took his way home through the wet shrubberies. He felt sorry for Virginia, whom he regarded as injured by Alvar, but he thought that she ought to be angry with Ruth, never supposing that the latter's delinquencies were unknown to her.

As he walked on he passed by a cart shed belonging to a small farm of his father's above which was a hay loft, reached by a step ladder, to the foot of which Buffer and Rolla both rushed, barking rapturously, and trying to get up the ladder.

"Hullo! what's up?—rats, I suppose," thought Jack; and mounting two or three steps of the very rickety ladder, he looked into the loft, his chin on a level with the floor. Suddenly a blinding heap of hay was flung over his head; there was a scuffle and a rush, and Jack freed himself from the hay to find his head in Nettie's very vigorous embrace; and to see Dick Seyton swing himself down from the window of the loft and run away.

"Stop, I say. Nettie, let go, what are you doing here? Dick, stop, I say," cried Jack, scrambling up the ladder and rushing to the window; but Dick had vanished.

"Don't stamp, Jack, you'll come through; you should have run after him," said Nettie saucily.

Jack turned, but caught his foot in a hole and fell headlong into the hay, while Nettie sat and laughed at him, and the dogs howled at the foot of the ladder.

Jack picked himself up cautiously, and sitting down on the hay, for there was hardly room for him to stand upright, said severely,—

"Now, Nettie, what is the meaning of this?"

"The meaning of what?"

"Of your being here with Dick. I told you in the summer that I didn't approve of your being so friendly with him, and now I insist on knowing at once what you were doing with him."

"Well, then, I shan't tell you," said Nettie coolly.

"I say you shall. I couldn't have believed that my sister would be so unladylike. Just tell me how often you have met him, and what you were doing here?"

"It's no business of yours," said Nettie, making a sudden rush at the ladder; but Jack caught her, and a struggle ensued, in which of course he had the upper hand, though she was strong enough to make a considerable resistance; and he felt the absurdity of fighting with her as if she were a naughty child, when her offence was of such a nature.

"Now, Nettie," he said, in a tone that she could not resist. "Stop this nonsense. I mean to have an answer. What has induced you to meet Dick Seyton in secret, and how often have you done so? You can't deny that you have."

"No," said Nettie, "I have, often, and I shall ever so many times more."

"I couldn't have believed it of you, Nettie," said Jack, so seriously and so mildly that Nettie looked quite frightened, and then exclaimed,—

"Jack, if you dare to venture to think that I meet Dick that we may make love to each other, or any nonsense of that kind, I'll—I'll kill you—I'll never speak to you again, *never!*"

"Why—why what else can I think?" said Jack, blushing, and by far the more shamefaced of the two.

"Well, then, it's abominable and shameful of you. Do you think I would be so horrid? As if I ever meant to marry any one. I shall live with Bob."

"Don't be so violent, Nettie. You have acted very deceitfully."

"Deceitfully! Do you think I'd tell you a story?"

As Nettie had never been known to "tell a story" in her life, Jack could not say that he thought she would; but he replied, —

"You *have* acted deceitfully. You have run after Dick when we all thought you were somewhere else, and—there's no use in being in a passion—but what do you suppose any one would think of a girl who behaved in such a manner?"

Nettie blushed, but answered, —

"I can't help what any one thinks, Jack. I know I'm right, and I must go on doing it."

"Indeed you won't," said Jack angrily; "for unless you promise never to meet him any more, I shall tell father at once that I found you here. What do you think Cherry would say to you?"

"Cherry would say I was perfectly right, and would do *exactly* the same thing himself," said Nettie, triumphantly. "I am not doing any harm; and I must go on. I can't tell you why I am doing it, because I promised not, and I'll do it nearer home if you like it better. Bob and I quarrelled about it many a time, *he* knows."

"Oh, he knows, does he? What a fool he must have been to let you do it."

"He won't tell of me," said Nettie, "and he never did let me when he was at home. But I am not a silly, horrid girl, Jack, whatever you think; and I'm not flirting with Dick, nor—nor—engaged to him; and when—when—it's right, I don't mind people thinking so!"

But this speech ended in a flood of tears, as poor Nettie's latent maidenliness began to assert itself.

"And pray," said Jack, "does Dick come after you because it's right?"

"No—no," sobbed Nettie; "because I make him."

"And how can you *make* him, I should like to know?"

Nettie made no answer but renewed tears. At last she sobbed out, "Oh, Jack, Jack, I wish you were Cherry!"

"I wish I were with all my heart," said Jack. "Would you tell me if I were Cherry?"

"No; but I know *he* would be kind, and not think me horrid."

"Well, Nettie, I'll try to be kind; but you frighten me by all this. Now just listen. I believe I ought to tell father directly."

"Oh, Jack! dear Jack! Don't, don't—it would be dreadful! Don't you believe me?"

"Yes," said Jack, "I believe you; but how do I know about a young scamp like Dick? You tell me the whole truth, and then I can judge, or I shall tell my father this moment. You're my sister, and I shall take care of you. You've done a thing that may be told against you all your life, and nothing can make it right, say what you will."

"But I *can't* tell you, Jack; I've promised."

"Well, then, I shall have it out first with Dick."

"Oh, Jack, everything will be undone then!"

"And pray, if you don't care about him, why does it matter to you so much about him?"

"Indeed—indeed, Jack, I'm not in love with him in the least. I never was with anybody, and I never mean to be," said Nettie, fixing her great blue eyes full on Jack, and speaking with convincing eagerness.

"And how about him?" said Jack crossly.

"No, it's nothing to do with it," said Nettie; but the tone of her voice altered a little, and Jack had a sort of feeling that there was more in the matter than she herself knew, for he never thought of disbelieving her.

"Will you tell, and will you promise?" he said.

"No, I won't," said Nettie.

"Then you are a very naughty, disobedient girl, and you shall come home with me this minute."

"I hate you, Jack. I'll never forgive you," said Nettie passionately, as she followed him; and all the way home she sobbed and pouted, with an intolerable sense of shame, while Jack, utterly puzzled, walked by her side, a desire to horsewhip Dick Seyton contending in his mind with a dread of making a row.

They came in by the back-door, and Nettie rushed upstairs at once; while Jack, virtuous and resolute, went into the study.

Resolute as the girl was, she listened trembling, till her father's loud call of "Nettie, Nettie, come here this moment!" brought her down to the study, where were her father, her grandmother, and Jack.

"Eh, what's all this, Nettie?" said Mr Lester. "I can't have you running about the country with young Seyton. What's the meaning of it?"

"Papa," said Nettie, "I haven't run about the country. Dick and I have got a secret; it's a very good secret."

"Well, what is it, then?" said her father.

"I don't mean to tell. I never tell secrets," said Nettie, with determination. "We have had it a long time."

"My dear," said Mr Lester, much more mildly than he would have spoken to any of his boys, "I must put an end to it. You have been running wild with your brothers till you forget how big a girl you are getting. Never go out with Dick again by yourself—do you hear?"

Nettie made no answer, and her father continued, more sternly,—

"I am sorry, Nettie, that you did not know better how to behave. Never let me hear of such a thing again."

Still silence; and Jack said,—

"She won't promise. I shall see what Dick says about it."

"Then you'll just do nothing of the sort, Jack," said his grandmother, "making mountains out of mole-hills. Nettie is going to London to stay with her aunt Cheriton, and have some music and French lessons with Dolly and Kate. I'd settled it all this morning. She doesn't attend enough to her studies here. You'll take her up when you go to Oxford, and there'll be an end of the matter."

"Yes, yes," said Mr Lester. "Grandmamma and I were talking it over just now."

"Not that it is on account of your remarks, Jack," said Mrs Lester. "That would be making far too much of her foolish behaviour; but in London she'll learn better."

"To be sure," said Mr Lester, who had been stopped on his way out riding by Jack's appeal, and was now glad to escape from an unpleasant discussion. "Nettie will come back at Christmas, and we shall hear no more of such childish tricks."

Nettie looked like a statue, and never spoke a word; but there was a look of fright through all her sullenness. Jack was not accustomed to think much of her appearance, but he knew as a matter of fact that she was handsome, and it struck him forcibly that she looked "grown-up."

"You've done more harm than you know," she said; "but I will not tell, and I will not promise." And with a sort of dignity in her air, she walked out of the room.

"What does she mean?" said Jack.

"Never you mind," said his grandmother, "and don't you raise the countryside on her by saying a word to Dick or any one. Hold your tongue, and be thankful. The Seytons are the plague of the place, and we'll ask them all to dinner before Nettie goes, Dick included."

"Ask them to dinner?" said Jack.

"Yes; we'll have no talk of a quarrel. And besides, your father finds that people are apt to think that it was Virginia's fault that your half-brother left her in the lurch; and that's not so, though she *is* a Seyton."

"No, indeed!"

"So my son means to have a dinner-party, and to show that we are all good friends, and pay them proper attention. A bad lot they are; there's not one of them to be trusted."

"But, Granny," said Jack anxiously, "what do you think about Nettie? What secret can she have?"

"Eh, I can't tell. He may be getting her a puppy or a creature of some kind; but Nettie's secret may be one and Dick's another. I always blamed Cherry for encouraging the Seytons about the place."

"Poor Cherry!" muttered Jack to himself, with a great longing to throw the burden of his difficulty on to Cherry's shoulders.

Nettie remained sullen and impenetrable. She treated Jack with an intense resentment that vexed him more than he could have supposed. Neither her father nor her grandmother asked her any questions; but she was watched, though not palpably in disgrace, and she suffered from an agony of shame and of self-reproach which contended strangely with the motive that in her view justified the stolen meetings. Whether her womanly instincts, roughly awakened, justified the warnings given her, or whether, she merely resented the unjust suspicion, she herself scarcely knew, and not for worlds would she have explained her feelings. The dread of giving an advantage, the intense sulky self-respect that leads to an exaggeration of reserve and false shame, was in her nature as in that of all the Lesters, and if Cheriton had been present she could not probably have uttered a word to him. Being absent, she could venture to soften at the thought of him, and cried for him many a time in secret.

Chapter Thirty One
Broken Links

"Love is made a vague regret."

Virginia, when she parted from Jack, walked slowly homewards through the mist and the falling leaves, and thought of the bloom and the brightness of that fair Seville which she had so often pictured to herself. How happy the two brothers would be there together, among all the surroundings which she had heard described so often! Alvar would never think of her. "At least, I should have had letters from him if I had not sent him away," she thought; and though she did not regret the parting in the sense of blaming herself for it, she felt in her utter desolation as if she had rather have had her lover cold and indifferent than not have him at all.

For life was so dreary, home so wretched, and Virginia could not mend it. Indeed in many ways a less high-minded girl with stronger spirits and more tact might have been far more useful there. Virginia held her tongue resolutely; but she could not shut her eyes. She had lost her bearings, and could not possibly understand the proportion of things. Thus even in her inmost soul she never blamed her father for his life-long extravagance, for the vague stories of his dissipated youth—these things were not for her to judge; but the conversation, which he intended to be perfectly fit for her ears, was full of small prejudices, small injustices, and trifles taken for granted that grated on her every hour. She tried very hard to be gentle and pleasant to her aunt; but she could not bring herself, as Ruth could, to laugh at scandalous stories, old or new, or even to think herself right in listening to them. And though her father and aunt *so far as they knew how*, respected her innocence, the latter only laughed at the ignorance that thought one thing as bad as another. For there *were* virtues, or at least self-denials in their lives, for which, with all her love and with all her charity, she could not possibly credit them. It was something that Mr Seyton had pulled through without utterly succumbing to debt and difficulty, it was something that when writhing under an injury which she never forgot or forgave, his sister stuck to him and kept things as straight as they were. It was a godless, idle, aimless household, above stairs and below; but it was not a scandalous one, and, with all the antecedents, it easily might have been. But the obvious outcome of this hard narrow life was a deadness to all outer or higher interests, an ignorance of the ordinary views of society, and of modern forms of thought never attained save by selfish people, an absence of restraint of temper, a delight in utter littleness, which were intensely wearying. Higher principles would have made life more interesting if nothing more. The narrowest form of belief in religion and goodness would have given a wider outlook. Virginia was sick to death of tales of little local incidents spiced with ill-nature, or incessant complaints of someone's ill-behaviour about a fence or a cow. If she had lived at Oakby she would have heard a good deal of the same sort of thing; but there there would have been something else to fall back on, and she would not have heard small triumphs over small overreaching, which Mr Seyton did not mix enough with his kind to hear commented on.

Virginia used to wonder if she would grow like her aunt, her life was so empty. All her young-lady interests, the essay and drawing clubs, the correspondence and the art needlework, with which like other girls she had amused herself, had languished entirely during her engagement, and she did not care to resume them. She would have liked to be a resource to Dick; but she was not used to boys, and had not much faculty for amusing them, and Dick did not care for her. Her Sunday class tired her, and were naughty because her teaching was languid; the children by no means offering the consolations to her depression which they are sometimes represented as doing in fiction. The Ellesmeres, who were always kind to her, were away for their annual holiday, and the library books for which she subscribed, and which might have amused her, could never, by any chance be fetched from the station when she wanted them.

Her uncle showed his sympathy by scolding her roundly for fretting for a black-eyed foreigner, till she was almost too angry to speak to him.

Under all these circumstances Ruth's urgent invitation had been welcome, and as she received others from her friends at Littleton, she resolved to go and try to pick up the threads that Alvar had broken. Soon after she parted with Jack she met the Parson, and told him what she knew would be welcome news, that Cherry was better. "Ay," said Mr Seyton, "Jack brought me a message from him that he would write me an account of a bull-fight. Wonder he's not ashamed to go near one. Cruel, unmanly sport—disgraceful!"

"Well, uncle," said Virginia, "I think you ought to be pleased that Cherry is well enough to go."

"Eh? I'll ask him if he'll come and see a cock-fight when he comes home. Plenty of 'em here—round the corner. So you're going to London to get a little colour in your cheeks, I think it's time."

"Yes, uncle; Mrs Clement will teach the children while I'm away."

"Very well, and tell Miss Ruth she was blind of one eye when she made her choice, but *I* can see out of both."

"Uncle, I shouldn't think of telling her such a thing. What do you mean?"

"Never mind, she'll understand me. Good-bye, my dear, and never mind the Frenchman."

Virginia smiled, but she could not turn her thoughts away, not merely from Alvar, but from her life without him. Fain would she have refused the invitation which soon arrived to a solemn dinner-party at Oakby; but it had been accompanied by a hint from Mr Lester to her aunt which caused the latter to insist on accepting it, and they went accordingly to meet Sir John and Lady Hubbard, and one or two other neighbours. Mr Lester was markedly polite to Virginia. Mrs Lester wore her best black velvet, and a certain diamond brooch, only produced on occasions of state. Jack looked proper, silent, and bored. Every one wished to ask after the universally popular Cheriton, but felt that Alvar was an awkward subject of conversation, so that the adventures of the travellers could not be used to enliven the dulness. Nettie did not of course appear at dinner, and afterwards sat in a corner of the drawing-room in her white muslin, apparently determined not to open her mouth. Dick strolled up to her when the gentlemen came in, and was instantly followed by Jack, who stood by her silent and frowning. Nettie looked up under her eyebrows, and said, "Dick, I am going to London."

"So I hear," said Dick, with a smile and a slight shrug.

"I hate it, but I can't help it. *You go on.*"

Dick smiled again and nodded, and then looked at Jack with an air of secret amusement, indescribably provoking. "All right," he said, but he turned away and made no further demonstration; and Mrs Lester desired Nettie to show Miss Hubbard "Views on the Rhine," a very handsome book reserved for occasions of unusual dulness.

Altogether the evening did not raise Virginia's spirits, and she was half inclined to resent the special kindness shown to her by Mr Lester, as implying blame to his absent son.

It was a wonderful change of scene and circumstance, when she found herself, some few days later, sitting in Lady Charlton's pleasant London drawing-room, full of books, work, plants, and pretty things, with Ruth, bright-eyed and blooming, sitting on the rug at her feet, ready for a confidential chatter.

She was to be married directly after Christmas, she told Virginia. Rupert did not mean to sell out of the army; she did not at all dislike the notion of moving about for a few years, and now the regiment was at Aldershot she could see Rupert often while she remained in London to get her things.

"And, Queenie, you must choose the dresses for the bridesmaids. Grandmamma will have a gay wedding. *I* think it will be a great bore."

"Your bridesmaids ought to wear something warm and gay and bright, like yourself, Ruthie. Are you going to ask Nettie Lester?"

"Oh, no!" said Ruth hurriedly. "Why should I?"

"She is Rupert's cousin, and she is so handsome."

"I never thought of her! I am angry with them all since Don Alvar has made you miserable. My darling Queenie, I should like to stamp on him! Now, don't be angry; but tell me how it all came about?"

"I don't think I could ever make you understand it, Ruth. He did nothing wrong. It was only that—that I did not suit him, and I found it out," said Virginia, with a sort of ache in her voice, as she turned her head away.

"The more—well, I won't finish the sentence. Any way, he has spoiled your life for you; for I am afraid he is *your* love if you are not his," said Ruth, scanning her sad face curiously. "Queenie, weren't you ready to kill him and Cherry, too, when they went off comfortably together?"

"No," said Virginia, "he could not help going—*that* was not it. And as for Cherry, he was the only person who understood anything about it—he was so kind! Oh, I hope he is really better!"

"I dare say he is, by this time," said Ruth, rather oddly; "but they are all so easily frightened about him—they spoil him. I wonder what they would all say if *he* fell in love with a naughty, wicked siren—a female villain, who broke his heart for him—just for fun."

"She would break something worth having," said Virginia indignantly. "But, do you know anything about Cherry, Ruth?"

"I? I don't believe in sirens who break hearts just for fun and vanity. And as for Cherry, if he did meet with a little trouble, he'd mend up again, heart and lungs and all. There's something happy-go-lucky about him— don't you think so?"

"I think Cherry is too many-sided to be left without an object in life, if that is what you mean," said Virginia. "Besides, it is so different for a man, they can always do something."

Then Ruth put aside the little uneasy feeling of self-reproach and doubt that had prompted her to talk about Cherry, and put her arms round Virginia, kissing her tenderly.

"My darling Queenie! You have been fretting all by yourself at Elderthwaite till things seem worse than they are."

"No," said Virginia; "but my life has all gone wrong. When I found that he did not love me everything seemed over for me."

Ruth interposed a question, and at last acquired a clearer knowledge of the circumstances under which Alvar and her cousin had parted. She had a good deal of knowledge of the world, and some judgment, though she did not always use it for her own benefit, and she did not think that the case sounded hopeless. She tried an experiment.

"If you gave him up, Queenie, because you discovered that he did not come up to your notions of what he ought to be, why there's an end of it, for he never will; but it looks to me much more like a very commonplace lovers' quarrel aggravated by circumstances. He isn't a bad sort of fellow in his own way; but it's not the way that you think perfection."

"I did not quarrel with him, and I think the failure was in myself. Why should he love me?—it does not seem as if I was very lovable."

There crossed Virginia's young gentle face a look that was like a foretaste of the bitterness and self-weariness that had seized on so many of her race—a sort of self-scorn that was not wholesome.

"Why should you think so?" said Ruth.

"I think I should have got on better at home if I had been."

She spoke humbly enough, but there was utter discouragement in every line of her face and figure.

"Nonsense!" said Ruth briskly. "Nobody would get on, in your sense, at Elderthwaite. I don't think you ought to stay there. You know it is quite in your power to arrange differently. You might make them long visits and—come fresh to every one."

"I'll never have it said that I could not live there," said Virginia, colouring deeply. "And if I was away—I could not.—I would not—"

"Go back into the neighbourhood? Well, at any rate you are going to have a holiday now, and see something besides moors and mud."

The change of scene could not fail to do Virginia good, though there might be something in the courtship of Ruth and Rupert to remind her, with a difference, of her own. It was sometimes breezy, for Rupert loved to tease his betrothed, and having got his will, was a free-and-easy and contented lover, not much liking to be put out of his way, and not quite coming up to Ruth's requirements.

Ruth, though very kind to her cousin, believed that she had lost her lover in great measure through a feminine scrupulosity and desire to bring him up to her own standard. Ruth would never be so narrow and unsympathetic, *she* would be prepared to understand *all* the story of her hero's life; and being young, and much more simple than she believed herself to be, thought that her indiscriminate reading of somewhat free-spoken novels, gave her the necessary experience. But Rupert took quite another view. He was not aware of having any particular story to tell, and had no intention whatever of telling it. He did not in the least desire Ruth's sympathy with his past, which was quite commonplace. He was not in a state of repentance, desirous of making a confession; nor had his heart ever been withered up by any frightful experiences. No doubt he could remember much that was not particularly creditable, and which he rightly thought unfit for discussion with his betrothed. Moreover, he did not care at all for poetry, and very little for novels, and at last actually told her that one she mentioned was unfit for her to read.

Ruth was very angry, and had a sense of being put aside. Had Rupert— like herself—a secret, or was she going to be "only a little dearer than his horse?" as she expressed it to herself, and with tears to him. Rupert laughed, and then grew a little angry, and then they made it up again; but he teased her for her romance, laughed at her most muscular and strong-souled heroes, and never would put himself in a heroic attitude. Ruth quarrelled with him, made it up with him, was vexed by him, and sometimes was vexatious; but all the while she never told him about Cheriton.

Chapter Thirty Two
Don Juan

"I wonder if the spring-tide of this year
Will bring another spring both lost and dear;
If heart and spirit will find out their spring,
Or if the world *alone* will bud and sing."

It was a bright sunny day in December, fresh enough to make the Sevillanos pull their picturesque cloaks over their shoulders out of doors, and light scraps of wood-fire in their sitting-rooms, but with the sun pouring down in unveiled splendour over quaint painted relics of a bygone world, when the Moor employed his rich fancy in decorating the city, and over dark Gothic arches and towers that seemed to tell of a life almost equally remote from nineteenth-century England. It was a very new sort of Christmas weather for Jack Lester as he tried to find his way from the railway station to Don Guzman de la Rosa's house. He soon discovered that he had lost it, and stopped by a fruit-stall piled with grapes, oranges, and melons to ask the brown, skinny old woman in a gay handkerchief who kept it, for some directions, hoping that she would at least understand the name of the street. So she did, but it seemed to him that she pointed in every direction at once, and Jack stared round bewildered as a young lady stepped across the street towards the fruit-stall. Jack looked at her and she looked full at him from under her straw hat, with a pair of eyes dark as any in Andalusia, but direct and clear, level and fearless, as her face broke into a smile just saved from a laugh.

"If you are looking for Don Guzman de la Rosa's," she said in distinct and comprehensible English, "I can direct you; but your brothers, Mr Lester, are much nearer, at my father's, Mr Stanforth's. Will you come there with me when I have bought some fruit?"

"Oh, thank you immensely! I—I thought I would walk up, and I couldn't find the way. Thank you," said Jack, colouring and looking rather foolish.

"They did not expect you to be here till to-morrow. What have you done with your things?"

"I've lost them, Miss Stanforth," said Jack; "I can't think how. You see no one understands anything, and the stations coming from Madrid are so odd."

"Oh, I think you will get them; we had one box detained for ages. Thank you," as he took her basket of fruit. "Shall we come?" and then, looking up at him, "Your brother is so much better."

"I—I am very glad of that," said Jack, in a sort of inadequate way.

He was nervous about the meeting, and felt conscious that he was dusty with his journey, and sure that he must have looked foolish staring at the old woman.

Gipsy took him down the street, and into a house with a balcony covered with gay-striped blinds, and led him upstairs till she came to a door, or rather curtain, which she lifted, putting her finger on her lip.

It was a long, low room, with the lights carefully arranged and shaded, containing drawing-boards and unframed sketches, a wonderful heap of "art treasures," in one corner, Algerine scarves and stuffs, great, rough, green pitchers, and odds and ends of colour. Some one sat with his back to the door drawing, but Jack only beheld his brothers who were together at the further end of the room, and did not immediately see him, for they were looking at each other and appeared to the puzzled Jack oddly still and silent.

Miss Stanforth gave a little laugh, and Alvar looked round and exclaimed. Cheriton sprang up, and with a cry of delight seized on Jack, with an outburst of greetings and inquiries, in which all the surroundings were forgotten. Gipsy laughingly described her encounter to Alvar; while "father," and "granny," "the old parson," "no good in having a Christmas at all at home without you," passed rapidly between the other two.

"Come, Jack, that's strong! But, indeed, I think you have brought Christmas here. How rude we are! You have never spoken to Mr Stanforth. Mr Stanforth, let him see the picture. Jack, do you think father will like it?"

"Yes. You look much jollier than in the photograph," said Jack, as Mr Stanforth turned the picture round for his inspection.

It was a small half-length in tinted chalk showing Cherry seated and looking up, with a bright interested face, at Alvar, who was showing him a branch of pomegranates. The execution was of the slightest, but the likenesses were good, and the strong contrast of colouring and resemblance of form was brought out well. "*Brothers*," was written underneath, and Jack looked at them as if the idea of any one wishing to make studies of them was strange to him.

"Jack is bewildered—lost, in more senses than one," said Cherry, smiling.

"Come, it is time we went home, and then for news of every one! Mr Stanforth, we shall see you to-night."

Jack's arrival was an intense pleasure to Cheriton, whose reviving faculties were beginning to long for their old interests. He had recovered his natural spirits, and though he still looked delicate, and had no strength to spare, was quite well enough to look forward to his return to England and to beginning life there. Indeed the ardent hopes and ambitions, so cruelly checked in their first outlet, turned—with a difference indeed, but with considerable force—to the desire of distinction and success; and in return for Jack's endless talk of home and Oxford, he planned the course of study to begin at Easter, and the hard work which he felt sure with patience must ensure good fortune. Cheriton was very sanguine, and since he had felt so much better, had no doubt of entire recovery; and Jack was accustomed to follow his lead, and was much relieved both by his liveliness and by his resolute mention of Rupert, and inquiry as to the arrangements for his marriage.

If Cheriton had not won the battle, he was at least holding his own in it bravely—the bitter pain was first submitted to, and then held down with a strong hand. But surely, he thought, there was *something* in store for him, if not the sweetness of happy love, yet the ardour of the struggle of life.

He could not say enough of Alvar's care for him, and Jack found Alvar much more easy of access than at home, and more interested than he had expected in the details of the home life; and in the course of conversation the dinner-party to the Seytons, and its motive, came out.

Alvar coloured deeply; he was silent then, but as soon as he was alone with Cheriton he said with some hurry of manner,—

"My brother, I am ashamed. What can I do? It is not endurable to me that any one should blame Miss Seyton."

"I suppose my father did the only thing there was to be done. When an engagement is broken people generally say that there were faults on both sides."

"That is not so," said Alvar. "She is as blameless as a lily. Can I do nothing? I am ashamed," he repeated vehemently.

"Perhaps when you go home you will be able to show the world that you are of a different opinion," said Cherry very quietly, but with difficulty suppressing a smile.

"You do not understand," said Alvar in a tone of displeasure, turning away, and thinking that he had never before known Cheriton so unsympathetic.

Jack did not make much way with the de la Rosas, he did not like committing himself to foreign languages, and was shy, but they were very polite to "Don Juan," a name that so tickled Cheriton's fancy that he adopted it at once.

Jack began by somewhat resenting his brother's intimacy with the Stanforths as a strange and unnecessary novelty, but he soon fell under the charm, and pursued Mr Stanforth with theories of art which were received with plenty of good-humoured banter. Gipsy, too, set to work to enlighten him on Spanish customs; and having rescued him from one difficulty, made it her business to show him the way he should go, so that they became very friendly, and the strange Christmas in this foreign country drew the little party of English closer together. There was enough to interest them in the curious and picturesque customs of Andalusia, but the carols which Gipsy insisted on getting up gave Cherry a fit of home-sickness; and a great longing for Oakby, and the holly and the snow, the familiar occupations, the dogs, and the skating came over him. It had been a long absence; he thought how his father would be wishing for him, and he experienced that sudden doubt of the future which people call presentiment. Would he ever spend Christmas *at home* again? He was beginning to weary a little of the wonder and admiration that had stood him in such good stead, and to want the time-honoured landmarks which showed themselves unchanged as the flood-tide of passion subsided.

He was quite ready, however, to enter into the plans for a tour through some of the neighbouring towns before the Stanforths should return home at the end of January. Jack's time was still shorter; and as Cheriton himself had hitherto seen nothing but Seville, a joint expedition was proposed, with liberty to separate whenever it was convenient, as Alvar would consent to nothing that involved Cherry in long days on horseback lasting after sundown, or in extra rough living; and Mr Stanforth backed up his prudent counsels.

But Cordova, Granada, and Malaga could be managed without any extreme fatigue, and Ronda could be reached easily from the latter place. So in the first week in the new year the three Lesters, Mr Stanforth and his daughter, and Miss Weston set off together for a fortnight's trip. Afterwards they would all separate, and Alvar and Cheriton, after returning for a few weeks to Seville, were to make their way gradually northwards, stopping in France and Italy till the spring was further advanced.

The tour prospered, and in due time they found themselves at Ronda, and strolling out together in the lovely afternoon sunshine, reached the new bridge across the river; Jack and Gipsy engaged in an endless discussion on the expulsion of the Moors, lingering while they talked, and looking down into the deep volcanic chasm that divides the old town of Ronda from the new, while nearly three hundred feet below them roared, dashed, and sparkled the silvery waters of the Guadalvin. On either side were the picturesque buildings of the two towns, fringed with wood—in front, miles of orchards, and beyond, the magnificent snow-crowned mountains of the Sierra; while over all was the sapphire blue, and sun, which, though the year was but a fortnight old, covered the ground with jonquils, and hung the woods with lovely flowers hardly known to our hothouses.

They had marvelled at the Alhambra, and Cheriton had disclaimed all sense of feeling himself in the Crystal Palace. They had noticed and admired the mixture of Moorish and Christian art in Granada and Cordova, and had discussed ardently all the difficult questions of the Moorish occupation and expulsion—discussions in which Gipsy's fresh school knowledge, and Jack's ponderous theories, had met in many a hearty conflict. They had sketched, made notes, collected curiosities, or simply enjoyed the beauty according to their several idiosyncrasies, and had remained good friends through all the ups and downs of travel; while Cheriton had stood the fatigue so well that he had set his heart on riding with the others across country to Seville, and could afford to laugh at the discomforts incidental to eating and sleeping at Ronda. There was much to see there, and they did not mean to hurry away. Cherry remarked to Alvar that Jack had improved, and was less sententious than he used to be; but the cause of this increased geniality had struck no one. Every one laughed when Gipsy reminded him of things that he had forgotten, talked Spanish for him because he was too shy to commit himself to an unknown tongue, and stoutly contradicted many of his favourite sentiments. Writing an essay, was he? on the evil of regarding everything from a ludicrous point of view. There were a great many cases in which that was the best point of view to look at things, and Gipsy wrote a counter essay which afforded great amusement. But no one perceived when Gipsy's sense of the ludicrous fell a little into abeyance; and when she ceased to contradict Jack flatly, and began to think that she received new ideas from him, still less did his brothers dream of the new thoughts and aspirations that were rushing confusedly through the boy's mind; he was hardly conscious of them himself.

The pair were a little ahead of their companions, who now came up and joined them.

"Well, Jack," said Alvar, "I have been making inquiries, and I find that we can take the excursion among the mountains that you wished for. Mr Stanforth prefers making sketches here, and it would be too rough for the ladies, or for Cherry."

"I suppose the mountains *are* very fine?" said Jack, not very energetically.

"Jack found the four hundred Moorish steps too much for him. He has grown lazy," said Cherry. "For my part, I think the fruit market is the nicest place here; it has such a splendid view. I shall go there to-morrow and eat melons while you are away."

"Miss Weston and I are going to buy scarves and curiosities in the market," said Gipsy; "but they say we should have come here in May to see the great fair; that is the time to buy beautiful things."

"Yes," said Alvar, "and Mr Stanforth might have studied all the costumes of Andalusia. But, I think, since we ordered our dinner two hours ago, it is likely now to be ready. I hope the ladies are not tired of fried pork, for I do not think we shall get anything better."

"Oh!" said Gipsy, "I mean to get mamma to introduce it at home; it is so good."

"Do you, my dear?" said her father. "I am inclined to think that with the ordinary accompaniments of clean tablecloths and silver forks it might be disappointing."

Without a table-cloth and with the very primitive implements of Ronda, the fried pork was very welcome; and when their dinner was over, as it was too dark to go out any more, they went down into the great public room on the ground floor of the inn, where round a bright wood-fire were gathered muleteers, other travellers and natives, both men and women.

It was a wonderful picturesque scene in the light of the fire, and Mr Stanforth's sketching so delighted his subjects that they crowded round him, only anxious that he should draw them all, while the "English hidalgos" were objects of the greatest curiosity. The men came up to Jack and Cheriton, examining their clothes, their tobacco pouches and pipes; and one great fellow in a high hat, and brilliant-coloured shirt, looking so much like an ideal brigand that it was difficult to believe that he was only an olive-grower, after looking at Cheriton for some time, put out a very dirty hand, and touched his hair and cheek as if to assure himself that they were of the same substance as his own. Gipsy's dress and demeanour interested them greatly, and one or two of them made her write her name on a bit of paper for them to keep.

The next day's ride was fully discussed, and much information given as to route and destination. Then, at Cherry's request, some of the muleteers sang to them wild half-melancholy airs, and one of the men danced a species of comic dance for their edification, and then the chief musician diffidently requested them to give a specimen of *their* national music. Gipsy laughed and looked shy; but her father laid down his pencil, and in a fine voice, and with feeling that told even in an unknown language, sang "Tom Bowling," and then, as this gave great satisfaction, began "D'ye ken John Peel," in the chorus of which his companions joined him.

"That," he explained, "was a hunting song. Now he would give them a really national air;" and in the midst of this strange audience, he struck up the familiar notes of "God save the Queen."

The English rose to their feet; the men lifted their hats, and all joined in and sang the old words with more patriotic fervour than at home they might have thought themselves capable of; and the Spaniards, with quick wit and ready courtesy, uncovered also, and when they had finished the musician picked out the notes on his guitar.

The weather next morning proving all that could be wished, Alvar and Jack, with a couple of guides, set off before daybreak on their ride into the mountains, intending to ascend on foot a certain peak from which the view was very fine, and which was accessible in the winter. The expedition had been entirely planned for Jack's benefit, and perhaps he was not quite so grateful as he might have been. The others had no lack of occupation. They went down to the "Nereid's Grotto," a cave filled with clear emerald water, near which stand an old Moorish mill, built on rocks, fringed with masses of maidenhair fern. Mr Stanforth remained there sketching the building, white with a sort of dazzling eastern whiteness, the strange forms of cactus and aloe crowning the cliffs, and the washerwomen in gay handkerchiefs and scarlet petticoats kneeling on the flat stones by the river. Cheriton, with the ladies, went on their shopping expedition to find presents that might be sent home by Jack, and having found some silk handkerchiefs for his father, a wonderful sash for Nettie, and a striped rug for his grandmother, to whom Alvar intended to despatch some Spanish lace already bought in Seville, he helped Gipsy to choose a present for each of her numerous brothers and sisters, and himself hunted up smaller offerings for his friends of all degrees.

This occupied a long time, especially as the children followed them wherever they went, "as if one was the pied piper," said Cherry; and afterwards they bought bread and fruit, and ate it for luncheon, and Gipsy reflected that in three weeks' time she would be back in Kensington, very busy and rather gay, and would probably never buy pomegranates and melons in Ronda again in all her life.

Cheriton employed himself in the evening in writing to his father, while the Stanforths went down again to the mixed company below. He did not expect his brothers till late, and was not giving much heed to the time, when he looked up and saw Gipsy cross the room.

"Have they come back?" he said.

"No," said Gipsy. "Don't you think they ought to be here soon?"

Cherry glanced at his watch.

"Nine o'clock? Yes, I suppose they will be here directly, for the guides told us eight. People never get off mountains as soon as they expect they will. I'll come down. I have finished my letter."

Some time longer passed without any sign of an arrival, and the landlord of the inn, and some of the muleteers, began to say that either the Ingleses must have changed their route, or that something must have detained them till it was too dark to get down the mountains, so that they must be waiting till daylight to descend. Cheriton did not take alarm quickly; he knew that a very trifling change of path or weather would make this possible, and he was the first to say that they had better go to bed, and expect to see the wanderers in the morning; and Mr Stanforth, very anxious to avoid frightening him, chimed in with a cheerful augury to the same effect. But when Cheriton had left them, he said, anxiously,—

"I don't like it; I am sure Alvar would not delay if he could help it—he would not cause so much anxiety."

"But some very trifling matter might have detained them till after dark," said Miss Weston.

"Oh, yes; I trust it may be so."

Gipsy said nothing; but before her mind's eye there rose a vision of more than one little wayside cross which she had been shown on their ride to Ronda, with the inscription, "Here died Don Luis or Don Pedro," and the date.

These were erected, she was told, where travellers had been killed by *saltiadores* or brigands; but there were very few of such breakers of the law in Andalusia now. Still, their party had thought it right to carry arms. What if they had been driven to use them?—what if—? Even to herself Gipsy could not finish the sentence; but she lay awake all night listening for an arrival, till her ears ached and burnt with the strain; till she heard in the night-time, that had hitherto seemed to her so silent, sounds innumerable; till she felt as if she could have heard their footsteps on the mountain side. And all the time the worst of it was that she heard nothing. And for fear that Miss Weston would guess at her terror, for speaking of it seemed to remove it from the vague regions of her imagination and give it new force, and also for fear of missing a sound, she lay as still as a mouse, till, spite of an occasional doze, the night seemed endless, and the most welcome thing in the world was the long-delayed winter dawn.

Gipsy was thankful to get up and dress and find out what was going on, and as soon as possible she ran downstairs and went out to the front of the inn. Her father was just before her, and Cheriton was standing talking to a group of guides and muleteers. He turned round and came up to them saying,—

"I have been making inquiries, and they say that if they kept to their intended route—and I feel sure that they would not change it—there is no reason to fear any dangerous accident such as one hears of on Swiss mountains. And the men all laugh at the notion of any brigandage nowadays. What I think is, that one of them may have got some slight hurt, twisted his foot, for instance, and been unable to get on; and if they don't turn up in an hour or so I think we ought to go after them." Cherry looked anxiously at Mr Stanforth as he spoke, as if, having worked up this view for his own benefit, he wanted to see others convinced by it also.

"Yes," said Mr Stanforth, "I have been thinking of the possibility of strained ankles too."

"You see," said Cherry, "they must have left their mules somewhere; at least we shall fall in with them."

"Ah—ah! they are coming," cried Gipsy, with a scream of joy, as the sound of hoofs were heard along the street.

Cherry dashed forward, but as the party came into sight he stopped suddenly, then hurried on to meet them; for only Pedro, one of the mule-drivers who had accompanied them, appeared, riding one mule and leading the other.

In the sudden downfall, Gipsy's very senses seemed to fail her; as she saw Cherry lay his hand on the mule as if to support himself, and look up, unable to frame a question; she could hardly hear the confusion of voices that followed.

Soon, however, she gathered that no terrible news had come—no news at all. Don Alvar and Don Juan had ascended the mountain with their guide José, and had never returned; and, after waiting for their descent in the early morning, Pedro had come back without them. What could have happened? *They might* have gone a long way round, in fact a three days' route—there was no other, or they might have fallen from a precipice.

"In short, you know nothing about them. We must go and see," interrupted Cherry, briefly; "at least, I will. What mules have you? Who is the best guide now in Ronda?"

"My dear boy," said Mr Stanforth gently and reluctantly, "you must not try the mountain yourself. You know it must be done on foot, and the fatigue—"

"How can I think of that now? What does it matter?" said Cherry, with the roughness of excessive pain. "It is far worse to wait."

"Yes, but depend upon it, *they* are as anxious as you are. Certainly I shall go, and the guides; but, you see, speed is an object."

"Oh, I shouldn't cough and lose my breath *now!*" said Cherry. "Indeed, I can walk up hill."

Mr Stanforth could hardly answer him, and he went on vehemently,—

"You know Alvar is much too fidgety; he thinks I can do nothing. But, at least, let us all ride to the foot of the mountain; perhaps we shall meet them yet."

"Yes, that at any rate we will do. Give your orders, and then come and get some chocolate."

Miss Weston had taken care that this was ready, and Cherry sat down and ate and drank, trying to put a good face on the matter before the ladies.

After they started on their ride he was very silent, and hardly spoke a word till they came to the little inn where the mules had been left the day before. Then he said very quietly to Mr Stanforth,—

"Perhaps I had better wait—I might hinder you."

"I think it would be best," said Mr Stanforth, with merciful absence of comment, for he knew what the sense of incapacity must have been to Cherry then.

The kindest thing was to start on the steep ascent at once. Miss Weston, in what Gipsy thought a cold-blooded manner, took out her drawing materials, and sat down to sketch the mountain peaks, Cheriton started from his silent watch of the ascending party, and asked Gipsy to take a little walk with him: and as she gladly came, they gathered plants and talked a little about the view, showing their terror by their utter silence on the real object of their thoughts. Then he exerted himself to get some lunch for them; so that the first hours of the day passed pretty well. But as the afternoon wore on, he sat down under a great walnut-tree, and watched the mountain—the great pitiless creature with its steep bare sides and snowy summits. He gave no outward sign of impatience, only watched as if he could not turn his eyes away; and Miss Weston, almost as anxious for him as for the missing ones, thought it best to leave him to follow his own bent.

No one was anxious about poor Gipsy, who wandered about, running out of sight in the vain hope of seeing something on the bare hill-side on her return.

At last, just as the wonderful violet and rose tints of the sunset began to colour the white peaks, Cheriton sprang to his feet, and pointed to the hill-side, where, far in the distance, were moving figures.

"How many?" he said, for, in the hurry of their start, they had left the field-glasses, which would have brought certainty a little sooner, behind.

"Oh, there are surely a great many," said Gipsy.

Cheriton watched with the keen sight trained on his native moorlands; while the ladies counted and miscounted, and thought they saw Jack's white puggaree.

"*No*," said Cherry, "there are only Mr Stanforth and the two guides. I *cannot* wait," he added, impetuously, and began to hurry up the hill, till he stopped perforce for want of breath.

"There can have been no accident; we have found no one—nothing whatever," cried Mr Stanforth, as soon as he came within speaking distance. "They must have gone the other way; there is no trace."

He spoke in a tone of would-be congratulation, but an ominous whisper passed among the guides, *bandidas,* and the utter blank was almost more terrifying than direct ill news.

"We must go back to Ronda, and see what can be done to-morrow."

"But," said Cherry, rather incoherently, "I don't know—you see, I must take care of Jack."

"Yes," said Mr Stanforth, "but any little detention would not hurt either of them, and they must not find that you are knocked up. We can consult the authorities at Ronda."

"Yes, thank you; I hope you are not over-tired," said Cherry, half dreamily. "I? oh, no; I am quite well; but I can't help being anxious."

"No, it is very perplexing; but I feel quite hopeful of good news myself," said Mr Stanforth.

But somehow the necessity of this assurance struck a sharper pang to Cherry's heart than his own vague forebodings.

Chapter Thirty Three
Civis Romanus Sum

"The mightiest of all peoples under Heaven!"

"I tell you, you stupid, blundering blockheads, that he *is* my brother; and we *are* Englishmen, and we know nothing whatever of your Carlist brigands, or whoever they are! We are British subjects, and you had better let us go, or the British Government will know the reason why," thundered Jack Lester, in exceedingly bad Spanish, interspersed with English epithets, at the top of his voice.

"Gentlemen, it is true; our passports are at Ronda; conduct us thither, if you will. We are travelling for pleasure only, and have no concern with any political matters at all," said Alvar, in far more courteous accents.

The scene was the mountain side, the time evening, and Alvar and Jack were just beginning their descent, when they were confronted by an official, and surrounded by a small troop of soldiers in the government uniform. They had been suddenly encountered and stopped, and desired to produce their passports, and, these not being forthcoming, their account of themselves was met with civil incredulity, and they were desired to consider themselves under arrest.

"But—but don't you see that you're making an utter fool of yourself," shouted Jack, in a fury. "I tell you this gentleman *is* my brother, and we are the sons of Mr Lester, of Oakby Hall, Westmoreland, and have nothing to do with your confounded Carlists. I'll knock the first fellow down—"

"Hush, Jack! Keep your temper," whispered Alvar, in English. "Señor, I am the grandson of Señor Don Guzman de la Rosa, of Seville, well known as a friend to the government, and this is my half-brother from England."

"One of the De la Rosas, señor, is exactly what we know you to be; but as for this extraordinary falsehood by which you call yourself an Englishman—and the brother of this gentleman—why, you make matters worse for yourselves for attempting it."

"Ask the guide," said Alvar.

"Ah, doubtless; the fellow was known as having been engaged in the late war. Come, señores, you may as well accompany me in silence."

"Will you send a message by the direct route to Ronda, asking for our passports, and informing our friends of our safety?" said Alvar.

No, informing their friends was the last thing wished for. In the morning they would see.

"Do not resist, Jack," said Alvar; "it is quite useless; we must come."

"Don't you *hear* he is talking English to me?" said Jack, as a last appeal, and, of course, a vain one.

"I am sure they haven't got a magistrate's warrant," said Jack, as his alpenstock was taken away from him, and, closely guarded, he was made to precede Alvar down the hill, in a state of offended dignity and incredulous indignation. He was very angry, but not at all frightened; it was incredible that any Spanish officials should hurt *him*. Indeed, as he cooled down a little, the adventure might have been a good joke, but for the certainty that Cherry would be imagining them at the bottom of a precipice.

After walking for some way along a different road from the one they had come by, they stopped at a little wayside tavern, where they were given to understand that they were to pass the night.

"But it's impossible; they *can't* keep us here," cried Jack. "Isn't there a parish priest, or a magistrate, or a policeman, or some one to appeal to?"

"No one who could help us," answered Alvar. "I do not think there is anything to be afraid of for ourselves; we can easily prove that we are English when we get to some town; it is of Cherry that I think—he will be so frightened."

"You don't think they'll go and take him up?"

"Oh, no; I hope they will send to Ronda for our passports in the morning. But, Jack, do not fly in a passion. We must be very civil, and say we are quite willing to be detained in the service of the government."

"I'm hanged if I say anything of the sort," muttered Jack, whose prominent sensation was rage at the idea that he, an Englishman, a gentleman, a man with an address, and a card—though he had unluckily left it at home—should be subjected to such an indignity, stopped in his proceedings by a dozen trumpery Spaniards!

Alvar was not so full of a sense of the liberty of the subject; he felt sure that he was mistaken for Manoel, and more than suspected that the government might have been justified in detaining his cousin. He did not, however, wish to confide this to Jack, of whose prudence he was doubtful, and knew that if the worst came to the worst, his grandfather could get them out of the scrape.

There might be no danger, but it was very uncomfortable, and provisions being scarce in the emergency, the captain—who looked much more like a bandit than an officer—gave his prisoners no supper but a bit of bread. Alvar was Spaniard enough to endure the fasting, but Jack, after his day of mountain climbing, was ready to eat his fingers off with hunger; and as the hours wore on, began really to feel sick, wretched, and low-spirited, and though he preserved an unmoved demeanour, to wonder inwardly what his father would say if he knew where he was, and to remember that the Spaniards were a cruel people and invented the Inquisition! And then he wondered if Gipsy was thinking of him.

Moreover, it was very cold, and they were of course tired to begin with, so that, when at length the morning dawned, Alvar was startled to see how like Jack looked to Cheriton after a bad night, and made such representations to the captain that Englishmen could not bear cold and hunger, that he obtained a fair share of bread and a couple of onions—provisions which Jack enjoyed more than he would have done had he guessed what Alvar had said to procure them.

"I'm up to anything now," he said. "If they would only let us put a note in the post for Cherry, it would be rather a lark after all."

"I do not know where you will find a post-office," said Alvar disconsolately, as they were marched off in an opposite direction to Ronda. "If Cherry only does not climb that mountain to look for us!"

"I should like to set this country to rights a little," said Jack.

"That," said Alvar dryly, "is what many have tried to do, but they have not succeeded."

The prisoners were very well guarded, and though Alvar made more than one attempt to converse with the captain, he got scarcely any answer. Still, from the exceedingly curious glances with which he regarded them, Alvar suspected that he was not quite clear in his own mind as to their identity. After a long day's march they struck down on a small Moorish-looking town, called Zahara, built beside a wide, quick-rushing river.

And now Alvar's hopes rose, as here resided an acquaintance of his grandfather, a noted breeder of bulls, who knew him well, and had once seen Cheriton at Seville. Besides, the authorities of Zahara might be amenable to reason.

However, they could get no hearing that night, and were shut up in what Jack called the station-house, but which was really a round Moorish tower with horseshoe arches. Here Alvar obtained a piece of paper, and they concocted a full description of themselves, their travelling companions, and their destination, which Alvar signed with his full name,—

"Alvaro Guzman Lester, of Westmoreland, England," and directed to El Señor Don Luis Pavieco, Zahara, and this he desired might be given to the local authorities. He also tried hard, but in vain, to get a note sent to Ronda.

They hoped that the early morning might produce Don Luis, but they saw nothing of any one but the soldier who brought them their food, which was still of the poorest.

Alvar's patience began to give way at last; he walked up and down the room.

"Oh, I am mad when I think of my brother!" he exclaimed. "My poor Cheriton. What he will suffer!"

"Don't you think they'll let us out soon?" said Jack, who had subsided into a sort of glum despair.

"Oh, they will wait—and delay—and linger. It drives me mad!" he repeated vehemently, and throwing himself into a seat he hid his face in his arms on the table.

"Well," said Jack, "it's dogged as does it. I wish I hadn't used up all my tobacco though."

Early the next morning their door was opened at an unusual hour, and they were summoned into a sort of hall, where they found "el Capitano," another officer in a respectable uniform, and, to Alvar's joy, Don Luis Pavieco himself.

The thing was ended with ludicrous ease. Don Luis bowed to Alvar, and turning to the officer declared that Don Alvar Lester was perfectly well known to him, and that the other gentleman was certainly his half-brother and an Englishman. The officer bowed also, smiled, hoped that they had not been incommoded; it was a slight mistake.

"Mistake!" exclaimed Jack; "and pray, Alvar, what's the Spanish for apology—damages?"

Alvar turned a deaf ear, and bowed and smiled with equal politeness.

"He had been sure that in due time the slight mistake would be rectified. Were they now free to go?"

"Yes;" and Don Luis interposed, begging them to come and get some breakfast with him while their horses could be got ready. Their guide?—oh, he was still detained on suspicion.

"Well," ejaculated Jack, "they are the coolest hands. Incommoded! I should think we have been incommoded indeed!"

In the meantime no hint of how matters had really gone reached the anxious hearts at Ronda. The authorities had scouted the idea of brigands, and had revealed the existence of a dangerous ravine, some short distance from the mountain path. Doubtless the darkness had overtaken them, and they had been lost. The guides declared that nothing was more unlikely, as it was hardly possible to reach the ravine from the path, the rocks were so steep. A search was however made by some of the most active, it need not be said, in vain. Cheriton, afterwards, never could bear a reference to those days and nights of suspense—suspense lasting long enough to change the hope of good tidings into the dread of evil tidings, till he feared rather than longed for the sounds for which his whole being seemed to watch.

Nothing could exceed Mr Stanforth's kindness to him, and he held up at first bravely, and submitted to his friend's care. On the third morning they resolved that Don Guzman should be written to, and Cherry, who had been wandering about in an access of restless misery, tried to begin the letter; but he put down the pen, turning faint and dizzy, and unable to frame a sentence.

"I cannot," he said faintly. "I cannot see."

"You must lie down, my dear boy; you have had no rest. I will do it."

"My father, too," Cheriton said, with a painful effort at self-control. "I think—there's no chance. I must try to do it; but—oh—Jack—Jack!"

He buried his face on his arms with a sob that seemed as if it would tear him to pieces.

"You must not write yet to your father," said Mr Stanforth. "I do not give up hope. Courage, my boy!"

Suddenly a loud scream rang through the house, and an outburst of voices, and one raised joyously,—

"My brother—my brother—are you here?—we are safe!" and as Cherry started to his feet Alvar, followed by Jack, rushed into the room, and clasped him in his arms.

"Safe! yes, the abominable, idiotic brutes of soldiers! But we're all right, Cherry. You mustn't mind now."

"Yes, we are here, and it is over."

"Thank Heaven for His great mercy!" cried Mr Stanforth, almost bursting into tears as he grasped Alvar's hand.

"Bandits, bandits?" cried half-a-dozen voices.

But Cherry could not speak a word; he only put out his hand and caught Jack's, as if to feel sure of his presence also.

"*Mi querido*," said Alvar in his gentle, natural tones, "all the terror is over—now you can rest. I think you had better go, Jack. I will take care of him," he added.

"Yes," said Mr Stanforth; "this has been far too much. Come, Jack—come and tell us all that has chanced."

Chapter Thirty Four
Jack on his Mettle

"Lat me alone in chesing of my wyf,
That charge upon my bak I wol endure."

Chaucer.

That same morning, when Jack and Alvar had ridden hurriedly up to the hotel, looking eagerly to catch sight of those who were so anxiously watching for them, their eyes fell on Gipsy's solitary figure, standing motionless, with eyes turned towards the mountain, and hands dropped listlessly before her. Jack's heart gave a great bound, and at the sound of the horses' hoofs, she turned with a start and scream of joy, and sprang towards them, while Jack, jumping off, caught both her hands, crying,—

"Oh, don't be frightened any more, we're come!"

"Your brother!" exclaimed Gipsy, as she flew into the house; but her cry of "Papa! papa!" was suddenly choked with such an outburst of blinding, stifling tears and sobs, that she paused perforce; and as they ran upstairs, Mariquita, the pretty Spanish girl who waited on them, caught her hand and kissed her fervently.

"Ah, señorita, dear señorita; thanks to the saints, they have sent her lover back to her. Sweet señorita, now she will not cry!"

A sudden access of self-consciousness seized on Gipsy; she blushed to her fingertips, and only anxious to hide the tears she could not check, she hurried away, round to the back of the inn, into a sort of orchard, where grew peach and nectarine trees, apples and pears already showing buds, and where the ground was covered with jonquils and crocuses, while beyond was the rocky precipice, and, far off, the snowy peaks that still made Gipsy shudder. Unconscious of the strain she had been enduring, she was terrified at the violence of her own emotion, for Gipsy was not a girl who was given to gusts of feeling. Probably the air and the solitude were her best remedies, for she soon began to recover herself, and sat up among the jonquils. Oh, how thankful she was that the danger was over, and the bright, kindly Cheriton spared from such a terrible sorrow! But was it for

Cheriton's sake that these last two days had been like a frightful dream, that her very existence seemed to have been staked on news of the lost ones? No one—*no one* could help such feelings. Miss Weston had cried about it, and her father had never been able to touch a pencil. But that foolish Mariquita! Here Gipsy sprang to her feet with a start, for close at her side stood Jack. At sight of him, strong and ruddy and safe, her feeling overpowered her consciousness of it, and she said, earnestly,—

"Oh, I am so thankful you are safe! It was so dreadful!"

"And it was not dreadful at all in reality, only tiresome and absurd," said Jack.

"It was very dreadful here," said Gipsy, in a low voice, with fresh tears springing.

"Oh, if you felt so!" cried Jack ardently; "I wish it could happen to me twenty times over!"

"Oh, never again!" she murmured; and then Jack, suddenly and impetuously,—

"But I *am* glad it happened, for I found out up in that dirty hole how I felt. There was never any one like you. I—I—could you ever get to think of me? Oh, Gipsy, I mean it. I love you!" cried the boy, his stern, thoughtful face radiant with eagerness, as he seized her hand.

"Oh, no—you don't!" stammered Gipsy, not knowing what she said.

"I do!" cried Jack desperately. "I never was a fellow that did not know his own mind. Of course I know I'm young yet; but I only want to look forward. I shall work and get on, and—and up there at school and at Oakby I never thought there was any one like you. I disliked girls. But now—oh, Gipsy, won't you begin at the very beginning with me, and let us live our lives together?"

Boy as he was, there was a strength of intention in Jack's earnest tones that carried conviction. Perhaps the mutual attraction might have remained hidden for long, or even have passed away, but for the sudden and intense excitement that had brought it to the surface.

"Won't you—won't you?" reiterated Jack; and Gipsy said "Yes."

They stood in the glowing sunshine, and Jack felt a sort of ecstasy of unknown bliss. He did not know how long was the pause before Gipsy, starting, and as if finishing the sentence, went on,—

"Yes—but I don't know. What will they all say? Isn't it wrong when we are so young?"

"Wrong! as if a year or two made any difference to feelings like mine!" cried Jack. "If I were twenty-five, if I were thirty, I couldn't love you better!"

"Yes—but—" said Gipsy, in her quick, practical way. "You *are* young, and—and—papa—If he says—"

"Of course I shall tell him," said Jack. "I am not going to steal you. If you will wait, I'll work and show your father that I am a man. For I love you!"

"I'll wait!" said Gipsy softly; and then voices sounded near, and she started away from him, while Jack—but Jack could never recollect exactly what he did during the next ten minutes, till the thought of how he was to tell his story sobered him. Practical life had not hitherto occupied much of Jack's mind; he had had no distinct intentions beyond taking honours, and if possible a fellowship, till he had been seized upon by this sudden passion, which in most lads would probably have been a passing fancy, but in so earnest and serious a nature took at once a real and practical shape. But when Jack thought of facing Mr Stanforth, and still worse his own father, with his wishes and his hopes, a fearful embarrassment seized on him. No, he must first make his cause good with the only person who was likely to be listened to—he must find Cherry. However, the first person he met was Mr Stanforth, who innocently asked him if he knew where his daughter was. Jack blushed and stared, answering incoherently,—

"I was only looking for Cherry."

"There he is. I heard him asking for you. Perhaps Gipsy is in the orchard." Jack felt very foolish and cowardly, but for his very life he could not begin to speak, and he turned towards the bench where Cherry sat in the sun, smoking his pipe comfortably, and conscious of little but a sense of utter rest and relief.

"Well, Jack, I haven't heard your story yet," he said, as Jack came and sat down beside him. "I don't think you have grown thin, though Alvar says they nearly starved you to death."

"Where is Alvar?" asked Jack.

"I got him to go to the mayor, *intendant*, whatever the official is called here, and see if anything could be done for poor Pedro. His mother was here just now in an agony. Jack, I think the 'evils of government' might receive some illustrations."

"Cheriton," said Jack, with unusual solemnity, "I've got to ask your advice—that is, your opinion—that is, to tell you something."

"Don't you think I should look at it from a ludicrous point of view?" said Cherry, whose spirits were ready for a reaction into nonsense.

"I don't know," said Jack; "but it is very serious. I have made up my mind, Cherry, that I mean to marry Miss Stanforth, and I shall direct all my efforts in life to accomplish this end. I know that I am younger than is usual on these occasions; but such things are not a question of time. Cherry, *do* help me; they'll all listen to you."

Cheriton sat with his pipe in his hand, so utterly astonished, that he allowed Jack's sentences to come to a natural conclusion. Then he exclaimed,—

"Jack! You! Oh, impossible!"

"I don't see why you should think it impossible. Anyhow, it's true!"

"But it is so sudden. Jack, my dear boy, you're slightly carried off your head just now. Don't say a word about it—while we're all together at least; it wouldn't be fair."

"But I have," answered Jack, "and—and—" in a different tone, "Cherry, I don't know how to believe it myself, but she—it is too wonderful—she will."

Cherry did not answer. He put his hand on Jack's with a sudden, quick movement.

"I suppose you think I ought to have waited till I had a better right to ask her," said Jack presently.

A look of acute pain passed over Cheriton's face. He said doubtfully, "Are you quite sure?"

"Sure? Sure of what?"

"Of your own mind and hers?"

"Did I ever not know my own mind? I'm not a fool!" said Jack angrily. "And, if you could have seen just the way she looked, Cherry, you wouldn't have any doubts."

"I am afraid," said Cherry very gently, and after a pause, "that you have been very hasty. I don't think that father, or Mr Stanforth either, would listen to you now."

"I want you to ask them," said Jack insinuatingly. "Father would do anything for you now; and, besides, we are young enough to wait, and I've got the world before me, and I mean to keep straight and get on. Why should Mr Stanforth object? I feel as if I could do anything. You don't think it would make me idle? No, I shall work twice as hard as I should without it."

"Yes," said Cherry quietly; "no doubt." Something in his tone brought recent facts to Jack's remembrance, as was proved by his sudden silence. Cherry looked round at him and smiled.

"You know, Jack, I wasn't prepared to find the schoolboy stage passed into the lover's. I'll speak to Mr Stanforth, if that is what you want, and even if things don't fit in at once, if you feel as you say, you won't be much to be pitied with such an aim before you!"

"I'm not at all ashamed of telling my own story," said Jack, "but—"

"*But* there is Mr Stanforth coming out of the house, so if you mean to run away you had better make haste about it."

Jack rose, but he paused a moment, and as Mr Stanforth came towards them, said bluntly,—

"Mr Stanforth, I want Cheriton to tell you about it first;" then deliberately walked away.

Poor Mr Stanforth, who had little expected such an ending to his tour with his favourite little daughter, was feeling himself in a worse scrape than the lovers, and though he had romance enough to sympathise with them, was disposed to be angry with Jack for his inconsiderate haste, and to feel that "What will your mother say?" was a more uncomfortable question to himself than to his daughter.

Cheriton, on his side, would have been very glad of a few minutes for reflection, but Mr Stanforth began at once,—

"I see I have not brought news to you."

"No," said Cherry. "Jack has been talking to me; I had no idea of such a thing. But, Mr Stanforth, there is no doubt that Jack is thoroughly in earnest," as a half smile twinkled on the artist's perplexed countenance.

"In earnest, yes; but what business has he to be in earnest? What would your father say to such a proceeding? What can he say at your brother's age, and of people of whom he knows nothing, and of a connexion of which, knowing nothing, he probably would not approve?"

Cheriton blushed, knowing that this last assertion contained much truth.

"But he does know," he said, "of all your kindness, and he will know more—and—and when he knows you, he could not think—"

"Excuse me, my dear fellow, but he will think. He will think I have thrown my daughter in the way of his sons—for which I have only my own imprudence, I suppose, to thank. And he would no doubt dislike a connexion the advantages of which, whatever they may be, are not enumerated in Burke's 'Landed Gentry.'"

Mr Stanforth smiled, though he spoke with a certain spirited dignity, and Cheriton could not contradict him; for though Mr Stanforth had not risen out of any romantic obscurity, he certainly owed his present position to his own genius and high personal character. He had himself married well, and all would depend on the way in which it was put to a man like Mr Lester, slow to realise unfamiliar facts. Cheriton could not take the liberty of saying that he thought such an objection would be groundless, or at least easily overcome; but he was afraid that his silence might be misconstrued, and said,—"But on your side, Mr Stanforth, would you think it wrong to give Jack a little hope? I think he has every prospect of success in life. And he is a very good fellow. Sudden as this is, I feel sure that he will stick to it."

"As to that," said Mr Stanforth, "I like Jack very well, and for my part I think young people are all the better for having to fight their way; but whatever may take place in the future I can allow no intercourse till your father's consent is obtained. That will give a chance of testing their feelings on both sides. Gipsy is a mere child, she may not understand herself."

"I think," said Cheriton, "that if Jack writes to my father now, or speaks to him when he gets home, that no one will attend to him. But if it could wait till we all go back, I could explain the circumstances so much better. It is always difficult to take in what passes at a distance."

"Well," said Mr Stanforth, "all I have to say is that when Jack applies to me, with his father's consent, I will hear what he has to say, not before. Come, Cheriton," he added, "you know there is no other way of acting. This foolish boy has broken up our pleasant party, and upset all our plans."

"Perhaps I ought to have made more apologies for him," said Cherry, with a smile. "But I want things to go well with Jack. It would be so bad for him to have a disappointment of that kind just as he is making his start in life."

Mr Stanforth noticed the unconscious emphasis, "I want things to go well with *Jack*," and said kindly, "Jack couldn't have a better special pleader, and if he has as much stuff in him as I think, a few obstacles won't hurt him."

"Oh, Jack has plenty of good strong stuff in him, mental, moral—and physical, too," added Cherry hurriedly.

Mr Stanforth was touched by the allusion, which was evidently intended to combat a possible latent objection on his part.

"Jack is excellent—but inconvenient," he said, thinking it better not to make the subject too serious. "The thing is what to do next." As he spoke, Jack himself came up to them, and Mr Stanforth prevented his first words with, "My dear fellow, I have said my say to your brother, and I don't mean to listen to yours just yet."

"I believe, sir," said Jack, "that I—I have not observed sufficient formalities. I shall go straight home to my father, and I hope to obtain his full consent. But it is due to me to let me say that my mind is, and always will be, quite unalterable. And I'm not sorry I spoke, sir—I can't be!"

"No," said Mr Stanforth; "but I must desire that you make no further attempt at present."

"I hope, Mr Stanforth, that you don't imagine I would attempt anything underhand!" cried Jack impetuously.

"I shall have every confidence in you," said Mr Stanforth gravely; "but remember, I cannot regard you as pledged to my daughter by anything that has passed to-day." Jack made no answer, but he closed his lips with an expression of determination.

When Alvar came back, having succeeded in instituting an inquiry into the merits of Pedro's character, there was a discussion of plans, which ended in the three brothers agreeing to go by the shortest route to Seville, whence Jack could at once start for England; while the Stanforths followed them by a longer and more picturesque road, and after picking up their own property, would also go home *via* Madrid some week or two later. Alvar was not nearly so much astonished as the others, nor so much concerned.

"It was natural," he said, "since Jack's heart was not preoccupied, and would doubtless pass away with absence."

Jack was so excessively indignant that he did not condescend to a reply, only asking Cherry if he was too tired to start at once.

This proposal, however, was negatived by Mr Stanforth, who remarked that he did not want to hear of any more adventures in the dusk; and it was agreed that both parties should start early on the following morning. In the meantime the only rational thing was to behave as usual. Jack was, however, speechless and surly with embarrassment, and stuck to Cheriton as if he was afraid to lose sight of him; while Gipsy bore herself with a transparent affectation of unconsciousness, and, though she blushed at every look, coined little remarks at intervals. Miss Weston kindly professed to be seized with a desire to inspect the Dominican Convent, and carried her and Alvar off for that purpose; while Jack held by Cherry, who was glad to rest, though this startling incident had one good effect, in driving away all the haunting memories of the late alarm.

The next morning all were up with the sun, Gipsy busily dispensing the chocolate and pressing it on Cheriton as he sat at the table. Suddenly she turned, and, with a very pretty gesture, half confident, half shy, she held up a cup to Jack, who stood behind.

"Won't you have some?" she said, with a hint of her own mischief in her eyes and voice. Jack seized the cup, and—upset it over the deft, quick hands that tendered it to him.

"Oh, I have burnt you!" he exclaimed, in so tragic a voice that all present burst out laughing.

"No," said Gipsy, "early morning chocolate is not dangerously hot; but you have spoiled my cuffs, and spilled it, and I don't think there's any more of it."

"Jack's first attention!" said Cherry, under his breath; but he jumped up and followed Alvar, who had gone to see about the mount provided for them. Miss Weston was tying various little bags on to her saddle.

"I say, Mr Stanforth," called Cherry, "there's such a picturesque mule here; do come and see it."

He looked up with eyes full of mischievous entreaty as Mr Stanforth obeyed his call. "Well," said the latter with a smile, "I may ask *you* to come and see me at Kensington, for I must get the picture finished."

"That was a much prettier picture, just now," said Cheriton; "and I'm sure Jack would be happy to sit for it *any* time."

When Gipsy, long afterwards, was pressed on the subject of that little parting interview, she declared that Jack had done nothing but say that he wouldn't make love to her on any account; but however that might be, she soon came running out, rosy and bashful; while Cheriton put her on her mule and gave her a friendly hand-squeeze and a look of all possible encouragement. Mr Stanforth went into the house and called Jack to bid him a kind farewell. After the party had set off, Gipsy looked back and saw the crowd of mule drivers and peasants, the host and hostess, with Mariquita kissing her hands, and the three brothers standing together in the morning sunshine, waving their farewells. As they passed out of sight, her father touched her hand and made her ride up close to his side.

"My little girl," he said, "this is a serious thing that has come to you; I do not know how it may end for you. I am sure that it will bring you anxiety and delay. Be honest with yourself, and do not exaggerate the romance and excitement of these last few days into a feeling which may demand from you much sacrifice."

Gipsy had never heard her father speak in this tone before—she was awed and silenced.

"Be honest," repeated her father, "for I think it is a very honest heart that you have won."

"Papa," said Gipsy, "I *am* honest, and I think I know what you mean. But I don't mind waiting if I know he is waiting too. He said 'begin at the beginning' with him."

"Well," said Mr Stanforth with a sigh, "*Che sará sará;*" but with a sudden turn, "*He* is young, too, you know, and many things may happen to change his views."

"I cannot help it now, papa," said Gipsy, who felt that those days and nights of terror had developed her feelings more than weeks of common life. She gave her father's hand a little squeeze, and looked up in his face with the tears on her black eyelashes. She *meant* to say, "I love *you* all the better because of this new love which has made everything deeper and warmer for me," but all she managed to say was—"There! There are all the things tumbling out of your knapsack! I'm not going to have *that* happen again even if—if—whatever should take place in the future."

"I hope, my dear, that nothing more will happen, at least till we are at home again," said Mr Stanforth meekly; but Gipsy put the things into the knapsack, and after a little silence they fell into a conversation on the scenery as naturally as possible.

Chapter Thirty Five
A Summons

"Once from high Heaven
Is a father given.
Once—and, oh, never again!"

After Jack returned home, with the understanding that the disclosure of his holiday occupation should await his brother's return, and after the Stanforths had also left Seville, Alvar and Cheriton spent several weeks there without any adventures to disturb their tranquillity. Alvar was a good deal with his grandfather, whose health was not at this time good, but who had evinced great curiosity as to the details of their detention on the mountains. He used also to go to the different clubs and meet acquaintances, where they talked politics and scandal, and played at cards, dominoes, and billiards. It was an aimless existence, and Cheriton sometimes fancied that Alvar grew restless under it, and would not be sorry to return to England. This, however, might have been owing to Cheriton's own decided dislike to the young *Sevillanos*, who struck him as almost justifying his grandmother's preconceived theory of Alvar's probable behaviour.

"Ah, they do not suit you, that is not what you like," Alvar said cheerfully; but he never said, "It is not *good*, this sort of life does not make a nation great or virtuous."

Manoel was of another type, and perhaps a more respectable one; but they saw very little of him. Cheriton liked the ladies, who were kind, and possessed many domestic virtues; and at Don Guzman's country place there was something exceedingly pleasant in the cheerfulness and gaiety of the peasants. He would have liked to have found out something of the working of the Church, of the views of the clergy, and how far they differed, not only from those of an Anglican, but of an intelligent Roman priest in more civilised countries, but on these subjects no one would talk to him. He heard mutterings of hatred towards the priests in some quarters, and a good deal of chatter about processions and ceremonies from the young ladies, but nothing further. He did not want for occupation. He could now read and speak Spanish easily; and although the Cid, Ferdinand and Isabella, the Armada, and the Inquisition had been about the only salient points in his mind previously, he made a study of Spanish history, without much increase of his admiration for the Spaniards. He was able, also, to do much more sight-seeing than at first, and of the cathedral he never tired, and never came to the end of its innumerable chapels, each with some great picture, which Mr Stanforth had taught him how to see; never ceased to find something new in the mystery and solemnity of its aisles with their glory of coloured lights.

These quiet weeks formed a sort of resting-place, during which he was able to think both of the past and of the future; he could dare now to look away from the immediate present. Cheriton's eyes were very clear, his moral sense very keen, and he saw that he had been under a delusion, that Ruth and he were as the poles asunder, that her deliberate deception, her want of any sense of honour, had marked a nature that never could have satisfied his. Love in his case was no longer blind, but it was none the less passionate, and, whatever else life might hold for him, the memory of all his first, best hopes could never bring him anything but pain. This pain had been as much as he could bear, but others, he thought, had suffered as keenly, and had led lives that were neither ignoble nor unhappy. Because one great love had gone out of his life was nothing else worthy or dear? "Nothing" had been the answer of his first anguish, but Cheriton's nature was too rich in love for such an answer to stand. The help for which he had prayed had been sent to him, and it came in the sense that home faces were still dear—*how* dear his late alarm had taught him—home duties still paramount, that he could be a good son and brother and friend still. And he thought with a sort of surprise of the many pleasant and not unhappy hours he had passed of late; how much, after all, he had "enjoyed himself." He hardly knew that his quick intelligence was a gift to be thankful for, or that his unselfish interest in others brought its own reward. On another side of his nature, also, he resisted the aimlessness of his lost hopes. The thought of Ruth had sweetened his success at Oxford, but he would not be such a coward as to give up all his objects in life, he would make a name for himself still, and show her that she had not brought him to utter shipwreck. This motive was strong in Cheriton, though it ran alongside with much higher ones.

One picture in the cathedral exercised a great fascination over Cheriton's mind. It hangs in the Capella del Consuelo, over a side altar, dedicated to the *Angel de la Guarda*, and is one of the many masterpieces of Murillo to be found in Seville. It represents a tall, strong angel with wide-spread wings, and grave, benevolent face, leading by the hand a child—a subject which has been of course repeated in every form of commonplace prettiness. But in this picture the figure of the angel conveys a sense of heavenly might and unearthly guardianship which no imitation or repetition could give. It is called the "Guardian Angel;" but Cheriton had been told by one of the priests that the name given to it by the painter himself was "The Soul and the Church," which for some reason or other had been changed by the monks of the Capuchin Convent, to whom the picture had originally belonged. It was a thought and a carrying out of the thought which, seen among such surroundings, was full of suggestion, how and why that Divine Guidance seemed here in great measure to have gone astray, how the great angel's finger had not always pointed upward, and yet how utterly helpless and rudderless the nation was when it cast off the Guide of its fathers. Then his thoughts turned to his own life and to the Hand that held it, to the Guidance that was sometimes so hard to recognise, so difficult to yield to, and yet how the sense of a love and a wisdom above his own, speaking to him, whether in the events of his own life, the better impulses of his own heart, or in the visible forms of religion, was the one light in the darkness.

"O'er moor and fen, o'er crag and torrent, till
The night is gone."

As he murmured the words half aloud a hand touched his shoulder. He looked up and saw Alvar standing beside him.

"*Mi querido,* I have been looking for you. Will you come home? I want you," he said.

"There is something the matter," said Cheriton quickly, as he looked at him. "What is it?"

"Ah, I *must* tell you!" said Alvar reluctantly. "It is bad news, indeed. Sit down again—here—I have received this." He took a telegraph paper out of his pocket and put it into Cherry's hand.

"Mrs Lester to Alvar Lester.
"Your father has met with a dangerous accident. He wishes to see you. Come home at once. He desires Cheriton to run no risk."
Cheriton looked up blankly for a moment, then started to his feet, crushing up the paper in his hand.

"Quick," he said, "we must go at once. When? By Madrid is the shortest way."

"Yes—I—" said Alvar; "but see what he says."

"I *must* go," said Cheriton. "Don't waste any words about it. I *know* he wants me. I'll be careful enough, only make haste."

But he paused, and dropping on his knees on the altar step, covered his face with his hands, rose, and silently led the way out of the cathedral.

Alvar, with his usual tact, perceived at once that it would be impossible to persuade him to stay behind, and did not fret him by the attempt, though this hasty journey and the return to Oakby in the first sharp winds of March were more on his own mind than the thought of what news might meet them at the journey's end.

It was still early in the day, and they were able to start within a few hours, only taking a few of their things with them, amid a confusion of tears, sympathy, and regret; Don Guzman evidently parting from Alvar with reluctance, and bestowing a tremendous embrace on Cheriton in return for his thanks for the kindness that had been shown to him. Manoel, on the other hand, was evidently relieved at their early departure.

Some days later, on a wild, blustering morning in the first week of March, Jack Lester stood on the step of the front door of Oakby. The trees were still bare, and scarcely a primrose peeped through the dead leaves beneath them; pale rays of sun were struggling with the quick driven clouds, the noisy caw of the rooks mingled with the rustle of the leafless branches. Jack was pale and heavy-eyed. He looked across the wide, wild landscape as if its very familiarity were strange to him, then started, as up the park from a side entrance came a carnage and pair as fast as it could be driven, and in another minute pulled up at the door.

"Oh, Cherry, we have never dared to wish for you!" cried Jack, as Cheriton sprang out and caught both his hands. "Come in—come in! Oh, if you had *but* come last night!"

"Not too late—not too late altogether?" Jack shook his head, his voice choked, but they knew too well what he would tell them, and the two brothers stood just within the door, holding by each other, Jack sobbing with relief from the strain of responsibility and loneliness, and Cheriton dazed and silent, unable to utter a word.

The servants began to gather round them. "Oh, Mr Cheriton, it's some comfort to see you back, sir!" said the butler; and—"Thank heaven, sir, you're come to help your poor grandmother!" cried the old housekeeper; while Nettie, flying downstairs, threw herself into Cheriton's arms, as if they were a refuge from the agony of new and most forlorn sorrow, while he held her fast with long speechless kisses.

Alvar stood still. In that instinctive mutual clinging in the first shock of their common grief he had no share, and for the moment he stood as much a stranger among them as when, more than a year before, he had come into the midst of their Christmas merry-making, and had silenced their laughter by his unwelcome presence.

Jack was the first to awaken to a sense of present necessity.

"You have been travelling all night," he said. "Come and sit down—you must be tired out."

"We had some breakfast at Hazelby, while we waited for the carriage," said Alvar; and Cherry, as Nettie released her hold, unfastened his wraps, and moved over to the hall fire, sitting down in the great chair, as they began to exchange question and answer.

"What happened—how was it?"

"Didn't you get my telegram?" said Jack.

"No; only granny's. Where is she?"

"Asleep, I hope. The meet was at Ashrigg, and old Rob fell in taking the brook, just by Fletcher's farm. And so—so he was thrown, and it was an injury to the spine; but he was quite conscious, and sent that telegram to Alvar. After that he didn't often know us—till—till last night. And it was over before eleven. We did not think you could possibly get here till to-night, and we had no news of you, so I telegraphed again as soon as I got home; but I suppose you missed the message."

"We wrote and telegraphed from Madrid," said Alvar; "it is quite possible that there should be delay there; and in Paris and London we had hardly a moment to catch the trains. Cherry has been too anxious to feel the fatigue, but he *must* rest now."

"There must be a great many things to attend to," said Cheriton, standing up, and passing his hand over his eyes as if he were rousing himself out of an unnatural dream.

"Not yet," said Jack, "it is so early. Mr Ellesmere will come back by-and-by."

Cherry looked round. He noticed that a pair of antlers had been removed from one of the panels, and an impulse came to him to ask why, and then the oddest sense of the incongruity of the remark. He rather knew than felt the truth of the blow that had fallen on them, and all the different aspects of this great change, even to remote particulars, passed over his mind, as over the mind of a drowning man, but as thoughts, not as realities. Suddenly there was a bark and a scutter, and Buffer, in an ecstasy of incongruous joy, rushed into the hall, jumped upon him, yelping, licking, dancing, and writhing with rapture. He was followed by Rolla, who came slowly in, and laid his great tawny head on his master's knee, looking sorrowfully up in his face as much as to say that *he* knew well enough that this was like no other home-coming.

Cheriton started up and pushed them all aside. He walked away to the window and stared out at the park, into the library and looked round it, evidently hardly knowing what he was about. Alvar, who had been standing pale and silent, roused himself too, and followed him, putting his arm over his shoulder.

"Come," he said; "come upstairs. Jack, where is there a fire?"

Cheriton yielded instinctively to Alvar's hand and voice, and Jack led them upstairs, saying that granny had insisted on their rooms being kept ready for them. Nettie withheld Buffer from following them, and crouched down on the rug by the hall fire till Jack returned to her.

"They have both gone to bed for a little while," he said; "even Alvar is tired out. Nettie, you had better go to granny, as soon as she is awake, and tell her that they are here, and that Cherry is pretty well."

"I suppose Cherry will tell us what to do," said Nettie, as she stood up.

Discipline and absence from home had improved Nettie; she was less childish and more considerate, remembering to tell Jack that he had had no breakfast, and to order some to be ready when the travellers should want it.

Bob, who had been sent for a day or two before, now joined them. He had grown as tall as Jack, but grief and awe gave him a heavy, sullen look, and indeed they said very little to each other. Jack wrote a few necessary letters, and sent them off by one of the grooms, and telegraphed to Judge Cheriton, who was coming that same evening, the news of what he would find. But their father had been so completely manager and master, that Jack felt as if giving an order himself were unjustifiable, and as soon as he dared, he went to see if Cherry were able to talk to him.

"Come, Jack," said Cherry, as the boy came up to him; "come now, and tell me everything."

Jack leaned against the foot of the bed, and in the half-darkened room told all the details of the last few days. There had not been much suffering, nor long intervals of consciousness, so far as they knew. Cherry could have done no good till last night. Granny had done all the nursing. "I never thought," said Jack, "she loved any one so much." Mr Ellesmere had been everything to them, and had written letters and told them what to do. "But last night father came more to himself, and sent for Mr Ellesmere, and presently he fetched me, and father took hold of my hand, and said to me quite clearly, 'Remember, your eldest brother will stand in my place; let there be no divisions among you.' And then—then he told me to try and keep Bob straight, and that I had been a good lad. But oh, Cherry, if he had but known about Gipsy! But I couldn't say one word then. And then Mr Ellesmere said, 'Shall Jack say anything to Cherry for you?' And he smiled, and said, 'My love and blessing, for he has been the light of my eyes.' And then he sent for Bob and Nettie, and sent messages to old Wilson and some of the servants. And he said that he had tried to do his duty in life by his children and neighbours, but that he had often failed, especially in one respect, and also he had not ruled his temper as a Christian man should; and he asked every one to forgive him, and specially the vicar, if he had overstepped the bounds his position gave him; Mr Ellesmere said something of 'thanks for years of kindness.' And then—we had the communion. And after a bit he said very low, 'If my boy should live, I know he will keep things together.' Then I think he murmured something about—about your coming—and the cold weather—and—and—you were not to fret—it was only waiting a little longer. And then quite quite loud he said, 'Fear God, and keep His commandments,' and then just whispered, 'Fanny.' That was the last word; but he lived till eleven. And poor granny, she broke down into dreadful crying, and said, 'The light of *my* eyes—the light of *my* eyes is darkened.' Nettie was very good with her; but at last we all got to bed—and—oh, Cherry, it isn't quite so bad now we have you!" and Jack pressed up to his side.

Cheriton had listened to all this long, faltering tale leaning on his elbow, his wide-open eyes fixed on his brother, without interrupting him by a word. Jack cried, and he put his arm round his neck, and said, "Poor boy!" but no tears came to him.

"I never thought—" said Jack, whose natural reserve was dispelled by stress of feeling, "I never thought what a good man he was, and how much he cared."

"Yes, he loved goodness," said Cherry, with a heavy sigh.

It was true. With some prejudices and many weaknesses, Gerald Lester had set his duty first; he had lived such a life that those around him were the better for his existence, he had left a place empty and a work to be done. Who would fill the place—how would the work be done?

Through all the crush of personal grief, his two sons could not but ask themselves this question; but they could not bring themselves to speak of it to each other; and after a few minutes Cheriton said, "I think I will get up now. We must talk things over together; and I want to see granny."

"If you have rested."

"Oh, yes, as much as is possible. I am quite well, indeed. Go down, my boy. I will come directly."

Jack went with a lightened heart. If Cherry were well and able to take the lead among them, everything could be borne. When Cheriton came into the library he found that Alvar had already appeared, and was eating some breakfast, for it was still only twelve o'clock, while Mr Ellesmere was standing by the fire. The vicar greeted him kindly and quietly, and Alvar poured out some coffee for him; and then Mr Ellesmere began to explain some of the arrangements he had been obliged to make, and that he had sent to their father's solicitor, Mr Malcolm, to come in the afternoon. Cheriton thanked him, and asked a few questions; but Alvar did not seem to take the conversation to himself, till the butler, having taken away the breakfast things, paused, and after looking first at Cheriton, turned to Alvar, and said rather awkwardly,—"Do you expect the judge by the five o'clock train, sir, and shall the carriage be sent to Hazelby to meet him?"

There was a moment's silence, the three younger brothers coloured to their very hair roots, and Cheriton made a half step away from Alvar's side. The sudden pang that shot through him by its very sharpness brought its own remedy. He put his hand on Alvar's arm as if to call his attention.

"The train comes in at five—we had better send, hadn't we?" he said.

"Oh, yes!" said Alvar.

He had grown a little pale, and he turned his large black eyes on Cheriton with a look half-proud, half-appealing, and so sad as to drown all Cheriton's momentary shrinking in self-reproach.

"Alvar," said Mr Ellesmere, "if you will come with me, I have a message for you from your father."

He led the way into Mr Lester's study, and Alvar followed him to the room, of which his last vivid recollection was of the painful dispute after the breach of his engagement. He stood by the fire in silence, and the vicar said,—

"Alvar, your father desired me to tell you that, of all the actions of his life he most regretted the neglect which for so many years he showed you. He bid me say that on his death-bed he desired his son's forgiveness."

"My father made me every amends in his power," said Alvar, in a low voice.

"He commended your grandmother and your sister to your protection and kindness; your brothers also, and thought thankfully of all that you and Cherry have become to each other."

Alvar was much agitated, for some moments he was unable to speak, then he said vehemently, —

"This is my inheritance, as it was my father's; but to my brothers I seem an interloper. This is the wrong my father did to me, he made me a stranger in my own place."

"It was a wrong of which he deeply repented."

"It does not become me to speak of it," said Alvar proudly.

"You must not exaggerate," said Mr Ellesmere. "It would be hard for Cheriton to see any one in his father's place; but you have won from him, at any rate, a brother's love."

"I am his dear friend," said Alvar; "but it is different with Jack."

"Don't draw these fine distinctions. *Be* a worthy successor to your father; live here among your people, as he did, in the fear of God, and doing your duty as an English gentleman, and be, as you have ever been, patient and kind to your brothers. Doubtless it seems a hard task to you, but I earnestly believe that by God's blessing you may be all to them that even Cheriton might be in your place. Nay, the very differences between you may be, — nay have been — the means of good."

"You are very kind to me, sir, and I thank you," said Alvar courteously; but Mr Ellesmere felt as if his words had fallen a little flat. He felt sorry for Alvar, but he could not look forward to the future without uneasiness. He saw that the wrong was neither forgotten nor forgiven, and that there was in the young Spaniard's nature a background of immovable pride that promised ill for accommodating himself to unfamiliar duties, and a want of moral insight that would be slow in recognising them.

It seemed rather inconsistent when Alvar said meekly, "Cheriton will tell me in all things what I should do," and led the way back to the library.

Here they found the others gathered in a group by the fire; Nettie sitting on a stool at Cheriton's feet, Jack leaning over the back of his chair, and Bob close at hand. How much alike they looked, with their similar colouring and outline, and faces set in the same sorrowful stillness and softened by the same feelings! Alvar paused and looked at them for a moment, but Cheriton, seeing him, rose and came forward.

"We have been waiting for you, Alvar," he said. "I have been to see grandmamma, but I did not stay — she could not bear it; but now — will you come upstairs with us?" He gave a look of invitation to Mr Ellesmere also, and he followed them silently into the chamber of death.

There lay their father, all the irritable marks of human frailty smoothed away, and the grand outline and long beard giving him a likeness to some kingly monument. The twins held by each other, their grief almost overpowered by shrinking awe. Jack frowned and set his mouth hard, and wrung Cherry's hand in his stress of feeling till he almost crushed it, while Cheriton stood quite still and calm by Alvar's side.

"Let us pray," said Mr Ellesmere; and as they all knelt down he repeated the Lord's Prayer, and such other words as came to him.

When they rose up again Cheriton bent down and kissed his father's brow, and one by one the younger ones followed his example. Only Alvar stood still, till Cheriton turned to him, and taking his hand, with a look that Mr Ellesmere never forgot, drew him forward.

Alvar obeyed him, but as his lips touched his father's face the thought suddenly struck Cheriton that it must have been for the first time—that never, even in babyhood, had a caress passed between the father and son; and then, in contrast, he thought of himself, and the grief, hitherto unrealised, broke forth at last. He hid his face in his hands, and hurried out of the room into his own, away from them all.

The Squire of Oakby

"A lord of fat prize oxen and of sheep,
A raiser of huge melons and of pines,
A patron of some thirty charities,
A quarter-sessions chairman."

Chapter Thirty Six
The Funeral

"Wild March wind, wilt thou never cease thy sighing?"

It was on a wild March morning, when sudden gleams of radiant sunlight contended with heavy storm-clouds, that Mr Lester of Oakby was buried. There was no rain, but the violent wind carried the sound of the knell in fitful gusts over the mourning village, through the well-cared-for fields and plantations of Oakby, away to Ashrigg and Elderthwaite, bringing all the countryside in a great concourse to the funeral. For it was a real mourning, a real loss. Long years ago, Fanny Lester, with her bright smile, and clear, upward-looking eyes, had said to her husband, "We have a piece of work in the world given to us, Gerald; let us try and do it." And under her strong influence the dutiful and honourable traditions of conduct to which Gerald Lester was born, widened and were drawn higher; the various offices he held were exercised with conscientious effort for the benefit of his neighbours; and his tenantry, mind, soul and body, were the better for his life among them. They could trust him, and if he sometimes made mistakes from which the wise Fanny might have saved him, her death had consecrated for him every simple duty that she had pointed out. Now, while "the old Squire" still meant his father, while he was still in the strength of his manhood, he was gone; and at the head of his grave there stood, not the son they knew, with his father's fair face and his mother's fair soul, but the dark, stately stranger, who—among all those north-country gentlemen, farmers, and labourers who crowded round, those "neighbours" all so well known to each other—looked so strangely out of place.

So thought another stranger who, when he had travelled northwards, had little thought to find himself present at such a scene.

The Stanforths had long since returned to London, and Gipsy found herself once more in the midst of as pleasant a home-circle as ever a girl grew up in, while her attention was claimed by numerous interests, social, intellectual, and domestic. Her mother shook her head over the story of Jack's proposal; but she said very little about the matter, secretly hoping that Gipsy would cease to think of it on returning to another atmosphere. All the advances, she said to her husband, must now come from the other side, and she could not but regard the future as doubtful, and was slightly incredulous of the charms of the travelling companions whom she had not herself seen. But Jack, while he was at Oxford, wrote to Mr Stanforth, about once a fortnight, rather formal and sententious epistles, which did not contain one word about Gipsy, but which in their regularity and simplicity impressed her mother favourably. One long, pleasant letter arrived from Cheriton during his last weeks at Seville, and of this Gipsy enjoyed the perusal. She did not show any symptoms of low spirits, and being a girl of some resolution of character, held her tongue and bided her time. Perhaps a bright and fairly certain expectation was all she as yet wanted or was ready for. She was young in feeling, even for her eighteen years, and in truth they were "beginning at the beginning."

Still she wished ardently that her father should accede to a request from Sir John Hubbard, that he should come down to Ashrigg Hall, and paint a companion picture of his wife to the one that he had taken of himself long ago. Lady Hubbard was infirm and could not come to London, or Sir John would not have made such a demand on Mr Stanforth's time, now, of course, even more fully occupied than it had been ten years before.

Mr Stanforth hesitated; he did not like the notion of any possible meeting with Mr Lester, while Jack's views remained a secret from him; but Sir John had shown him a good deal of kindness, and he felt curious to hear something of his young friends in their own neighbourhood. So the first week in March found him at Ashrigg, in the midst of a large family party, for the eldest son and his wife were staying there, and there were several daughters at home.

"We had hoped to give a few of our friends the pleasure of meeting you, Mr Stanforth," said Sir John, after dinner, when the wine was on the table, "but our neighbourhood has sustained a great loss in the death of a valued friend of ours, Mr Lester, of Oakby."

"Mr Lester of Oakby! You don't say so! Surely that is very sudden," said Mr Stanforth, infinitely shocked. "I saw a great deal of his sons in the south of Spain," he added in explanation.

"Indeed! They are at home now, poor fellows. They were just too late. I had this note from Jack—that's the second son—no, the third—this afternoon."

"I know Jack, too," said Mr Stanforth, as he took the note. It was a very brief one, merely announcing his father's death, and adding,—

"My brothers returned from Spain this morning. We hope that the journey has done Cheriton no harm."

"Ah, poor Cheriton!" said Mr Stanforth. "I fear he must have run a great risk. It will be a terrible blow to him. We formed something more than a travelling acquaintance."

"Poor Mr Lester was here only a fortnight ago, speaking with delight of Cheriton's entire recovery," said Lady Hubbard.

"Yes, he was much better," said Mr Stanforth, a little doubtfully, "and full of enjoyment. But this will be indeed a startling change."

"Yes," said Sir John; "one does not know how to think of Alvar in his father's shoes. It was a sadly mismanaged business altogether."

"There is a great deal to like in Alvar Lester," said Mr Stanforth; "but of course the circumstances are very peculiar."

"Yes. You see while the elder brother, Robert, was alive, no one thought much of Gerald, and when this Spanish marriage came out, it was a great shock. And he was too ready to listen to all the excuses about the boy's health. If he had come home and been sent to school in England he might have grown up like the rest, and black eyes instead of blue ones would have been all the difference."

"I have always thought his long absence inexplicable."

"Well, Lester hated the thought of his boyish marriage, and these other boys came, and Cherry was his darling. His wife did make an effort once, and Alvar was brought to France when he was about seven years old; but they said he was ill, and took him back again. Then when old Mrs Lester came into power she opposed his coming, and things slipped on. I don't think he was expected to live at first, and, poor fellow! no one wished that he should."

"The second Mrs Lester must have been a very remarkable person," said Mr Stanforth.

"She was," said Lady Hubbard warmly. "She was a person to raise the tone of a whole neighbourhood. She made another man of her husband, and he worshipped her. She was no beauty, and very small, but with the brightest of smiles, and eyes that seemed to look straight up into heaven. No one could forget Fanny Lester. She influenced every one."

There was much more talk, and many side lights were cast on Mr Stanforth's mind when he heard of Alvar's broken engagement to Virginia Seyton, and of her pretty cousin Ruth's recent marriage to Captain Lester, "though at one time every one thought that there was something between her and Cheriton." He could not but think most of how his own daughter's future might be affected by this sudden freeing of her young lover from parental control; but he was full of sympathy for them all, and the note that he wrote to Cheriton was answered by a request that he would accompany Sir John Hubbard to the funeral: "They could never forget all his kindness in another time of trouble."

It was a striking group of mourners. Alvar stood in the midst, dignified and impassive, and by his side a tall, girlish figure, with bright hair gleaming through her crape veil, the three other brothers together, looking chiefly as if they were trying to preserve an unmoved demeanour; Rupert's face behind them, like enough to suggest kindred, and Judge Cheriton's keen cultivated face; Mr Seyton, pale, worn, and white-haired, and his brother's tanned, weather-beaten countenance, ruddy and solemn, above his clerical dress. Many a fine, powerful form and handsome outline showed among the men, whose fathers had served Mr Lester's; and behind, crowds of women, children, and old people filled the churchyard and the lanes beyond.

As the service proceeded the heavy clouds parted, and a sudden gleam of sunlight fell, lighting up the violet pall and the white wreaths laid on it, the surplices of the choristers, and the bent heads of the mourners. Cheriton looked up at last away from the open grave, through the break in the clouds, but with a face strangely white and sad in the momentary sunlight. Jack, as they turned away, caught sight of Mr Stanforth, and the sudden involuntary look of pleasure that lightened the poor boy's miserable face was touching to see. When all was over, and, in common with most of those from a distance, Mr Stanforth had accompanied Sir John Hubbard up to the house, Jack sought him out, hardly having a word to say; but evidently finding satisfaction in his presence.

"Oh, we have nothing picturesque at home, but still I should like to show you Oakby," Cheriton had said, as they walked together in the beautiful streets of Seville; but the long table in the old oak dining-room, covered with family plate, the sombre, faded richness of colouring that told of years of settled dignified life, were not altogether commonplace, any more than the pair of brothers who occupied the two ends of the table. It was not till there was a general move that Cheriton came up and put his hand into his friend's.

"We all like to think that you have been here," he said. "You will come again while you are at Ashrigg?"

"I will, indeed. And you,—these cold winds do not hurt you?"

"No, I think not. My uncle wishes Sir John Hubbard to hear some of our arrangements; you will not mind waiting for a little."

He spoke very quietly, but as if there were a great weight upon him, while his attention was claimed by some parting guest.

"Well, Cheriton, good-bye; this is a sorrowful day for many. You must try and teach your poor brother to fill your father's place. We are all ready to welcome him among us, and we hope he will take an interest in everything here."

"You are very land, Mr Sutton," said Cheriton, rather as if he thought the kindness too outspoken.

Then a much older face and voice took a turn.

"Good-bye, my lad. Your grandfather and I were friends always, and I little thought to see this day. Keep things going, Cherry, for the old name's sake."

"I shall be in London soon," said Cherry ungraciously, for the echoes of his own forebodings were very hard to bear. Then Rupert came up with a warm hand-shake.

"Good-bye, my dear fellow. I hope we shall see you in London. Don't catch another bad cold. I hope you'll all get along together."

"I dare say we shall. But thank you, it was very good of you to come just now."

"Just off your wedding trip, as I understand?" said the old gentleman.

"Yes; we came back from Paris a few days ago, and I must get back to town to-night," said Rupert, as Cheriton moved away to join his uncle for a sort of explanation of the state of affairs to the younger ones, and for the reading of the will, though, its chief provisions were well known to him.

Alvar, as his father had done before him, inherited the estate free from debt or mortgage, with such an income as sounded to his Spanish notions magnificent; but which those better versed in English expenditure knew would find ample employment in all the calls of such a place as Oakby.

It was quite sufficient for the position, but no more. The estate, of course, still remained chargeable with old Mrs Lester's jointure. Mr Lester had enjoyed the interest of his wife's fortune during her life, the bulk of which had come to her from an aunt, and was secured to her daughter; her three sons succeeding to five thousand pounds apiece, and for this money Judge Cheriton, and a certain General Fleming, a relation of the Cheritons, were joint trustees. So the will, made almost as soon as Mr Lester inherited the property, had stood, and indeed most of its provisions had been made by his father. Since his illness, however, a codicil had been added, stating that Mr Lester had intended to leave the small amount of ready money at his disposal equally among his three younger sons, but that now he decided to leave the whole to Cheriton, "whose health might involve him in more expenses, and prevent him from using the same exertions as his brothers." He also joined his two elder sons, with their uncle, Judge Cheriton, in the personal guardianship of John, Robert, and Annette. There were a few gifts and legacies to servants and dependants, and that was all.

"Nothing," remarked Judge Cheriton, after a pause, "could be more proper than this decision with regard to Cheriton, though we hope its necessity has passed away; but under the very peculiar circumstances every one has felt that it would have been well if a somewhat larger proportion of his mother's fortune could have come to him."

"Of course," said Jack, "it is all right."

"But my father might have trusted him to me," said Alvar.

"Such things should always be in black and white," said the judge. "Your father has shown marked confidence both in you and in Cheriton by giving you a share in the charge of the younger ones, and this desire will, of course, naturally affect our arrangements for them. Annette's home at least must be fixed by her grandmother's."

"But my grandmother will stay here," said Alvar, in a tone of surprise. "Why should she change? It will be all the same. And the boys too, and my sister, and Cheriton—of course—we must be together."

He spoke warmly, and crossing over to Cheriton, took his hand as he spoke.

"This is your home, my brother, always."

"You are *very* good to us, Alvar, thank you," said Cheriton, hardly able to speak.

"Most kind," said the judge; "whatever may be decided on, your offer is suggested by a most proper feeling, of which I hope all are sensible."

"Alvar is very kind," said Jack shyly.

"Would you not expect that Cheriton should be 'kind' to you? Then why not I, as well?" said Alvar.

"Such an arrangement," said the judge, "would not be *binding* on Cheriton even in your place. I am rejoiced to see so good an understanding between you. Alvar has a great deal of business before him, and it would be a pity to make any changes at present. But as for you, Cheriton, is it wise to remain here so early in the year?"

"No," said Alvar; "I think we should go to the south for a little."

"I think the calls upon your time—" began the judge, but Cheriton interposed.

"I don't think I am any the worse for the weather," he said, "and I should not like to go away now. We shall all have a great deal to do."

Sir John Hubbard spoke a few friendly words and offered any assistance or advice to Alvar in his power, and then took his leave, as did Mr Malcolm. Alvar and Jack, with the judge, accompanied them into the hall; and no sooner had the door of the study closed than Nettie, who had been a silent spectator of the scene, suddenly burst out,—"I don't care! I will say it! It may be very kind of Alvar, but it is horrible, *horrible* to think *he* is master and may do what he pleases with us. I hate to stay here if *he* is to give us leave."

"I told you, Nettie," said Bob, with masculine prudence, "that no one ought to *say* those things."

"Nor feel them, I hope," said Cherry. "Nettie, my dear child, you must not make it worse for us all. We feel our great loss; but you know the future will not be easy for Alvar himself."

"I know," sobbed Nettie, with increasing vehemence, "that he will not be like—like papa. I can't *bear* to think that the dear place all belongs to *him*, and the things, and the animals even, and the horses. *He* doesn't love them, nor the place, and ice do!"

"Be silent, Nettie," said Cheriton, with unusual sternness; "I will never listen to one word like this. There is nothing wrong about it. Think of all that Alvar has done for me, and then say if such words are justifiable."

The severity of the tone silenced Nettie—it was meant to silence poor Cheriton's own heart. He was stern to his sister because he felt severely towards himself; but Nettie thought him unjust, and only moved by partiality for Alvar. He saw complications far beyond her childish jealousy, and yet he shared it. And above all was the anguish of a personal loss, a heavy grief that filled up all the intervals of perplexing anticipations and business cares.

The twins went away together, and Cherry sat down in his father's chair and leaned his head back against the cushion of it. It was all over, all the love that had had so many last thoughts for him, and, alas! no last words. They had indeed parted for ever in this life; but how differently from what he had expected last year. Over! and the future looked difficult and dark. "*He* does not love them, and we do." It was too true. Cherry was tired out with the long, hasty journey, the succeeding strain of occupation, and with the sorrow that weighed him down—a sorrow that only now seemed to come upon him in all its strength. He was not conscious of the passing of time till a hand was laid on his shoulder, and Alvar's voice said softly, "I have been looking for you, *Cherito mio*."

"Oh, I am very tired," said Cherry.

How strange it was to rouse himself from thoughts in which Alvar's image brought such a sense of trouble and perplexity, to feel the accustomed comfort of his presence! How strange to shrink so painfully from the thought of his foreign brother's rule in his father's place, and yet to feel the fretting weariness soothed insensibly by the care on which he had learned to depend. He could not think this crooked matter straight, he could not even feel compunction for his own fears. He was tired and wretched, and Alvar knew just what was restful and comforting to him.

Chapter Thirty Seven
The New Master

"Against each one did each contend,
And all against the heir."

By the next morning Cheriton's thoughts had cleared themselves, and matters began to take some shape; he could make up his mind to a certain line of conduct, or at least could place a distinct aim before him. He had often before been forced to acknowledge that Alvar's character, as well as his position, had its own rights; they must take him as they found him; neither his faults nor his excellencies were theirs—and how much Cherry owed to those very points in Alvar which had come on them like a surprise! Was it not the height both of ingratitude and of conceit to think of him as of one to be altered and influenced before he could be fit for his new station? Why would not Alvar's gentleness, honour, and courtesy, his undoubted power of setting himself aside, make him as valuable a member of society as industry, integrity, and regard for those about him had made of his father? It was his misfortune, not his fault, that he was a square man in a round hole; and what could Cherry do but try to round off a few angles or poke a few corners for them to stick into? Was it prejudice and unworthy jealousy that made him unable to accept this view, or was there something in Nettie's vehement disapproval, however unkindly and arrogantly it was expressed? If Alvar chose he could make a very good Squire Lester. Yes, if—There was the question. The English Lesters sometimes did right, and sometimes— some of them very often—did wrong; but they one and all recognised that doing right was the business of their lives, and that if they did wrong they must repent and suffer. They certainly believed that "conduct is nine-tenths of life," in other words, that they must "do their duty in that state of life to which they were called."

But in Alvar this motive seemed almost non-existent. He did not care about his own duty or other people's. Only such a sense, or the strong influence of the religion from which in the main it sprang, or a sort of enthusiasm equally foreign to him, could have roused an indolent nature to the supreme effort of altering his whole way of living, of caring for subjects hitherto indifferent to him—in short, of changing his entire self.

No doubt Alvar would think something due to his position, and something more to please Cheriton, but he would not regard shortcomings as of any consequence; in short, it was not that Alvar's principles were different from theirs, but that as motives of action he had not got any; not that he had Spanish instead of English notions of property, politics, or religion, but that he did not care to entertain any notions at all.

Cheriton understood enough now of the shifting scenes of Spanish life to understand that this might be their effect on an outsider who saw many different schemes of life all produce an equally bad effect on society; but it was none the less peculiarly ill-adapted to an owner of English property; and he took leave to think that if Spanish gentlemen in past generations had administered justice in their own neighbourhoods, mended their own roads, and seen to the instruction of their own tenants, a happier state of things might have prevailed at the present time in the peninsula. Anyhow, to him, as to his father, the welfare of Oakby was very dear—dearer now than ever, for his father's sake. One thought had troubled Mr Lester's last hours, that by his own conduct he had allowed Alvar to become unfit to succeed him: all, therefore, that Cheriton could do to remove that unfitness was so much work done for his father's sake; all, too, that made Alvar happy, was an undoing of the wrong that he had suffered. There was no real discord between what was right by Alvar and by Oakby and by his own sense of right. To make the best of Alvar, to allow for all his difficulties, to help him in every possible way, was not only due to that loving brother, but was the right way to be loyal to his father's higher self, and to clear his memory from those weaknesses and errors which cling to every one in this mortal life—was, too, the only way to see his work carried on.

This "high endeavour" came to Cheriton, indeed, as "an inward light" to brighten the perplexed path before him. Sorrow, he had already learnt, could be borne, difficulties might be overcome, now that his inmost feelings were at peace.

Certainly he had enough on his hands. Much of the correspondence with old friends fell naturally to his share. English "business" was unintelligible to Alvar without his explanations, and though the new Squire showed himself perfectly willing to receive from Mr Malcolm an account of the various sources of his income, and submitted to go through his father's accounts, and to hear reports from farmers and bailiffs, he always insisted on Cheriton's presence at these interviews; and though he was too easily satisfied with the fact that "my brother understands," no one could have expected him to find it all quite easy to understand himself.

Cherry apologised for putting his finger in every pie.

"Oh," said Alvar cheerfully; "I could not make the pie if I put in both my hands."

But Cheriton knew perfectly well that the parish and the estate believed themselves to be entering on the reign of King Log. Any breakers, however, in this direction were still far ahead; but within doors difficulties and incongruities came sooner to a point, and Alvar was by no means always to blame for them.

On the day after the funeral, Mrs Lester resumed her place in the family; but her son's death had aged her much, and to see Alvar in his place was gall and wormwood to her. She accepted his offer of a home, and thanked him for it with dignity and propriety; but she did not attempt to conceal from the young ones that she grudged him the power to make it.

The household arrangements went on as usual, and Alvar's behaviour to her was irreproachable in its courtesy and consideration, nor did she ever clash with him, but reserved her fears and her disapprobations for Cherry's benefit.

Nettie had come back from London at Christmas, and nothing more had been heard of Dick Seyton, who was then absent from home; but the recollection of that episode prompted Mrs Lester to give a ready consent to Judge Cheriton's proposal that she should go at Easter to school for a year. Bob, too, who had been taken away from school at Christmas, where his career had not lately been satisfactory, was at present reading with a clergyman at Hazelby, and was to be sent to a tutor by-and-by. In the meantime, both he and Nettie were as unhappy as young creatures can be when their world is all changed for them; with their hearts yearning towards what they already called old times. And all the force of their natures concentrated into a sort of fierce, aggressive loyalty to every practice, opinion, and tradition of the past, and to this code they viewed Cherry as a traitor. It was a cruel offence when he happened to say that he liked to drink chocolate, and when Alvar made a point of his having some; when Alvar now and again used Spanish expressions in speaking to him, when he pronounced Spanish names in Spanish fashion, or, worst of all, regretted Spanish sunshine; when he yielded to Alvar's care for his health, or seemed to turn to him for sympathy—a hundred such pin-pricks occurred every day. And yet the foolish twins scrupulously did what they thought their duty. That Alvar owned their father's horses cost Nettie floods of tears; but she insisted on Bob asking his permission before he took one to ride to Hazelby, and she always showed him a kind of sulky deference.

"How can you be so silly, Nettie?" said Jack, in answer to a pettish remark. "Do you want Cherry to quarrel with Alvar?"

"No," said Nettie; "but I didn't think he would have *liked* Spain, and have talked so much about the pictures and things. Last night he asked Alvar to play to him."

"I should think you might be glad to see him pleased with anything; he looks wretched enough."

"Well, I like what I'm used to," said Nettie, in a choked voice. "I don't care to hear about all the stupid people you met in Spain."

"The friends we made in Spain," said Jack, in high indignation, "were people with whom it was a privilege to associate."

"I daresay," said Nettie; "but old acquaintances are good enough for me; and old weather and everything. Yes, Buffer, *I'll* take you out, if it *is* a nasty cold morning."

And Nettie went off, with a train of dogs behind her, angry with all her brothers, for even Bob had had the sense to grumble out "that people must do as they pleased, and she had better let Cherry and Alvar alone," and feeling as if she only were faithful to the dear home standard.

As Jack stood by the hall fire, heavy-hearted enough himself, in spite of his rebuke to his sister, there was a ring at the bell, and the cloud cleared from his brow as he started forward to greet Mr Stanforth with an eagerness unusual with him.

He was too unaffectedly pleased to be embarrassed, and began almost at once, —

"My uncle Cheriton comes back to us to-night. He had to leave us on the day after we saw you; Cherry has promised to speak to him, that we may come to an understanding before I go back to Oxford." Mr Stanforth smiled a little.

"When do you come of age, Jack?" he said.

"I shall be twenty next week," said Jack, in a tone of humiliation. "If I take a fair degree, I shall try for a mastership in one of the public schools. I should like that, and—and it is suitable to getting married," concluded Jack blushing.

"Very well," said Mr Stanforth. "Then you shall come and tell me of your intentions for the future in a year's time from next week. Wait a bit," as Jack looked exceedingly blank. "If circumstances had not so sadly changed, no other decision would have been possible for you. I have no objection, in the meantime, to see you occasionally at my house, as I think you should both have every opportunity of testing the permanence of such quick-springing feelings."

Mr Stanforth smiled as he spoke; but Jack said after a moment,—

"You mean that I must earn her? Well, I will."

There was a solemn abruptness in Jack's manner that provoked a smile; but his self-confidence was tempered by a look of such absolute honesty and sincerity in his bright blue eyes, he looked such a fine young fellow in all the freshness and strength of his youth, that it would have been difficult to doubt either his purposes or his power of carrying them out.

"Don't you think you might have asked Mr Stanforth to take off his coat and come into the library before entering on such an important subject?" said Cheriton, joining them.

"I beg your pardon," said Jack. "Please come in; I was not thinking—"

"Of anything but your own affairs? No, that's very unfair, for I am sure you have taken heed to every one else's," said Cherry, as he led the way into the library, where on the table was a great accumulation of papers, looking like the materials for a heavy morning's work.

Cherry sent Jack to find Alvar, and told him to order some wine to be brought into the library, apologising to Mr Stanforth for not asking him to lunch, as their grandmother was unequal to seeing a stranger; and then, in Jack's absence, he listened to Mr Stanforth's ultimatum, and owned that it was a great relief not to have to startle his relations just now with what would seem an incongruous proposal; but praising Jack's sense and consideration in their trouble, and speaking of him with a kind of tender pride, unlike the tone of one so nearly on the same level of age, and whose life also was but beginning. He said that he should come to London at Easter, but that in the meanwhile there was much to be done at home. English affairs were naturally puzzling to Alvar, and a great deal of the business concerned them all.

"You must remember that you ought to be still taking holiday," said Mr Stanforth.

"Oh, yes. At least Alvar and Jack never let me forget it. But, indeed, I am quite well, and though I feel the cold, I don't think it means to hurt me. It is better to have plenty to do."

Cherry's manner was not uncheerful, and though he looked pale and delicate, there was no longer the appearance of broken health and spirits which had marked him at their first acquaintance; but the quick, changeable brightness was gone also. He was like one carrying a load which took all his strength; but he carried it without staggering.

Alvar now came in with Jack, looking bright and cordial.

"My brother is teaching me how to be the Squire," he said to Mr Stanforth, with a smile, as he put aside the papers to make room for the tray that had been ordered; "but I am not a good scholar."

"You must go regularly to school, then," said Mr Stanforth.

"Ah," said Alvar; "I must know, it seems, about rents, and tenants, and freeholds—so many things. But there is something that we wish to ask of Mr Stanforth, is there not, Cherry?"

"Yes—we spoke of it."

"It is that he will try to make a drawing of our father for us, for there is none that my brothers like."

"I will try with pleasure, but I am afraid likenesses, under the circumstances, are rarely quite satisfactory. You have a photograph?"

Jack produced a very bad daguerreotype, and a photograph taken for Cheriton before he left home.

"This is a good likeness," he said; "but Cherry thinks it wants fire and spirit."

"I will take both," said Mr Stanforth, seeing that Cherry had turned aside from the photograph, and took no part in the discussion. "I will make a little sketch, and when you are in London you can tell me what you wish about it. And now I think I must be getting back to Ashrigg; to-morrow I go home."

Jack eagerly said that to-morrow he was going to London on his way to Oxford, and received the longed-for permission to call at Kensington. Poor boy! he could not keep himself from looking ecstatically happy even while he told Mr Stanforth, as he walked through the park with him, how sorry he was to leave Cheriton with so much on his hands.

Cheriton himself would gladly have kept Jack beside him. He was capable of seeing both sides of the difficult question, and was, moreover, so individual and independent in his modes of thought, that home matters were less personal to him. He had, too, his own hopes, and had chalked out his own career, so that, young as he was, he was a support to Cherry's spirits, even while more than half the reason why his own were less overpowered was that the brother who was all in all to him was still left. His presence did not always conduce to peace with Bob, for he had grown away from him, and was disposed to lecture him; but though he departed with more good advice to his family than was necessary, he left another gap, and Cherry, trying to rouse himself from the added feeling of loneliness, went over to Elderthwaite to see the old parson. He had been away so long that every familiar place brought fresh associations, and he tried to get the first sight of each one over quickly and alone.

He could not walk past the stables and through the farm-buildings without the image of his father meeting him at every turn. Here they had planned a new fence together, in this direction the very last walk he had had strength for before leaving home had been taken. How well he remembered *then* sitting on that bench under the stable wall, and watching his father with a sad wonder if he should ever sit there again. This was the short way from the station by which he used to come home from school. Here his father used to meet him—nay, suddenly he recollected, with a memory that started into life after lying asleep for years, *here* he had parted for the last time from his mother, and the long-past grief seemed to come back in the light of the new one. He said to himself that he ought to rejoice in the thought that his parents were once more together; but in the strangest way he longed for this long-lost mother to comfort him in the new grief of his father's death.

And then he walked on through the fir plantation, across the bit of bare, bleak fell, into the woods of Elderthwaite. And as he walked he thought of Jack's bright hopes, and of that sweet and promising future that was to make up to him for all that the past had taken from him. Here, by the broken stile and ruinous wall, all hope of such a future had been dashed away from Cheriton's heart. *This* memory had no sweetness to temper its pain; and he hurried on through the plantation and down the lane that led to the vicarage. As he passed the church he saw that some one was trimming the ivy round the windows, and it struck him that they had been cleaned, and that the whole place had a somewhat improved appearance. A little girl made him a curtsey; she wore a smart red flannel hood, and had a clean face; he thought that he had never seen an Elderthwaite child look so respectable. Nay, as he passed one of the larger cottages, it shone upon him resplendent with whitewash, and looking in at the open door he beheld a row of desks, and sundry boys and girls seated thereat, and with curiosity much excited by this evidence of reform, he hastened on towards the vicarage.

Chapter Thirty Eight
Plans and Experiments

"I am sick of the hall and the hill, I am sick of the moor and the main."

Virginia Seyton had spent her Christmas at Littleton, and after returning to London for her cousin Ruth's marriage, had come home again at the end of January. At Littleton, more than one old friend had advised her to reconsider her resolve to live at Elderthwaite; but Virginia did not feel herself tempted by any proposal of cottage, however charming, or companionship, however congenial. She had been lonely, unhappy, and forlorn at Elderthwaite; but somehow it pulled at her heart-strings. She could not rejoice over all the well-ordered services at Littleton, much as they refreshed her spirits, as she did over the new hymn which she and Mrs Clements drilled into the Elderthwaite children; and she found herself believing, when receiving the correct answers of her former scholars, that there was after all "something" in the north-country intellect, however untrained, that was superior in quality, if not in quantity, to that of the south. When she went back to London, common acquaintances brought her into contact with the Stanforths. She and Ruth went to an evening party at their house, just as Mr Stanforth and Gipsy returned from Spain, and were invited to come afterwards and see the Spanish sketches. Ruth was glad to make all the business that pressed on her an excuse for refusing; but Virginia went, and was happier than she had been for months in hearing Alvar spoken of, and spoken of in terms of praise. Neither girl was conscious of the other's interest in this meeting— how Gipsy listened to "some one who had known Jack all his life," how Virginia watched Alvar's recent companion; but Gipsy's blushes came in the right place, and in spite of her extreme amaze at the idea of Jack in this new capacity, Virginia guessed where the spark had been lighted, and so could listen fearlessly to the story of the adventures at Ronda, and could look with pleasure at the sketches of which Alvar's figure was a picturesque element. It was a pleasant peep at a new life linked with her old one.

Ruth's was a very brilliant wedding. Everything was arranged by her grandmother, and bridesmaids, dresses, breakfast, and even church, were all chosen with exact regard to the correct fashion of the moment. Ruth wished it all to be over that she might find herself away with Rupert; then perhaps she would feel at rest. As it was, their rapid, interrupted surface intercourse tantalised her almost as much as their occasional interviews in the days of secrecy and silence. And when they were alone, Ruth was afraid to go deep. Often had she said, "In *my* love there shall be perfect confidence; there shall be nothing between my soul and his." And now her past transgression, however excusable it might seem, erred against this perfect confidence. And Rupert's "soul" was not at all ready to display itself to her, or to himself either, partly because he was not serious in his emotions, any more than in his principles, but partly also because he not unnaturally considered that when his deeds were satisfactory to Ruth, it was quite unnecessary to analyse his feelings. So she had no encouragement to confidence, and the perfect union for which she had longed, disappointed her, partly through her past falsity, but more from the want of any common aim or principle to unite them. Ruth was fairly happy; but she was the same Ruth still, with a nature that could never be satisfied without earnestness equalling her own, an earnestness from the purity and simplicity of which she had turned aside to seek a sort of consecration of life *which only a man of high principle and strong purpose could really have helped her to find*, in a love which she thought more powerful because it was more regardless of duty, in which view she did but follow much teaching and many writers.

Ruth did not make the confession which would have set her right with herself if not with Rupert, she had practised too much self-pleasing to find the courage for it. She married; and as life went on her aspirations would either die into the commonplace she had despised, or she might be driven to satisfy them elsewhere than with Rupert.

And Virginia, who equally with Ruth idealised life and its relations, and who also found her ideal unfulfilled—unfulfilled, but not destroyed. She had lost her lover, but the good and holy life which she had thought to lead with him, though its beauty took a sterner cast, was possible without him. Life was not purposeless, though it was very difficult, and poor Virginia was diffident of her own powers, and was, moreover, in many ways ill-fitted to live with those whose views of life were uncongenial to her.

"If I had more tact I should get on better at home; if I had had more patience, more charity, I should not have quarrelled with Alvar," she thought, and with some truth. But when she came back to Elderthwaite it *was* coming home. Dick and Harry were glad to see her; her father said it looked cheerful to have her about again; the little housemaid, whom she had taught for an hour on Sundays, was enchanted, and had written copies and learnt hymns in her absence; while she could not but be welcome to her aunt, whom she found suffering from a severe attack of rheumatism, which confined her to her room. Virginia had no natural skill in nursing, and Miss Seyton was not fond of attentions. But, though she was severely uncomplaining, Virginia's companionship was enlivening, and, moreover, while she was incapacitated, her niece was obliged to manage the house. She had bought enough bitter experience now not to be frightened and startled at the state of things, and she perceived how much Miss Seyton had done to keep things straight. But the young, fresh influence brightened up the old dependents, and she managed, too, to introduce some little comfort. But a piece of home work really within her powers came to her in an unexpected quarter. Dick's examination was to take place in about six weeks, and she found from Harry that he had been really reading for it, and to her great surprise and pleasure he did not resent her interest in it. Her French, and history, and arithmetic were quite enough in advance of Dick's to make her aid valuable to him, and finding how much he was behindhand, spite of some honest though fitful efforts, she gave him some lessons with the tutor at Hazelby to whom Bob Lester was sent, and as Dick always brought his papers to her afterwards, there was no question that he actually availed himself of the opportunity.

As for the old parson, he greeted her with a perfect effusion of delight. He had come to love her better than anything in the world except Cheriton, whose illness had been a real sorrow to him. The little improvements had not been allowed to languish—indeed others had been projected. Mr Clements had not been idle. A poor widow, whose continued respectability had certainly been partly owing to her attachment to Mr Seyton's rival or assistant, "the old Methody," had a niece who had been trained as a pupil-teacher in a parish belonging to a friend of Mr Ellesmere's, and, her health failing, the girl had come to live with her aunt. Hence a proposal for a little day-school; and actually a subscription set on foot by Mr Clements.

(This of course took place before the passing of the Education Act.)

"So you see, Miss Seyton," he had said, "we have not been quite idle in your absence."

"Indeed," said Virginia, smiling, "you seem to have done better without me."

"No, Miss Seyton, whatever better things we may succeed in doing in Elderthwaite in the future, it is your doing that the wish to improve had been awakened."

Virginia blushed at this magnificent compliment; but it was true. High principle, recommended by gentleness and humility, must in the end win its way.

These various changes formed a safe subject of conversation in a meeting that could not fail on many accounts to be trying, when Cheriton, as he came up to the vicarage, met Virginia going in there also. He did not want to talk about his own health or home difficulties, she could not fail to be conscious; but the parson was only restrained, or *not* restrained, by her presence from lamentations over Alvar's succession, and looked unspeakably wicked when Cherry implied that they were getting on smoothly. So the new school came in handy, and Parson Seyton talked about a "Government grant," and winked at Cherry over his shoulder.

"It's all getting beyond me, Cherry," he said; "I'm not the man for these new lights."

"You'll have to get a curate, parson," said Cherry.

"Nay—nay!" said the parson sharply. "I'll have no strangers prying into all our holes and corners, and raking out the dust. I don't like curates—hate their long coats and long faces."

"You might put in the advertisement 'round and rosy preferred,'" said Cherry.

"Nay, nay, my lad; no curates for me, unless *you* will apply for the situation."

"Cherry has a *very* long coat on," said Virginia, smiling and pointing to his "ulster."

"And not too round a face nowadays, eh? Never mind, if he came here I'd let him wear—"

"A cassock, perhaps," said Cheriton. "I feel all the force of the compliment. But I think Queenie is the best curate for Elderthwaite at present."

Virginia's heart danced at the familiar brotherly name by which Cheriton had learned from Ruth to call her in the days of her engagement, but which had never become her home appellation, and something in her face made him whisper under his breath as she rose to take leave,—

"Though Oakby grudges her to you." Virginia hurried away, but she was presently overtaken by Cheriton as she paused at a cottage door, and they walked up the lane together, and talked of the Stanforths; and when Virginia praised Gipsy, neither could help a smile of implied comprehension and sympathy.

It was a bright, pleasant day, the puddles and ditches of the Elderthwaite hedgerows sparkled in the spring sunshine, the blackthorn put out its shy blossoms on each side. Virginia smiled and looked up gaily, and Cheriton's voice took its natural lively tone as he related some of the humours of their Spanish journey.

"I must turn off here," said Cherry, as they came to a stile. But Virginia did not answer him, for, leaning against the fence, stood Alvar, watching them as they approached. A hayrick and tumble-down cart-shed, and a waggon with its poles turned up in the air, formed a strangely incongruous background for his graceful figure, his deep mourning giving him an additional air of picturesque dignity.

There was no escape for Virginia. She turned exceedingly pale, but with a self-command that, in Cheriton's opinion, did her infinite credit, she bowed—she had not courage to put out her hand—and said timidly,—

"Good morning."

Alvar's olive face coloured all over; he bowed, for once utterly and evidently at a loss, while Cherry plunged into the breach.

"Hallo, Alvar, have you come to look for me? I have been to see Parson Seyton. You have no idea what grand doings there are now in Elderthwaite."

"I did not come to look for you," said Alvar, with some emphasis.

"Well, I was coming home."

Then Alvar turned, and with a sort of haughty politeness hoped that Mr and Miss Seyton were well; and Virginia, in the sweet tones unheard for so many months, replied to him, and after shaking hands with Cheriton, walked away down the sunny lane, from which she could not turn aside, and which afforded no shelter from any eyes that might choose to follow her.

Alvar, however, turned away, and Cherry following, said,—

"I think a little light will dawn on Elderthwaite one day, thanks to Virginia."

Alvar did not make any answer, and Cheriton was not at all sorry to see how much the meeting had disturbed him.

He never alluded to it again, but whether from any feelings connected with it or from the worries of his new position, he was less even-tempered than usual.

There was much to try him. So many matters pressed on him, and he was so very much at fault as to the way of dealing with them. Mr Lester had kept a considerable portion of his property in his own hands; he had also been a most active magistrate, sat upon innumerable county committees, and had united in his own person the chief lay offices of the parish. In all these capacities he had done a considerable amount of useful work, and though no one expected Alvar to take up the whole of it, he ought to have endeavoured to make himself master of the more necessary parts.

But the real defect of Alvar's nature—the intense pride, that made the sense of being at a disadvantage hateful to him—worked at first in a wrong direction. The great effort of bending himself to learn to do badly what those around him could do well, was beyond one who had never felt the need of repentance, never acknowledged an error in himself; nor did the sense of duty to his neighbour, that counteracted this tendency in others of his name, appeal to the conscience of one who inherited the selfish instincts of the Spanish grandee. After the very first he grew impatient of the tasks that were so new to him, and yet resentful of any comment on his behaviour. He resented the standard to which he would not conform, all the more because an unspeakable soreness connected it with Virginia's rejection of him.

Perhaps this was more hopeful than his former good-humoured indifference, but it was with exceeding pain that Cheriton, before Easter came, began to perceive that though Alvar would let him please himself in any special instance, his hopes of exerting any general influence were vain, and that Alvar would resent the attempt even from him.

"*Did* you expect to make the leopard change his spots by the force of your will, Cherry?" said Mr Ellesmere to him, when some instance had brought this prominently forward. "You cannot do it, my boy, and excuse me for saying that I think you should not try."

"I only wanted to help the leopard to accommodate his coat to our climate," said Cherry, with rather a difficult smile.

"He must do that himself when stress of weather shows him the need. If he had married, such an influence as your mother's might have come into his life; but, my dear boy, *even* that could not have sufficed, unless it had appealed to something higher."

"I know," said Cherry slowly. "I know what you mean about it. No man ought to stand dictation as to his duty, and we all lay down the law to each other. But I cannot break myself of feeling that matters here are my own concern."

"I think that is a habit of mind common to a great many people hereabouts," said Mr Ellesmere kindly; "and, after all, what I said was only meant as a warning."

"Much needed! But I believe Alvar will find things out in time; and we none of its make half enough allowance for him."

Jack came home for a few days at Easter, and there was a final discussion and arrangement of plans, which resulted after all in a general flitting. Alvar declared that Oakby was too dull without his brother, and that he should himself go to London for some time. No one could exactly find fault with this scheme, and if he had exerted himself hitherto to get his new duties in train, they would have welcomed it, as his resolute avoidance of the Seytons produced social difficulties, and Jack thought Cheriton's London life so much of an experiment as to be glad that he should not have to carry it out entirely alone. But they both knew that without any difference that would strike outsiders, there was just the essential change from good to bad management, from care to neglect, in every matter with which the master of Oakby was concerned.

Nettie was to go to a London boarding-school for a year. This was the express desire of Mrs Lester, who thought this amount of "finishing" essential. Lady Cheriton was choosing the school, and the brothers of course consented, though Cheriton felt that it was like caging a wild bird, and Alvar remarked with much truth, —

"My sister is a woman; it is foolish to send her to school."

Nettie wept torrents of tears over Rolla, Buffer, her pony, nay, every living creature about the place; but she did not resist, it was part of the plan of life to which she was accustomed.

If Mrs Lester herself had not insisted on sending Nettie away, the others would have made no proposal which involved a separation; but to the surprise of them all, she proposed spending the ensuing three months at Whitby. Lady Milford would be there, and it had always been an occasional resort of Mrs Lester's, and with her old favourite maid, she declared that she should be perfectly comfortable there; and if she was dull, she would ask Virginia Seyton to stay with her.

One other member of the family remained to be disposed of, and while Cheriton and Jack were consulting with each other what they could say to their uncle with regard to Bob, he took the matter into his own hands, and as he walked across the park with Cheriton to view some drainage operations which had been begun by their father, and which Alvar was very glad to let them superintend, he remarked suddenly,—

"Cherry, I wish you would let me go to Canada, or New Zealand, or some such place, and take land. It is the only thing I'm fit for."

Cheriton was taken by surprise, though the idea had crossed his own mind.

"Do you really wish it?" he said.

"Yes," said Bob. "I'm not going to try my hand in life at things other fellows can beat me at."

"I'm afraid that rule would limit the efforts of most of us!"

"Well," said Bob, "I hate feeling like a fool; and besides, I don't see the good of Latin and Greek. But I mean to do some thing that's some use in the world. I approve of colonising."

"Really, Bob," said Cherry, "I don't think you were ever expected to go in for more Latin and Greek than would prevent you from feeling like a fool. There's a great deal in what you say; but have you thought of a farm in England or Scotland?"

"Yes; but I think that is generally a fine name for doing nothing. Now, I shall have some capital, and I'm big and strong, and can make my way. Cherry, don't you think I should have been allowed to go?"

"Yes, Bob, I think you would; but you are too young to start off at once on your own resources."

"Well, I could go to the agricultural college for a year, and there are men out there who take fellows and give them a start. You can talk it over with Uncle Cheriton, and if you agree, I don't care for the others."

"Does Nettie know about it?"

"Yes," said Bob; "she wouldn't speak to me for a week, she was so sorry. But she came round, and says she shall come out and join me. Of course she won't—she'll get married."

They had reached a little bridge which crossed a stream, on either side of which lay the swampy piece of ground which they had come to inspect. Looking forward, was the wide panorama of heathery hills, known to them with life-long knowledge; looking back, the wide, white house, in its group of fir-trees, with the park stretching away towards the lake. All the woods were tinted with light spring green, and the air was full of the song of numberless birds, and with that cawing of the rooks, which Cheriton had once said at Seville was to him like the sound of the waves to a person born by the sea.

"Of course," said Bob, "if one went a hundred thousand miles, one would never forget this old place."

"No," said Cheriton; "nor, I sometimes fancy, if one went a longer journey still!"

"But I hate it as it is now, and I shall come back when you're Lord Chancellor, and Jack, Head Master of Eton."

"Well, Bob," said Cherry, "wherever we may any of us go, or whatever we may be, I think we cannot be really parted, while we remember the old place, and all that belongs to it."

Chapter Thirty Nine
The Dragon Slayer

"Life has more things to dwell on
Than just one useless pain."

There are few places where the charm of a bright June day is felt more perfectly than in a London garden. The force of contrast may partly account for this; but The Laurels, as the Stanforths' house was called, was a lovely place in itself, dating from days before the villas by which it was now almost surrounded. Within its old brown sloping walls flourished white and pink acacias, magnolias, wisterias, and quaint trees only found in such old gardens; a cork-tree, more curious than beautiful; a catalpa, which once in Gipsy's memory had put out its queer brown and white blossoms; and a Judas-tree, still purple with its lovely flowers. The house, like the garden-walls, was built of brown old brick, well draped with creepers; and Mr Stanforth's new studio had been so cunningly devised that it harmonised wonderfully with the rest. That garden was a very pleasant place in the estimation of a great many people, who liked to come and idle away an hour there, and was famous for pleasant parties all through the summer; while it was a delightful play-place for the little Stanforths, a large party of picturesque and lively-minded children, who, in spite of artistic frocks and hats, and tongues trained to readiness by plenty of home society, were very thoroughly educated and carefully brought up. They were a great amusement to Cheriton Lester, who was always a welcome guest at The Laurels, and felt himself thoroughly at home there.

Cheriton's London life was in many ways a pleasant one. He found himself in the midst of old friends and schoolfellows, he could have as much society as he wished for, he was free of his uncle's house and of the 'Stanforths', and he had none of the money anxieties which troubled many of those who, like him, were beginning their course of preparation for a legal life. He saw a good deal, in and out, of Alvar, who had established himself in town, and was an exceedingly popular person in society; and as the obligations of his mourning, which he was careful to observe, diminished, was full of engagements of all sorts, enjoyed himself greatly, and thought as little of Oakby as business letters allowed. Lady Cheriton thought that he ought to have every opportunity of settling, "so much the best thing for all of them," and arranged her introductions to him accordingly; but Alvar walked through snares and pitfalls, and did not even get himself talked of in connexion with any young lady. Cheriton was much less often to be met with; he found that he could not combine late hours and anything like study, and so kept his strength for his more immediate object—an object which, however, was slowly changing into an occupation. Cheriton soon found out that the pleasures and pains of hard and successful labour were no longer for him; that though he did not break down in the warm summer weather, the winter would always be a time of difficulty, and that his strength would not endure a long or severe strain—in short, that though reading for the bar was just as well now as anything else for him, and might lead the way to interests and occupations, he could not even aim at the career of a successful lawyer. Besides, London air made him unusually languid and listless.

"Yes, he is a clever fellow, but he is not strong enough to do much. It is a great pity, but, after all, he has enough to live on, and plenty of interests in life," said Judge Cheriton; and his wife made her house pleasant to Cherry, and encouraged him to come there at all hours, and no one ever said a word to him about working, or gave him good advice, except not to catch cold; while he himself ceased to talk at all about his prospects, but went on from day to day and took the pleasant things that came to him. And sometimes he felt as if his last hope in life was gone—and sometimes, again, wondered why he did not care more for such a disappointment. But now and then, in these days that were so silent and self-controlled, there came to him an indifference of a nobler kind, an inward courage, a consoling trust, the reward of much struggling, which a year ago he could never have brought to bear on such a trial.

Mr Stanforth's presence always gave him a sense of sympathy, and he spent so many hours at The Laurels, that his aunt suspected him of designs on Gipsy, though Jack's secret, preserved in his absence, was likely to ooze out now that the end of the Oxford term had brought him to London for a few days, previous to joining a reading party with some of his friends.

The Laurels, with its pretty garden, might be a pleasant resting-place for Cheriton, but it was a very Arcadia, a fairy-land to Jack, when he found his way there late on one splendid afternoon, so shy that he had walked up and down the road twice before he rang the bell, happy, uncomfortable, and conscious all at once, looking at Gipsy, who had just come home from a garden party, in a most becoming costume of cream colour and crimson, but quite unable to say a word to her, as she sat under the trees, and fanned herself with a great black fan, appealing to Alvar, who was there with Cheriton, whether she had quite forgotten her Spanish skill. Gipsy was very happy, and not a bit shy as she peeped at her solemn young lover over the top of the fan, and laughed behind it at Jack's look of disgust when Cherry remarked that he had grown since Easter.

"Don't be spiteful, Cherry," said Mr Stanforth, with a smile. "Shall we come and see the picture?"

Jack and Gipsy were left to the last as they came up towards the house, and she made a little mischievous gesture of measuring herself against him.

"Yes, I think it's true!"

"Well," said Jack gruffly, though his eyes sparkled, "I shall leave off growing some time, I suppose. I say, are you going to dine at my aunt's to-morrow?"

"Yes," said Gipsy. "Lady Cheriton has been here, and she brought your sister. How handsome she is; but she was so silent. I was afraid of her. I wonder if she liked me," said Gipsy, blushing in her turn.

"Shy with Nettie?" exclaimed Jack. "You might as well be shy of a wild cat. She doesn't like any one much but Bob and her pets."

"All, young ladies grow as well as young gentlemen," said Gipsy. "Next year—"

"Yes; next year—" said Jack; but Gipsy opened the studio door, and ended the conversation.

Mr Stanforth's studio was arranged with a view more to the painting of pictures than to the display of curtains, carpets, and china; but it was still a pretty and pleasant place, with a few rare works of art by other hands than those of its owner. There were few finished pictures of Mr Stanforth's there then; but one large canvas on which he was working, and, besides various portraits in different stages, the drawing of Mr Lester, which Jack had not hitherto seen. Mr Stanforth brought it forward, and asked him to make any comment that occurred to him. It was a fine drawing of a fine face, and brought out forcibly the union of size and strength with beauty which none of the sons fully equalled, though there might be more to interest in all their faces. For, after all, the little imperfections of expression, that which was wanting as well as that which was present in the coming out and going in, the pleasures, the duties, and the failures, the changes of mood and temper, the smiles and the frowns of daily life, had made the individual man, and could not be shown in a likeness so taken. It was a picture that would satisfy them better as the years went by. Indeed Alvar thought it perfect, and Jack could hardly say that he saw anything wanting; but Cherry, after many praises and some hesitation, had said, "Yes, it is very like, but it is as if one saw him from a distance. Perhaps that is best."

After this picture had been put away, Jack began to look round and to relieve the impression made on him by a little artistic conversation, evidently carefully studied from the latest Oxford authorities. He looked at the pictures on the wall, found fault so correctly with what would have naturally been pleasing to him, and admired so much what a few months before he would have thought hideous, that Cheriton's eyes sparkled with fun, and Alvar, for once appreciating the humour of the situation, said,—

"We must ask Jack to write a book about the pictures at Oakby;" while Gipsy, seeing it all, laughed, spite of herself.

"Ah, Gipsy, he is carrying his lady's *colours*, like a true knight," said Cherry softly, as Jack faced round and inquired,—

"What are you laughing at?"

"Who lectures on art at Oxford, Jack?" said Cherry. "What a first-rate fellow he must be!"

"Ah, he is indeed a great teacher," said Alvar, "who has taught Jack to love art."

"A mighty teacher," said Cherry, under his breath.

"Of course," said Jack, "as one sees more of the world, one comes to take an interest in new fields of thought."

"Why, yes," said Gipsy, recovering from Cherry's words, and flying to the rescue, "we all learned a great deal about art at Seville."

"My dear," said Mrs Stanforth, "aren't you going to show them the knights?"

For she thought to herself that if a year was to pass before Jack's intentions could meet with an acknowledgment, his visits had better be few and far between, especially in the presence of Cherry's mischievous encouragement. "Mr Stanforth himself being as bad," as she afterwards remarked to him.

Now, however, Mr Stanforth turned his easel round and displayed the still unfinished picture for which he had begun to make sketches in Spain, when struck with the contrast of his new acquaintances, and with the capabilities of their appearance for picturesque treatment.

The picture was to be called "One of the Dragon Slayers," and represented a woodland glade in the first glory of the earliest summer—blue sky, fresh green, white blossoms, and springing bluebells and primroses, all in full and yet delicate sunshine—a scene which might have stood for many a poetic description from Chaucer to Tennyson, a very image of nature, the same now as in the days of Arthur.

Dimly visible, as if he had crawled away among the brambles and bracken to die, was the gigantic form of the slain dragon, while, newly arrived on the scene, having dismounted from his horse, which was held by a page in the distance, was a knight in festal attire—a vigorous, graceful presentment of Alvar's dark face and tall figure—who with one hand drew towards him the delivered maiden, a fair, slender figure in the first dawn of youth, who clung to him joyfully, while he laid the other in eager gratitude on the shoulder of the dragon slayer, who, manifestly wounded in the encounter, was leaning against a tree-trunk, and who, as he seemed to give the maiden back to her lover, with the other hand concealed in his breast a knot of the ribbon on her dress; thus hinting at the story, which after all was better told by the peculiar beaming smile of congratulation, the look of victory amid strife, of conquest over self and suffering—a look of love conquering pain, which was the real point of the picture.

Jack stood looking in silence, and uttering none of his newly-acquired opinions.

"Is it right, Jack?" said Mr Stanforth. "Yes, I know," said Jack briefly; and then, "Every one will know Alvar's portrait. And who is the lady?"

"She is a little niece of mine—almost a child," said Mr Stanforth; while Cheriton interposed,—

"It is not a group of photographs, Jack. Of course the object was the idea of the picture, not our faces."

"Well, Cherry," said Mr Stanforth smiling, "your notion of sitting for your picture partakes of the photographic. You did not help me by calling up the dragon slayer's look."

"That was for the artist to supply," said Cherry; "but it seems to me exactly how the knight ought to have looked."

"For my part," said Alvar, "I should not have liked to have been too late."

"It is very beautiful," said Jack; "but I don't think I approve of false mediaevalism. At that date these fellows would have fought, and the best man would have had the girl."

"Pray, at what date do you fix the dragon?" said Cherry.

"Jack is as matter-of-fact as the maiden herself," said Mrs Stanforth, "who will not be happy because her uncle will not tell her if the knight got well and married somebody else."

"No—no, mamma," said one of the Stanforth girls, "he did no such thing; he was killed in King Arthur's last battle. We settled it yesterday—we thought it was nicer."

"You don't think he gave in to the next dragon?" said Cherry, half to tease her.

"No, indeed, that knight never gave in. Did he, papa—did he?"

"My dear Minnie, I am not prepared with my knights' history. There they are, and I leave them to an intelligent public, who can settle whether my object was to paint sunlight on primroses, or a smile on a wounded knight's face—very hard matters both."

"Don't you really like it?" said Gipsy aside to Jack.

"Oh, yes," said Jack uneasily, "I have seen him look so. I know what your father means. But I hate it. I'd rather have had a picture of him as he used to be, all sunburnt and jolly. Yes, I know, it's the picture, not Cherry; but I don't like it."

Gipsy demurred a little, and they fell into a long talk in the twilight garden. Jack kept his promise, he did not "make love" to her, but never, even to Cheriton, had he talked as he talked then, for if he might not talk of the future, he could at least make Gipsy a sharer in all his past. When Cheriton came out upon them to call Jack away, they looked at him with half-dazzled eyes, as if he were calling them back from fairy-land.

The dinner-party at Lady Cheriton's offered no such chances, though it was a gathering together quite unexpected by some of the party. Lady Cheriton, when the question of a school for Nettie had been discussed, had renewed her offer of having her to share the studies of her younger daughters; and Cheriton, who thought that Nettie in a London boarding-school would be very troublesome to others and very unhappy herself, had succeeded in getting the plan adopted. So here she was, dignified and polished, in her long black dress, and bent, so said her aunt, in a silent and grudging fashion, on acquiring sufficient knowledge to hold her own among other girls. She was wonderfully handsome, and so tall that her height and presence marked her out as much as her intensely red-and-white complexion and yellow hair. There, too, were Virginia and her brother Dick, Cherry being guilty of assuring his aunt that there was no reason why Alvar should not meet them. For Dick's examination had at length been successfully passed, and an arrangement had been made that he should board with some friends of Mr Stanforth's, and Virginia had availed herself of an invitation from Lady Cheriton to come to London with him.

"You did not tell me she was coming," said Alvar angrily to Cheriton.

"It is impossible that you should avoid so near a neighbour," replied Cherry.

"I do not like it," said Alvar; and the effect on him was to shake his graceful self-possession, make him uncertain of what he was saying, and watch Virginia as she talked to Cherry of Dick's prospects, with a look that was no more indifferent than the elaborate politeness of Jack's greeting to Miss Stanforth. She was more self-controlled, but she missed no word or look. But if Cheriton had played a trick on his brother, he himself received a startling surprise when Mr and Mrs Rupert Lester were announced. "You cannot avoid meeting your cousins" was as true as his excuse to Alvar; but he could not help feeling himself watched; and as for Ruth, her brilliant, expressive face showed a consciousness which perhaps she hardly meant to conceal from him as she looked at him with all the past in her eyes. Ruth liked excitement, and the situation was not quite disagreeable to her; but while her look thrilled Cheriton through and through, the fact that she could give it, broke the last thread of his bondage to her. She made him feel with a curious revulsion that Rupert was his own cousin, and that she had tried to make him forget that she was his cousin's wife; and as, being a man, he attributed far too distinct a meaning to the glance of an excitable, sentimental girl, it repelled him, though the pain of the repulsion was perhaps as keen as any that she had made him suffer. He did not betray himself, and it was left to Jack to frown like a thunder-cloud.

When Cheriton came out of the dining-room, Nettie pursued him into a corner, and began abruptly, —

"Cherry, I want to speak to you. When Jack went to Spain did he tell you anything about me?"

"Nothing that I recollect especially," said Cherry, surprised.

"Well, I am going to tell you about it. Mind, I think I was perfectly right, and Jack ought to have known I should be."

"Have you and Jack had a quarrel, then?"

"Yes," said Nettie, standing straight upright, and making her communication as she looked down on Cherry, as he sat on a low chair. "*I* taught Dick to pass his examination."

"*You!*"

"Yes. You know he wouldn't work at anything, and I used to make him come and say his lessons to me—the kings of England, you know, and the rivers, and populations, and French verbs. Well, then, if he didn't know them, I made him learn them till he did. But of course he didn't wish any one to know, so we had to get up early, and sit in the hay-loft, or down by the bridge. I could not help the boys knowing that Dick and I went out together, and at last Jack found us in Clements' hay-loft. Dick ran away, but Jack was very angry with me, and insulted me; and Cherry—he went and told papa, and they sent me to London. But I never told the reason, because I had promised Dick. Now, Cherry, wouldn't it have been very wrong to give up the chance of doing Dick good because Jack chose to be ridiculous? It just made him succeed, and perhaps he will owe it to me that he is a respectable person, and earns his living. *You* would have helped him, wouldn't you?"

"Why, yes," said Cherry; "but that is not quite the same thing."

"Because I am a girl. Cherry, I think it would be mean to have let that stop me. But now he is through, I shall never do it again, of course; and, Cherry, indeed I meant it just as if he had been a ploughboy." Here Nettie hung her tall head, and her tone grew less defiant.

"But, after all, Nettie, you should not have done what you knew granny and father would not like," said Cherry, much puzzled what to say to her.

"It was because papa never knew that I told *you*," said Nettie rapidly.

Cheriton asked a few more questions, and elicited that Nettie had, very early in their intimacy, taken upon herself the reform of Dick, and had domineered over him with all the force of a strong will over a weak one. Nettie had acted in perfect good faith, and had defied her brother's attack on her; but as the lessons went on, her instinct had taught her that Dick found her attractive, and came to learn to please himself, not her. The girl had all the self-confidence of her race, and having set her mind on what she called "doing good" to Dick, she defied her own consciousness of his motives, having begun in kindness dashed with considerable contempt. But lazy Dick had powers of his own, and by the time of her quarrel with Jack, Nettie had felt herself on dangerous ground. "I shan't marry—no one is like our boys," she said to herself; but there was just a little traitorous softening and an indefinite sense of wrong-doing which had made her seek absolution from Cheriton, and with the peculiar absence of folly, which was a marked characteristic of the slow-thinking twins, she gave herself the protection of his knowledge.

Cheriton's impulse was to take up Jack's line and give her a good scolding, but he was touched by her appeal, and had learned to weigh his words carefully. He said something rather lame and inadequate about being more particular in future, but he gave Nettie's hand a kind little squeeze, and she felt herself off her own mind. It had been a curious incident, and had done much to make Nettie into a woman—too much of a woman to look on her *protégé* with favouring eyes. Dick, too, was likely to find other interests, but Nettie had helped to give him a fair start, and her scorn of his old faults could never be quite forgotten.

Chapter Forty
A New Suggestion

"Once remember
You devoted soul and mind
To the welfare of your brethren
And the service of your kind,
Now what sorrow can you comfort?"

Soon after the scenes recorded in the last chapter, Alvar received a letter from Mrs Lester, in which she thanked him, in a dignified and cordial manner, for his proposal that the home at Oakby should go on as usual, but said she did not consider that her residence there would be for the happiness of any one. During her son's married life she had lived in a house at Ashrigg, which was part of the Lester property, and was called The Rigg. This was now again vacant, and she proposed to take it, making it a home for Nettie, and for any of her grandsons who chose so to consider it. The great sorrow of her dear son's death would be more endurable to her, she said, anywhere but at Oakby. The neighbourhood of the Hubbards would provide friends for herself and society for Nettie, who would be very lonely at Oakby in her brothers' constant absences. Alvar was sincerely sorry. He was accustomed to the idea of a family home being open to all, and did not, in any way, regard himself as trammelled by his grandmother's presence there, while Cheriton was utterly taken by surprise, and hated the additional change and uprooting. He did not think the step unwise, especially as regarded Nettie, but he marvelled at his grandmother's energy in devising and resolving on it. He had expected a great outcry from Nettie, but she proved not to be unprepared, and said briefly, "that she liked it better than staying at home *now*."

"But you will not desert me?" said Alvar. "Shall I drive you too away from your home?"

"No," said Cherry. "No, I'll come home for the holidays, and the boys, too, if you will have them; though I suppose granny will want to see us all sometimes."

"I wish that I could take you home now," said Alvar. "I think you are tired with London—you see too many people."

Cheriton coloured a little at the allusion, but he disclaimed any wish to leave London then, shrinking indeed from breaking through the externals of his profession. It ended by Alvar going down to meet his grandmother at Oakby, and to make arrangements for the change, during which he proved himself so kind, courteous, and helpful to her, that he quite won her heart; and Nettie, on her return, was astonished at hearing Alvar's judgment deferred to, and "my grandson" quoted as an authority, on several occasions.

Jack, after a few days in London, joined a reading party for the first weeks of the vacation; and Bob, on his return from the gentleman who was combining for him the study of farming and of polite literature, joined Nettie in London, and took her down to Ashrigg; so that the early part of August found only Cheriton and Alvar at Oakby.

Cherry liked this well enough, for though the house could not but seem forlorn and empty to him, daily life was always pleasant with Alvar, and he would have gladly helped him through all the arrears of business that came to hand. These were considerable, for Mr Lester's subordinates had not been trained to go alone, and none of them had been allowed universal superintendence. Cheriton thought that Alvar required such assistance, and that he ought to have an agent with more authority; but oddly enough he did not take to the proposal, and in the meantime he made mistakes, kept decisions waiting, failed to recognise the relative importance of different matters, and, still worse, of different people.

One afternoon, towards the end of August, Cheriton went over to Elderthwaite. What with business at home, expeditions to Ashrigg, and a great many calls on his attention from more immediate neighbours, he had not seen very much of the parson, and as he neared the rectory he beheld an unwonted sight in the field adjoining, namely, some thirty or forty children drinking tea, under the superintendence of Virginia and one of the Miss Ellesmeres.

"Hallo, Cherry," said the parson, advancing to meet him; "where have you been? Seems to me we must have a grand—what d'ye call it?—rural collation before we can get a sight of you."

"As you never invited me to the rural collation, I was not aware of its existence," said Cherry laughing, as Virginia approached him.

"Oh, Cherry, stay and start some games," she said. "You know they are so ignorant, they never even saw a school-feast before."

"Then, Virginia, I wonder at you for spoiling the last traces of such refreshing simplicity. Introducing juvenile dissipation! Well, it doesn't seem as if the natural child wanted much training to appreciate plum-cake!"

"No; but if you could make the boys run for halfpence—"

"You think they won't know a halfpenny when they see one."

"Do have some tea!" said Lucy Ellesmere, running up to him. "Perhaps you are tired, and Virginia has given them *beautiful* tea, and really they're very nice children, *considering*."

So Cherry stayed, and advanced the education of the Elderthwaite youth by teaching them to bob for cherries, and other arts of polite society, ending by showing them how to give three cheers for the parson, and three times three for Miss Seyton; and while Virginia was dismissing her flock with final hunches of gingerbread, the parson called him into the house.

"Poor lassie!" he said; "she is fond of the children, and thinks a great deal of doing them good; but it's little good she can do in the face of what's coming."

"How do you mean?" said Cheriton. "Is anything specially amiss?"

"Come in and have a pipe. A glass of wine won't come amiss after so much tea and gingerbread."

They went into the dining-room, and the parson poked up the fire into a blaze, for even August afternoons were not too warm at Elderthwaite for a fire to be pleasant, and as he subsided into his arm-chair, he said gravely,—

"Eh, Cherry, we Seytons have been a bad lot—a bad lot—and the end of it'll be we shall be kicked out of the country."

"Oh, I hope not!" said Cherry, quite sincerely. "What is the matter?"

"Well, look round about you. Is there a wall that's mended, or a plantation preserved as it ought to be? Look at the timber—what is there left of it? and what's felled lies rotting on the ground for want of carting. There's acres of my brother's hay never was led till the rain came and spoiled it. Look at the cottages. Queenie gets the windows mended, but she can't make the roofs water-tight. Look at those woods down by the stream, why, there's not a head of game in them, and once they were the best preserves in the country!"

"Things are bad, certainly," said Cherry.

"And yet, Cherry, we've loved the place, and never have sold an acre of it, spite of mortgages and everything. Well, my brother's not long for this world. He has been failing and failing before his time, and though he has led a decent life enough, things have gone more to the bad with years of doing nothing, than with all the scandals of my father's time."

"Is Mr Seyton ill?" said Cheriton.

"Not ill altogether; but mark my words, he'll not last long. Well, at last, he was so hard up that he wrote to Roland—and I know, Cheriton, it was the bitterest pill he ever swallowed—and asked his consent to selling Uplands Farm. What does Roland do but write back and say, with all his heart; so soon as it came into his hands he should sell every acre, house and lands, advowson of living and all, and pay his debts. He hated the place, he said, and would never live there. Sell it to the highest bidder. There were plenty of fortunes made in trade, says he, that would give anything for land and position. So there, the old place'll go into the hands of some purse-proud stranger. But not the church—he shan't go restoring and improving that with his money. I'm only fifty-nine, and a good life yet, and I'll stick in the church till I'm put into the churchyard!"

Cherry smiled, it was impossible to help it; but the parson's story made him very sad. He knew well enough that it was a righteous retribution, that Roland's ownership would be a miserable thing for every soul in Elderthwaite, and that the most purse-proud of strangers would do something to mend matters; and yet his heart ached at the downfall, and his quick imagination pictured vividly how completely the poor old parson would put himself in the wrong, and what a disastrous state of things would be sure to ensue.

"I'd try and not leave so much 'restoration' for any stranger to do," he said.

"Eh, what's the good?" said the parson. "She had better let it alone for the 'new folks.'"

"Nay," said Cherry, "you cannot tell if the 'new folks,' as you call them, will be inclined for anything of the sort, and all these changes may not take place for years. It doesn't quite pay to do nothing because life is rather more uncertain to oneself than to other people."

Cheriton spoke half to himself, and the parson went on with his own train of thought.

"Ay, I'll stick to the old place, though I thought it a heavy clog round my neck once; and if you knew all the ins and outs of that transaction, you'd say, maybe, I ought to be kicked out of it now."

"No, I should not," said Cherry, who knew, perhaps, more of the Elderthwaite traditions than the parson imagined. "Things are as they are, and not as they might have been, and perhaps you could do more than any one else to mend matters."

The parson looked into the fire, with an odd, half humble, half comical expression, and Cherry said abruptly, —

"Do you think Mr Seyton would sell Uplands to me?"

"To you? What the dickens do you want with it?"

"Why—I don't think it would be a bad speculation, and I should like, I think, to have it."

"What? Does your brother make Oakby too hot to hold you?"

"No, indeed. He is all that is kind to me," said Cherry indignantly. "Every one misconstrues him. But I should like to have a bit of land hereabouts, all the same."

"Well, you had better ask my brother yourself. He may think himself lucky, for I don't know who would buy a bit of land like that wedged in between the two places. Ah, here's Queenie to say good-night. Well, my lassie, are you pleased with your sport?"

"Yes, uncle; and the children were very good."

Cheriton walked a little way with Virginia, beyond the turning where they parted from Lucy Ellesmere. He found that she was unaware of the facts which the parson had told him, and though somewhat uneasy about her father, very much disposed to dwell on the good accounts of Dick and Harry, and on the general awakening in the place that seemed to demand improvements. Oakby offered a ready-made pattern, and other farmers had been roused by Mr Clements to wish for changes, while some, of course, were ready to oppose them.

"They begin to wish Uncle James would have a curate, Cherry," she said; "but I don't think he ever will find one that he could get on with. No one who did not know all the ins and outs of the place could get on either with him or with the people."

"It would be difficult," said Cheriton thoughtfully; "yet I do believe that a great deal might be done for parson as well as people."

"Ah, Cherry," said Virginia, with a smile, "if you hadn't got another vocation, Uncle James would let *you* do anything you liked. I wish *you* were a clergyman, and could come and be curate of Elderthwaite; for you are the only person who could fit into all the corners."

Virginia spoke in jest, as of an impossible vision, but Cheriton answered her with unexpected seriousness.

"It would be hard on Elderthwaite to put up with a failure, and an offering would not be worth much which one had waited to make till one had nothing left worth giving; I'm afraid, too, my angles are less accommodating than you suppose—ask Alvar." Cherry finished his sentence thoughtlessly, and was recalled by Virginia's blush; but she said as they parted, "That is a safe reference for you."

Cheriton laughed; but as he walked homeward he turned and looked back on the tumble-down, picturesque village at his feet. Loud, rough sounds of a noisy quarrel in the little street came to his ears, and some boys passed him manifestly the worse for drink, though they pulled themselves up and tried to avoid his notice. It was not quite a new idea which Virginia had put into shape; but as the steep hill forced him to slacken his steps, he could not see that the strength which had proved insufficient for a more selfish object was likely to be worth consecrating to the service of his neighbours.

Chapter Forty One
A New Ambition

"Like a young courtier of the king's—like the king's young courtier."

In the first week of September Jack came home, and Bob also came over from Ashrigg to assist in demolishing the partridges. The empty, lonely house affected the spirits of the two lads in a way neither of them had foreseen; the unoccupied drawing-room, the absence of Nettie's rapid footsteps, the freedom from their grandmother's strictures on dress and deportment—all seemed strange and unnatural; and when they were not absolutely out shooting, they hung about disconsolately, and grumbled to Cheriton over every little alteration. Jack, indeed, recovered himself after a day or two, but he looked solemn, and intensified Cherry's sense that things were amiss, strongly disapproving of his principle of non-interference. He contrived, too, whether innocently or not, to ask questions that exposed Alvar's ignorance of the names and qualities of places and people, and betrayed delays in giving orders, misconceptions of requirements, and many a lapse from order and method. Moreover, the way in which some of the excellent old dependents showed their loyalty to the old *regime*, was by doing nothing without orders. Consequently, a hedge remained unmended till the cows got through into a plantation, and ate the tops off the young trees,—"Mr Lester had given no order on the subject;" and a young horse was thrown down and broke his knees through Mr Lester desiring the wrong person to exercise him. Then, of two candidates for a situation, Alvar often managed to choose the wrong one, and with the sort of irritability that seemed to be growing on him, would not put up with suggestions.

"What?" said Jack; "one of those poaching, thieving Greens taken on as stable-boy! And Jos, too—the worst of the lot! Why, he has been in prison twice. A nice companion for all the other lads about the place! I saw little Sykes after him this morning. I should have thought you would have stopped *that*, Cherry, at least!"

"I did not know of it, Jack, till too late," said Cherry quietly.

"Well," said Jack, driving his hands into his pockets and frowning fiercely, "I don't think it's right to let such things pass without a protest.

Something will happen that cannot be undone. I don't approve of systems by which people's welfare is thrown into the hands of a few; but if they are—if you are those few, it's—it's more criminal than many things of which the law takes cognisance, to neglect their interest. It's destroying the last relics of reality, and bringing the whole social edifice to destruction."

"What I think," said Bob, "is that if a man's a gentleman, and has been accustomed to see things in a proper point of view, he acts accordingly."

"A gentleman! A man's only claim to be a gentleman is that he recognises the whole brotherhood of humanity and his duties as a human being."

"Come, I don't know," said Bob, not quite sure where these expressions were leading him.

"His duty to his neighbour," said Cheriton.

"You worry yourself fifty times too much about it all," said Jack, with vehement inconsistency.

"Well, perhaps I do," said Cheriton, glad to turn the conversation. "Come, tell me how you got on in Wales, I have never heard a word of it."

Jack looked at him for a moment, and with something of an effort began to talk about his reading party; but presently he warmed with the topic, and Cherry brightened into animation at the sound of familiar names and former interests; they began to laugh over old jokes, and quarrel over old subjects of disputation; and they were talking fast and eagerly against each other, with a sort of chorus from Bob, when, looking up, Cherry suddenly saw Alvar standing before them with a letter in his hand.

He was extremely pale, but his eyes blazed with such intensity of wrath, he came up to them with a gesture expressive of such passion, that they all started up; while he burst out,—

"I have to tell you that I am scorned, injured, insulted. My grandfather has died—"

"Your grandfather, Don Guzman? Alvar, I am sorry," exclaimed Cheriton; but Alvar interrupted him,—

"Sorrow insults me! I learn that he has made his will, that he leaves all to Manoel, that I—I, his grandson—am not fit to be his heir, 'since I am a foreigner and a heretic, and unfit to be the owner of Spanish property.'"

"That seems very unjust," said Cheriton, as Alvar paused for a moment.

"Unjust!" cried Alvar. "I am the victim of injustice. Here and there—it is the same thing. I have been silent—yes, yes—but I will not bear it. I will be what I please, myself—there, here, everywhere!"

"Nay, Alvar," said Cherry gently; "*here* at least, you have met with no injustice."

"And why?" cried Alvar, with the sudden abandonment of passion which now and then broke through his composure. "*You* are doubtless too honourable to plot and scheme; but your thoughts and your wishes, are they not the same—the same as this most false and unnatural traitor, who has stolen from me my inheritance and my grandfather's love? What do you wish, my brothers—wish in your hearts—would happen to the intruder, the stranger, who takes your lands from you? Would you not see me dead at your feet?"

"We never wished you were dead," said Bob indignantly, as Alvar walked about the room, threw out his hands with vehement gestures, stamped his foot, and gave way to a violence of expression that would have seemed ludicrous to his brothers but for the fury of passion, which evidently grew with every moment, as if the injury of years was finding vent. All the strong temper of his father seemed roused and expressed with a rush of vindictive passion, his southern blood and training depriving him at once of self-consciousness and self-control.

"What matter what you wish? Am I not condemned to a life which I abhor, to a place that is hateful to me, despised by one whose feet I would kiss, disliked by you all, insulted by those who should be my slaves? What is this country to me, or I to it? I care not for your laws, your magistrates, your people—who hate me, who would shoot me if they dared. And this—this—has lost me the place where I was as good as others. I lose my home for this—for you who stand together and wonder at me. I curse that villain who has robbed me; I curse the fate that has made me doubly an outlaw; most of all, I curse my father, whose neglect—"

"Silence!" said Cheriton; "you do not speak such words in our presence."

The flood of Alvar's words, half Spanish, half English, had fairly silenced the three brothers with amazement. Now he faced round furiously on Cheriton,—

"I will speak—"

"You will *not*," said Cheriton, grasping his hand, and looking full in his face. "You forget yourself, Alvar. Don't say what we could never forget or forgive."

But Alvar flung him off with a violence and scorn that roused the two lads to fury, and made Cheriton's own blood tingle as Jack sprang forward,—

"I won't have that," he said, in a tone as low as Alvar's was high, but to the full as threatening.

"I'll give you a licking if you touch my brother," shouted Bob, with a rough, schoolboy enforcement of the threat.

"Hush!" said Cheriton; "for God's sake, stop—all of you! We are not boys now, to threaten each other. Stop, while there is time. Stand back, I say, Jack, and be silent!"

The whole thing had passed in half a minute; Alvar's own furious gesture had sobered him, and he threw himself into a seat; while Cheriton's steady voice and look controlled the two lads, and gave Jack time to recollect himself.

There was a moment's silence. Then Alvar stood up, bowed haughtily, like a duellist after the encounter, and walked out of the room. Jack, after a minute, broke into an odd, harsh laugh, and, pushing open the window, leant out of it.

"One wants air. That was a critical moment," he said.

"I'll not stand that sort of thing; I'll go back to Ashrigg; I'll not come here again," said Bob. "What did you stop us for, Cherry, when we were going to show him a piece of our minds?"

"I did not think anybody's mind was fit to be exhibited," said Cheriton. "Don't begin to quarrel with me too, Bob; and do not go away to-day on any account."

"Well!" said Bob; "if you like such a hollow peace—but I'll not shoot his partridges, nor ride his horses; I'll go for a walk, and I shan't come in to dinner!"

Bob flung out of the room, banging the door behind him.

At first the other two hardly spoke a word to each other. Cherry sat down a little apart, and mechanically took up a newspaper. Jack sat in the window, and as his heat subsided, thought over the scene that had passed. He felt that it was more than a foolish outburst of violent temper; it had been a revelation to themselves and to each other of a state of feeling that it seemed to him impossible any longer to ignore. He knew that Cheriton's presence of mind had saved them from words and actions that might have parted them for ever; but what was the use of pretending to get on with Alvar after such a deadly breach? Better leave him to do the best he could in his own way, and go theirs. And Jack's thoughts turned to his own way in the future that he hoped for, success and congenial labour, and sweet love to brighten it. After all, a man's early home was not everything to him. And then he looked towards Cheriton, who had dropped his newspaper, and sat looking dreamily before him, with a sad look of disappointment on his face.

"What are you going to do, Cherry?" said Jack.

"Do? Nothing. What can I do?" said Cherry. Then he added, "We must not make too much of what passed to-day; let us all try and forget it. Alvar has been ill-treated, and we are none of us so gentle as not to know what a little additional Spanish fire might make of us."

"To be rough with you!" said Jack.

"Oh, that was accidental. It is the terrible resentment. There, I did not mean to speak of it. Let us get out into the air, and shake it off."

"It is too wet and cold for you," said Jack, looking out.

Cheriton flushed at the little check with an impatience that showed how hardly the scene had borne on him.

"Nonsense; don't be fanciful," he said. "It won't hurt me—what if it did?"

Jack followed him in silence, and as they walked Cherry talked resolutely of other matters, though with long pauses of silence between.

In the meantime Alvar endured an agony of self-disgust. He could not forgive himself for his loss of dignity, nor his brothers for having witnessed it. Cheriton had conquered him, and the thought rankled so as to obscure even the love he bore him; while all the bitter and vindictive feelings, never recognised as sinful, took possession of him, and held undisputed sway. He was enough of an Englishman to reject his first impulse of rushing back to Seville and calling out his cousin and fighting him. After all, the bitterness was here; and at dinner-time he appeared silent and sullen in manner. Cheriton looked ill and tired, and could hardly eat; but Alvar offered no remark on it, and the younger boys (for Bob did come back) were shy and embarrassed. Alvar answered when Cheriton addressed him with a sort of stiff politeness, and by the next morning had resumed a more ordinary demeanour; but when Bob again suggested going back to Ashrigg, Cheriton and Jack agreed that he had better do so, only charging him not to let Nettie or their grandmother guess at any quarrel.

"And, Cherry," Jack said, "suppose we come somewhere together for a little while? A little sea air would do you good—and you could help me with my reading. No one could think it strange, and I am sure you want rest and quiet."

"No, Jack," said Cherry. "It is very good of you, my boy, but—I'll try a little longer. Alvar and I could not come together again if I went away now, and I'll not give up hoping that after all things may right themselves. Think of all he has been to me. But you must do as you think best yourself."

"I shall not leave you here without me," said Jack; "but I don't see the use of staying."

"Well—I shall stay," said Cherry.

Alvar never alluded again to his letter from Spain; and the others were afraid to start the subject. He was very polite to them, and together they formed engagements, went over to Ashrigg, and led their lives in the usual manner; but there was no real approach, and Cheriton missed Alvar's caressing tenderness, and the tact that had always been exercised on his behalf.

He did not, with all this worry, find as much strength to face the coming winter as he had hoped for, and while he thought that going back to London would put an end to the present discomfort, he believed that he would do no good there; and would not a parting from Alvar now be a real separation?

Alvar, meanwhile, took a fit of attending to business. He spent much time about the place, insisted on being consulted on all subjects, and still more on being instantly obeyed; King Log had vanished, and a very peremptory king Stork appeared in his place. The gentle, courteous, indifferent Alvar seemed possessed with a captious and resentful spirit that brooked no opposition. No one had ever dared to disobey Mr Lester's orders; but then they had been given with a due regard to possibility, and often after consultation with those by whom they were to be obeyed.

Alvar now proved himself to be equally determined; but he was often ignorant of what was reasonable and of what was not, and though the sturdy north-countrymen had given in against their inclination to their superior, they thought it very hard to be driven against their judgment when they were right and "t' strange squire" was wrong, or at least innovating. Now Alvar did know something about horses, and his views of stable management differed somewhat from those prevailing at Oakby, and being based on the experience of a different climate and different conditions, were not always applicable there, and could only of course be carried, as it were, at the sword's point.

Full of this new and intense desire to feel himself master, and to prove himself so, Alvar not unnaturally concentrated his efforts on the one subject where he had something to say. He *could* not lay down the law about turnips and wheat; but he did think that he knew best how to treat the injuries the young horse had received by his own mistaken order.

Perhaps he did; but so did not think old Bill Fisher, who had been about the stables ever since he was twelve, and who, though past much active work, still considered himself an authority from which there was no appeal.

Alvar visited the horse, and desired a certain remedy to be applied to a sprained shoulder, taking some trouble to explain how it was to be made.

Old Bill listened in an evil silence, and instead of saying that so far as he knew one of the ingredients was unattainable at Oakby, or giving his master an alternative, said nothing at all in reply to Alvar's imperious—"Remember, this must be done at once;" but happening soon after to encounter Cheriton, requested him to visit the horse, and desired his opinion of the proper treatment.

Cheriton, ignorant of what had passed, naturally quoted the approved remedy at Oakby, adding,—

"Why, Bill, I should have thought you would have known that for yourself."

"Ay, no one ever heard tell of no other," muttered the old man, proceeding to apply it with some grumbling about strangers, which Cheriton afterwards bitterly rued having turned a deaf ear to.

The next morning Alvar went to see if his plans had been carried out, and discovering how his orders had been disregarded, turned round, and said sternly,—

"How have you dared to disobey me?"

"Eh, sir," said Bill, rather appalled at his master's face, "this stuffs cured our horses these fifty year."

"You have disobeyed me," said Alvar, "and I will not suffer it. I dismiss you from my service—you may go. I will not forgive you."

Old Bill lifted up his bent figure, and stared at his master in utter amaze.

"I served your honour's grandfather—me and mine," he said.

"You cannot obey me. What are your wages? I will pay them—you may go." Neither the old man himself, nor the helpers who had begun to gather round, belonged to a race of violent words, or indeed of violent deeds; but there was more hate in the faces that were turned on Alvar than would have winged many an Irish bullet. All were silent, till a little brother of Cherry's friends, the Flemings, called out, saucily enough,—"'Twas Mr Cherry's orders."

As if stung beyond endurance, Alvar turned, caught the boy by the shoulder, and raising his cane, struck him once, twice, several times, with a violence of which he himself was hardly conscious.

This was the scene that met Cheriton's startled eyes as he came up to the stable to inquire for the sick horse.

He uttered a loud exclamation of astonishment and dismay, and put his hand on Alvar's shoulder.

Alvar, with a final blow, threw the lad away from him, and faced round on Cheriton, drew himself up, and folded his arms, as he said, regardless of the spectators,—

"I will not have it that you interfere with me, to alter my orders, or to stop me in what I do. You shall not do it."

"I have never interfered with you!" cried Cheriton fiercely. "Assuredly I never will. I—I—" He checked himself with a strong effort, and said, very low, "We are forgetting ourselves by disputing here. If you have anything to say to me, it can be said at a better moment."

Then, without trusting himself with a word or look, he walked slowly away.

Alvar said emphatically,—

"Remember, I have said what I desire," and turned off in another direction; while those left behind held such an "indignation meeting" as Oakby had never seen.

Chapter Forty Two
No Use

"Learn that each duty makes its claim
Upon one soul, not each on all;
How if God speaks thy brother's name,
Dare thou make answer to the call?"

Cheriton had encountered greater sorrows, he had met with more startling disappointments, but never, perhaps, had he endured such a complication of feeling as when he turned away and left Alvar in the stable yard. Perhaps he had never been so angry, for Alvar's accusation was peculiarly galling, peculiarly hard to forgive, and impossible to forget. And then there was the bitter sense of utter failure—failure of influence, of tact, of affection, and, in so far as he identified himself with the place and the people, there was yet a deeper sense of injury. Every old prejudice, every old distaste, surged up in his mind, and yet he loved Alvar well enough to sharpen the sting. He walked on faster and faster, till want of breath stopped him, and brought on one of the fits of coughing to which overhaste or agitation always rendered him liable. He just managed to get back to the house and into the library, where Jack started up, as he threw himself into a chair.

"Cherry, what *is* the matter?"

Cherry could not speak for a moment; and Jack, much frightened, exclaimed,—

"What *have* you been doing? Let me call Alvar."

Cheriton caught his arm as he turned away; and, after a few moments, as he began to get his breath,—

"Don't be frightened. I walked too fast up hill."

"How could you be so foolish?"

"Jack, I suppose I must tell you; indeed, I want to find out the rights of it; and *I* can ask no questions," he added, with a sudden hurry in his accent.

"What do you mean? What has happened?"

The instinct of not irritating Jack enabled Cheriton to control his own indignation, and he said very quietly,—

"When I went up to the stable I found Alvar giving little Chris Fleming a tremendous licking. He was very much vexed with me for—I suppose for trying to interpose; but there were so many people about that we could not discuss it there. I wish you would go and ask old Bill what Chris had been doing, then come and tell me. Don't say anything to Alvar about it."

Jack was keen enough to see that this was not quite an adequate account of the matter. He saw that Cheriton was deeply moved in some way; but he was so unfit for discussion just then, that Jack thought the best course was to hurry off on his errand.

He came back in about half-an-hour, looking very serious—too much so to be ready to improve the occasion.

"Alvar has given old Bill warning—do you know that?"

"*No*. What was that for?" cried Cheriton, starting up.

"He would not speak a word to me, and Chris had gone off to his brother's; but John Symonds told me what had passed." Here Jack repeated the story of the ointment, old Bill's disobedience, and Chris's declaration that it had been done by Cheriton's orders.

Cheriton's face cleared a little.

"Ah, I understand now. No wonder Alvar was vexed! I can explain that easily. But old Bill, it *was* very unjustifiable; but if Alvar will not overlook it I do believe it will kill him."

"I don't see what he would have to live on," said Jack. "You know that bad son spent his savings. But Alvar will let him off if you ask him, I daresay."

"I think you had better do so," said Cheriton quietly.

At this moment Alvar came into the room, and Cheriton addressed him at once.

"Alvar, when old Bill asked me about the ointment, I did not know that you had been giving any orders about it. I am very sorry for the mistake."

"It is not of consequence," said Alvar. "Do not trouble yourself about it."

The words were kind, but the tone was less so; and there was something in Alvar's manner which made it difficult even for Jack to say,—"I'm afraid old Bill Fisher was provoking. He should have told you that he could not get the stuff; but he is such an old servant, and so faithful. I hope you won't dismiss him for it. He seems to belong to us altogether."

"I shall not change," said Alvar.

"But it's an extremely harsh measure, and will make every one about the place detest you," said Jack, still considering himself to be speaking with praiseworthy moderation.

"I will judge myself of the measure." Then Cherry conquered his pride, and said pleadingly,—

"I wish it very much."

"I am sorry to grieve you," said Alvar, more gently; "but I have determined."

"Well," said Jack, losing patience, "we spoke as much for your sake as for Bill's. Every one will consider it harsh dealing and a great shame. You'll make them hate you."

"I will make them fear me," said Alvar.

"Claptrap and nonsense!" said Jack; but Cheriton interposed,—

"Hush, Jack, we have no right to say any more. What must be must."

To do Alvar justice, he was not aware how deeply he was grieving Cheriton; he felt himself to be asserting his rights, and in the worst corner of his heart knew that any relenting would be ascribed to his brother's influence.

It was a very miserable day. After some hours of astonished sulking, the poor old groom put his pride in his pocket, and came humbly "to beg t' squire's pardon," and to entreat Cheriton to intercede for him, recapitulating his years of long service, and his recollections of the old squire's boyhood, till he nearly broke Cherry's heart; and induced him to promise to make another attempt at interceding—a promise which was not given without quite as severe a rebuke as Alvar had ever inflicted, for disrespect to his master's orders.

He was closely followed by the eldest of the Fleming brothers, in great indignation.

Nowhere but at Oakby, as the young man took care to observe, would Chris have been allowed to take such a situation, in spite of his love of horses, and troublesomeness at home.

"Chris was impertinent to Mr Lester," said Cheriton, hardly knowing what line to take.

Young Fleming was very sorry; in that case he was better at home, and he hoped it would not be inconvenient if he took him away at once.

"I suppose it might be best," said Cheriton, thoroughly sympathising with the grievance, and thankful to Fleming for not obliging him to hear or say much about it.

"Then, sir, maybe you will tell the squire that such is our wish."

"No; I think you had better write him a note about it."

The two young men looked at each other, and though Cheriton turned his eyes quickly away, he knew well enough that Fleming understood the whole matter.

"As you please, sir," he said; "I wouldn't wish for *you* to be annoyed, Mr Cherry, and *so* I'll keep out of the squire's way. But Westmoreland men are not black slaves, which no doubt the squire is accustomed to, and accounts for his conduct. It's plain, sir, to any one that can read the newspapers, that there's no liberty in foreign parts, where they're all slaves and papists. Education, sir, teaches us that. And folks do remark that the squire doesn't keep his church as others do; and I *have* heard that he means to establish a Popish chapel like the one at Ravenscroft."

"Then you have heard the greatest piece of nonsense that ever was invented. Education might cure you of such notions," said Cherry. "You must do as you think best for Chris. I am very sorry."

The last words were involuntary, and Cherry hurried away before he was betrayed into any further discussion.

Some hours later, as it was growing dusk, he was lying on the window-seat in the library, thinking of how he could plead old Fisher's cause without giving offence, and coming slowly to the conclusion that his presence there was doing far more harm than good, that he was risking peace with Alvar, and had better give up the straggle, when Alvar himself came into the room, and came up to him.

"Are you not well?" he said, rather constrainedly.

"Only very tired."

"What have you been doing?" said Alvar, sitting down on the end of the broad-cushioned seat, and looking at him.

The words certainly gave an opening; but Cheriton, famous all his life for the most audacious coaxing, could not summon a smile or a joke.

"I have been tired all day," he said, to gain time for reflection.

"See," said Alvar suddenly, "you are unhappy about this old man, whom I have dismissed."

"Yes. I don't defend him, far from it; but he is old and crochety, and I think you were harsh with him," said Cherry resolutely.

"But it is I who should decide what to do with him," said Alvar.

"Of course. Don't imagine I dispute it," said Cheriton, thinking this assertion rather foolish.

"You tell me that I should be master; you have told me so often. Well, then, I can be harsh to my servants if I please."

"If you please, remembering that you and they serve the same Master above."

Alvar paused for a moment, then said, —

"I do not please, at present. I have grieved you, as when I hurt Buffer. I will not be ruled by any one, but the old man shall live in his cottage, and have his wages; but he shall not come into the stables nor near my horses. Does that please you, my brother?"

Cherry had his doubts as to how old Bill might regard or fulfil the conditions, and certainly forbidding a servant to do any work was rather an odd way of punishing him; but he answered gratefully, —

"Yes, thank you, you have taken a great weight off my mind."

"You cough," said Alvar, after a few moments; "the weather is getting too cold for you."

"I thought," said Cherry, forcing himself to take advantage of the excuse, "that I would go to the sea for a little while before the winter."

"Yes; where shall we go?" said Alvar, in a tone of interest. "Look," he continued, with wonderful candour; "here we vex each other because we do not think the same. We are angry with each other; but we will come away, and I will take care of you. Then you shall go to London, and I shall come back, and you will see, I will yet be the squire. Where shall we go, *mi caro*?"

It was almost a dismissal, and so Cheriton felt it to be; but after all it was his own decision, and the return of Alvar's old kindness was very comfortable to him.

"I had hardly thought about that," he said.

"Well," returned Alvar, "we can talk about it. Now, it is cold here in the window; come nearer to the fire and rest till dinner-time."

As Cheriton sat up and looked out at the stormy sunset, he saw little Chris Fleming coming up the path that led round to the back door.

"Ah," said Alvar cheerfully, following his eyes, "I do not wish to punish that boy any more. He has had enough, that little rascal."

Evidently, Alvar's conscience was quite at ease, and he did not suppose that he had in any way compromised himself. He began to perceive that Alvar had his own ideas as to what would make him really master of Oakby.

Just after dinner a note was brought to Alvar.

"If you please, sir, this note was found in the passage, just inside the back door."

Alvar took the letter, lit one of the candles on the chimney-piece, and proceeded to read it.

"Moor End Farm, *September 29th.*
"Honoured Sir,—After the events of this morning, I consider it for the best that my brother Christopher should leave your service at once. I have no objection to forfeit any wages due to him, as I do not feel able to give the usual month's notice after what has passed.
"I remain, honoured sir,—
"Your obedient servant,—
"Edward Fleming."

Alvar coloured deeply as he read. "What is this?" he exclaimed. "May I not punish even a little boy, who insults me? Look!" and he threw the letter to his brother.

"It is very awkward," said Cheriton.

"I think it is insolent," said Alvar.

"I think there is a great effort to avoid any want of respect in the letter."

"To take the boy away because he was punished!"

"Well, Alvar, if you or I were in Ned Fleming's place, we shouldn't have liked it."

"Did you know that this letter was coming?"

"Yes, I did."

"It is perhaps as you have advised Fleming?"

"No. I gave him no advice; but I knew he would not let the boy stay here."

"Do you then approve?" said Alvar, in a curious sort of voice.

"From their point of view—yes. You are right in saying that you must make yourself felt as the master; but there is no good in enforcing your authority in a way that is not customary, to say the least of it. In England we can't lay hands on other people; and they *might* have summoned you for an assault, you know."

"What! before a judge?"

"Before a magistrate."

"I?" exclaimed Alvar, in a tone of such amazement that Cheriton nearly laughed. "Who would listen to that little boy against me, who am a gentleman and his master?"

"The little boy is your equal in the eyes of the law, and might meet with more attention just because you *are* his master. Not that I mean to say it would not be regarded as very annoying to convict you," said Cheriton, thinking of the feelings of Sir John Hubbard on such an emergency.

"I will myself be a magistrate," said Alvar.

"That you never will," said Cherry, losing patience, "while these stories get about, for no one would trust you."

"Can I not be a magistrate if I choose?"

"Not unless the Lord Lieutenant gives you a commission, of course."

"I think there is power for every one but me!" said Alvar. "I may not punish that little—what is your word?—vulgar, common boy. I do not like so much law. Gentlemen should do as they wish. You talk so much about my being landlord and squire. What is the use of it if I may not do as I will? Well, I will send away Fleming from his farm—that is mine at least."

"I am afraid he has a twenty-one years lease in it," said Cheriton, rather wickedly, and Alvar, fancying himself laughed at, suddenly put the letter in his pocket and turned away, as the gong sounded for dinner. He disappeared afterwards when they went back to the library, and Cheriton had the forbearance to abstain from giving Jack the benefit of Alvar's peculiar views on the British constitution, though they could not fail to speak of the events of the morning, and Jack said,—

"Well, at least he has heard reason about old Bill, and that was of most consequence; but I should think you would be glad to be back in London, and out of the way of it all."

"I am not quite sure about London, Jack," said Cheriton, after a moment.

"What, don't you feel well enough?"

"I don't think I shall ever be good for much there; and besides—I think I should like to talk to you a little, Jack, if you'll listen."

"Well?"

"You know how I always looked forward to settling in London, and how Uncle Cheriton wished it, and meant to help me on. In fact I never thought of anything else."

"Yes, I know," said Jack, briefly.

"There was a time when I desired that sort of success intensely, and when things were very much changed for me, I thought it would still—be satisfactory."

"Yes?"

"But of course, as you know, I soon perceived that the hard continuous work, necessary for anything like success, was quite out of the question for me—I feel sure that it always will be; and, moreover, I never felt well in London. I was much better here when I first came back."

Poor Jack looked as if the disappointment were much fresher and harder to him than to the speaker himself.

"You must know," Cheriton continued, "that a doctor once told me at Oxford that the damp soft air there was very bad for a native of such a place as this, and I see now that the last few months there began the mischief; and London has something the same effect on me. That seems to settle the question."

"I suppose so," said Jack, so disconsolately, that Cherry half smiled, as he resumed,—

"Otherwise the pleasant idle life there might have its charms. Though, after all, Jack, I shouldn't like it as things are now. When I expected to be a London man, I expected, as you know—a good deal else. And afterwards even, while all home ties here were safe and sound, one would not get selfish and aimless. But now I couldn't be happy, I think, without a home-world that really belonged to me."

"And so home is being spoilt for you too?" said Jack.

"I see," returned Cheriton, "that it won't do. If Alvar is left to himself here, he will fight his way now, I think, to some means of managing proper to himself."

"Or improper," said Jack.

"Well, to be honest, I am afraid he will make a great many mistakes, and do a great deal of mischief. But if I were here—I mean if this place were still to be home to me so that I still felt—as I should feel—a personal concern in all the old interests, Alvar would quarrel with me. I might prevent individual evils; but in the long run I should do harm. He thought at first that I should guide him. Perhaps I thought so too; but it is a false and impossible relation, and it must be put a stop to."

"But, Cherry, I think father looked to you to keep things straight."

"Yes," said Cherry, "but not to make them more crooked, by such disputes as we have had lately."

Cheriton spoke resolutely, though with a quiver of the lip, and Jack could guess well enough at the pain the resolve was costing him. "Alvar is quite changed to you!" he said, savagely.

"Yes, because he himself is changing. He is different in many ways, and conscious of all sorts of difficulties."

"But what do you mean to do?"

"Oh, nothing desperate, nothing till the winter is over. Probably I shall go to the sea with Alvar, as he suggests. Then if I am pretty well, I shall go and see granny. I have a notion that I should be better here in the cold weather than in London. I want to try."

"Had you all this in your mind when you settled to buy Uplands?" said Jack suddenly. "Yes—in part I had."

"But, you are not thinking of living *there*! What are you driving at, Cherry, I can't understand you?"

"Well, Jack," said Cherry, slowly and with rising colour, "I will tell you, but I wanted to show you the process. And you must remember that it is only an idea known to no one, and very probably may prove impossible, perhaps undesirable."

"Tell me," said Jack, more gently. Any scheme for the future was a relief from listening to the laying aside of hopes which he knew had been so much a part of Cheriton's being.

"Well," said Cherry again, "I'm afraid my motives are rather poor ones. You see, after Oakby there's no place for me like Elderthwaite. I want the feeling, as I say, of a place and neighbours of my own. I suppose I am used to playing first fiddle, and to looking after other people's concerns. Granny always said I was a gossip. Then I'm narrow-minded, perhaps I have had too much taken out of me to think of starting fresh. And you know the old parson will always put up with me, and so will Elderthwaite people. And I want an object in life—if you knew how dreary it is to be without one! If they had a strange curate he would set them all by the ears, and the parson would make a fool of himself! So if Mr Ellesmere thinks the bishop would consent, and approves, and if I am fit for anything, I thought that I would try."

Jack was silent for some moments. He understood Cheriton well enough to "follow the process," but it affected him strongly, and at last he said, gravely,—

"I am afraid all the vexation here has put this into your head."

"Partly," said Cherry, simply, "this actual thing. I can't say anything of other motives of course, Jack. I know that it looks like, that in fact it *is* turning to this—which ought to be the offering of all one's best—when other careers have failed me. And I know that those who sympathise the least will be the most inclined to say so. But it is not quite so. I *have* always wished to be of use, of service, here especially. I thought I saw how. I have the same wish still, and this seems to offer me a way. It is but a gathering up of the fragments, but I trust He will accept."

Jack's view rather was that the plan was not good enough for his brother, than that his brother was not good enough for it.

"You were always good enough for anything, if that is what you mean," he said. "But I do understand, Cherry, about wanting an object; only—only it's such an odd one."

"I tell you," said Cherry, brightly, for the disclosure was a great relief to him, "that that's the very point. I don't think I get on amiss with any one, even with the *Sevillanos*, but down at the bottom of my heart, Jack, I'm not far removed—we none of us are—from 'There's a stranger, 'eave 'alf a brick at him,' and when I think of any direct dealing with people, anything like clerical work, why, except to my own kith and kin, I should have nothing to say. The self-denial of missionaries seems to me incredible. I could not do as Bob means to do, I think, if health and strength were to be the reward of it. It's a very unworthy weakness, I know, but I can't help it."

"You would get on very well anywhere," said Jack; "that is all nonsense. I don't believe Elderthwaite would agree with you, and you could overwork yourself just as well there as anywhere else."

"Well, as to the place agreeing with me, that remains to be proved. It's a very small church, and a small place; and I hope I might be able to do the little they are fit for—at present. But I know it may prove to be out of the question."

Jack was silent. He could not bear to vex Cherry by opposing a scheme which seemed to offer him some pleasure in the midst of his annoyances, and if his brother had proposed to take orders with more ordinary expectations, it would have been quite in accordance with the Oakby code of what was fitting. But there was something in the consecration of what Cheriton evidently viewed as a probably short life and failing powers to an object so unselfish, and yet, as it seemed to Jack, so commonplace, it was so like Cherry, and yet showed such a conquest of himself—there was such humility in the acknowledgment that he was only just fit for the sort of imperfect work that offered itself, and yet such a complete sense that no one else could manage that particular bit of work so well—it was, as Jack said, "so odd," that it thrilled him through and through, and he was glad that Alvar's entrance saved him from a reply.

Chapter Forty Three
Revenge

"'Now, look you,' said my brother, 'you may talk,
Till, weary with the talk, I answer nay.'"

Alvar, having avoided his brothers after dinner, came back into the hall, and, sitting down by the fire, lighted a cigarette. As he sat there in the great chair by himself, the flames flickering on the oak panels, and the subdued light of the lamp failing to penetrate the dark corners of the old hall, his face took an expression of melancholy, and there was an air of loneliness about his solitary figure—a loneliness which was not merely external. He was perplexed and unhappy, and the fact that his unhappiness had roused in his breast pride and jealousy and anger, did not make it less real. He had not come to the point of owning himself in the wrong, and yet he felt puzzled. He could not see how he had offended. It was a critical moment. Gentle and affectionate as Cheriton was, and happy as the relations had hitherto been between them, Alvar felt himself judged and condemned by his brother's higher standard, now that he had at last become aware of its existence. He had never been distressed by Virginia's way of looking at things, she was a woman, and her view's could not affect his; and for a long time, as has been said, he had regarded Cheriton's ideas of duty as as much an idiosyncrasy as his fair complexion, or his affection for Rolla and Buffer. Now he perceived that Cheriton himself did not so regard them, but with whatever excuses and limitations, expected them to be binding on Alvar himself; and Alvar's whole nature kicked against the criticism. Cheriton had been clear-sighted enough to perceive this, and so judged it better to draw back; but Alvar, through clouds and darkness, had seen a glimpse of the light. He *knew* that Cheriton was right, and the knowledge irritated him. In a fitful, dark sort of way he tried to assert his independence and yet justify himself to Cheriton. It was doubtful whether he would gradually follow the light thus held out to him, or decidedly turn away from it, and just now his wounded pride prompted him to the latter course. He would go his own way; and when he had settled his affairs to his mind, his brothers should own that he was right. And yet—did he not owe a debt, never to be forgotten, to the kind hand that had welcomed him, the bright face that had smiled on him, long ago, on that dreary Christmas Eve? Alvar did *not* say to himself, as he perhaps might have done with truth, that he had repaid Cheriton's early kindness to him tenfold; but he thought of the joyous, active youth, whose animal spirits, constant activity, and frequent laughter had been such a new experience to him.

As Alvar thought how great the change had been, his softer feelings revived, and with them the instinct of caving for his brother's comfort in a thousand trifling ways. He remembered that Cheriton had hardly eaten any dinner, and rose, intending to go to him and persuade him to have some of the chocolate for which he had never lost the liking gained in Spain. As he moved towards the library the butler came into the hall, and, with some excitement, told him that Fletcher, his farm bailiff, wanted to speak to him.

"But it is too late," said Alvar. "He may come to-morrow."

"Indeed, sir, I think it is of consequence. Some ill-disposed persons, sir, have set one of your ricks on fire, as I understand," said the butler, with the air of elevation with which the news of any misdemeanour is usually communicated.

"Tell him, then, to come in," said Alvar, coolly; and Fletcher appearing, deposed that a certain valuable hayrick, in a field about a mile from the house, on a small farm called Holywell, which had always been managed, together with the home farm, by Mr Lester himself, had been discovered by one of the men going home from work to be on fire. In spite of all their efforts, a great part had been burnt, and the rest much injured by the water used to put out the fire.

"And how did the hay catch fire?" asked Alvar, with composure.

"Well, sir, that young lad Fleming was found hanging about behind a hedge, as soon as we had eyes for anything but the flames; and after this morning's work, and words that many have heard him drop, the constable thought it his duty to take him up on suspicion, and he is in the lock-up at Hazelby."

Fletcher eyed his master as he spoke, to see how the intelligence would be received.

"Ah, then," said Alvar, "he will be sent to prison."

"The magistrates meet on Thursday, sir—day after to-morrow; but arson being a criminal offence, he'll be committed for trial at quarter-sessions," said Fletcher, in an instructive manner. "Wilfully setting fire to property we name arson, sir; the sentence is transportation for a term of years, sir."

"It is the passion of revenge," said Alvar, calmly. "It does not surprise me."

Fletcher looked as if the squire surprised him greatly; but Alvar wished him good-night, and dismissed him.

"Why—the old squire would have been up at Holywell and counted the very sticks of hay that was left!" he thought to himself as he withdrew; while Alvar went and communicated the intelligence to his brothers.

Cheriton listened, dismayed, while Jack exclaimed,—

"I don't believe it! No Fleming ever was such a fool."

"But he was angry with me," said Alvar. "He might have stabbed me out of revenge."

"Nonsense! we don't live in Ireland, nor in Spain either! They'll never forgive you, of course, to their dying day, but they won't put you in the right by breaking the law—we're too far north for that."

"Fletcher doesn't belong to these parts, you know," said Cherry; "He might take up an idea. I do think it most unlikely that a boy brought up like Chris would commit such an act. Besides, we saw him down here. When was the fire seen?"

"I do not know," said Alvar; "but Fletcher said that he was there."

"It can't be," said Cheriton; "I cannot believe it. But they'll never get over the boy being taken up at all. Why on earth did they never let us know what was going on! I wish I had been there."

"Yes; a fire, and for us never to know of it!" said Jack, regretfully.

"I think that Chris is a bad boy, and that he has done it," said Alvar. "But I do not care about the hay. What does that matter?"

"Why, the rick was worth forty pounds," said Cherry.

"I do not care for forty pounds. I care that I shall be obeyed," said Alvar.

A great deal more discussion followed, chiefly between Alvar and Jack; the latter at last relieving his mind of much of the good advice which he had long been burning to bestow. He showed Alvar his errors at length, and in the clearest language. Alvar took it very coolly, and without much more interest than if it had been an essay. He was not, as they would have expected, enraged at the burnt rick; indeed Cheriton could not help fancying that he regarded it as a justification of his violence towards Chris. As usual, it was the sense of Cheriton's opposing view rather than the thing itself that annoyed him.

"Don't worry yourself, Cherry," said Jack, as he wished him good-night. "I'll go the first thing in the morning and find out the rights of it."

Accordingly, before either of his brothers appeared, Jack started off through wind and rain, and investigated the story of the burnt rick.

He returned in high feather, and found them still at breakfast; for Alvar by no means held his father's opinion as to the merits of early rising.

"Well," said Jack, "it's clear that Chris had nothing to do with it. He left home at half-past four, went straight to old Bill's cottage, where Alice Fisher gave him some tea, and where no doubt they indulged in a good crack, left them at half-past five, and came straight up here with the note for Alvar, when you saw him."

"Yes," said Cherry, "I looked at the clock when I came over to the fire."

"Well, then, John Kitson saw the rick on fire exactly at half-past five, he heard the church clock strike; so if you and Alvar go over to Hazelby to-morrow, and prove that Chris came here on his way from old Bill's at that time, you can set it all to rights in a moment. And if that idiot Fletcher had sent for you—for Alvar—last night, poor Chris would never have been suspected."

"Well, Jack, you have done a good morning's work," said Cherry, much relieved.

"Yes. Give me some coffee, I had hardly any breakfast," said Jack, cutting himself some cold beef. "It is such a cold morning, too."

"And who did set the rick on fire, then?" said Cherry.

"Ah, that's not so clear. Fletcher and Jos Green had a shindy a day or two ago, and that lad is capable of anything; but, after all, it may have been an accident."

Alvar all this time had eaten his breakfast in silence. He did not disbelieve Jack's evidence, but perhaps he hardly felt its force, and the sense of having been nearly concerned in committing an injustice, did not strike him as forcibly as it did the others. He felt, perhaps not unnaturally, a sense of intense irritation against the whole Fleming family, and a wish never to hear their names again. Besides, Jack was openly triumphant, and he could not doubt that Cherry was secretly so.

The conversation dropped therefore, and Alvar, as the weather brightened, ordered his horse and went out. Jack retreated to his books; and presently came the vicar, to hear the rights of the story about Chris Fleming.

Cheriton said as little as he could, declaring that the arrest had been an entire mistake, which they much regretted, and that Alvar would take care that it was set right to-morrow.

"Have you heard of the outbreak of reforming zeal at Elderthwaite?" asked Mr Ellesmere.

"Yes," said Cheriton, colouring. "Miss Seyton told me about it, and besides, Clements was full of it when I saw him last. You see some new blood has come into the place, and there is a violent reaction, of course only among the few."

"Yes. Clements came to consult me about writing to the bishop. They want to have a curate; but I am afraid the old parson has set all his strength against it, and there are plenty to back him up. Besides, I don't see how the payment could be managed, as, of course, Miss Seyton will not act against her uncle. I told Clements to have patience; but a good deal of ill-feeling is cropping up. I wish you would go over and see if you can smooth things down a little."

"Do you think I could?"

"Why, yes; you always take Elderthwaite abuses under your protection. You would be the only curate to please the parson and his parishioners, too!"

Mr Ellesmere spoke entirely in jest, and was exceedingly surprised when Cheriton answered seriously,—

"Indeed, I have thought so;" and then proceeded, at greater length than he had done with Jack, to unfold his project. He did not try to prepossess the vicar in its favour, nor touch on his home difficulties, save by saying that an idle life at Oakby would not suit him. He said plainly that he felt that only the peculiar circumstances of Elderthwaite, and his own independent means, could justify such a step in one who believed himself likely to have but little time and less strength before him. Would Mr Ellesmere explain the whole state of the case to the bishop, and ask—other matters being satisfactory—would he ordain him if the next spring he found himself capable of doing anything.

"And would this really content you, Cherry?" said Mr Ellesmere. "It would be clerical work in its most unattractive form, among, I should say, very unattractive people?"

"Not to me," said Cheriton. "It would not be a distasteful life to me."

"And then the climate here—"

"That the doctors shall decide next spring," said Cherry, smiling.

"I don't see my way to it, my boy," said Mr Ellesmere, struck by his fragile look. "You must not run risks, and you would take responsibilities upon you which would make each particular risk seem unavoidable." Cheriton evidently did not see his way to a reply. His face fell. The vivid, vigorous nature, checked at every turn, was ever striving after a fresh outlet. The instinct to be up and doing, to put his hand to everything that came to it, could not be stifled by loss and disappointment, or even by want of physical health and strength. After a pause he said, in an altered voice,—

"There are things that make it seem as if that did not much matter. I mean it is my own concern *now*. A short life and a busy one is better than a few more months, or years even, like mine."

"I do not think your life has ever been useless yet, Cherry, even under the limitations that have been laid on it," said Mr Ellesmere, quietly.

Cheriton sat looking into the fire in silence, then he turned round and smiled with much of his old playful defiance, though there was a deeper undercurrent.

"You can keep a look-out on me all the winter, and tell the Elderthwaite reformers that they don't know what may happen, if they will only have patience. Then next spring I'll come and ask your advice again, and if you make out a very good case against me, why, *I'll give in*."

He uttered the last words slowly, and Mr Ellesmere fully understood all that they implied. He feared that the question might be answered for him before next spring.

Cherry himself felt that he had not taken a very favourable moment for putting forward his designs, for he was neither looking nor feeling well; and could hardly point to himself as a proof of the suitability of his native climate. Still the communication had given a certain point to look forward to, and was an individual interest apart from the confusing worry of affairs at Oakby. If, after the present crisis had subsided, Alvar still held to his intention of going to the sea with him, their old friendliness would soon supersede the present irritation. Then, afterwards, he would go to London, break up his arrangements there, and see the Stanforths, and would then spend Christmas with his grandmother. In the meantime he would be exceedingly prudent; and having regard both to the bad weather and to the charge of interference, would leave Alvar to go by himself to Hazelby to-morrow.

Alvar's ride had been interrupted by an encounter with Edward Fleming, full of resentment, by no means unnatural, though it was by this time somewhat unreasonable, for he could hardly help believing that the accusation against Chris had been intentional. A very sturdy and recalcitrant north-countryman he showed himself, respectful indeed in word to the squire, but intensely conscious of his injuries, and giving the squire very plainly to understand that a full explanation before all the magistrates at Hazelby, not to say a full apology, was no more than his duty, and fully to be expected of him. It was an unfortunate meeting. An appeal to Alvar's generosity and protection would have been instantly responded to; but the one form of pride roused the other, and stirred up the fear of dictation in his mind. He looked down at the sullen, resolute face of the young farmer with an expression of intense haughtiness, a look which, on the dark foreign face, seemed utterly hateful to Fleming, and said, as he made his horse move on, —

"That is as I shall please."

"If you let my brother be wronged, sir," said Fleming, "mark me, you'll repent it. 'Tis not the way your father would treat an old tenant, nor your brother either. A dog had his rights at their hands."

And in a rage, intensified by his consciousness of Alvar's scorn, he flung off with a sense of injury which would have led an Irishman to fire a shot, but which, in the English farmer, meant opposing the squire in Church and State, disobliging him on every private and parochial question, taking on every occasion the other side, and carrying on this line of conduct till his dying day.

He was young, too, and, as he had remarked to Cheriton, had education, and he might confide his grievance to the county paper. But he was both too proud and too generous to appeal again to Cheriton; and, besides, he never supposed for a moment that the squire would withhold his evidence.

But Alvar's wrath was hot within him. As master against servant, as head of the family against his juniors, above all, as gentleman against peasant, he felt bound to assert himself and his authority. No one should threaten him into begging off the boy who had insulted him, and whose family had so defied him. He would not yield to any one's view of his duty. Let the insolent boy have a few weeks more of suspense; what did it matter? When the real trial came he would condescend to give evidence in his favour (*subpoenas* did not at that moment occur to his mind), and would explain to the judge why he had chosen to delay his evidence. Then every one would see with what vigour he could administer his estate; and perhaps he would, to please Cheriton, then of his own free will confer some benefit on the Flemings which would make everything smooth.

Of course Alvar was not so foolish as his intentions, but all his past negligence had resulted in an amount of present ignorance of his surroundings which made such a scheme appear possible to him. It did strike him that Cheriton might take the matter into his own hands, and go to Hazelby himself; but so great a point had been made of his own going that he hardly knew how far this would supersede the need for it, and he did not mean to provoke a discussion.

Circumstances favoured him; Jack was going to dine and sleep at Ashrigg, he himself had another dinner engagement, and on the next day he had really promised to go early and shoot with Lord Milford. Cheriton had forgotten all about this, and, anxious not to irritate Alvar, said nothing about the magistrates' meeting during the short time they were together.

Chapter Forty Four
A New Life

"His peaceful being slowly passes by
To some more perfect peace."

The next morning Cheriton slept late, and awoke to the consciousness that he had caught a slight cold, "which," as he said to himself, "might happen to any one."

"Will you ask Mr Lester to come to me before he goes to Hazelby?" he said, not feeling quite able to satisfy himself that Alvar had all the needful evidence clear in his head.

"Mr Lester is not going to Hazelby, sir," said the man; "he went to Lord Milford's early this morning in the dog-cart. He left word that he would not disturb you, sir."

The engagement at Milford flashed across Cheriton's mind, and with dismay and indignation he perceived that Alvar had not thought it worth while to break it on Chris Fleming's account. In a moment he recognised the utter ruin that would fall on all chance of Alvar's success with his tenants, still more the disgrace that he would bring on himself in the eyes of the whole bench of magistrates, by the neglect of such an obvious duty, while on his own part he felt that it was such an unkindness as he hardly knew how to forgive. His first impulse was to let the matter alone, and to leave Alvar to bear the brunt of his own misdoings. But then the thought came of the distress to the Flemings, of the fatal injury to the boy from the weeks of undeserved detention, and, after all, the discredit would fall on them all alike. He forgot all his intention of nursing his cold, forgot its very existence, as he perceived, on looking at his watch, that he had barely time to reach Hazelby for the meeting.

"It is all the same," he said, "my going to Hazelby will answer every purpose. Tell them to bring Molly round at once. As Mr Lester has the dog-cart, I will ride."

"There is a very cold wind, and it looks like rain, sir."

"That can't be helped," said Cheriton, "there is no time to lose."

He tried to make his expedition seem a matter of course; but every one in the house believed that he went because the squire had gone off on his own pleasure, or out of what the old cook did not hesitate to call "nasty spite," had refused to justify little Fleming. Indeed, as Cheriton rode hurriedly away, he could hardly divest himself of the same opinion.

In the meanwhile, Alvar no sooner found himself well on the way to Milford than he began to feel pangs of compunction. The cold wind and drizzling rain beat in his face, as the conviction was borne in upon him, that Cheriton would certainly go to Hazelby in his place. He had not been at Milford since the day of the great rejoicing, when Cheriton, with all his fresh honours, had met them there, had wooed, and, as he thought, won Ruth Seyton; when he himself was Virginia's acknowledged lover. He called her to mind, as she had walked by his side in smiling content, as she played with the children—felt *now*, as he never had then, the wistfulness of her eyes when they met his, and almost for the first time he recognised that the want of devotion had been on his side. He had not loved her enough. A sense of discouragement and despondence seized on him, a deep melancholy softened the resentment which he had been cherishing. As he looked back on the years of his father's neglect, on Virginia's dismissal, on his brother's views of what his position required, for once the sense of his shortcomings overpowered his sense of the many excuses for them. His indifference to the chance of Cheriton's running a great risk touched him with a self-reproach for which his theories of life offered no palliative. He could not rest, and with a suddenness and vehemence of action most unusual with him, he turned to Lord Milford as they prepared to start on their day's sport, declared that he had suddenly recollected an important engagement, and must beg them to excuse him at once; overruled all objections on the score of his horse wanting rest by declaring that he would only drive to the station, and go by train to Hazelby.

"I am humiliated by my want of courtesy to your lordship, but it is necessary that I should go," he said; but what with the delay of starting, and the absence of a train at the last moment, the magistrates' meeting was over long before he reached Hazelby, every one had dispersed, and the court-house was shut.

He could not bring himself to ask any questions; but ordered a conveyance and started on his way back to Oakby, hardly knowing whether to reveal his change of purpose or not. On the road he passed the three Fleming brothers, trudging home through the mud. They looked away, and omitted to touch their hats to him. Alvar said to himself that he did not care; but the sense of unpopularity can never be other than bitter. He thought to himself that after all English gentlemen did not always live on their estates. There were hundreds of his father's rank who did not hold his father's view of their duties. He could shut Oakby up, let it, go where he would never see it again. But where? Never as the disinherited heir would he set foot in Seville, and he had no craving to hunt tigers in India, or buffaloes on the prairies. He did not wish to go yachting; did not care to travel; he hated the fogs and the colourlessness of London. He was as little ready to cut himself loose from all his moorings as Cheriton himself. Suddenly, as he drove on, he saw one of the Oakby grooms riding fast towards him. The man pulled up as he passed.

"Mr Cheriton is ill, sir; Mrs Lester is there, and she sent me for the doctor."

Alvar felt as if he had been shot.

"Ride on," he said, breathlessly; then seized the driver of the trap by the shoulder—"Drive fast; I will give you five pounds if you will drive fast. My brother is ill; he will want me."

"Ay, sir—all right, sir," said the lad, lashing up his horse.

Alvar felt as if a telegraph would have been slow; but he folded his arms, and sat like a statue till they reached the door, when he sprang out, and at the foot of the stairs saw Jack.

"Alvar! you here!" he exclaimed.

"What is it?—where is he?—what has happened?—tell me!" cried Alvar.

"Cherry went to Hazelby, of course, to clear Chris, as you were out of the way. He was so done up when he came back, and seems so evidently in for just such a bad attack as he had before, that granny, who came back here with me, sent for Mr Adamson. Yes, he is in bed; he was wet through."

Jack's face was like thunder; but Alvar dashed past him upstairs, and opened the door of his brother's room.

Cheriton was sitting up in bed. He had recovered a little from the exhaustion of his hasty ride, and though suffering much pain and oppression, was spending some of the little breath he had left, in trying to explain matters to his grandmother.

"You always were a perverse lad, or you would not be using your voice now, Cherry," she said. "When your brother comes back, I shall give him a piece of my mind."

"There he is," cried Cherry. There was a look in his eyes for a moment as if he hardly knew how they were to meet; but as Alvar advanced into the room, all his vehemence subsided. He came up to the bed, and laid his hand on Cheriton's with the old tender touch.

"You are ill, *mi caro*. I think you must not talk so much just now."

Cheriton looked up in his face, and read in it, steady as was the voice, an altogether new terror and trouble.

"*This* is my own fault," he said. "I was in such a hurry—that—I would not wait for the carriage. After all, there would have been time."

"Oh, my brother—my brother!" cried Alvar, losing his self-control, "your fault! Grandmother, it is I who have let him kill himself."

"You are just crazy," said Mrs Lester, agitated and angry, as Alvar rushed up to her, and threw himself on his knees beside her chair, clasping her hands in his. "I don't care whose fault it is. No doubt you are one as bad as the other. For the last half hour I have been trying to make Cherry hold his tongue, and now you make a worse turmoil than ever. Since my poor son went there is no one to look to."

Mrs Lester was shaken and terrified by the shock of sudden alarm, and agitated by Alvar's extraordinary behaviour, and thus her still fresh grief came back on her, and she burst into tears.

"Oh, granny, don't—don't!" cried Cherry, and the distress of his tone recalled Alvar to his senses.

"Oh, I am a fool!" he said, and getting up, he applied himself to soothe his grandmother with all the tact of which he was master, and was so successful, that in a few minutes she went away in search of some remedy for Cheriton, who, as he was left alone with his brother, felt, spite of his increasing suffering, the old sense of repose in Alvar's care creep over him.

"As violent an attack as the last, and much less strength to meet it," was the doctor's verdict, and the great common terror hushed for the time all disputes and differences.

Mrs Lester remained at Oakby, Nettie had returned to London a few days previously, and both she and Bob held themselves ready for a sudden summons.

Mrs Lester questioned Alvar on that first evening about all that had passed, in a dry, caustic fashion, while he answered, meekly enough. "Why, ye'll have made yourself a laughing-stock to the whole place," was her only comment on the story of the horsewhipping.

Alvar coloured to his temples, but said nothing; the reproach of Jack's silent misery was much harder to bear. He who knew how all the last weeks had been troubled by Alvar's fault, could not forgive, and felt that if Cheriton died, he could never bear the sight of Alvar again.

Alvar himself was shaken and disturbed as he had never been before. He had lost all the calm hopefulness and power of living in the present, that had made him such a support in Cheriton's previous illness; and though he was still a devoted and efficient nurse to him, there were times when he was quite unable to control his distress. He was frightened, and expected the worst; and poor Jack had to try to encourage him, a process that much softened his indignation.

All this was fully apparent to Cheriton. There was no longer the daze and confusion of that first attack of illness, the boyish astonishment at the fact of being ill at all, the novelty of all the surroundings, now, alas! so familiar; no longer, too, the sense that the exceeding sweetness of life made death incredible; no longer the same instinctive dependence on those around. Since then Cheriton had travelled a long way on the road of life, had looked across the dark river, and grown familiar with the thought of its other shore; he was no longer frightened at his own suffering, or at its probable result, and, as his senses were generally clear, except sometimes at night, or when under the influence of the remedies, he was able to think for others—a habit in which he had gained considerable skill.

He made Alvar write to Mr Stanforth, and beg that Gipsy might write to Jack, knowing that the surprise and joy of such a letter, and the relief of pouring out his heart in the answer, must lighten the heavy weight of the poor boy's anxiety; and so, in truth, it did, though Jack could never trust himself to thank Cherry for his kind thought. He also made the vicar go to Edward Fleming, and tell him that Alvar had only been a few minutes too late in coming to give evidence, and to entreat him to lay aside any ill-feeling for the misunderstanding "which," he said, "was partly caused by my bad management." He thought much about the state of affairs at Elderthwaite, or rather, perhaps, recalled at intervals much previous thinking. He was not equal to anything like a connected conversation, and he knew that no one would let the poor vehement old parson come near him; but he greatly astonished his grandmother by telling her that he had an especial desire to see Virginia Seyton.

"I cannot talk enough to tell you why," he said; "but, granny, do get her to come."

Mrs Lester promised; for how could she refuse him? He gave a good many directions to Mr Ellesmere, and in especial desired that a certain cup, won many years ago at some county athletic sports in a contest with his cousin Rupert, should be given to him as a remembrance.

From only one thing Cheriton's whole heart shrank, and that was from forcing Jack to listen to parting words. He had several things to say to him, but he put them off; he could not bear the sight of Jack's grief, and in this case could not trust his own self-command. It was the one parting that he could not yet face.

With Alvar it was different. In one way, he had with him much less sense of self-restraint, and in another, things lay between them that must be cleared away.

This state of things lasted for several days, and all the while the hard struggle between the remedies and the disease went on, a hand-to-hand fight indeed, and Cheriton's strength ebbed away, till he knew that he dared wait no longer for what he wanted to say.

It had been raining, but the yellow, level light of an October evening was shining through the thinly-clothed boughs of the great elms, and lighting up the russet and amber of the woodlands; while the purple hills beyond were still heavy with clouds—clouds receding more and more as the clear blue spread over the sky.

As Cheriton listened to the noise of the rooks, and looked out at the sunset, he recalled the awe and strange curiosity, the clinging to the dear home, to the dearer love which had made life so dear; the attempted submission, the dim trust that death, if it came, must be well for him, with which he had first said to himself that he must die; remembered, too, other hours, when, in weakness of body and anguish of soul, he had found it still harder to believe that it must be well for him that he should live. The passionate joy, the passionate sorrow, had passed away, or rather, had been offered at last as a willing sacrifice, and the loving kindly spirit had found sweetness in life without the first, while much anxiety, much trying disappointment, had succeeded to the second. Now there came over him a wonderful peace, as he summoned his strength for what he had in his mind to say.

With a look and sign he called Alvar over to him; and Jack, who was sitting apart in the window, watched and listened.

"Alvar," he said, taking hold of his hand, "I see it clearly." And the intent, wide-open eyes, seemed to Jack as if they could indeed look beyond the mists of life. "We were wrong to wish you like ourselves. Forgive me. You—yourself—can be as good for Oakby as—I—yes—as my father. But there is only one way for us both—to love God with all our hearts, and our neighbour as ourself. To take pains about it for His sake. That is the truth, Alvar—the truth as I know it!"

"Ah!" cried Alvar, "but I do not love my neighbours! that *is* the difference. But I love you, oh! my brother—my brother! Is it religion that will make me what you wish? I will be religious; I will no longer be careless; but oh, *caro—caro mio!* if I lose you, I have no heart to change. I have grieved you. Oh! what punishment is there for me? I would do penance like Manoel. What can I do?"

Alvar flung himself on his knees, the tears started in his eyes and choked his voice. At last he was stirred to the depths, and instincts deeper than teaching or training came to the surface.

"You know Who bore our sins for us," said Cheriton, "because He loved us."

How much, or how little, Alvar knew, after his formal teaching, and careless, unmoved youth, would be hard to say; probably Cheriton could not conceive how little; but face, voice, and manner had moved Alvar's soul to a great conviction, however little he realised what Cheriton had meant to say.

He called on that name which his brothers had never heard from his lips before, save in some careless foreign oath.

"I swear," he said—"I swear that I will be a religious man, and that I will be a good squire to Oakby. I make it a vow if my brother recovers—"

"Oh, hush—hush!" interposed Cheriton. "If not—we shall meet again—and you *must* be good to Oakby. Let me know you will!"

"I will! I will!" cried Alvar, completely carried away. He would have thrown his arms round Cheriton, but Jack interposed—

"Alvar! Alvar! this is enough. He *must* not have this agitation." Alvar yielded, but, too much overcome to control himself, rushed out of the room.

As he hurried blindly down the stairs he met Mr Ellesmere, and with a sudden impulse caught hold of his hand.

"Mr Ellesmere, you are a priest. I have sworn to him that I will change, that I will be religious. I give myself up to you. I will do whatever you wish. I swear to obey you—"

"Gently, gently!" said the astonished vicar. "You are too much agitated to know what you say. Come with me into the study; tell me what has passed. Believe me that I desire to help you in this great sorrow."

Alvar followed him, and as Mr Ellesmere talked and listened to him, he began to hope that, in spite of an ignorance which he had hitherto had neither the conscientious desire nor the intellectual curiosity to diminish, in spite of blind impulses rashly followed, the will for good that must bring a blessing had at last been awakened, even in this strange longing for vow and penance, an instinct that seemed inherited without the faith from which it had sprung. Alvar was in the mood which might have made his Spanish ancestors vow all their worldly goods away and think to buy a blessing, and to listen to him without unduly checking his vehemence, and yet to lead his thoughts upward, was a hard task; since Alvar was left subdued and quieted, and yet with an inkling of what had been really wrong with him, it may be inferred that Mr Ellesmere succeeded better than he had hoped to do.

Meanwhile, to poor Jack, every word of Cheriton's had thrilled with a thousand meanings. He knew that silence was imperative, and did not mean to say another word; but Cherry felt his hand tremble as he gave him some water, and looked up at him with a smile.

"You will have Gipsy soon," he whispered, "my own dear boy."

Jack pressed his hand. "To take pains for His sake." With his whole heart Jack recognised this key-note. Nothing else would do. Even Gipsy could not by herself give his life the full joy of a sufficient purpose; but as he thought of all the currents through which he must steer, and knew too well which way they often set, he shuddered.

"If I had not you to talk everything out with!" he said, inadequately enough.

"Oh, Jack, if I can't help you still, it will be because the work is done better. I don't fancy now that everything hangs on me. I am content."

And Jack felt that the memory of that perfect contentment could never pass away from him.

Chapter Forty Five
My Lady and My Queen

"Let all be well—be well."

"So, Queenie, you see there will soon be an end of it all!"

The speaker was Miss Seyton. She stood looking down at her niece with an odd quiver in lip and voice, even while her tone was not altogether a sad one. Virginia sat in dismayed silence; she had been arranging a bunch of autumn leaves and berries to brighten up the dark old drawing-room, which bore many a trace of her presence in bits of needlework and tokens of pleasant occupation, though the house was duller and quieter than ever now that Mr Seyton's rapidly failing health gave him the habits of an invalid, and that both the boys were absent. Miss Seyton looked more faded than ever, but she was kind and friendly with Virginia, even though she could not divest her voice of its sarcastic tone as she continued,—

"You are a person of consequence, and you ought to understand the state of the case."

"That Roland means to sell Elderthwaite?" said Virginia, slowly.

"Yes. We can't afford, Virginia, to make pretences to each other, and we know that it will come before many months. Then what are we to do?"

However much it went against Virginia to discuss the results of her father's death, she felt that there was some truth in her aunt's words, that they ought to be prepared for so great a change; and she had also learnt to practise great directness in dealing with Miss Seyton.

"I have sometimes supposed that you would live at the vicarage, Aunt Julia," she said.

"Not if I have a penny to live on elsewhere," replied Miss Seyton. "James and I were never friends, and I'll not see the place in the hands of strangers. Besides, I've had a thirty years' imprisonment, and I'd like my freedom. Look here—when I was a girl I was just like the others; I loved pleasure as well as they did, and had it too. I was as daring as ever a Seyton of them all. However, I meant to marry and live in the south, and I was quite good enough, my dear, for the man I was engaged to. Then he quarrelled with James, and that began the breach. I didn't marry, as you may see, and when *my* father died my portion couldn't be paid off without a sale, and things were in such a mess I had no power to claim it. So here I stayed, and, let me tell you, I've stopped up a good many holes, and been quite as great a blessing to my family as they deserved."

Virginia laughed in spite of herself, though her answer was grave.

"Yes, I know that, now."

"But *now*, d'ye see, Virginia, I'm tired of it. I'm only fifty, and it'll go hard if I don't get some pickings out of the sale of the estate. Do you know, we have some old cousins living in Bath, a Ruth and Virginia of another generation? I'm inclined to think I should like to go into society—to 'come out,' in fact, in a smart cap, and to live within reach of a circulating library and scandal. That's my view, and that's what I mean to aim at when the time comes. What do you say?"

"I should like the boys to have a home somehow," said Virginia. "Perhaps that would make some place into home for me."

"I don't wish to desert you," said Miss Seyton, "but candidly I think we should be happier apart. We shouldn't amuse each other if we lived together. But won't James want to keep you?"

"I don't know," said Virginia. "I am afraid it would not be a good plan for the boys to go there for holidays—if this place is to be given up. But oh, Aunt Julia, how *can* we tell what will happen? I can't make plans; I don't feel as if it mattered; and Roland seems to want to cast us all off."

"Yes; he's a selfish fellow. But, my dear, just consider how much worse it would be, if we had to *take him on*. Thank your stars that he means to stay in India. And as for the place, with its paint and its fences and its broken glass, let it go. We're better free of it. He is right, there. The worst part of the story is poor old James who must stay."

"He can't forgive Roland."

"No—you see, Queenie, it's wits that tell.—James hasn't brains, and he has never thought of cutting himself loose. He couldn't live away from Elderthwaite, any more than he could live without his skin. But when he hasn't the family dignity to keep him up, I'm afraid he'll go down."

"He is so wretched now about Cheriton Lester."

"Yes. He is the only Lester worth fretting for. As for that prig Jack, I'd like to see him make a fool of himself. I'd like to see him 'exceed his allowance considerably.' There's a pretty way of putting it for you!"

With which parting shot Miss Seyton went away, and Virginia sat sorrowful and perplexed, and with something of the family bitterness in her heart. Life was very hard to her. Her love for each one of her relations was a triumph over difficulties, and the sweet spontaneous passion that had promised to make her happy had been in its turn triumphed over by the uncongeniality of her lover. The softness of early youth and of her previous training had been replaced by something of the strength that expects little and makes the best of a bad business, but at a risk, the risk of the sense that evil is inevitable. Virginia was always outwardly gentle; but she had been thrown back on herself till she had gained a self-reliance that the Seyton blood in her was ready to exaggerate into scorn. For even Ruth was slow in answering her letters, and never wrote as in her girlish days.

As she sat musing a note was brought to her. It was from Mrs Lester, containing Cheriton's imperative request that she would come and see him. Would she come at once?

Virginia's cheeks flamed as if the missive had been from Alvar himself. She got up and put the note in her pocket, dressed herself, and leaving word with one of the servants that she meant to take a walk, set forth without delay for Oakby, walking through the plantations, across the fell, and through the fir-wood, as she had scarcely ever done alone before. She remembered going as Alvar's betrothed to ask for Cheriton during his first illness, and Alvar's absorption and indifference to her presence. Now that would be natural enough. Still she could scarcely think of Cheriton in her dread and wonder as to who might greet her, as she rang at the bell, and asked for Mrs Lester, who came forward into the hall to receive her.

"My dear," she said, "I do not know what Cherry wants with you; but we can't refuse him. Will you come at once?"

Virginia was afraid to ask questions, she followed the old lady's slow progress up the dusky staircase, and into Cheriton's room.

The daylight was now fast fading, but its last rays fell on Cheriton's wide-opened eyes and flushed face.

He took hold of her hand, and said with extreme difficulty, —

"Thank you — my love to the parson. Ask Jack what I meant to do — and then tell him. Tell him — I say — he must reform Elderthwaite for my sake. He must do it himself. I know he can. Don't let him *be* one of the abuses. Don't get into despair." He paused for breath, and then with an accent and smile that through all the suffering had something of his old playful daring, "I *mustn't* say anything else to you, but that will come right too."

"I will tell him," faltered Virginia, awed, bewildered, and yet with a strange sense of encouragement; she let herself be drawn away, heard Mrs Lester say that it was too dark for her to go home alone, she should send Jack with her to get a breath of air, while Cherry was suffering less. He was so fully himself it was hard to believe in the danger, but the attacks of coughing were most exhausting, and he could hardly take anything, she was very hopeless, and "my grandson"—this always meant Alvar—thought badly of him. "Come in here, my dear, and I will fetch Jack."

As Mrs Lester put her into the library, and left her there alone in the dusk, the tears that she had hitherto restrained broke forth.

She thought that she was crying for Cheriton, but all her own sad future, all her yearnings for the lost past, mingled together, and she wept the more because, she knew not how, Cheriton had given her a sort of indefinite comfort.

She did not hear the study door open, nor see Alvar come through the room, nor did he see her in the dim light, till he heard her sobbing.

"Who is it?" he exclaimed, becoming aware of a woman's figure near the fire. She started up, and with her first movement he knew her. "*Mi dona!*" he cried in his astonishment.

"Cherry asked to see me," she faltered. "He is so ill—I could not help crying."

"Ah, no!" said Alvar; "and *I* may not comfort you!"

But he came close and stood by her side, and she saw that he too was greatly agitated. She wanted to speak about Cheriton, but she could not command her voice, nor think of a word to say.

Suddenly Alvar turned and clasped her hand.

"Ah!" he cried, with such vehemence as she had never seen in him before. "My heart is breaking! Can you never forgive? I love you; I have always loved you. When you sent me from you, it was my pride that let me submit! In my own country I knew that for your sake I was English— English altogether. I am not worthy, but I repent. I have confessed. Help me, and I will be a good Englishman! For I have now no other country, and I cannot live without you. Give me your hand once more!"

Alvar poured forth this torrent with such burning eagerness, such abandonment of entreaty, that he did not see how weak were the defences he was attacking.

"Indeed," she whispered, "it was not *that*—not that I thought you were—not good—I thought you did not love me—much."

"I did—I do love you—I love you as my life! But you?"

"I have always loved you. I could not change," she said, with something of her old gentle dignity. "But—I have been very unhappy all this time."

"Ah, now you shall be happy! Yet, what do I say? How can *I* make any one happy! I who have grieved and vexed my brother with my unkindness—nay, caused his illness even—I cannot make you happy!" said Alvar, in a tone of real self-blame.

"I think you can!" said Virginia softly; but the words had hardly passed her lips when she started away from him, as Jack came into the room.

"Granny says I am to walk home with you, Virginia. What, Alvar, are you here? they have been looking for you. Do go to Cherry—he is so restless now!"

"I will go," said Alvar. "Take care of her, Jack, for I must not come. Farewell, *mi regna!*" He took both her hands and kissed them, then put her towards Jack, and hurried away; while poor Virginia glanced in much confusion at her escort; but he was too much absorbed in grief and anxiety to take in what had passed, or to heed it if he did. He walked on by her side without speaking; till she, trying to collect her thoughts, and actuated by a very unnecessary fear of what he would think of her silence, bethought herself to ask him what Cheriton wished her to tell her uncle.

"He said I was to ask you?"

"He wanted to take orders, and be curate of Elderthwaite," said Jack. "You know London did not suit him, and the work was too hard, and life at home was so worrying for him. Besides, he hated being idle. He thought that he could manage to get things right at Elderthwaite, and he said that he should like it, and be happy there."

Jack spoke in a dull, heavy voice, his use of the past tense marking how completely he regarded the possibilities of which he spoke as at an end; and something in the tone showing that the proposal had been distasteful to him.

"Would Cherry have given himself for *that?*" exclaimed Virginia.

"Yes," said Jack. "I didn't like it. It seemed a great sacrifice, and besides—he was not half strong enough."

"But did he care so much? I don't mean that I can't understand his wishing to take orders—but just for *Elderthwaite!*"

"He is very fond of Elderthwaite. And he said that it was only because he fancied that he could be more useful there than any one else; and because he has money, that he was justified in proposing it—because he was ill, I mean."

"Indeed, he could do good there! He always did!"

"You know," said Jack, rather more freely, "that Cherry has a notion that when a person seems specially marked out for any situation, he is likely, in the long run, to be the best person for it. He says you can't destroy evil without good. That people *fit* their own places, and so he believes that Elderthwaite would do better, in the long run, if Parson Seyton could be encouraged to make things a little more ship-shape, than it would with a new man, if he were driven away. You see he gets fond of people. *I* don't see it; I think it's fanciful. All reformers begin with a clean sweep. Then Cherry said valuables were sometimes found in the dust; nobody would reform if you ran at them with a besom. Of course *he* could persuade people; at any rate, he always thought he could."

"He thinks the sun is more powerful than the north wind," said Virginia. "I am sure Uncle James would have given in to him."

"So he said. But he was mistaken in one case, and then he blamed himself, and I suppose—I suppose—he has conquered at last! Any way, Virginia, you were to tell your uncle what he wished to do."

"I will tell him. He is breaking his heart about Cherry now."

"I suppose so. I can't come in. Good-bye; we'll send over in the morning." Jack turned away. Cheriton's kindly theories might seem fanciful to him; but he would never have the chance of knocking them on the head any more. He was so miserable that even the thought of Gipsy only made him feel her absence, and wonder if so bright a creature could continue to care for him, when he had grown into a stern, hard-hearted person, without any power of softening. Poor Jack's hard heart was very heavy, and beat so fast as he came up to the house, that he could hardly ask if there was any change.

Chapter Forty Six
My Dear!

"But still be a woman to you."

Early the next morning Virginia received a letter from Alvar, written at intervals during his night watch in Cheriton's room. Perhaps it was the first real communication she had ever received from him, and in it he made a sort of confession of his shortcomings, as far as he himself understood them. He told her that he had been "revengeful" towards his father, and that in the affair of the Flemings he had allowed "the passion of jealousy" to overcome him. He recounted his promise to Cheriton, and with the simplicity that was at once so strange and so engaging a part of his character, assured her "that he was no longer indifferent to religion," but would follow the instructions of Mr Ellesmere. "I think," he added, "that this will give you pleasure."

There was a great deal about Cheriton, Alvar declaring that he could not *now* despair of anything, but that he should have written to *her* at such a time, and about *himself*, was enough to mark the change in his former relations with Virginia.

The change in himself she was ready to take for granted. All must be right where there was such humility and power of repentance; and perhaps she did him more justice than even Cheriton could have done. For Alvar had undergone no change of intellectual conviction, that element was wanting, both in his former carelessness, and in his present acceptance of a new obligation, and in the excitement of feeling under which he was acting love and remorse towards his brother had the largest share. But he had recognised himself as erring, and intended to amend, and such a resolution must bring a blessing. But as his brothers would only have altered any settled line of conduct, after infinite heart-searchings and perplexities, they could not have conceived how simple the matter appeared to Alvar, when he had once made up his mind that he could possibly have been in fault.

Virginia had said nothing the night before of her changed prospects; she knew that the Lesters could have no thought to spare for her; but when her aunt suggested sending over to inquire, she could not pretend ignorance, and her blush and few words of explanation were enough for Miss Seyton.

"Ah, well," she said, "you might have saved yourselves a great deal of trouble if you had found this out a little sooner."

"We cannot speak of it just now, auntie."

"No; but you say, don't you, that everything happens for good? Now this good has come out of Cherry's illness; perhaps he'll get well."

After these characteristic congratulations Virginia took her way to the vicarage. She found her uncle in his "study," a room which was sufficiently well lined with ancient and orthodox divinity to merit the name, though the highly respectable volumes, descended from some unwontedly learned Seyton vicar, did not often see the light.

The parson was looking out of the window down the road.

"Ah, how d'ye do, my dear?" he said, in unwontedly quiet accents. "I was just looking out, for I sent over to Oakby to inquire how that poor lad is to-day."

"We have heard," said Virginia. "I don't think he is any worse. And, uncle, I saw him yesterday; he sent for me to give me a message for you."

"A message! Well, my lassie, what did he say?"

Virginia came and stood behind the chair in which her uncle had seated himself.

"He wished me to tell you that he had been making up his mind to take orders, and that he loved Elderthwaite so much that he meant to ask you if you would let him come and be your curate, that you and he together might set things right here. But he said that now that will never be. And he sent his love, and I was to ask you to reform Elderthwaite for his sake. He said, 'Tell him I know he can, better than any one, if he will.'"

Virginia paused, as her voice faltered.

"Why, bless my soul," cried the parson, "what does the lad mean? Why, I'm one of the old abuses myself."

"Yes—yes—uncle. But that is what he said. You must not be one of the abuses. He said you might do it all, if you would, because you love the place more than any one can."

There was a silence. The parson sat still.

"He is a good lad—he always was a good lad," he said, after a pause. "And did he think to come here, to spend his time over a parcel of scamps and drunkards? Eh! I shouldn't have believed it. He had heard that they want me to have a curate, I suppose," he added, quickly.

"Oh, yes, uncle; but he was afraid that you would not like it."

"Look here, my lassie, I like the old methody in his proper place; but I'll have no psalm-singers in my church. I'm a sound Churchman, and I don't approve of it."

Virginia, finding an objection to psalm-singing in church rather difficult to reply to, was silent, and her uncle went on rapidly, —

"I hate the whole tribe of your *earnest*, hard-working, 'self-devoted' young fellows—find it pay, and bring them into the society of gentlemen— write letters in trumpery newspapers, and despise their elders. Newspapers have nothing to do with religion. The Prayer-book's the Prayer-book, and a paper's a paper. Give me *Bell's Life*. Bless you, my dear, do you think I keep my eyes shut?"

"You are not just, uncle," said Virginia. "But Cheriton would not have been like that."

Mr Seyton's twinkling eyes softened, and the angry resistance to a higher standard, that mingled with the half-shrewd, half-scornful malice of his words, subsided, as he said, in quite a different tone, —

"I would have had Cheriton for my curate, my dear."

He said no more, and Virginia could not press him; and when he spoke it was only to question her about Cheriton's condition.

But when she went away he took his hat and walked out through his bit of garden towards the church, and sitting down on the low stone wall, looked over the churchyard, where a fine growth of nettles half smothered the broken gravestones; and as he sat there he thought of his past life, of his dissipated, godless youth, of the sense of desperation with which, to pay his debts, he had "gone into the Church," of the horrible evils he had never tried to check, and yet of the certain kindliness he had entertained towards his own people. How he had defied censure and resisted example till his fellow-clergy looked askance at him, and though he might affect to despise them, he did not like their contempt. He thought of the family crash that was coming, and he was keen enough to know how he would be regarded by new comers—"as an old abuse." And he thought of Cheriton's faith in him, and the project inspired as much by love for him as by the zeal for reform. He thought of the first time he had read the service, the sense of incongruity, of shame-facedness; how a sort of accustomedness had grown upon him till he had felt himself a parson after a sort, and how, on a low level, he had in a way adapted his life to the requirements of his profession.

Then he thought of the way Cheriton had proposed such a step to himself, and, without entering into any of those higher feelings which might have repelled rather than attracted him, he contrasted with his his own the unselfishness of the motive that prompted Cheriton.

He made no resolutions, drew no conclusions, but unconsciously he was looking at life from a new standpoint.

Virginia did not see Alvar, nor hear directly from him all that day; and but for the letter in her possession, her interview with him would have seemed like a dream.

The next morning was sunny and still. She stood on the steps at the garden door, looking over the lawn, now glistening with thick autumn dew. The sky was clear and blue, the wild overgrown shrubberies that shut out the landscape were tinted with brown and gold, an "autumn blackbird" sang low and sweet. All was so peaceful that it seemed as if ill news could not break in upon it; yet, as the old church clock chimed the hour, and through the still air that of Oakby sounded in the distance, Virginia started lest it should be the beginning of the knell. As the sound of the clock died away, the gate in the shrubbery clicked, a quick step sounded, and Alvar came up the path.

Virginia could wait no longer. She ran to meet him, gathering hope from his face as she approached.

"Yes, he is better. There is hope now; but all yesterday he grew weaker every moment. I thought he would die."

Alvar's voice trembled, and he spoke with more abandonment than was usual with him; he looked very pale, and had evidently gone through much. He added details of their suspense, and of Cherry's condition, "as if," Virginia thought, "he *wanted* to talk to me."

"You are very tired," she said. "Come in and have some breakfast. Auntie and I always have it here."

She took him into the drawing-room, where there was a little table near the fire, and made him sit down, while she waited on him, and poured out the tea. She did not feel a bit afraid of him now, and, spite of his punctilious gallantry, he submitted to her attentions without any of the forms and ceremonies with which he had previously made a distance between them.

"You have been up all night. I think you ought to have gone to bed, instead of coming here," she said, sure of a contradiction.

"It is a great deal better than going to sleep to see you, my dear!" said Alvar, quaintly; and Virginia thought she liked the homely English better than the magnificent Spanish in which he had been wont to term her his lady and his queen.

"I am getting very hungry, Virginia," said Miss Seyton, opening the door. "May I come in to breakfast?"

"Oh, but that is shocking!" cried Alvar, springing up and advancing to meet her. "Miss Seyton, I have brought good news of my brother. But I must go home now, he may want me. Perhaps if he is still better I can come again by-and-by."

"Only think," said Virginia, as she went with him through the garden on her way to the vicarage to tell the good news to her uncle, "only think, when the clock struck just before you came, I was afraid it was the beginning of the knell!"

"Ah, I trust we shall not hear that terrible sound now!" said Alvar, gravely.

And yet before that day closed the old bell of Elderthwaite church was tolling, startling every one with the sudden conviction that that morning's hope had proved delusory. It frightened Mr Ellesmere as he came home from a distant part of his parish, though a moment's reflection showed him that his own church tower was silent. What could be the matter elsewhere?

There was a rush of people to the lodge gates at Oakby, to be met there by eager questions as to what was the matter at Elderthwaite?

"It must be old Mr Seyton, took off on a sudden," they said. "Well, so long as Mr Cherry was getting better—"

But before curiosity could take any one down the lane to verify this opinion, up came the parson's man from Elderthwaite with a letter for Mr Lester, and the news that a telegram had been received two hours before at the hall, to say that Mr Roland had been killed out tiger-hunting in India.

There was more consternation than grief. Roland had not felt nor inspired affection in his own family; in the neighbourhood his character was regarded with disapproval, and his sarcastic tongue remembered with dislike. He had intensified all the worst characteristics of the family.

Virginia had scarcely ever seen him; his father and uncle had so resented his determination to sell the estate, though it had perhaps been the wisest resolve he had ever come to, that he had been to them as an enemy.

But still the chief sense in all their minds was that the definite, if distasteful, prospect, to which they had been beginning to look forward, had melted away, and that all the future was chaos.

Dick, suddenly became a person of importance, and now within a month or two of coming of age, was sent for from London. He had improved in looks and manner, and seemed duly impressed with the gravity of the situation. He was told what Roland's intentions had been, and that his father's life could not be prolonged for many months; listened to Mr Seyton's faltering and confused explanations of the state of affairs, and to his uncle's more vigorous, but not much more lucid, denunciation of it. Dick said not a word in reply, he asked a few questions, and at last went down into the drawing-room where his sister was sitting alone. He walked over to the window and stood looking out of it.

"Virginia," he said, "*I* don't wish to sell Elderthwaite."

"Do you think it can be helped, Dick?" she said, eagerly.

"I don't know. *I'm* not in debt like Roland—that is, anything to speak of. I don't want to wipe the family out of the county for good and all. Why couldn't the place be let for a term of years?"

"But—it is so much out of repair!"

"Yes," said Dick, shrewdly, "but it's an awfully gentlemanly-looking place yet. Fellows who have made a fortune in trade want to get their position settled before they *buy* an estate, or to make a little more money first. I heard Mr Stanforth talking about some old place in the south where there were fine pictures, which had been let in that way. Well then, of course, some sacrifices must be made; something was done with the money Cheriton Lester paid for Uplands. Then there's all that part out Ashrigg way—Cuddiwell, you know, and High Ashrigg. Those two farms have always paid rent. If they were sold—they're handy either for the Lesters or the Hubbards—we might put things to rights a little in that way."

"I am *glad* you care about Elderthwaite, Dick," said Virginia, impetuously.

"Oh, as to that," returned Dick, "I don't know that I go in for any sentiment about it. Of course, I couldn't live here for years to come. I'm not quite such a fool as I was once, Virginia, thanks to you and some others I could name; and I should go on as I am for the present. But it makes a difference in a man's position to have a place like this in the background, even if it is tumbling to pieces. A girl with money might think twice whether she wouldn't be Mrs Seyton of Elderthwaite."

"Oh, Dick! don't marry a girl for her money," said Virginia, half laughing; but she could never have imagined herself listening with so much respect to Dick's sentiments.

In truth, want of sense and insight had never been the cause of the Seytons' errors; but just as in some men a warm heart and tender conscience fail to make head against violent passion, so that they feel their sins while they commit them, so in the Seytons a shrewd *mental* sense of their own folly had always co-existed with the headstrong self-will which had overridden it. Dick had a less passionate nature, and was, moreover, less at the mercy of circumstances than if he had been brought up as the heir, and his friends in London were sensible people.

"Perhaps," said his sister, "you might ask Alvar what he thinks of it."

"Alvar? Oh, ho! is that come to pass again? So, you've made it up. Well, it is a good thing that you have some one to take care of you," said Dick, sententiously.

Alvar was taken into counsel, and the results of much discussion and consideration may be briefly told.

Dick's plans were hailed by his father and uncle as an escape from a prospect, which had made death doubly bitter to the one, and the rest of life distasteful to the other. And an unexpected purchaser of the two farms was found in Judge Cheriton, who had been talking for some time of buying a small property which might be a home for him when his public career was over, and a holiday retreat for the present. There was a farm-house at High Ashrigg which might be improved into a modern antique of the style at present admired. The two farms were therefore purchased at once of Mr Seyton himself, and with his full consent and approval.

The rest of Dick's plan could not be carried out in his father's lifetime, but it was agreed to by Mr Seyton as the best thing his heir could do.

All this time Cheriton was mending slowly, but with much uncertainty as to how far his recovery would be complete. He very soon detected the turn that Alvar's affairs had taken, much to his satisfaction; but Jack, guessing that the news of Roland's death would be a shock to him, it was not till he had begun to insist that his own state must not again delay Alvar's marriage, that he heard the story of which it might have been said "that nothing in Roland Seyton's life became him like the leaving of it;" for it proved that he had met his death by an act of considerable bravery, which had saved the lives of others of the party. Perhaps Cheriton, unable to be untender to the memory of his boyish ideal, gave him a truer regret than any of his own family.

He listened with great interest to all the future arrangements, and was the first to suggest that his old acquaintance, Mr Wilson's son, was to be married to a young lady of fortune, and might form a possible future tenant for Elderthwaite.

As for the rest, even setting her deep mourning aside, Virginia would not hear of marrying while her father grew daily weaker; nor was Cheriton at all equal to the inevitable excitement and difficulty of arranging plans for the winter which must have ensued.

It ended, as soon as he was able to bear the journey, in his going to Torquay with Alvar, to stay for the present. Mrs Lester went back to Ashrigg, and Oakby was once more left solitary.

Chapter Forty Seven
The Yeomanry Meeting

"All's right with the world."

It was a bright morning just before Whitsuntide in the ensuing year, when the bluebells were still adorning the Elderthwaite plantations, and the ivy on the church was fresh with young green shoots. Once more Parson Seyton sat on the churchyard wall watching his nettles, which now, however, were falling beneath the scythe, while a space had previously been carefully cleared and trimmed round a handsome cross-marked stone of grey granite, which showed the spot where Mr Seyton had rested, now for nearly three months. Suddenly a step came up the lane and through the gate, and the parson sprang up joyfully as Cheriton Lester came towards him.

"Well, my boy—well? So here you are, back at last. And how are you?"

"Oh, I am very well—quite well now," said Cheriton.

And indeed, though the figure was still very slight, the hand he held eagerly out still over-white and thin, the colour too bright and variable for perfect health and strength, he looked full of life and spirits, overjoyed, as he said, to find himself at home again.

"Oh, yes, Alvar is here, of course, and we started together; but we met Virginia in the lane, and then—I thought I would come and find you. How lovely it all looks!"

"Ah, more to your taste than Mentone?"

Cherry laughed. "My taste was always a prejudiced one," he said; "but Mr Stanforth and I were very jolly at Mentone, especially when Jack joined us. How did Alvar get on up here by himself at Christmas?"

"He got on very well *here*—if by here you mean Elderthwaite. As for Oakby, he attended all the dinners and suppers and meetings and institutions like a hero. But I suspect he and his tenants still look on one another from a respectful distance."

"All, they won't be able to resist him next week, he'll look so picturesque in his yeomanry uniform. We shall have a grand meeting."

"The volunteers keep the ground, I understand?" said the parson.

"Yes, myself included. There doesn't seem to be much for them to do, and they wished me to come very much. Then, you know, we have had a grand explanation about Jack's affairs, and granny and Nettie have got Gipsy with them; so Sir John found out that the pictures wanted Mr Stanforth, and he is coming down. Then Jack couldn't resist, and managed to get a couple of days' leave. So the only thing to wish for is fine weather. But I am not forgetting," continued Cherry, in a different tone, "that *here* you have all had a good deal of trouble."

"Well," said the parson, "it was a great break up and turn out; and I'm bound to own your brother was a great help in getting through it. Julia, she is gone off to Bath, and writes as if she liked it; and I was very glad that Virginia should stay here with me for the present. Mr Wilson has taken the place for his son, and it is being put in order. But all in the old style, you know, Cherry," said the parson, with a wink, "no vulgar modernisms."

"Fred Wilson's a very nice fellow," said Cherry.

He had sat down on the wall by the parson, and now, after a pause, began abruptly,—

"I saw Dr A— again as we came through London. He says that I am much better; indeed, there is nothing absolutely the matter with me. I haven't got disease of the lungs, though of course there is a tendency to it, and I shall always be liable to bad attacks of cold. He says I should be better for some definite occupation, partly out of doors. He does not think London would suit me, but this sort of bracing air might do better than a softer one, as I was born here, except perhaps for a month or two in the winter. I *may* get much stronger, he thinks, or—But it was a very good account to get, wasn't it?"

"Yes, my lad, I'm glad to hear it—as far as it goes," said the parson, looking intently at him. Cheriton looked away with deepening colour, and said, rather formally,—

"I thought that I ought to tell you all this, sir, because I have never yet felt justified in referring to what I asked Virginia to tell you last year. But my wishes remain the same, and if you think with such doubtful health I could be of any service to you or to the place—I—I should like to try it."

"Why, if you have your health, you might do better than be my curate," said the parson.

"But I won't exemplify a certain proverb! In short," said Cherry, looking up and speaking in a more natural manner, "if you'll have me, parson, I'll come."

"And suppose I say I won't have you?"

"Then I should have to ask the bishop to find me another curacy," said Cheriton. "I have quite made up my mind; even if I could follow the career I once looked forward to, which is impossible, I should not wish it. I've had some trouble, only *one* thing has made it bearable. I should, like to help others to find that out. But I want to help my old neighbours most. I made up my mind with this place chiefly in my thoughts. I care for it, for many reasons. But nothing now would induce me to change my intention of taking orders if I have the health to carry it out."

An odd sort of struggle was evident in the old parson's weather-beaten face.

"They'd work him to death in some fine church at a watering-place, with music and sermons, and all sorts of services," he muttered to himself.

"Yes; I don't think that that would suit me as well as Elderthwaite."

"Then, my lad," said the parson, with some dignity, "I will have you. And, Cherry, I—I *understand* you. I know that you have stood by me, ever since you dusted out the old church for the bishop."

"That's just what I want to do now!" said Cherry. "Thank you; you have made me very happy. There are Alvar and Queenie," and with a hearty squeeze of the hand he started up and went to meet them. The parson remained behind, and as Cheriton moved away from him he lifted his rusty old felt hat for a moment, and said emphatically,—

"I'm an old sinner!"

The morning of the Yeomanry Review dawned fair and bright, and brought crowds together to the wide stretch of moorland above Ashrigg, where the review was to take place. Whitsuntide was a time to make holiday, and half Oakby and Elderthwaite was there to see. The only drawback was that Virginia's mourning was still too deep to admit of her sharing in so large a county gathering, for which she cared the less, as Alvar, in his blue and silver, mounted on the best horse in the Oakby stables, and looking as splendid as a knight of romance, rode round by the vicarage to show himself to her.

But Parson Seyton was present in a new black coat and a very conspicuous white tie, mounted, he assured Cheriton, to do credit to his future curate.

Cheriton himself appeared in the grey and green to which he had once been enthusiastically devoted, and which was now worn for the last time before he began his preparation for the autumn ordination. In the meantime he could stay at Oakby, while Uplands was being made habitable, and could begin to feel his way among the Elderthwaite people, while Virginia was still there to help him, for she and Alvar meant to be married quietly in the summer.

But the happiest of all happy creatures on that bright morning, was perhaps Gipsy Stanforth, as she sat with Nettie and Sir John and Lady Hubbard, while Jack was on horseback near at hand. The two young ladies excited much interest, for it was Miss Lester's first appearance on leaving school, and people had begun to say that she was a great beauty, as she sat perfectly dressed and perfectly behaved, her handsome face with its pure colouring and fine outline as impassive "as if," thought Dick Seyton, "she had never seen a hay-loft in her life."

Gipsy, on the other hand, could not help sparkling and beaming at every pleasant sight and sound. This was Jack's world, and it was such a splendid one, and every one was so kind to her; for Nettie, though she secretly thought Gipsy rather too clever, knew how to behave to her brother's betrothed. Gipsy could not keep her tongue still in her happy exultation, and very amusing were her remarks and comments, till, if people came up to the carriage to look at Miss Lester, they frequently remained to talk to Miss Stanforth.

Her father was in another carriage with the rest of the Hubbard party, enjoying the brilliant scene perhaps more than any one present, since no quaint incident, and no picturesque combination escaped his keen and kindly notice.

"Nettie looks like coming out sheep-farming in Australia in that swell get-up, doesn't she?" said Bob to Jack, as they had drawn off to a little distance together.

"She doesn't look like it," said Jack; "but if she set her mind to that or to anything else, she would do it."

"Oh," said Bob, "it's all nonsense. I sha'n't marry out there. I shouldn't like a colonial girl; but I shall come home in a few years' time, and look about me. Nettie will be married before then, I hope, in a proper way. I hope you'll all be very careful about her acquaintances."

"Well, we'll try," said Jack, smiling. "She will have Virginia to go about with."

"Yes, I like Virginia. She'll do Alvar good," said Bob, condescendingly. "And I like Gipsy too, Jack; she's very jolly."

"Thank you," said Jack, "she is."

"I suppose you'll be a master in a school somewhere when I get back, and Cherry will be a parson. Well, he'll make a very good one."

"Yes," said Jack, shortly. He did not like discussions as to Cherry's future; it hung, in his eyes, by too slender a thread.

"Good heavens!" cried Bob, suddenly, "look there!"

Sir John Hubbard had left his carriage, and his young horses, which had been already excited by the numbers and the noise; frightened by some sudden chance movement among the crowd, no one could tell what—the bark of a dog, the sudden crossing of an old woman with a tray of ginger-beer—shied so violently that the coachman, who was holding the reins loosely, was thrown off the box, the horses dashed forward down the hillside, towards an abrupt descent and break in the ground, at the bottom of which ran a little stony brook.

Jack and Bob were far behind, and even as they spurred forward they felt it would be all in vain; while Nettie, springing on to the front seat, tried to climb up and reach the reins; but they swung far beyond her reach. She looked on and saw all the danger, saw the rough descent ahead, heard the cries of horror on all sides, saw too, one of the yeomanry officers gallop at headlong speed towards them, dash in between them and the bank, and seize the reins. A violent jolt and jerk, as the horses were thrown back on their haunches, and she recognised Alvar, as he was flung off his own horse and down the bank by the shock and the struggle, as other hands forced the carriage back from its deadly peril, and Jack, dashing up, his face white as marble, dismounted and caught the trembling Gipsy in his arms.

Nettie heeded none of them; she sprang out and down the bank, and in a moment was kneeling by Alvar's side, who lay senseless. She had lifted his head and unfastened his collar, before her brothers were beside her.

"No, no; I'll do it," she cried, pushing Jack's hand aside.

"Hush, Nettie, nonsense; let us lift him up. Get some water."

There were a few moments of exceeding terror, how few they never could believe, as they carried Alvar to smooth ground, and tried to revive him, before he opened his eyes, looked round, and after a minute or two, said faintly,—

"What has happened? Ah—I remember," trying to sit up. "Are they safe?"

"Yes—yes—but you? Oh, Alvar, are you killed?" cried Nettie.

"No, no," said Alvar, "my arm is hurt a little. I think it is sprained—it is nothing. Do not let Cherry be frightened."

"I never thought of him!" said Jack. "Oh, he won't know anything of it—he is not here. You are sure your arm is not broken?"

"No. Ah, there he is! Help me up, Jack! Cherry, it is nothing."

Cheriton, who had been considerately summoned with the news of a dreadful accident, but they hoped Mr Lester was not killed, was speechless with mingled terror and relief. He knelt down by Alvar's side, and took his hand, hardly caring to ask a question as to how the accident had come about; but now Sir John Hubbard's voice broke in,—

"I never saw such a splendid thing in my life, never—the greatest gallantry and presence of mind! A moment later and they would have been over! My dear fellow, I owe you more than I can say—Lady Hubbard, and your own sister, and Jack's pretty little Gipsy—my horses starting off in that way. I can never thank you—never. I couldn't have believed it. And I thought it was all over with you!"

"I am not seriously hurt, sir," said Alvar, sitting up, "and there was nothing else to be done; it is not worth your thanks."

"Is not it?" cried Mr Stanforth, unable to restrain himself. "More thanks than can be spoken."

"I'll accept them all for him," said Cheriton, looking up, his face full of triumph; while Nettie, hitherto steady, broke down, to her own disgust, into sobs.

"I'm not frightened—no!" she said, as Gipsy tried to soothe her. "But I thought he wasn't worth anything—and *he is*!"

"Come," said Sir John, "we must not have any more heroics, and the hero must go home and rest—to Ashrigg, I mean. And you too, Cherry, go and look after him; here's your grandmother's carriage, while I see if my horses are fit to be trusted with the ladies."

Alvar was still dizzy and shaken, though he said that the hurt to his arm was a trifle, and now stood up and inquired after his horse, which had been caught by a bystander, and was unhurt. Sir John's coachman had also escaped with some severe bruises; and there was a general move. Jack, seeing Gipsy with her father, followed his brothers, anxious about them both, and overflowing with gratitude towards Alvar for his darling's safety.

But as they turned to drive away they were obliged to cross the ground, and there rose from all sides such a thundering shout as threatened a repetition of the former danger; yeomanry, volunteers, and spectators, all joining in such an outburst of enthusiasm as had never echoed over Ashrigg

Moors before. Their driver pulled up in the centre of the field with the obvious information,—

"They're cheering, sir; it's for you." Alvar stood up, with his hand on Jack's shoulder, and bowed with a grace and self-possession from which his pale face and hastily extemporised sling did not detract, and which his brothers—agitated, and ashamed of their agitation, were far from rivalling, as Jack desired the driver to "get on quick," and Cheriton bent down his head, quivering in every nerve under the wonderful influence of that unanimous shout.

Some hours later, as Alvar lay on a sofa at Ashrigg, resting in preparation for the public dinner at Hazelby, for which every one had declared he *must* be well enough, the doctor included, he looked at Cherry, who sat near him, and said, with a smile,—"*Cherito mio*, I think they would all have grieved for me—the twins and all—if I had been killed. They would have been sorry for me—now."

"Don't—don't talk of it. Of course they would," said Cherry, with a shudder.

"Ah! I fear you will dream of it, as you used of the mountain at Ronda. It will hurt you more than it has hurt me."

"No," said Cherry; "but if we had lost you! We can hardly believe yet that we have you safe."

"But," said Alvar, with unusual persistency, "then *you* would have been the squire, after all. Ah! I am cruel to hurt you; but, Cheriton, *once* they would not have grieved."

Cheriton could not command an answer, and Alvar quitted the subject; but the unmistakable affection showed to him at last by his brothers and sister healed the old wounds as nothing else would have done.

No one would own that the fright and agitation demanded a quiet evening, and the ladies all repaired to Hazelby, to sit in the gallery at the Town-hall to hear the speeches, Mrs Lester, who had happily not been present in the morning, accompanying them; and Jack, going to fetch Virginia, and after overwhelming her with the story of the alarm, assuring her that she *must* come and hear Alvar's health drunk. Sir John Hubbard intended it should be done.

And so, when the usual toasts were over, old Sir John rose, and, full of compunction for past prejudices, and of gratitude for what Alvar had done for him, said that this was really the first public occasion they had had of welcoming Mr Lester among them; spoke of his father's merits, of the difficulty a stranger might have in accommodating himself to their north-country fashions; touched lightly and gracefully on the reason of Alvar's recent absence, and their pleasure in welcoming back again "one long known and loved," and how much was owing to the elder brother's care; hinted how Alvar had won "one of the best of their county prizes;" and then, out of the fulness of his heart, thanked him for his heroic behaviour in saving the life of Lady Hubbard, and himself from an irreparable loss, and, moreover, a frightful sense of responsibility.

Then Alvar's health was drunk with all the honours, and it was long before the enthusiasm subsided sufficiently to allow him to reply.

He stood up, in his unusual height and dignity, and said, slowly and simply, "I thank you *much*, gentlemen. Sir John Hubbard need not thank me for rescuing my sister, and the betrothed of my brother. I was at hand, and of the danger I did not think." ("No, no; of course not," cried a voice.) "I have been a stranger, but I have no other country but England now, and it is my wish to be your friend and your neighbour, as my father was. I will endeavour to fill his place to my tenants; but I am ignorant, and have little skill. I think it is not perhaps permitted to me to name the one who will most help me in future, one of whom I am all unworthy. But there is another, who has always given me love, whom I love most dearly, as I think you do also. My brother Cheriton has taught me how to be an English squire."

And among all those who cheered Alvar's speech, the voice that was raised the loudest was Edward Fleming's.

The next morning Cheriton went alone along the path from Oakby to Elderthwaite. His great wish was granted; his father's place would be worthily filled. Alvar would never be a nobody in the county again, would never seem again out of place as their head. All old sores were healing, all were turning out well—how much better than he could ever have hoped!

Even for hopeless Elderthwaite things looked hopeful; and Cheriton's quick and kindly thoughts turned to his share in the work of mending them. "If I may," he thought, "but if not, I think I shall never fear for any one or any place again."

Too much, perhaps, for the impetuous spirit to promise for itself; but come what might, those who loved Cheriton Lester had little cause to fear for the real welfare of one who loved them so well and looked upward so steadily.

Epilogue

"Mr Ellesmere! I saw your name in the visitors' book. So you are taking a holiday in Switzerland?"

"Mr Stanforth! Very glad to meet you. You will put us up to all we ought to see and admire. Are you alone?"

"Yes; you know I have lost my travelling companion. My next girl is still in the schoolroom, and I think will never be so adventurous as Gipsy."

"You have good accounts, I hope, of Mrs Jack, as we irreverently call her."

"Excellent; she adores the boys, and the boys adore her; her letters are very educational and aesthetic. She has picked up more 'art' as a schoolmaster's wife than ever she learnt as an artist's daughter, and could, doubtless, set me right on tones and colours."

"Cherry told me that Jack had taken to the new culture."

"Yes, he was much amused at the development produced by house-furnishing. But double firsts have a right to vagaries. But tell me something of the Oakby world. It is a very long time since I have been there, and one does not see much of people at a wedding, though I thought Cheriton looking very well."

"Yes, he is fairly well, *very* useful, and, I think, quite content. Alvar has settled into his position, and fills it well. He is indignant if he is supposed to be ignorant of anything English; and his sweet graceful wife guides him as much as 'Fanny' did his father thirty years ago. His one trouble is that little Gerald is as dark as all his Spanish ancestors, and even Frances is like the Seytons, but that he can forgive."

"Does she promise to rival her aunt? What a beautiful creature Miss Lester is!"

"Splendid! and still Miss Lester, which is rather a trouble to her grandmother. Whether she will ever be Lady Milford—or whether—Any way, Nettie can keep her own counsel."

"And now, tell me about Elderthwaite. Has Cheriton justified his experiment?"

"Yes, I think I may say that he has. He has done a great deal. No one else could have done so much good, and certainly no one would have done so little harm."

"And the old parson is resigned to improvements?"

"Yes, but there have been fewer external changes than you would expect, or than Cherry would wish if he were his own master, or even if he could depend on himself. But of course his health has weighted him heavily, and he cannot promise perfect regularity in services or arrangements."

"I wonder he can manage at all."

"Well, I think on the whole his health *has* improved, and he is well enough off to contrive things—has a horse and waggonette for bad weather; and his house is near the church, and he has built on a great room to it, and fitted it up with books and games, and he makes a sort of club of it for the boys and young men. His sitting-room opens into it, and he has classes and talks, and gets them to come and see him one by one. If he cannot do one thing he does another. And they have evening services in the summer, and early ones when it is possible. I think the sort of resolute way in which Cheriton has recognised the need of special care of himself, if he is to be useful, and carries it out, is one of the most remarkable things about him. Many young men might have killed themselves with hard work, and many would forget the danger when well and in good spirits, but he has recognised the limitations set to him, and bows to them."

"Yes, and he does not offend his vicar."

"Rarely, he has never failed to recognise his right to respect—never allowed the Wilsons, who are ardent and enthusiastic, to force anything on him. And there's a great change. I don't mean that the old fellow is cut after any modern pattern yet; but he is considerably more decorous, and sometimes there's a sort of humility about him in admitting his shortcomings that is very touching. Cherry is the very light of his eyes."

"And how does Cherry hit it off with the modern element?"

"Well, there I think his position has been a great advantage to him; they are a little afraid of him. But he gets on admirably with them, and you know they have improved the church immensely this last year, and what is more to the point, perhaps, it is filled with good congregations."

"Is Cheriton a fine preacher?"

"Well, his people like him. I have rarely heard him; he is very difficult to get. Yes, I like his sermons; but he has not much voice, you see, and his manner is very quiet. He has not the sort of vehement eloquence you might have expected. I made some comment once to him, and he looked at me, and said, 'I daren't get eager and tire myself.' I saw then how little strength he had to work with."

"Poor fellow! But this life—does it satisfy him? Is he happy in it?"

"He is just as merry and full of fun as ever. He has a wonderful capacity for taking an interest in every one and everything; and though Alvar does not depend on him in the old exclusive way, he is most tender and careful of him, and Cherry delights in the children. I *think* Jack's marriage *was* rather a wrench; those two do cling together so closely, and Jack was a great deal with him; but still there are grand plans for the holidays, and he is very fond of your daughter."

"I don't think that marriage will loosen the tie."

"No; and he is much too unselfish really to regret it. Then all his village boys bring him pets; he says everything makes a link from a horse to a hedgehog. And my curates and the Ashrigg ones run after him, and think it a privilege to take a service for him; and he has done one rather feather-pated fellow, I know, a world of good."

"That I can believe."

"Yes; for, after all, Mr Stanforth, it is not his being a Lester of Oakby, nor a man of means, nor his wonderful tact, nor even his great charm of manner in itself that counterbalances his weak health and frequent absences, or makes a life spent among rather uncongenial elements sufficient to him. It is that he has the root of the matter in him as very few have. What he does and says may be less in quantity, but it is infinitely above in quality the ordinary work of his profession. He looks deep and he looks high, and men feel it. He has come through much tribulation, and—well, Mr Stanforth, the dragon slayers have their reward."

"Yes, one must touch a high note in thinking of him."

"So high, that one fears 'to mar by earthly praise,' one who I verily believe is as true a saint, as full of love and zeal.—Well, being so, as I truly think, he has what some holy souls have lacked, the gift of a gracious manner and a most sympathetic nature; and if a few more years and a little more experience could be granted to him, I believe he will have a great spiritual influence, if not wide, deep. Any way he will leave in one place the memory of a pure and holy life, and will lead others to follow the Master he loves so well."